WINGS AND TAILS

ISAAC LEE

Copyright © 2024 by Isaac Lee

All rights reserved.

No part of this book may be reproduced in any form or by any electronic or mechanical means, including information storage and retrieval systems, without written permission from the author, except for the use of brief quotations in a book review.

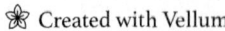 Created with Vellum

CONTENTS

Chapter 1	1
Chapter 2	11
Chapter 3	22
Chapter 4	34
Chapter 5	42
Chapter 6	55
Chapter 7	66
Chapter 8	76
Chapter 9	88
Chapter 10	102
Chapter 11	120
Chapter 12	132
Chapter 13	147
Chapter 14	157
Interlude 1: Hope & Madeline	171
Chapter 15	182
Chapter 16	192
Interlude 2: Hope	203
Chapter 17	208
Chapter 18	218
Chapter 19	229
Chapter 20	238
Chapter 21	250
Interlude 3: Addison	261
Chapter 22	267
Chapter 23	278
Chapter 24	293
Chapter 25	305
Chapter 26	314
Chapter 27	328
Chapter 28	337
Chapter 29	348
Chapter 30	358

Chapter 31	368
Interlude 4: Jayden	378
Epilogue 1:	384
Epilogue 2:	389
Acknowledgments & Thank You	397

CHAPTER ONE

"CAPTAIN WALKER, this is Samuel Jennings down here on the beach with all these fine Americans, can you hear me?"

"This is Captain Walker, I hear you loud and clear Mr. Jennings."

"That's fantastic! I want to let you know that all eyes are on you. Show this crowd what the Mustang can do!"

"Roger that," I said as I banked the fighter to the left and put the plane into a dive, gaining speed as I fell out of the sky. The beach below filled my forward field of view, getting closer and closer before I pulled up on the stick and leveled out the plane, screaming over the heads of the onlookers of South Beach. As I went by, I could pick up the emotions of the crowd below while they marveled and cheered for me and my warbird.

People called it empathy as I was growing up, but I knew it was more than that. I could sometimes feel more than someone's feelings, in fact it sometimes felt like they were mentally telling me what they were going to do before they did it. Some would call it mind reading, but it wasn't complete images or thoughts, just quick flashes.

Now, I could feel the excitement of the children as they

jumped up and down, the pride of the veterans from the first great war as they saluted, and the joy of Samuel as he got back on the microphone to read his script like the showman he was.

"That right there ladies and gentleman is the North American P-51D Mustang. Captain Walker just flew past at over four hundred miles per hour, can you believe it? This is the best of what American engineering is capable of!" He rambled to the crowd and over my radio so I would know when to move on to the next part of the act.

Pulling up, I entered a wingover to my right and brought the Mustang around again, this time going through a series of barrel rolls as I passed over the crowd. I smiled to myself as I soaked up the excitement and joy radiating off my audience.

This was my second year of demonstrating war planes to the American public in air shows. Though I hated not being used for combat, I told anyone who asked that the feelings of elation I received from the crowd were better than the feelings of fear and hate I got from squad members and enemy pilots during combat as they reached the end of their life.

"The Mustang isn't just fast, it's agile and maneuverable, and in the hands of a double ace like Captain Walker, it's something the pilots of the Luftwaffe have nightmares about," continued Jennings from his stand next to the crowd.

Reaching the end of the beach, I pulled the plane up to gain altitude for the live fire demonstration.

"Next, you will see the firepower that the six wing-mounted .50 caliber Browning Machine guns can bring to any target on the ground. That's right! The legendary firepower of the Browning M2 machine gun gives the Mustang all the bite old Adolf can handle!"

Banking left again, I spotted the targets anchored below in the water, let the nose of my plane dip into a dive and lined up the first old sailboat with my gun sights. My mind started to wander as I bore down on the bobbing boat and I went into a state of autopilot, going through the same familiar motions I had done hundreds of times over the past few years.

God, am I bored, I thought.

After seeing combat in England as an American volunteer, I had reached double ace status before a damn Messerschmitt brought me down over the Channel in early 42'. Luckily, I was plucked out of the water before I froze to death. Unluckily, that earned me a ticket back to the States. When I got home and joined the Army Air Corp, they told me they had a special mission only I could do.

Raise funds for War Bonds.

So here I was, a pilot who was deemed to have more value flying in air shows than combat over Europe.

The guns screamed as I pulled the trigger, letting off two bursts of lead down on the first boat. It splintered and shattered as it was ripped apart by the quick rain of bullets, and as I pulled up, my mind picked up another wave of excitement from the crowd on the beach.

Who didn't like watching things get destroyed for fun?

"What a fine use of live rounds," I said over the radio as I pulled up and to the right, climbing to gain altitude so I could come around for another run.

"Don't be like that," Samuel said on our private channel. "That was perfect, the crowd loved it. Now bring her around and sink another one!"

"Roger that."

I applied full power to the Merlin engine and climbed into a large cloud bank. As I forged my way forward, my plane vibrated gently, shaking me in my seat.

"Captain Walker?" called Samuel over the radio, his voice breaking up and filled with static, "James...are you there-"

"I can hear you Samuel, but you're breaking up," I said into my headset.

I drifted through the soup of the cloud, my propeller the

only thing breaking up the white that engulfed me. I waited for Samuel to reply to me, but silence was all that answered.

"Hello, Samuel, are you there?"

A moment later the vibration stopped, and everything was smooth.

Then I lurched forward in my seat as my plane was hit with the strongest turbulence I had ever experienced in my life. The plane jerked up and then dropped, the metal frame rattling as it was shaken like it was the toy in a child's hand.

"What the hell….Ow! What the fuck?!" I screamed in the cockpit as a sudden headache built up from the base of my skull and washed over my head. Gritting my teeth, I did my best to push through the pain and focus on the controls. My brain felt like it was boiling. I forced my eyes open.

The gauges on my instrument panel were going berserk even though the plane was flying level.

Just when it felt like it couldn't get any worse, the pain and the shaking faded, and peace returned to my little world there in the clouds.

"Good lord that sucked. Samuel, give me a second, I hit some turbulence and got disoriented. I'm fine now, but I need a moment to clear my head before I enter the next dive."

I shook my head and waited.

"Samuel? Are you there?"

Static was all that replied as the plane buzzed along and finally cleared the clouds. My compass said I was still facing south, so I continued my right turn, but as the plane pointed west, I struggled to spot the Miami shoreline in the water below.

A shadow overhead made me crane my neck to look, and my eyes went wide.

In front and below was the ocean, where it should be, but above that was the land. Not just above, as in cliffs towering over the ocean, no, above as in *floating* over the water. Where open air should be was a hovering landmass that stretched as far as my eyes could see to the north west and back to the south east.

Looking at it, I estimated that this floating land was at least a mile or more over the surface of the ocean.

I shook my head, rubbed my eyes, slapped my cheeks, yelled, and even pinched myself, but nothing woke me up from the dream I thought I was in.

Flipping through the four channels on the plane's radio, I began calling out to air traffic control.

"Tower, Tower, Yellow Rose Copy."

Nothing.

"Miami Control, Yellow Rose Copy."

As I called out, I began a long spiraling climb and came to the conclusion that there was no one on the first channel, other than static. I checked the second and third channels and found the same, static and more static. It wasn't until the fourth channel that I finally got a response.

"Yellow Rose to any planes in the area, this is Captain James Walker of the United States Army Air Force, does anyone copy?"

"Yellow Rose?" echoed a voice with a thick accent, "I demand to know what or who is Yellow Rose?"

I sat there in silence for a second, trying to figure out how to respond.

"I am Yellow Rose," I finally replied. "I am Captain James Walker, United States Army Air Forces. I was flying a demonstration off the coast of Miami when I was hit by strong turbulence...Who am I speaking with?"

There was silence for a minute before the voice responded, "I-I am a radio operator running a test. We are installing radio towers across Crestia to help with long range communication, would you repeat again where you are from?"

"Sure, I am a pilot from the United States. What is Crestia?"

"What kind of pilot?" he asked, ignoring my question.

"A combat pilot, now please tell me, what is Crestia?" I demanded into my radio.

The receiver went quiet. I was still climbing, and ready to ask again when my peripheral vision caught flashes of light back to the southwest.

Leveling out the plane, I slowly worked the rudder and headed in that direction. As I got closer, I noticed the flashes were the reflection of sunlight off pressed aluminum as four planes were tangled in a dance to the death. Turning back to my right, I made sure to keep my distance to avoid being targeted or getting hit by stray rounds.

"Hey, radio operator, this is Yellow Rose here, there are four planes currently engaged in a dog fight, two are metallic with yellow and purple striped tails while the other two are...gray and with a red tail...nope, now it's just one red tail."

The two metallic planes were working harder than the red tails. One red tail went wide on his turn, allowing the yellow tail to get inside and pump the plane full of lead. The red started smoking and spiraling down to the ocean below. I had seen spiraling like this before and knew that the pilot was already dead.

"Yellow Rose," came a new voice that spoke with an air of being in command, "did you say you are spectating a dog fight and that one of the red-tailed fighters was shot down?"

"Yes, a red tail was shot down, and the other one will be joining him soon. Who are the sides so I can know if I need to be worried about fighting, running or staying put."

"My subordinate says your plane is a combat plane. What type of plane is it?" asked the voice.

"I am flying a P-51D Mustang and I am fully loaded."

"And what was your name again?" asked the man I assumed was the commanding officer.

"Walker. Captain James Walker."

"Captain Walker," he said in a strange tone, "would you be willing to aid the pilot with the red tail? That is a Crestia Fighter, and possibly the son of a high-ranking noble. If you could aid him, that would be most appreciated."

"I don't want to engage without orders from-"

"Captain, I am sure by now you can see that you are not near anyone who can give you that order. However, Crestia are allies, and if you aid him, I will personally see to it that you are rewarded...handsomely," said the commander.

He had a point. If this was a dream, then nothing bad would come of my assistance. If this was something else, like another world, then surely I was on my own for making up my mind.

"Captain," said the commander, a sense of urgency in his voice, "the Crestia pilot is in need of assistance. The land closest to you is Crestia. If you aid him, they will allow you to land and answer all the questions you may have. There are people here who will help answer your questions. But first, please help this pilot."

His plea for help got to me, and I made up my mind.

Tightening my harness, I turned toward the action and moved in. As I got closer, I could start to pick up on the emotions and thoughts of the three pilots. One was feeling stressed and panicked while the other two felt confident and wanted to toy with their prey. The image of a pair of wolves circling another one that was backed into a corner popped into my mind. I shook my head to clear it away, but it stayed there, lingering in my thoughts.

This was new...

"Don't let him go Lone Wolf," said a voice in the vision.

"Worry about yourself, Jakle, and take the shot when you get it," replied a woman's voice.

Neither yellow-tailed fighter noticed that I had dropped in behind them. I followed and waited for the right opportunity, seeing their thoughts flash across my mind, clearer than ever now that I was closer to them. When the yellow tail I was focused on went wide, I moved with him, and when the opportunity came and I had the plane in my gun sights, I pulled the trigger.

The plane in front of me started to smoke as flames burst from the engine.

"Shit! I'm hit! Where did that plane come from?" shouted the pilot as waves of shock and panic filled his mind.

The pilot hesitated for a moment, and that allowed me to line up the final shot. A quick burst of .50 cal rounds made contact, ripping off the wing of the plane, sending it tumbling before exploding in mid air. I flinched as I felt the last moments and memories of the doomed pilot.

What is going on? I thought. I had picked up emotions before from enemy pilots, but this was more. I had seen what many see before they die, I saw his life flash before his eyes.

The second plane broke off from the red tail and began to climb as I moved to engage him, using the power of the Rolls Royce Merlin engine to catch up to them in the climb.

"Unknown fighter, thank you for your help," said a voice in my head with a slight mediterranean-sounding accent.

"What the hell?" I said as I looked around. The imagery in my mind showed two thoughts. One was a relieved person giving me a thumbs up, while the other gave off the feelings of fear and determination.

"Unknown silver fighter, can you hear me?" asked the mediterranean accented voice in my head again, *"This is Major Welch, the pilot of the plane with the red tail, do you copy?"*

"Yeah...sure I do," I said aloud, not sure how to talk to someone in my head.

"Yellow Rose, can you hear our pilot projecting to you telepathically?" asked the radio voice.

"Is that what that is? Sure, I can hear him."

Unnecessary talking while engaged in combat was something I could do without. My previous squad had used strict radio discipline while fighting in the skies of Europe, so all the back and forth was starting to annoy me.

"*Captain Walker, control tells me you can hear me. Since that is the case, let's bring this Thurnmar devil down!*"

The feelings of a second wind of confidence came from the Crestia pilot as he tried to aid me in wrangling in the last enemy combatant, but I thought he figured out that his plane couldn't do what my Mustang could. So instead of helping me, he decided he was going to sit back and watch as I got to work.

Here I was putting on another show, but at least I was getting to take part in actual combat.

The Thurnmar pilot on the other hand could not sit back and watch, their plane was just as maneuverable and fast as the Crestia plane, which was bad news for them. I respected the fact that they were not giving up and were doing everything they could to fly defensively while bullets whizzed past them from my guns.

As the plane maneuvered, I was finally able to take in its silhouette. It looked similar to the Brewster Buffalo we flew in my first few sorties with my squadron back in England before they switched us to the Hawker Hurricane. The only differences being that this plane had gull wings and two propellers on the nose. That kind of explained why the way the plane flew felt familiar to me.

The Thurnmar pilot had skill, I had to give them credit where credit was due, but sometimes you run into someone who matches you in skill, and at that point, the superior aircraft wins.

Today was that day for this pilot.

As the pilot of the enemy fighter started to get desperate, images of them going into a full dive for the water to try and outrun me filled my mind.

"Don't do it..." I said.

Then they did it. I got the feeling this was one clear advantage the Thurnmar planes had over those from Crestia. When they entered their dive, I was there to match them. As we both fell through the sky, their plane sat right in my sights, and I pulled the trigger. One short burst rang out before my guns went quiet.

"Shit, out of ammo," I hissed.

It didn't matter. Smoke started to flow from the yellow-tailed fighter as failure and disappointment flashed across my mind from the Thurnmar pilot. I disengaged and watched as the plane kept diving. The smoke grew darker, but I finally saw what I was hoping for when the Thurnmar pilot ditched the plane and their parachute deployed.

Better to live to fight another day.

"*Well done! Thank you for the assistance,*" projected the Crestian pilot as he pulled alongside my left wing. He waved to me and gave an energetic thumbs up. "*Once again, I'm Major Welch. Command is telling me you can't communicate like this, but let me tell you, I'm excited to greet you when we get on the ground. Follow me, my new friend!*"

The image of the pilot beckoning for me to follow him came across my mind, followed by glimpses of people throwing back a stiff drink.

That seemed like a good idea to me.

CHAPTER TWO

THE LAND we flew over once we got past the edge was beautiful and felt like the normal landscape I would fly over if I was in Tennessee or West Virginia. Really, anywhere around the Appalachian mountains in the summer would have fit the bill. Major Welch projected out the names of towns as we flew over them, he also gave me updates on how much further we had to go.

"*Up ahead is Imperial Base Gilmore,*" projected the Major as he lined his plane up to land.

I circled around once before landing behind him to give him time to get his plane out of the way before taxiing with the Major to the flight line. I cut the engine and relaxed into the seat, removing my sweat-soaked flight helmet and running my hands through my short sandy hair. I wasn't sure about where I was or what was going on, but the feeling of being in a parked plane after a "successful" mission was always something I made sure not to take for granted.

Seeing the other pilot climb out of their cockpit snapped me back to reality. I threw back the bubble canopy and let the fresh air swirl around me before doing the same. I pulled my lean frame from the cockpit of the fighter and stretched out my muscles as I stood on the wing, throwing my arms around to pop my back. From there, I jumped down to the ground and headed toward the smiling Major.

"My new friend, it's good to meet you face to face. I am Major Courtney Welch, Court for short. Thank you for saving my life up there," he said with his colorful accent as he extended his hand. The Major was about the same height as me, but seemed to be a little more muscular in his chest and shoulders by comparison. His face reminded me of a young Humphrey Bogart.

I shook his hand and returned the greeting, "Nice to finally meet you Maj-" as I shook the other pilot's hand, a series of imagery and thoughts came across his mind, cutting me off as I spoke...

Another Human? And this one brought a beautiful plane. I wonder if he would allow me to fly this machine?

I shook my head and tried to ignore the bombardment of thoughts as I continued to introduce myself, "...I'm Captain James Walker of the United States Army Air Forces, nice to meet you, Major Welch."

The images and thoughts went away when he released my hand. I looked down at my hand in confusion, opening and closing it to try and figure out what just happened.

"Is there a problem?" the major asked..

"I'm not sure, Major, but just now, I was able to see your thoughts as we shook hands."

Welch took a subtle step back. "Please, call me Court, and you heard all that? Are you a minder?" he asked with a look of concern as he pulled his own flight helmet off his head, revealing his black hair and a pair of black wolf ears sticking out of the top of his head.

Now it was my turn to step back, except I didn't, I froze. I stared at his ears, my mouth agape and eyes wide.

This 100% has to be a dream.

The major noticed where I was looking and gave a chuckle, "That's right, this is probably the first pair you have seen. You look like a boy who has seen his first pair of tits. I also have a tail."

Slowly I looked down at the black fluffy tail wagging behind Major Welch. "Is that real?" I asked.

"I would hope so. I am what we call a wolfkin, as are most of the men on this base," he said as he waved around.

I scanned the men working around us and noticed the mechanics of the airfield all had furry ears and tails of different colors. A hysterical laugh reverberated from my throat without my consent as my mind started to spiral. Thoughts from the mechanics and pilots nearby filled my mind, they were curious about my plane but hated that "another one of them" showed up. It was too much.

As I moved back toward my plane and leaned over the wing, hands holding my head, a gray jeep-like combat vehicle with an open top pulled up next to our planes. Two men with black helmets and soldier's uniforms climbed out carrying submachine guns. They didn't have their guns pointed at me, but were watching me while I tried to calm down.

"Gentleman," said the one who had been in the passenger's seat, "your presence is needed at Central Admin. Please come with me."

He gestured to the vehicle he had arrived in where another soldier was sitting in the driver's seat and looking over at us. All three men had black armbands on their left arms with the letters 'MP' in white. These guys were military police, so much for being rewarded.

The MPs drove us across the airfield, toward the buildings that made the barracks, mess hall, lounges, and meeting rooms of the airfield. They parked in front of a two story office building with the words *B-13: CENTRAL ADMIN* painted along the top, and led us in. We made a stop at the front desk to get me a visitor's pass, before heading down one of the hallways, past offices filled with men and women working on typewriters and looking over maps. We reached the end of the hallway and the MPs opened the door, motioning for me to enter.

"I'll see you later," the Major said as he turned to his right and walked down the next hall.

Inside, two officers were waiting for me at a table, a man and a woman. They both stood to greet me, and I took a moment to look each over.

The man was older but shorter than me, and a bit on the chubby side with gray hair and brown fur on his ears. He wore a gray officer's uniform with black trim and that was adorned with the right amount of decor for me to know he was probably a general.

The woman who stood next to him was beautiful and seemed to be the same age as me. She was considerably shorter than me, the top of her head maybe coming to my chin. The uniform that she wore was similar to that of the man, but with less accessories, and it fit well to her perky chest and lithe body in a way that I was glad no uniform fit any man. Her vibrant red eyes watched me from behind a pair of simple round glasses that sat on the nose of her pointed face. Large fluffy snow white ears protruded out of equally white hair that was pulled back in loose curls.

"Nice to meet you, I am Third Marshall Randall Altros of the Imperial Military," said the well-decorated gentleman with a gravelly voice, "and this is Agent Madeline Reynolds of the Ministry of State Security."

There were no handshakes, so I took the seat that the Marshall was gesturing toward on the opposite end of the table from them. The room was not small, or large, it didn't feel like an interrogation room, not that I had been in one before, but the image of one I had in my mind did not match this. I didn't see any of those double-sided mirrors, and the only windows were the two on the wall behind the two Crestia officials.

Marshall Altros nodded to the two MPs, and they left the three of us alone, shutting the door behind them.

"Do you mind if I smoke?" I asked as I pulled my pack of cigarettes from my jacket.

"I'd ask that you don't," said the woman, covering her nose as I lit up. "Our sense of smell is very strong and that is very unpleasant."

I rolled my eyes and shook my head as I took one more drag to calm my nerves before putting the cigarette out in one of the coffee mugs on the table.

"If this is a dream, then why can't I do what I want to do?" I whispered under my breath.

The white-haired woman's ears twitched. "Because this is not a dream."

I stared at the woman, my eyes going back and forth between her red eyes and large ears as I made a mental note to watch what I said around her.

Those ears are for more than show.

"Captain," the Marshall said while Agent Reynolds and I measured each other up and down. "Let me start by welcoming you to the Crestia Empire and thanking you for saving the life of one of our pilots. It would have been a tragic loss to the country if the son of Grand Duke Welch had died."

He took a deep breath before continuing, "This is my first time meeting a human, however Agent Reynolds assured me she has plenty of experience in dealing with the humans who have visited before you. She is going to be taking the lead for the rest of our meeting, but I want to assure you that you are in no danger, nor are you in any kind of trouble with The Empire."

"Humans before me?" I asked.

"Yes," Agent Reynolds replied, "as an intelligence officer of the Ministry of State Secrets, MSS for short, I have met a handful that have come to this world over the past few years."

I nodded, while my brain tried to process what was going on.

I could really use the rest of that smoke...

"Captain Walker, before we go any further, I wanted to let you know that this is not an interrogation," Agent Reynolds continued as she pulled out a journal. She wrote a few things down before looking up at me again. "I think the best way to explain what this is is a debriefing, for you and for us. I'm sure you have many questions, as do we, so just relax and let's take this a small bit at a time."

"I'll keep that in mind," I said as I tried to relax, which was difficult. Every second that went by made it more clear that this was not a dream, which meant I was seconds away from breaking down into hysterical laughter.

"Do you have any questions?" Agent Reynolds asked.

"Many, the first being where am I?"

She gave me a calming smile before answering, "I will do my best to answer them all. You are in another world, one we call Dione."

"Dione," I repeated before taking a deep breath, "and what are you? Because the guy who I saved said what he was outside, but the voices in my head and the shock of seeing everyone with animal ears and tails made me kind of not pay attention to him."

"Understandable," she said as she noted something, "I am a foxkin, and the Marshall and the Major you saved are both wolfkin. You can tell the difference in our kind by looking at our ears."

She blushed as she pointed at her ears, then pointed at the Marshall's, who was not amused to be used for this comparison. Both looked to be the same length, but her white ears had more fur and were a little wider, and twitched while I studied them.

"There are many races across Dione," she continued after clearing her throat, "but in Crestia, you will mostly find those of the canid variety, wolf and foxkin."

"Why is that?" I asked.

"Because this is the land Crestia herself made, she is the Goddess the Canids worship. Each race has their own God or Goddess that they worship too."

Marshall Altros nodded next to her, as if to add validity to her statement for my sake.

I nodded along as my mind processed everything. Or tried to. Wolf people? Really? How was a guy from the Texas panhandle supposed to accept something like that? No matter how much I tried to chew it over, I just couldn't wrap my head around it.

"Is this world at war?" I asked, assuming I knew the answer. I had just shot down two enemy nation fighters because someone on the radio asked. I didn't know how long I would be in this world, but I wanted to at least know the sides.

Marshall Altros leaned forward for this one. "Yes, the Crestia Empire is at war with a group of nations calling themselves *The Coalition*. They were against the marriage between then King William Fangburg of Crestia and Queen Sable Floray of the Floray Kingdom. Their marriage joined the countries and created what we now call the Crestia Empire."

"They started a war over that?" I asked, not fully believing what he was saying or thinking.

"There was also the annexation of neighboring countries who wished to join the growing empire. Thurnmar and Oshor were the loudest opponents to Imperial growth," he said with a chuckle.

"What's so funny?" I prodded.

"Oh, it's just that Thurnmar is the largest country on Dione and hated the idea of Crestia expanding. Thurnmarians think highly of themselves."

I looked at Agent Reynolds who nodded in agreement.

So here I was, on another world and I had ended up in the middle of another war.

"Do you have any other questions?" Agent Reynolds asked.

"I'm sure I do, but right now I'm trying to make sense of everything, just give me a second," I said. *And a cigarette,* I added internally as I licked my lips.

"While you are processing that, I have a question for you, Captain Walker," Agent Reynolds said as she looked over her notes, circling something she had written down earlier. "You said that you heard voices in your head, could you elaborate on that?"

"Um...sure, I could hear the thoughts of those around me. In fact, when I shook hands with the Major dude, I could see and hear his thoughts like they were my own-"

"Impossible," she murmured as she flipped through her notes, pulling out a page and reading over it. "No human that we have met has had any of these blessings."

"Blessings?"

"Yes, blessings." The Marshall chuckled as he butted in on the conversation. "That's what minders call the extra mental abilities they get beyond telepathy."

"They are blessings, Marshall Altros, how else would you explain them?" the foxkin asked.

The Marshall didn't answer, instead waving his hands for Agent Reynolds to move on.

She shook her head before continuing, "Blessings are gifts from the Gods, abilities such as telekinesis, mind reading and manipulation, as well as the ability to shapeshift."

She gave me a smile as if what she had said was perfectly normal.

I felt differently.

"That's terrifying," I said. I would hate to live in a world where anyone could read my mind at will, and now here I was stuck in one.

"You're telling me," agreed the Marshall as he gave me a nod and smile, showing that he thought I was alright for agreeing with him.

"It's only terrifying if someone is not trained properly," the foxkin added. "Take me for example," she said as she placed her hand on her chest and sat up straight, "I am a minder. The Goddess Crestia saw fit to gift me the ability to read minds, as well as the Reynolds family ability to shapeshift into my animal form at will."

Marshall Altros rolled his eyes while Agent Reynolds beamed with pride.

"That's incredible," I remarked, "I think I also have these minder abilities if that's the case."

"Surely you jest?" Agent Reynolds asked with a sympathetic smile. "I just said a moment ago that we have never documented a human who had any of the gifts."

"Well, that sucks for them, but I'm dead serious. I've been picking up the emotions and mental flashes of others ever since I was a little kid."

Agent Reynolds let out a soft laugh. "Captain Walker, empathy is not a power, it is simply being able to read the emotions of those around you better than others."

"It's not empathy, Agent Reynolds," I said defiantly.

All my life I'd had people tell me what it was. As a kid I had accepted that so kids would stop making fun of me, but when I got older, I knew it was more than how the dictionary defined it.

"I can feel more than that, and since crossing over to this world, I've been able to pick up more than before. Imagery and full thoughts have also started coming across. For example, the

Marshall here would rather be ogling the secretary he just hired instead of sitting through this."

The Marshall coughed and gagged on his coffee as he was caught off guard mid drink. "What? How did you know that?"

I shrugged. "I know it because it's what you've been thinking about this whole time. She has blonde hair and-now it's gone. All I see is a brick wall."

"Agent Reynolds!" he barked as he wiped coffee off his uniform, "you assured me that humans didn't have any minder abilities!"

"They don't! Every human we have met so far doesn't," said the flustered agent as she flipped through her notes. She then went back to the page where she had been taking notes while we were talking.

"Captain Walker, would you be willing to indulge me for a moment?" she asked with a curious smile. "Please take my hand, I want to see something."

I looked down at her outstretched palm, then back at her. "Why?"

"As I stated earlier, I am a minder, however I am having an impossibly hard time reading you. Physical contact will allow me to read your mind more easily. It will also allow you to see into my mind, that is, if you really are a minder," she said with a cheeky smile.

"So for your curiosity?"

"Yes, and for science."

"Then here is to science," I relented as I reached out and touched her hand.

I was prepared to get a flood of thoughts, like when I shook hands with Court, but nothing came. Instead, all I felt was the softness of her hand. When I thought about it, I realized I had not been able to sense anything from her this whole time.

"Are you trying to block me?" she asked.

"No...are you?"

"Yes, I always have my mental barriers up at all times, but...why can't I read you?" she asked with an air of curiosity in her tone. Then her expression changed to one of mischief. "I'm going to drop my barriers, if you can do what you claim you can, then you might enjoy it."

Her mind hit me all at once, much in the way a rogue wave hits a ship, knocking my mind back as her memories and thoughts washed over me.

"You are full of shit!"

We were suddenly alone in an empty room. I was sitting in my chair, and she was standing in front of me in her uniform.

"There is no way you have the gods' blessings, but if you do, I want you to know that I think your round ears are cute." She lowered herself to her knees and started crawling toward me. *"I also find you very handsome, Captain Walker, so I wouldn't mind having you be the first to bed me. That's right, I'm a virgin."* She started removing her clothes as she crawled onto my lap and pressed her lips to my ear, *"I'll do whatever you want, make me your naughty little..."*

"Woah! Down girl," I said as I pulled away from the foxkin, my heart racing.

Agent Reynold's eyes were filled with lust as she stared at me. "Did you like what you saw?"

"I think any man would have liked what I saw."

"What did she show you?" the Marshall asked.

"I shouldn't say."

"So you'll embarrass me, but not her?"

CHAPTER
THREE

I RUBBED my eyes and sipped on a mug of coffee while Agent Reynolds put away her notes. It was just the two of us as Marshall Altros had left about half an hour ago and had yet to return. I checked my wrist watch and was shocked when I saw it read just after midnight.

I craned my neck to look at the window. The sun was just starting to set outside. I tapped the face of my watch to see if it was broken, but it kept ticking.

"Well, Captain Walker, I'm done with you," Agent Reynolds said with a smile.

"That's good to hear. Hey, can you tell me the time?"

She reached into her coat pocket and pulled out a pocket watch, and popped open the cover. She looked at it for a moment before closing it and looking back at me. "It is 19:06."

I looked at my watch and adjusted it to 7:06, a whole five hours behind east coast time. A grumble from my stomach also reminded me that I hadn't had anything to eat since I had lunch back in Miami.

"That was a good one," Agent Reynolds said with a shy laugh, "would you like me to look into getting you some food?"

"Yes please-" I replied as another growl cut me off. "Could

you also tell me how I can get a hold of the humans who came before me?"

"They aren't here at the moment," she said, shaking her head, "but when they return, I am sure they will be more than happy to help you."

I nodded, feeling hopeful that I could get back to the States and my dad, so I could tell him stories about this place.

"What can you tell me about them?" I asked as I stretched in the chair.

"Well, I am not sure how to explain them. You all look the same to me." She crossed her arms and tapped her finger to her lower lip while she thought. "I don't really know how to describe them, but I do know one thing." She stopped, flashing me a playful smile. "I think you are the most attractive human I have met so far."

Our eyes met and my heart skipped a beat. I wasn't used to women coming onto me like this, much less being this forward. Then there were her red eyes, the way they glowed felt like they were beacons guiding me home.

Then I remembered what she told me when our minds connected.

Breathe James, breathe. Keep it cool...

Taking a deep breath, I flashed her a smile. "You know, I think you are the most beautiful foxkin I have met since coming to Diane," I said, throwing in a wink at the end for good measure.

Her ears perked up and her cheeks turned red. "That's nice of you to say, but I am afraid I am the only foxkin girl you have met." She grabbed her things and got up, moving to the door. "And it's Dione, not Diane."

My eyes were drawn to her shapely rump and the large white tail sticking out the back of her gray pencil skirt as she walked past me.

Has her tail always been that big?

"Captain Walker? My eyes are up here," Agent Reynolds said with a smile, catching me in the act.

"Oh, sorry about that," I apologized. I rose to my feet and scratched the back of my neck.

"I'll forgive you this time," she said as she opened the door, "right this way please."

She led me out the door and then proceeded to walk in front of me, giving me a great view of her ass and her swinging tail. As we walked, she glanced over her shoulder to make sure I was paying attention, her ears perking up each time she looked at me. As we got closer to the exit, I heard two familiar voices talking and laughing by the double doors. They were the voices of Marshall Altros and Major Welch.

Just before turning the last corner, Agent Reynolds stopped and grabbed my arm.

"James, hold on a second. I want to give you a word of warning."

"A warning? Am I in danger, Agent Reynolds?"

"No, you are not in danger," she said with a cute laugh. "It's about this war though, we have been at it for more than eight years. Many men have died, leaving a lot of women without mates, and Dionian women can get a little aggressive when we see a man we desire."

"So what's the warning? Look out for randy wolfkin girls?" I asked with a chuckle.

"And foxkin girls," she added with a wink. "Dionian women aren't like human women. I think 'less restrained' are the words previous humans have used to describe us."

"I'll keep that in mind."

With that we rounded the corner and came to the entry and waiting area of the building. I was greeted again by Marshall Altros and Major Welch. The two were standing in front of the counter of an older wolfkin woman who was the receptionist.

Two MPs stood by the door with sub-machines guns at their sides.

"Captain Walker," said the Marshall with a fake smile, "Major Welch wanted to thank you one last time before he departed for the evening."

"Yes, Captain Walker, I can not thank you enough for saving my life today, I must have you out to my estate soon to thank you properly. Show you proper Crestian hospitality."

"That sounds good, Major Welch," I replied, shaking his hand. I was flooded with feelings of overwhelming gratitude. "I'm glad I could help. I'm sorry I couldn't save your wingman though."

"Yes, it is a shame. Captain Timbers was a skilled pilot, and a good man. He will be missed, and I feel bad for his family. He was just a pup."

"To Captain Timbers," said Marshall Altros as we all bowed our heads for a moment of silence. "Life and death are the ways of war, but he is with the Goddess above, and we will run together with him on the Silver Plains when our time has come."

Agent Reynolds and Major Welch both nodded before making a crossing gesture across their chests.

"I must be going. I shall see you soon," the Major said as he shook my hand again. He then saluted Marshall Altros and Agent Reynolds before heading for a maroon luxury car that was waiting outside. He got in the back, but only after the driver opened the door for him.

"He's an interesting man," I said as his car drove off.

"The perks of being a noble, the Agent here can attest to that, can't you, Agent Reynolds?"

Her ears went flat along the top of her head. "Well, yes, I do come from nobility, but I'd rather focus on my position within the Ministry than who my father is."

"I respect that," said the Marshall with a nod before turning to me. "As for you, I am having private quarters set up for you with guards posted outside your door."

"There's no need to do all that," I said.

"Yes there is," he said with an annoyed tone. "I can't have you roaming around my base whenever you feel like it."

"Sounds like you're putting me in a fancy jail cell."

"I assure you, this is no jail, but if that is what you want, you can take the cell next to that Thurnmar mutt you shot down earlier today."

I was glad to hear that the pilot who had bailed out survived. Back on Earth I wouldn't have felt the same, but on Dione I didn't have a side. It would have been better if both pilots had survived, but one was better than none.

"Captain Walker, I am going to be honest with you," continued the Marshall as he crossed his arms. "I don't like you, and I don't trust you. The only reason you are getting private quarters is because you are a human and the Ministry ordered me to take care of you."

"I guess I should thank you?" I asked before thinking, "don't know what I did to get your panties in a wad-" I bit my tongue. I had not meant to say that out loud...

His and Agent Reynolds' eyes went wide as they looked at me. Reynolds' face was in shock while Marshall Altros started to turn red.

"What got my 'panties' in a wad you ask?" said the Marshall as he slowly walked towards me. "I am being told how to do things on my base because some smelly thing called a human showed up and saved the life of the Archduke's son. On top of all that, you are a minder, so now I have the Ministry crawling up my ass watching everything I do. Does that explain it? Or do I need to speak slower and louder?"

"I got it" I said, holding up my hands, "but do I really smell funny?"

"And now you are mocking me?" he yelled, his face wrinkled in annoyance.

"No, sorry, I was trying to see if I smelled funny."

His ears laid flat on his head and his face scrunched into a snarl

"Marshall Altros, if I may," Agent Reynolds said as she stepped in between us. "I do not think Captain Walker was trying to be disrespectful. In fact, humans do not have the heightened sense of smell that we canids do. Please show him some restraint."

She then turned to me and hissed, "Apologize!"

I stared at her before sighing and giving in, "Marshall Altros, I didn't mean to offend or insult you, I'm sorry."

The male wolfkin took a deep breath before smoothing out his hair and raising his ears back to their "normal" position. "Very well. Do learn our ways while you are here. I may be understanding, but nobles will take the slightest act of disrespect as an insult, and some can have you imprisoned or even killed on the spot."

I looked to Agent Reynolds, who nodded.

Marshall Altros knocked on the counter and the receptionist handed him a clipboard with some papers and an envelope. "This envelope has the key for your quarters. Room 112 in annex B," he said as he handed the envelope to one of the MPs and signed the papers before returning them to the receptionist. "These men will see you there. As I said earlier, you will stay in that room unless we call for you, and these guards will make sure you stay put. If you need anything, ask them."

"Understood," I said as the Marshall left without giving me another look.

Agents Reynolds and I stood there in silence for a moment before she leaned in and spoke softly, "I'll see about getting you some fresh clothes, also, you could use a shower."

"And don't forget the food, I'm starving," I added as the lead MP motioned for me to follow him.

"Don't worry, I won't let you waste away on me," she said with a wink.

I followed the first MP with the second one trailing close behind. The walk didn't take long, but it was a silent walk as the sun set and darkness set in. We followed a concrete path lined by the occasional lamp that gave off the same soft electric glow as lights back home.

Neither of the MP's who were assigned to "guard me" seemed to be very talkative, and even refused to give me their names when I asked, so I gave them names of my own. Laurel was the tall one in front of me while Hardy was the wide round one following behind.

The two did nothing to live up to the comedy duo I had named them after, but they were exemplary at the job assigned to them by Marshall Altros. They got me to the door of room 112, opened it for me and then shut it behind me, giving me all the privacy I could ask for.

The room was very simple with wooden floors, cinder block walls, and a wooden ceiling which looked like it could be the floor of the room above me. In the back of the room was the door to the bathroom, with just enough room for one person to use the toilet, sink and shower.

It came furnished with a single bed that was just large enough for one person, with the blankets and pillow rolled up at the foot. The bed was pressed up against the far wall, and next to it was a side table with a lamp on top of it. Across the room from the bed was a small three-drawer dresser with a dusty chair sitting next to it. The only thing I wished it had was a radio, but I had yet to see one of those.

Inside the top drawer were some towels, a wash cloth, a boxed up bar of soap and a large bottle of shampoo. Remembering Agent Reynolds' advice, I decided to have the shower she had requested I take before Laurel and Hardy had led me away.

I got undressed and removed my watch, staring at it as I sat down on the bed in my underwear. "There has to be a way back home," I said to the watch, flipping it over.

I'm proud of you, make it home safe. Dad. I ran my thumb over the engraving on the back. He had given me this watch the day after I had told him I was going to England to join the war. He and I were all we had, and following in his footsteps made him so happy.

"I'm going to do my best to make it home, old man," I whispered to the watch before setting it down on the bedside table. I then got up and went to the bathroom, turned on the shower, and jumped in once the water was warmed enough.

A good shower is something you sometimes don't know you need until you are already under the hot water. Getting cleaned off didn't take long, but before I reached to turn off the water, I had an idea.

Before I could change my mind, my hand reached out with a mind of its own and turned the knob to cut off the hot water. Almost instantly I was hit by frigged water that made me jump as it knocked the air out of me. I clenched my teeth and breathed frantically as I kept myself under the cold torrent for as long as I could.

"Wake up," I growled at myself repeatedly as I held my face under the shower head.

My resolve to withstand the cold water didn't last long as I had flashbacks to being pulled out of the frigid North Sea after being shot down. I turned off the water and jumped out of the shower. Without a doubt, I was awake. Anyone would be after that. The cold water had chilled me to the core while speeding up my heartbeat and breathing.

I dried off and wrapped a fresh towel around my waist, checking my reflection in the small mirror on the way out. "James, I don't think you're in Kansas anymore."

"I agree," said a soft voice from the other room.

I stood up straight and looked at the door, opened it slowly and stuck my head out to peek into my bedroom.

"Hello." Agent Reynolds waved from the armchair in the corner of the small room. "I brought you some fresh clothes to change into, as well as a late supper."

"Thanks...how did you get into my room?"

"You have guards outside your door who have your room key," she answered as she pointed toward the door of the small quarters.

"That makes sense," I whispered. "Sorry to expose myself to you in such a way, but I have nothing to cover up with," I added as I moved out of the bathroom and into the small bedroom.

Agent Reynolds blushed as she took in my body, wasting no time to look over my athletic build. She had laid the new clothes she had found for me on the bed, and I could feel her eyes watching me like a predator watches prey. Grabbing the clothes, I did the decent thing and went back into the bathroom to change, to the audible protests of the foxkin.

"Thank you for getting some clothes for me on such short notice, Agent Reynolds," I called as I put on the underwear, cotton white t-shirt, and gray twill pants.

"Please call me Madeline, and you're welcome. Did I get the sizes right?"

I checked myself in the mirror and did some stretching. "Yeah, you did pretty good," I said, commending her as I stepped back into the main room.

Her ears twitched as she smiled at me. "I also brought some food, it isn't much, but it should last you until morning," she added as she handed me a small brown paper bag.

I sat down on the narrow bed and removed the contents of

the bag. Inside was a sandwich wrapped in wax paper, an apple and a small package that looked to have some kind of candy in it, based on the design on the front. I unwrapped the sandwich and bit into it, sampling the flavors before continuing.

"What is the meat on this?" I asked between bites.

"It is a bird we call a ground goose."

I paused mid chew and stared at her.

"What? Was it something I said?" she asked, her ears laying flat.

"No," I said after I swallowed my current bite, "just curious as to what a ground goose looks like."

"Hmm." She put a finger to her lip and turned her head to the side. "They are fat birds with small wings and long necks, covered in black and brown feathers. They will often fluff up their feathers when trying to mate, and they make a weird gobble sound."

"Sounds like a turkey."

"A turkey?" she repeated slowly.

I grabbed a piece of the meat by itself and tossed it in my mouth, sure enough, it was turkey. *Ground goose is turkey, I wonder what other weird names they have for similar foods.*

To my surprise, bread was bread, cheese was cheese, and the apple was an apple. It seemed the meat was where the deviation occurred, and then there came the candy.

"I hope you like those," she said with a tinge of excitement, "they are my favorite type of chocolate."

Inside the package were small round candy shells that were either red, green, blue or yellow with milk chocolate in the middle. These were M&M's.

"We have something like this back on Earth," I said as I tossed one in my mouth, "what do you call them?"

"Choc Um's," she said excitedly, leaning forward as her tail wagged behind her.

"Do you want one?"

Her ears twitched before she nodded.

"Catch," I tossed one toward her, and instead of reaching out and catching it with her hand, she lunged forward and snagged it from the air with her mouth.

"Mmm," she moaned as she chewed on the candy-coated chocolate.

"Do you want some more?" I asked with a chuckle.

I didn't have too many "Choc Um's" after that, watching Madeline jump and dive for the chocolate treats that I tossed her way was the entertainment I needed to take my mind off things. She was quite skilled and didn't let a single one escape her maw.

"That was the last one," I said as I wadded up the packaging and put it in the paper bag that I was using for trash.

"That's the worst part of Choc Um's" she pouted as she leaned back in the arm chair, "but the last bite is always the best in my opinion."

"Really? Because I think the first bite is the best. In fact, I have found that the first of everything is always the best."

Her ears twitched again as she weighed the two. "I guess it depends on what kind of first we are talking about. I'll give you the first bite, as well as the first snow, first crush..."

"First kiss?" I asked with a wink.

She blushed and fidgeted with her hands as she licked her lips, "Yes...first kiss."

For a moment, we sat there, looking at each other in silence. I studied the lines of her beautiful face while I felt her eyes doing the same for me. The moment was interrupted by the sound of someone moving around on the floor above us.

Madeline looked away and pulled her watch out of her packet, "Oh my, it is late. I need to be going," she said as she rose to her feet.

I stood to walk her out.

"No need for that," she said softly.

"Sorry, I was trying to be polite."

"I know you were, and I appreciate it," she said as she opened the door. "Have a good night James, I'll see you in the morning."

"Same to you, Madeline."

CHAPTER
FOUR

IT HAD BEEN a miracle that I got any sleep that night. My active mind was still trying to process everything that had happened, and then there were the random dreams of strangers around me that would dance across my mind with no warning. Like anyone else, I was no stranger to having weird dreams that didn't make sense, but when you got to see glimpses of other peoples' without trying, well, let's just say I saw some weird things before sleep overtook me.

    I was lost in my own crazy dream about a raven and swarm of rabid dogs when the soft touch of a warm hand against my cheek brought me out of my sleep. As I began to stir, I slowly parted my eyes to see who had awoken me. Half of my brain had a good idea of who it was, while the other half hoped that the hand belonged to some spinster I had picked up on Miami beach after my airshow.

    "Hey there sleepy head," said the owner of the hand once she noticed I was beginning to wake.

    "Hey yourself," I yawned while stretching. "How long have you been sitting here watching me?"

    "Long enough to know that you look just as handsome asleep as you do awake."

I sat up and looked at Madeline, trying to figure out if what she said was a joke, or if it would even bother me if it wasn't. The white-furred foxkin was a beautiful woman, and though it was weird to see fluffy fox ears ears and a tail, I found they made her more alluring. Even her ruby eyes had a hypnotic effect on me, but I had to shake it off. I had been in Dione for half a day, and her military uniform reminded me that I was pretty much a captive.

In the end, I decided that falling for her lovely face was a bad idea…for the time being.

"You know," I began as I leaned against the headboard of my bed, "I don't mind being woken up by beautiful women like yourself, but this whole entering my quarters without permission has got to stop."

She sat up and her ears went flat, the smile on her face dissolving. "Sorry, I didn't mean to upset you."

"It's not that you are upsetting me, it's more…what if I wasn't dressed properly? Like yesterday, I was in the shower and came out to find you waiting for me."

"I announced I was here," she said defiantly as she crossed her arms.

"Yes, you did, but what if I'd come out without a towel on? I would have exposed myself to you. Even now, I'm in my underwear under these blankets."

Her ears twitched as the sides of her lips curled upward. "And what is wrong with that?"

My mouth opened to answer her, but a knot in my throat stopped me from saying anything. My mind started to wander down a naughty rabbit hole as I imagined what could have happened.

"That's what I thought," she said with a cute laugh. "James, there is no need to be so modest, especially around me."

"I'll keep that in mind."

I wasn't sure if she liked that response or not, but either

way, she got up, moved to the dresser, grabbed the tray that was sitting on it and brought it over to me in bed.

A mouth-watering aroma hit me as she lowered the tray onto my lap. On it was a covered plate, utensils, a glass of orange juice, and a steaming mug of coffee. Even though the plate had a cover, it did nothing to stop the strong smell of fresh cooked bacon from greeting me. When I removed the cover, savory steam rose up past my face, revealing the meal Madeline had brought.

Laid before me was a fluffy cheese omelet with three pieces of perfectly cooked bacon and two triangles of buttered toast. I admired the beautiful breakfast for as long as my stomach would let me before devouring it all.

Other than the omelet needing a bit more salt, the meal was perfect. While I ate, Madeline sat there, watching me while her tail wagged behind her. She bit her lips and made little sighs and whimpers every time I finished off a part of my meal.

"Do you want a piece of bacon?"

"No thank you, I ate before I came to see you," she replied as her eyes stayed glued to the bacon in my hand.

"That's not what I asked. Do you want a piece of bacon?"

She bit her lip and lowered her ears before gently nodding her head.

How much of their animal side do they have?

I extended my hand with the bacon, and Madeline swiped it from me before I had a chance to change my mind. She wolfed it down, her tail wagging more vigorously.

As I ate, the sounds of plane engines powering up before taking flight caught my ears. They had different tones than the planes I was used to hearing back on Earth, but the deep roar was unmistakable.

Madeline caught me turning my head to listen as a few of the planes flew over the dormitory. "What are you doing?" she asked.

"Listening to the planes. They sound so strange compared to the ones I am used to."

"Stange how?"

I got up and sat the tray of empty dishes on the dresser. I stretched a little more before answering her.

"Strange in how the engines hum, how their propellers sound as they pull through the air, and the whistle the wings make as they cut through the wind. Each plane has a different sound, and it's exciting to get to add new sounds to the mind."

"I've never thought of it that way. They all sound the same to me," she said with a shrug.

"I take it you don't fly much?"

She blushed before answering, "No. Believe it or not, I have a slight fear of heights."

"How? You live on a floating continent."

"And have you seen how long the drop is from land level to the water below?" she said with a shiver.

"How high is it?"

"Two miles, I think they say you would die from a heart attack if you fell for that long."

"It's not that bad," I offered as I put some pants on, feeling awkward being in my underwear while she visited.

"What isn't?" she asked.

"Falling through the air, well, as long as you know you have a parachute."

Madeline's eyes widened. "You have been shot down?"

"Yes, I have."

"Oh my Goddess, What was that like?"

"Humbling and terrifying. I'm lucky I was able to bail out and make it safely to the water."

She let out a nervous laugh, "That's another thing I have a fear of."

"You don't travel much, do you?" I asked as I sat down in the arm chair across from her.

"Growing up? No, my dad kept me on the estate with my mom. He and my older brothers traveled quite a bit, but not me. I didn't start going out until I was seventeen, and still, I only traveled by car, bus, or train."

Something felt so strange about her dad not letting her leave the estate, and I think she knew I was about to ask about it.

"Please don't ask about my upbringing. That is something I don't like to share with many people."

"Fair enough," I agreed with a nod.

"So, what made you want to be a pilot?" she asked as she leaned forward and pulled a journal out of the satchel on the floor. She then scooted back on my bed to lean against the wall and crossed her legs, resting her tail on her lap and using it to prop her journal on as she started writing.

"I always wanted to be one," I answered once I got past the image of me rubbing my face in her tail out of my mind. "My dad was a pilot. He flew in the first great war and became a mail and passenger pilot after that. He flew out to small communities around our city in the Texas panhandle, delivering the mail and clients to where they needed to go when they couldn't wait on a train."

"So, like father, like son?"

"I guess you could say that," I shrugged, "I learned how to fly a plane before I learned how to drive a car. We lived on the airfield my dad worked out of, so it was bound to happen."

"Sounds like it. Do you have any brothers or sisters?"

"Nope, only child. Did you say you have older brothers?"

"Yes, two, but we don't have a good relationship."

"Why?"

She set her journal down and stared at me.

"That's right, you don't want to talk about it."

"Not right now at least." She nodded before moving on, "So what made you want to be a fighter pilot?"

"Initially, I didn't. After I graduated high school, I became an air racer, and did that for three years."

"Were you good at it?"

"I found some success," I answered with a shrug, "Thompson Races were what I was best at, never won, but had a few top five finishes, had a sponsor and made good money."

"Thompson Races?"

"High speed, low altitude time trials over a closed course around pylons. Great training for eventual fighter pilots," I added as I waved my hands in the air like a plane flying around the obstacles.

The foxkin hid her face behind her journal and held back a laugh as she watched me. "I think I get the picture, so what made you stop doing that and become a fighter pilot?"

"War." I sighed. "When England declared war on Germany, all races were halted. A bunch of the guys I raced with joined their respective air forces and became enemies overnight. My country was late to join, but a few buddies and I went to England to volunteer."

I watched her eyes as she wrote, her brows furrowing a bit as she made some big movements and seemed to circle something on her page.

"Is something the matter?" I asked.

"No, just trying to keep up with all the names you are throwing at me."

"Have you heard of them?"

"In passing," she said with a shrug.

My eyes narrowed as I focused on her, "What country are the humans you have met from?"

She paused what she was doing and looked up to the right, tapping her pencil to her lips while she thought.

"Hmm, I don't really recall."

"I thought you were an intelligence officer?"

"I am," she said, dropping her head and ears, "just not a very good one."

Look what you did!

"I'm sorry Madeline, I didn't mean to insinuate that you weren't good at your job. I just assumed that someone who could read minds and shapeshift would be…"

"More valuable?" she said, finishing my thought.

Her red eyes looked at me over her glasses. She shut the journal and took a deep breath. "You're right. Someone with my skills should be in one of the Coalition countries, seducing dignitaries, befriending wives and girlfriends of lawmakers, and collecting anything I could to help the Empire."

She paused for a moment and removed her glasses. "However, I barely scored high enough to make it into the Ministry. Then there is my father. He made sure I couldn't do anything to embarrass him or my brothers, so he got me stationed here as a lowly Ministry grunt."

"I'm starting to dislike your father."

She faked a smile before getting up and stepping into the bathroom. I sat there in silence while she did what she needed to do. When she returned, she seemed to be doing better. Her head was held high and her ears stood tall.

"You are right James, I am a good minder," she said as she sat back on the foot of my bed. "And I am going to prove it by helping you with your minder abilities."

"Me?"

"Yes, you. You are the first human in our records to have minder abilities. It would be a disgrace to the Goddess Crestia to allow you to leave without helping you fully realize your gift. That is… if you want to?"

She leaned forward and gave me a pleading look, doing her best imitation of "puppy dog" eyes as she waited for my response.

"I'm in," I said, smiling back at her.

Her ears twitched and tail wagged as she did a small celebratory jump on my bed. "Thank you, you won't regret this. I-I need to go get a few things from my office. Wait here, I'll be right back!"

Madeline jumped to her feet and moved to the door, leaving before I had a chance to remind her that waiting here was all I could do. In her excitement, she forgot to shut the door behind her, so I got up to shut it for her.

Before doing so, I poked my head outside and saw Laurel and Hardy were still holding their posts on both sides of the door. They gave me a side eyed glance when I leaned out.

"You two working hard, or hardly working?" I asked.

They didn't answer. I stepped back in the room and grabbed my tray with dirty dishes from breakfast on it and sat it down on the floor next to Hardy.

"You know, I would take these back to the chow hall myself, but I feel like I am not allowed to leave. Will you make sure room service picks these up?"

Still no answer, but the feelings of annoyance that were dripping off him and his buddy Laurel made it clear I shouldn't push them any further.

"As you were," I said as I shut the door.

CHAPTER
FIVE

"YOU HAVE ALREADY DEMONSTRATED you can read people's minds, but now we need to establish your ability to talk to someone telepathically."

"Got it...how do I do that?" I asked, sitting cross legged on my bed.

"It's easy," said Madeline as she sat across from me, mirroring how I was sitting. "First you have to open your mind to receive. Once you start receiving someone's projected communication, you can grab their connection and send your own back to them."

Her tone and smile at the end made it seem like it was as easy as learning how to talk. Lost in all that was that it took most people twelve to thirteen years to be able to talk properly, and still some needed more work at it than others. But she was the teacher, and I was her student.

"Are you ready?" she asked.

"As ready as I can be."

"Then let's begin. Close your eyes, relax, and be ready to receive."

I did what she asked. I sat there and took slow shallow breaths with my eyes closed, waiting for something to happen.

"James? Can you hear me?" she asked, sending a shiver down my spine.

This was not the first time someone had spoken to me telepathically, Major Welch had communicated to me in this way yesterday as I flew to his aid. I was not able to talk back to him, but I had received his projections, and just like yesterday, it still felt strange.

I can hear you, can you hear me? I thought to myself.

Nothing.

"James," she called out again, "*can you hear me?*"

Yes.

We sat there in silence while she called out to me using her telepathic abilities. She sounded like we were on two different ends of the world's longest storm drain. Her projected voice was echoey and distant, almost muffled but still clear.

"*At this point, would you at least acknowledge that you can hear me?*"

"I can hear you Madeline," I said out loud, "I just can't seem to respond."

"Good, so it's you, not me."

I opened my eyes and stared at her, "Jeez thanks, you make it sound like I am broken."

"Compared to the humans we have met, you are," she said as she opened her eyes. "But don't worry, not every Dionian gets it right away."

"It must be entertaining when kids start talking to their parents telepathically," I said with a chuckle, imagining the silly things kids said, then picturing them saying them telepathically.

Madeline seemed less amused. In fact, the way her ears and head were leaning said she was more confused than anything.

"Is it not?" I asked. "Kids say the dumbest and funniest things while they are growing up. Having them being able to say those same things telepathically has got to be hilarious."

She still didn't laugh. "James, children don't have any gifts."

Now it was my turn to give her the confused look.

"The Gods and Goddesses do not hand out their gifts until our fifteenth birthday."

"Really?"

She nodded, her ears bouncing on top of her head as she did.

"Why fifteen?"

"No one knows," she shrugged, "but the moment is the same for everyone. You get a small headache in the base of your skull that moves through your entire head. It's a dull pain, and the more gifts you are given, the longer the pain lasts, but it goes away quickly when finished."

"No shit…"

The memories of yesterday came back to me like a flood. I didn't know how long I had been in that cloud that brought me here, but the headache and pain had happened to me, just as Madeline had described it. However, we needed to have a talk about what a "dull pain" was.

Did the Gods of this world give me a "gift?" I asked myself.

"James? Are you there?"

I saw Madeline's hand wave in front of my eyes and was snapped back to reality.

"There you are! You spaced out on me," she said with a concerned tone.

"Sorry, I was just thinking about yesterday."

"Must have been some thought, you were out of it for a good minute. I thought you were having a stroke."

"No, I'm fine," I said before changing the subject, "how long did it take you to make your telepathic connection?"

"Only a few minutes."

"Your parents must have been proud."

"My mom was," she said, faking a smile.

"But not your dad?"

The smile she had been faking shifted into a frown, matching the pain in her eyes. She didn't like talking about her father, she had made that clear, but my dumb ass kept asking about him.

"I'm sorry, I didn't-"

"He was there," she interrupted, "but for different reasons."

The melancholy beauty in front of me extended her hand, holding it out, beckoning for me to take it.

"I can't tell you and not lose control of my emotions, but I can show you," she said in my head. "Take my hand."

I did as she told me and took her hand in mine, and just like yesterday, everything around me went dark. Before me stood a wall that stretched as far as I could see in every direction.

This must be her mental barrier.

In front of me, a light appeared, creating a path for me to follow. While I walked, the scenery around me shifted until we arrived in a small room. There were three people in the room, an older man, a younger woman, and a child laying on the ground, crying. Their details were hard to make out as the memory before started to play out.

"You said you would keep an eye on her," said the man.

"I was, my lord, I looked away for a moment and-"

"And what?" scolded the man, "you allowed her to use her gift to run wild through the garden and my estate. Did you not understand that I had guests over?"

I looked closer at the man, he was blurry, but the more I focused, the more I could make out his details. He had white slicked back hair, white fox ears and red eyes. He wore a black pinstripe suit that had spots of dirt and mud on it.

"I am sorry, my lord. It was never my intention to embarrass you in front of your guests."

"Papa, I'm sorry," cried the girl on the floor.

The voice was familiar. She was crouched over, covering herself in a blanket with dried mud on her hands and feet. Her ears and tail were blurry, but I could make out the familiar white details of the woman whose mind I was in.

"If you were truly sorry, then you would not have done it," chided the man, looking down at her with disgust.

"My lord, she's still a child-"

"She is fifteen and my daughter, something that I am constantly reminded of. As long as she has my blood and lives under my roof, I will deal with her as I see fit."

The woman had nothing to say, nodding her head instead. She was the hardest of the three for me to focus on. The only detail I could truly pull out of the blur were the details of her face. She was a beautiful woman who had the same pointed facial features as Madeline, but she looked tired, and dirty.

"You do not know how lucky you are," he said as he looked down at the shaking Madeline. "You receive the Reynolds family gift from the goddess, and your first shift is a rabbit? How embarrassing."

Her mother was about to say something, but he held up his hand, silencing her before looking down on Madeline again. "You are lucky the hounds didn't get a hold of you before you led them into my house, but if they had, it would have saved myself and your brothers from embarrassment. They are currently having to explain to my guests why a rodent ruined their meal."

He turned to leave the room, fading as he moved away from the area that was being shown to me. There was the sound of a door opening, then her father spoke again, "Get her cleaned up, and for the love of Crestia, do not let her out of your sight again."

The door slammed and Madeline burst into tears on the floor as her mother dropped to her knees to console her.

"Why? Why did you do this to me?" Madeline cried as she pushed her mother away.

"Maddy, I'm sorry, I didn't..."

The memory quickly went black, and felt like the lamp of a projector had burned out mid movie. I then felt myself being pulled backwards until I stood back at the barrier I had seen at the start.

When I opened my eyes, Madeline still had one hand in mine, but pulled it from me to hide her face and her tear stained cheeks from my view. She wiped away the tears and looked at me with bloodshot eyes.

"See why I don't like to talk about my dad?" she asked between sniffles.

There was nothing I could say that would cheer her up, but there was something I could do. I got up and went to the bathroom, got one of the unused wash clothes, wetted it with warm water and returned to her.

I sat next to her on the bed and handed her the warm wash cloth so she could wipe off her face. Instead this made her break into more tears.

"Did I do something wrong?" I asked, confused by why she was crying.

She shook her head and leaned into me, wrapping her arms around my neck and burying her face into my shoulder. I held her for as long as she needed, gently rubbing her back as she let go. While she did, I felt her mental barrier crack and picked up trace thoughts as they crossed her mind.

"Why is he so sweet?" and *"Why did he have to be a human?"* were the two complete thoughts I was able to make sense of before she pulled herself together, and mended the cracks.

"Sorry about that," she said as she pulled away and sat on her feet, wiping her eyes with the washcloth.

"It's ok, thank you for showing me that, I know it must have been difficult."

"That's not even the worst. In his eyes, I didn't exist until I embarrassed him."

We sat there in silence until she got up to properly clean her face off.

"Oh my Goddess, I look terrible!" she grumbled from the bathroom.

"No you don't."

"You are too kind."

"I mean it," I said as I stood up and stretched, moving to lean against the door frame of the bathroom door. "Even when you are crying, you are beautiful, and you look so much like your mother."

Madeline froze and looked at me with wide eyes and alert ears, "What did you say?"

"I said you are beautiful-"

"Thank you," she said with a smile, "but after that."

"That you look like your mother?"

"Yes, that, how do you know what my mother looks like?"

"I saw her in your memory, she was blurry at first, but I was able to focus and her face came into focus."

"Oh yeah?" she asked as she crossed her arms, "Tell me what she looked like."

"Pointed face like yours, same eye shape as yours, except hers were brown, she looked tired and dirty."

Madeline had a worried look on her face, "You weren't supposed to see her."

"I wasn't?"

She moved past me into the small living space and started pacing back and forth. "When minders share their thoughts with others, we are able to show only the details we want to show. With a lot of training and practice, one can push past those restrictions and see hidden details."

I nodded to show I was still following her.

"James, I might be a terrible intelligence officer, but I am a damn good minder, A-ranked, to be more specific. The fact that you were able to see through any of my restrictions with no training at all is...impressive."

"Well I am glad you are impressed, because I have no idea what I did or how I did it."

She stopped pacing and flashed me a smile, "Then that's where I come in. Let's see if we can't get you a little more control."

My first two victims were Laurel and Hardy, the two guards outside my door. Madeline assured me that they didn't have any mental barrier training and tasked me to find something out about them.

It took me a few tries, but with a little focus, I was able to tell them apart by "brain signatures" and dive deeper into their minds than just surface thoughts.

"Victim one is Sergeant Paul Becker, code name: Laurel." I said between bites of one of the sandwiches that Madeline had gone out to get for us, along with a few other foods.

"Laurel?" she asked as she popped a Choc Um into her mouth.

"Victim two is Sergeant Jacob Horn, code name: Hardy."

"Hardy? Where are you getting these code names?" Madeline asked as she rubbed her forehead.

"They are a comedy duo back on earth. One is lean, while the other is hefty."

She shook her head and waved for me to go on, it had taken most of the day, but I was finally getting a hang on this mind reading thing.

"Sergeant Becker is a local kid who won't stop thinking about the lady running the commissary. Sergeant Horn comes from a military family and is tired of being compared to his brother and sister who outrank him."

"Not bad, but that's easy info that any C-rank could find, go in and find more."

I sighed and reached out again for Sgt. Horn. He had been the easiest of the two to read from the beginning, and I felt like he would provide good practice. Reaching out, I found the outer edge of his thoughts and pressed harder, forcing my mind deeper into his subconscious.

Memories and thoughts moved past me as I navigated his inner mind. I had to find something that was deeper than his shallow thoughts, something that he probably didn't want anyone to know. As I searched, I saw a memory that burned at his thoughts, it was being pushed aside, repressed and ignored at all costs.

"I can't believe another one rejected me!" shouted a young Sgt. Horn as he looked down at a collection of letters on the table he was hunched over.

"Well maybe now you can see how foolish the idea of making a living as an artist would be."

Sgt. Horn glared at the man who had spoken. He was built the same, and shared a few similarities. This memory was crystal clear, down to every detail when compared to the censored memory Madeline had shown me earlier. I peered over his shoulder and read the contents of the letters.

Rejection is what was layed out on the table. It seemed Sgt. Horn thought he was an artist and had applied to continue his studies at each of the major art institutes of the Empire. However, the judges felt his art was "basic" and had a lack of appreciation for the canid form.

Anger swelled up inside the young Sgt. Horn. He grabbed the letters, wadded them up and threw them into the fireplace off to the side, *"You win, father. I'll enlist in the morning."*

I let go of his mind and was pulled back to my own, blinking a few times to clear away the fog of his thoughts from my own.

"Sgt. Horn was rejected from multiple art institutes in the Empire, and that is what fuels his anger."

Madeline's face lit up as she looked at me, "Excellent! That is the type of information we can use, now dive deeper into Yanny."

"You mean Laurel?"

"Isn't that what I said?" she asked with a bewildered look.

Instead of diving down that rabbit hole, I turned my focus to Sergeant Becker, who I had named Laurel. Becker was more difficult for me to dive into, his mind was not as scattered as Horn's was, and was very well organized. If you thought an organized mind was easier to read, you would be wrong.

Madeline pointed out that an organized mind was better at hiding secrets in the details of the thoughts. While Horn's thoughts were all out in the open, Beckers were stored in neat rows and required me to scan them meticulously.

Important dates, names, places, and useless facts that would only be valuable for trivia rolled past my mind's eye. I had to work through the boring stuff before I could find anything of importance. My mind flicked faster and faster through his thoughts, and they started to blur as they went by.

Hold on, what was that?

I stopped and retraced my steps, returning to a memory that looked out of place, as if someone had placed an old comic book in the middle of leather bound novels. This is what I was looking for.

"Sergeant Becker is married," I whispered to Madeline.

"No shit? Where did you see that?"

"Between where he learned to ride a bike and his grandmother's funeral."

She went silent for a bit as her eyes went distant, "Oh...wow, there it is."

"But that isn't the best part," I said as I elbowed her, "let me know when you find the best part."

Her eyes went wide, mouth dropped and she looked at me in shock, "She's his-"

"Yup."

"And the family knows?"

"Yup, pretty disgusting isn't it?" I asked as she started shaking her head, "which makes me wonder about his crush on the commissary girl."

"What about it?" she asked, still shaking her head from time to time to clear away what she saw.

"Well, he's married, and his thoughts tell us that he's asked the commissary girl out on a date and she has accepted."

Madeline shrugged like she didn't understand where I was going with this.

"He's cheating on his wife," I said bluntly.

"No he isn't," she said, waving off my concern, "he's trying to add the commissary girl to his family so he can get harem benefits."

"Harem benefits?"

"Yeah, the more wives a soldier in the military has, the more pay he will receive, along with better assignments and a few other things...you look confused."

I nodded.

"It's the harem part, isn't it? I think I remember reading that humans don't have harems back on earth?"

"No, well, not anymore. They were a thing thousands of years ago in Asia, but not practiced in the modern day."

"Well on Dione, they are a big thing. Women outnumber men four to one because of the war, and the numbers are getting wider the longer the war goes on."

"So it's a war time thing?" I asked, trying to wrap my mind around another shocking revelation.

"I guess you could say that. Nobility has always practiced it, my dad has three wives, the emperor has five, oh, and Major Welch, he has four."

"Major Welch, that's the pilot whose life I saved?"

"Yes, I am friends with his first wife, you have no idea how grateful she is for what you did."

"Tell her it was nothing. I'm sure the pilots I shot down have loved ones who are worried about them."

Madeline smiled at me, her ears twitching, "You are a caring man, James, even if for the enemy."

"To be clear, they're not my enemy, I just answered a plea for help."

She nodded in understanding before popping another Choc Um into her mouth.

"Do I need to be worried about some fox or wolfkin trying to kick my ass because you just spent an entire day in my room?" I asked with a smug smile.

Madeline nodded as she swallowed the candy, "No, I am single."

"That's a shame. I figured a beautiful gal like yourself would have the men lined up to date you."

"That's kind of you to say," she said as her face turned red, "but men aren't doll dizzy over a girl who can read their mind."

"That's dumb, but I get it."

"Yeah, but that is why I like being around you," she said as her cheeks turned more red. "I can't read your mind, and you aren't scared of me."

"Because there is nothing to be scared of."

"You sweet man, if you only knew..."

I leaned forward, "Then tell me."

She smiled and leaned closer to me, "I should be going. It's getting late." she said, her breath tickling my lips.

"I'll walk you to the door."

She laughed but I did as I promised and walked her the few short steps to the apartment door.

"Before you go, I have a request-"

"Yes, I will knock tomorrow morning before coming in," she said, interrupting me.

"Thanks, but that's not it, I want to leave this room. Please ask the Marshall Altros if I can at least go running in the morning, I'm sure the guard dogs wouldn't mind the change of scenery."

They both turned their heads to say something, but Madeline held up her hand, silencing them, "I'm sure I can arrange something."

"Thank you, Agent Reynolds-"

She leaned forward and wrapped her arms around me, pressing her face into my chest. I returned the embrace, rubbing her back as one of her large ears twitched and tickled my chin.

"Thank you, James," she said before letting go and walking away without looking back.

I stood there and watched her leave, her tail and ass swaying hypnotically before she stepped out the door at the end of the hall.

"She's something else, isn't she?" I asked my guard buddies. Still no answer.

"Y'all are no fun," I said as I shut the door.

CHAPTER SIX

"EXPLAIN THIS GAME TO ME AGAIN?"

"*It's not a game, it's a minder training exercise,*" Madeline said telepathically as she walked beside me, "*and keep your voice down, don't forget that everyone around you has better hearing than you do.*"

"Got it."

She had gotten permission from Marshall Altros to escort me to certain locations around the airfield. I was limited to my apartment, the mess hall, and the commissary, even though I didn't have any of this country's money. I also had to wear an officer's hat and a long black duster style jacket that came down to my ankles over the clothes I was already being loaned by the Empire.

We left the mess hall and strolled in the early morning sunlight. There was a soft chill in the air as it appeared they were entering their autumn season, so the jacket did come in handy. Madeline was wearing a similar style jacket, and we looked like a couple since "we match!" Her words, not mine.

"*The game works by the two of us picking a target,*" the beautiful foxkin continued, intertwining her arm in mine, forcing us to walk close enough that her curvy hips would bump into mine. "*We will then have thirty seconds to see who can pull the most information out of their mind.*"

"What does the winner get?" I whispered.

"The loser has to buy the winner a treat of their choice at the commissary," she whispered back.

"But I don't have any money."

"Don't worry about that," she said, waving her free hand, "we will put it on credit and I'll worry about it later."

"Ok, I take it we are heading for the commissary?"

"Yes, I need Choc Um's!"

The first target we picked was a foxkin woman sitting on a bench by a memorial statue of one of the previous rulers of Crestia. She was reading a book and sipping on a mug of coffee as we approached her.

"I'm ready when you are," I whispered.

Madeline checked her pocket watch. "Ok...three, two, one, go!"

I pushed my mind toward the woman and entered her subconsciousness. The first thing to hit me were the words of the book she was reading. It was a story about a man who inherited a milk farm from his uncle that specialized in a special kind of milk that was provided by the farm's guests. I blushed a little as I scanned her imagery of the story, and couldn't believe she would read a book like that in the open.

Diving deeper, I saw she had a love for these kinds of stories, and tried to find anything on her mind other than the hundreds of erotic stories she indulged in. Eventually I did find some useful information, such as her name, how many siblings she had, how big her family was, yada yada. None of that was good enough to beat Madeline.

My mental clock was telling me that I was running out of time, and I had to find something, and then there it was. I memorized what I saw, and then pulled myself back and into my own mind where Madeline and I were still walking. How we managed that, I wasn't sure.

I waited for Madeline to say time, looking down at her hand holding her pocket watch. A minute went by before I looked closely and saw her face. Her ruby eyes were distant, she was breathing heavily, blushing and starting to get weak in the knees.

"Madeline," I hissed as I held her up, "Madeline!"

She lazily looked up at me, her eyes filled with lust as she wrapped her arms around my neck. "Kiss me, James."

I froze, allowing her to pull herself closer to me. For a moment, I went back and forth on if I should kiss her or not, but her full lips and lustful gaze was all the convincing I needed.

Leaning down, I pressed my lips to hers, pulling her into me as we kissed. She let out a muffled moan as her soft lips coaxed mine apart, allowing her tongue to venture into my mouth to find a friend waiting for it. She tasted like the chocolate candies she was always eating, and my tongue couldn't get enough.

We slowly pulled away from each other, smiling and breathing heavy as we did.

"So...who won?" I asked once I caught my breath.

Her eyes lost their lusty haze, became more alert, and her smile transformed into a face of shock and embarrassment.

"Oh no...I-I didn't mean to do that," she said as she backed away and covered her face.

"Hey, it's ok, calm down. You didn't do anything wrong," I assured her, holding up my hands and moving closer to her.

"But...we kissed..." she said softly, her face burning red as she tried not to look at me.

"I know, I was there," I said as I wrapped my arms around her, "and it was an amazing kiss."

"It was? You liked it?" she asked as she let me hold on to her.

"I did, why wouldn't I?"

She looked up at me and tried opening her mouth to speak. She shook her head, her ears brushing my face, then she buried her face in my chest. *"That was my first kiss..."*

"Oh," I said as I held her close, then it hit me, "Oh..."

I felt the eyes and thoughts of strangers as we stood there, but I didn't care. My number one priority was the beautiful woman in my arms.

"Did you enjoy the kiss?" I asked.

I felt her nod against me.

"Then there's nothing to be ashamed of. I liked it, you liked it, and if you don't mind me saying, I wouldn't mind doing it again, just in a more private location."

She let out a big sigh and stood up straight, smoothing out any wrinkles on her uniform.

"To the commissary?" I asked as I offered her my arm.

"Yes."

We walked arm in arm in silence as we simply enjoyed each other's company. It was Madeline who broke the silence.

"So what did you find?"

"Oh? Are we still playing?" I asked.

"Yes, even though I got lost in the story she was reading, we still need to work on your skills. Did you get caught by her... imagination?"

I let out a small chuckle as I remembered what I had seen when I first entered the woman's mind, "For a moment I was caught in what she was reading. It was very erotic, but also seemed caring and loving in a strange way. I was able to move past it and did find something that seemed valuable."

"What was it?" she asked.

"It seems she has family members living in Oshor who oppose the Empire."

"Not surprising." Madeline shrugged. "There is an organization named the Enclave that feels the need to let everyone know that the Goddess Crestia does not stand for the Empire's actions."

"And what actions are those?"

"Not in the open," she said as she shook her head. "I know you are not from here, but talking about our enemies' complaints about us in the open can be seen as treason."

I looked around and saw all the ears of those around us, wolf and fox ears, all up, all alert. Any one of them could be listening in on our conversation.

"Good morning and welcome to the commissary," said the comely wolfkin woman behind the counter as we entered the small general store looking building.

"Good morning Milli," Madeline called.

"Agent Reynolds, are you here for your daily Choc Um's round up?"

"Yes, and more," she said as she gestured to me standing behind her.

"Oh, hello," said Milli as she came out from behind the counter to greet me. "I am Millicent, but everyone just calls me Milli."

"James Walker," I said as I extended my hand.

Like when I shook hands with Major Welch, I got a flash of the woman's inner thoughts...

Wow, look at those little ears. No wonder Paul doesn't like to talk about him, he's handsome and smells nice.

"It's nice to meet you ma'am," I said, finishing the greeting.

"Enough of that," growled Madeline as she grabbed the woman's wrist before either of us had a chance to let go, yanking it free of my hand.

"Oww, you don't have to be so rough," said the shop keeper as she rubbed her wrist. "What's your problem?"

Madeline had a crazed look in her eye that faded away before she flashed Milli a smile. "Nothing, just don't do it again." She then turned, grabbed a hand basket, put it in my hands and pulled me down one of the aisles, leaving the shop manager looking bewildered.

There were three aisles in the shop. One had clothing such as underwear, shorts, pants, t-shirts and untailored uniforms. The second had snacks such as breads, crackers, cookies, chocolates, candies and dried and canned meats. On the last were a wide selection of drinks from juices and sodas to wines, liquors and beers.

Madeline bounced around like a kid in a candy store, especially in the candy section. At least six bags of Choc Um's were put in the basket, along with a summer sausage, crackers, candied nuts, and two bottles of wine. I was also able to get a few fresh clothing options so I could have something to wear when I did laundry.

"Do you want me to set you up a tab?" Milli asked as she rang everything up.

"Yes ma'am, though I don't know when I'll be able to pay you."

"Don't you worry, I'm sure Agent Reynolds will figure something out," she said with a wink.

"Stop flirting with him!" growled Madeline as she slammed her fist on the counter.

"Madeline, she wasn't."

The shop manager looked back and forth between us as she quickly bundled our items into two paper bags and slid them toward us. "You two have a nice day," she added before quickly turning and going into the back of the shop.

"What was that about?" I asked as we left the store.

"What was what?"

"Don't play coy with me, you snapped at her twice for no reason."

She took a deep breath. "I didn't like what she was thinking."

"Madeline, people are allowed to think what they want."

"I know, but I don't want to hear them, especially when they are thinking about you," she said as her ears dropped.

I shook my head as we walked, she was a grown ass woman but was acting like a jealous girl. I would have probably done the same though if I could read the minds of men who introduced themselves to her. Who was I to judge?

"Want to continue our game?" she asked as we walked in the direction of the dorm.

"Sure," I said with a shrug.

We took the long way back to my apartment, picking different people to use for our game. In the process, we uncovered some weird things about a few strangers on the base.

One was lying about their age and had bribed a minder to verify them, another was scared of cats and always looking over their shoulder to see if a feline assassin was behind them. The most bizarre had to be the pilot who walked by us who liked to role play as a rabbitkin with his wife. I thought it was hilarious, Madeline didn't agree with me at all.

It was past noon by the time we made it back to my apartment, and Sergeant Horn was the only one standing guard by my door.

"Did it go anywhere?" I asked him, pointing at the door as we approached.

Still no answer, but a lot more brain activity. It turned out they were ordered not to talk to me at all, which was fine by me.

Madeline popped the cork on one of the wine bottles and grabbed two glasses from the dresser drawer, filling them both with the red liquid.

"To new friends," I said as I took the glass.

"And more," she said with a wink before unbuttoning her uniform suit coat and hanging it on one of the wall hooks. She stood there in her gray pencil skirt and her white button-up undershirt as she quickly drank her glass of wine. After she refilled it, she grabbed a bag of Choc Um's and laid down on my bed, kicking off the black heels she had been wearing before rubbing the arches of her feet and groaning.

"Comfortable?" I asked as I sat down in the arm chair.

"Getting there," she said as she laid on her side, "I have spent a lot of time with you over the past two days, Captain Walker, are there any Earth women I have to worry about coming to fight me?"

I laughed as she flipped my question from last night around on me. "No, I'm quite single."

"Aww, why is that?"

I got up, filled my glass with more wine before topping hers off and sitting back down in the arm chair.

"I'm an air show pilot. We never spend more than a few days in any location before we pack everything up and move our fleet of planes on to the next city. I'll be in Atlanta for a few days, then off to Orlando or Miami, Nashville, and so on. I didn't have time to meet anyone to go steady with."

"Sounds lonely."

"It could be. There were nights I would not be alone, but-"

"I don't want to hear about them," she said, taking a sip of her wine.

I nodded and moved past those details, "So, I pretty much put my all into the planes I was flying, doing what I could to show the American people what they were spending money on."

"I thought you were a combat pilot?"

"I was, and I guess deep down I still am."

"What happened?"

"I was shot down, remember?"

She nodded as she took another sip, "But you survived?

Why wouldn't they put an experienced man like you back into combat?"

"That's what I asked. Apparently we didn't have a lot of well known pilots to use for pre movie newsreels, so I became that guy."

"That must have been exciting though?"

"It was, for a time, but then I got bored and started asking if I could get back into the air. I eventually annoyed them so much that they put together the air show circuit for me. It's not what I had in mind, but it was better than doing photo shoots, recording radio ads and making appearances in movies."

"You are one of a kind," she said as she sat up to get more wine. "I don't think many people would turn down celebrity status in order to go back to fighting."

"True, but it just never felt right to me, other men had flown just as hard as I had, some survived, others died. So I shot down thirteen planes, big deal? Let me go and get thirteen more."

I smiled as my face grew warm, the wine was starting to get to me. They say different alcohols have different effects on people's feelings, and wine tends to make me emotional. I took a deep breath and reached into the bags of food, grabbing some bread and summer sausage to snack on.

Madeline sat back down on the bed, her cheeks flushed and her lips stained red. "Sounds to me like you don't like to win."

"What do you mean?" I asked after I swallowed the mouthful of food I had been chewing on.

"You don't like to win, you like to survive," she said, her words starting to slur. "Those are two very different things, you know? You survived in the air, you survived being shot down, but when it came time for someone to reward you, you pushed it away."

"There...might be merit in what you're saying,"

"I am a survivor," she said, touching the now exposed cleavage of her chest.

When had she undone those buttons?

"I am also a winner," she continued. "I survived my fathers ridicule and neglect until I saw a chance to win, and do you know what I did when I saw my chance?"

"You took it?" I asked.

"Absolutely I did. I put on a dress I had had secretly made, I did up my hair and makeup and I strutted into his dinner party and made him introduce me to the nobility that was there."

She took a big sip and then kept going, "He couldn't deny me, not in front of the Grand Duke and his family. He finally had to acknowledge me, and I have not let that moment go to waste. He hates me every day for it, but after how he treated me, I do not give a fuck!"

There it was. Anger. Wine made Madeline an angry drunk.

She laid back on my bed, stretching and stressing the remaining buttons on her shirt before she stopped and looked at me.

"Remind me again, who won our game today?"

"You did, but barely," I said, raising my glass to her.

"A win is a win," she said as she laid there looking at me.

"What do you want for your reward?" I asked, "Do you want me to run to the commissary and-"

"No!" she barked, sitting up quickly, "you can't go there unless I am with you...Marshall Altros orders, remember?"

Technically, she was right, but I thought her jealousy issues were the real reason.

"Then what do you want?"

She bit her bottom lip before she answered, her ears laid back as she spoke, "I have two requests."

"I think I can handle two requests."

"First," she said as she blushed, "I want you to hold me. No funny business, just hold me."

"And two?" I asked as I leaned forward in my chair.

"Kiss me. Show me how it's really done."

I nodded and rubbed my chin. "And no funny business?"

Her tail slowly started to wag behind her. "No funny business, just holding and kissing...Maybe some petting?"

"Heavy petting?" I asked as I stood up and moved to the bed, setting down my glass on the side table before taking hers from her hands and doing the same.

"Very heavy petting," she growled as she waited for me.

"Then if that is what the winner wants," I said as I lowered myself on top of her, "then that is what the winner will get."

CHAPTER SEVEN

GRABBING the back of her head, I pulled her to me, and our wine-stained lips met in an explosion of passion. This time, my tongue parted hers and sought out its partner.

She was shy at first, but her tongue eventually found a rhythm with mine, and as it did, my taste buds were assaulted by the dry tartness of wine and sweet chocolate, a magical mixture.

I lowered her head onto the pillow as we made out like horny teenagers, holding my body above hers as she moaned into my mouth. I slowly lowered my body against her, the bulge in my pants growing harder as the softness of her body writhed under me.

"No funny business?" I asked as I pulled back, breathing heavily.

"No funny business," she replied with a whimper, biting her lip as I ground myself against her.

"Do you trust me?"

"I-I..." She nodded when she couldn't speak, her ears twitching as she did.

I kissed her again before getting up and flipping her onto

her stomach, a protesting yelp coming from her as I did so. I leaned over her and kissed the back of her neck as my hands unzipped the back of her skirt. Once loose, I pulled it down and exposed her round ass and the black panties that were hugging them.

"No funny business," she said, covering herself as I threw the skirt on the floor and rolled her back over.

"Madeline, I'm not going to do anything you don't want me to do, but that skirt was in the way of the heavy petting."

"Those stay on?" she asked, pointing at my pants.

"Yes, and the zipper up."

She moved her hands, letting me get a full look at her waist and legs. She was wearing black lace panties and a matching garter belt holding up her sheer stockings. Her skin was pale and flawless, allowing for a strong contrast between it and her undergarments.

Her hand reached out to me, letting me know that the time for viewing was over, and the time for action was now.

I crawled back on top of her, kissing her exposed cleavage, up her collarbone to her neck before planting another round of kisses on her soft lips. We exchanged moans as I ground my stiff member into her warm folds, and even though we had a few layers of clothing between them, I could feel the heat radiating off her.

As we kissed, my hand grabbed and rubbed at the back of her head, and with a mind of its own, worked up to the soft heaven that was her ear. Madeline froze when my hand touched it, but while my fingers gently rubbed the soft fur, I felt her leg start to spasm against mine. Stopping, I looked down.

"Why did you stop?" she panted.

"Which part? The kissing or the ear rubs?"

"Both?" she asked, pulling my lips back to hers and grabbing my hand and encouraging me to keep rubbing her ear.

I did as she wanted and felt her leg start to gently kick while she moaned against my lips. My fingers hit the sweet spot when those gentle kicks got quicker and more violent. Curious, I switched hands, rubbing her neglected ear with my other hand while I gripped her throat and kissed down to her collar bone.

Sure enough, her other leg started kicking, as well as triggering a torrent of groans and moans out of the mouth of the beautiful vixen.

I kissed and licked at her exposed cleavage, wanting to see more when her hands reached between us and undid the buttons, throwing back the shirt and giving me a full view of her upper body.

"Thank God," I said with a sigh of relief.

"What?" asked the blushing vixen as she tried to cover her chest.

"It's nothing, I just...thought you might have extra nipples or something weird like that."

She lifted an eyebrow as she gave me an unamused look.

"You look amazing, better than I expected, and deserve."

"That's better," she said as she moved her hands out of the way, exposing her black lace bra that matched the panties and garterbelt.

Her bra was fighting hard to keep her breasts from spilling over, so I brought my hands over to help them. I cupped her breasts, squeezing my face between her smooth mounds of flesh while I kissed and licked at her soft skin. My fingers dipped under the black lace, pushing them down and exposing her small pink nipples.

I worked my way to one, leaving a trail of kisses before teasing it with my tongue. She whimpered at me as she tried to direct her bud into my mouth. Her eyes fluttered as I gave her what she wanted, taking her tit into my mouth and suckling on it while gently pulling back. I moved back and forth between the two, doing my best to give her breasts the attention they deserved.

No nipple left behind!

While my tongue was in heaven, my throbbing cock was in hell. It was begging for more than what I could provide it through grinding motions alone, but a promise was made, and I wasn't bringing him out tonight. With that in mind, I had to change what I was doing, or I was going to lose control and be useless to my sexy foxkin.

Shifting to the side of the narrow bed, I pushed on her hip so she was laying on her side, her rump and tail pressed against my aching bulge.

She growled in protest as she looked back at me. "But how am I going to kiss you?"

"Patience Maddy," I whispered into the soft fluff of her ear as I wrapped the arm I was laying on around her, pinning her back to my chest. "Because from back here, I can hold and pet you properly."

The hand of the arm I had wrapped around her gripped and teased her nipple while my free hand traced its way down her hips before following the seam of her black panties to the space between her thighs. Her breathing picked up as my fingers got closer to heat radiating from her virgin pussy.

"Lift your leg," I whispered into her ears.

She nodded as she did as she was told. I could feel her heartbeat quicken as she parted her legs, and slowly my fingers brushed over the wet fabric that covered her womanhood. I caressed her through the satin fabric, teasing and coaxing moans of pleasure from her wine-stained lips before she pleaded for more.

Not wanting to be one to let a lady down, I pressed harder against her mound. My middle finger found the outline of her clit and rubbed her hidden pearl, causing her to throw her head back in ecstasy.

I gave her a kiss on the cheek before her writhing pulled it away from me. She grabbed a hold of the hand I was using to tease her breast and squeezed it, egging it on to do more, while her other hand went exploring. It soon found the waistband of my pants, but didn't stay there long before it moved down and rubbed my bulge before gripping my cock through its fabric prison.

Her hold on my length was firm and steady, causing me to shiver, and when she started stroking it, my body shuddered as I pulled her tighter to me. I moaned next to her ear, which sent goose bumps across her skin and a visible shudder down her spine. In turn, her stroking picked up its pace.

"I never knew a man's moans could make me feel so…" she said between heavy breaths. "I need more!"

Her hand grabbed at the zipper of my fly, pulling it down.

"Woah, we promised the zipper would stay up," I said, hating myself for saying that.

"You promised," she said, looking over her shoulder at me. She gave the hand over her breast a reassuring squeeze, "but I need to feel you while you moan in my ear."

"I can't argue with that."

She wasted no time weaving her hand through the opening and finding what she wanted. Her hand was soft and careful as she pulled my length out into the air, and once it was free of the restraints of the fabric, I let out a moan of excitement.

"That's what I wanted to hear," she said, cheering me on.

I remembered that I had a job to do as well, so while her soft hand stroked and rubbed my throbbing cock against her ass cheek, my fingers pressed and rubbed her slit, still hidden behind its fabric prison.

Feeling emboldened by the rush of her hand stroking my cock, I dipped my digits under the waist of her panties and pushed south. My fingertips pushed through a small tuft of soft hair before they moved over her pearl and into her valley. Her pussy lips were easy to spread with how wet they were, and though she was tight, it made it easy for my fingers to glide in and out of her.

We took turns vocalizing our pleasure to each other. Every twitch of my finger against her clit or dip of it deep into her slit made her give off the most lovely harmony of whimpers and moans. Meanwhile, the way her hand gripped and stroked my shaft, pulling all the way up to the head made me gasp and grunt into her ear, just like she wanted it.

She stroked me faster and faster, keeping pace with how fast I was fingering her. It felt amazing in her small soft hands, but amazing motions like that have a cost, and I was quickly building to that point.

"I'm about to cum Madeline, don't stop...Don't stop."

"Ohh...I-I'm almost there too."

Our hands worked hard and faster, rubbing, stroking and petting each other until we both shuddered as our individual orgasms washed over us.

My cock thickened in her grip before it sprayed rope after rope of cum onto her soft round ass and black panties. I groaned and curled my toes as her amazing hand kept stroking my length, milking every drop onto her skin.

As I painted her rump with my seed, she shook in my arms and soaked my fingers, her moans loud as she screamed out in pleasure. I didn't stop and continued to massage her clit and the inner depths of her folds until the shaking stopped and she collapsed in my arms. I soon followed suit and laid there holding her, breathing heavily, and the euphoria of the moment washed over me.

"That was amazing," I said as I nuzzled against her soft ear.

"You're telling me," she said as she gently caressed and teased my spent cock. "That felt like a lot, was that a lot?"

I looked at where my seed had landed. It was hard to say for sure, since my cum and her skin were close to the same color, but I could tell there was more there than I had seen in my twenty-five years.

"Umm...yeah, that's a lot."

"How does it taste?"

"Madeline, I have no idea, and I have no need to find out."

I lay in the small bed and let the wine and the post orgasm haze wash over me while I enjoyed the scent Madeline had left on my fingers. It was sweet, almost like honey and sugar, but there was also a heavy muskyness to it. As I breathed in her scent, I sank deeper and deeper into relaxation. All the stress of the past two days had been washed away by the wave of euphoria I felt while in the soft hands of a beautiful foxkin.

"I feel like a new man..."

"What was that?" Madeline asked as she walked out of the bathroom in her black lace undergarments. She was a short woman, but her features fit her height and lean body perfectly. I couldn't decide if I liked her breasts or ass more, I had always considered myself a boob man, but this vixen had me reconsidering my position.

My cock sprang back to life, but to its disappointment, Madeline started getting dressed.

"I wish you could stay," I said as I lay there watching her return to looking like a prim and proper military officer.

"As do I," she said as she straightened out her skirt, "but I do have a few things I need to do before this day ends."

I examined my narrow bed, amazed that we had had enough room to do what we had just done. Even if she did stay, it wouldn't be a comfortable night for either of us. We needed more room, and that was just for the simple act of sleeping next to each other. The activities we could do while we weren't sleeping were going to require a bed that was at least twice this size. But first I wanted to take her out on a proper date.

My mind wondered about how we would look for a night out on the town, her in my arms, making everyone we came across jealous.

"Wow, what are you thinking about?" the foxkin asked as she fixed her hair.

"I was thinking of how I would love to take you out on a date."

"Is that all you were thinking of doing with me?"

"There's more," I said with a smile, "but having you on my arm while we make the masses around us wish they were us was my number one thought."

She stood in front of me, looking like the proper Crestia officer that she was. "I wish we could do that as well, but the civilians outside of this airfield don't know about the existence of humans."

"Really?" I asked.

"Yes, and why did you say it like that?"

I sat up in my bed and stretched. "Look at the amount of mechanics and workers who have seen me over the past two days, you think they aren't talking when they get home?"

"No, they aren't," she responded confidently.

"How can you be so sure?"

She crossed her arms and adjusted her stance, pushing her hip to one side to what I called the "know it all" stance. "I am sure because I am not the only minder on this site. There are five others and part of our daily jobs is to mentally scan those who return to the base on leaving."

"Do the non-minders know this?"

She nodded.

"What happens if they tell someone about what they saw?" I asked, already having a good idea of what might happen.

"They are arrested, interrogated and punished. All in all, it's a quick process, a group of minders can fully scan a person's mind in a matter of minutes to find out what they said and who they told. From there, the people they spoke to are rounded up and dealt with accordingly."

The way she so nonchalantly spoke about arresting and interrogating people bothered me. *She's an intelligence officer,* I said to myself, thinking of how I was visited at times by officers of the OSS who reminded me what I could and could not share with the public about the planes I flew at airshows. *They would kill to have Madeline's abilities.*

"So about our date," I said, redirecting us back to what was really important, "how can I take you out and enjoy a night with you outside of these dull military clothes?"

Her arms were still crossed, but she brought her finger up to her lip and tapped it while she thought, then her ears twitched. "I've got an idea!"

"What is it?" I asked, rising to my feet.

"It could be a good one..."

"Lay it on me."

"But I would need to check with him first-"

"Say the idea!"

She snapped out of her thoughts and smiled. "Do you trust me?"

"If it gets me off this base so I can spend a night with you, then I do."

"Now you want a whole night?"

I stepped closer and pulled her to me, wrapping my arms around her as I looked down. "I've spent a whole day with you, twice, and both times I had to watch you leave when I wanted you to stay."

"You're greedy," she said, lifting herself up on her toes.

"I know," I said as I leaned down to meet her lips with mine. It was a simple kiss, but didn't lack passion, or meaning.

She pulled away and moved toward the door. "I should be

able to organize everything tonight. If I do, then you won't see me until you get off base, so I want you to be ready and waiting for the signal."

"Ok," I said with a grin while she talked like we were in a spy novel. "What will the signal be?"

"I think you'll know it when you see it."

CHAPTER EIGHT

THE IMAGES that I sometimes picked up from the strangers sleeping around me were getting easier to ignore as I slept. I assumed that being able to read and ignore people's minds took practice and time. Thanks to Madeline, I had been able to practice and gain some control, and thanks to Marshall Altros, I had time.

My third night of sleep was the most peaceful one yet, thanks in part to the wine and the amazing stress relief that a certain foxkin had provided me. Because of that, I was sleeping like a log when a thunder of knocks at my door dragged me away from the pleasant dream I was having.

I thought that if I ignored them, they would leave me alone, but that was not the case. The knocks continued, and then came the shouting.

"Captain Walker, wake up in there, we have places to go."

"Major Welch?" I yelled at the door.

"That would be correct," answered the boisterous voice.

My head pounded with a hangover from the wine. I sat up, flipped on the light and checked my watch. "Major Welch, it's 7:28 in the morning, why are you banging on my door?"

"A friend of a friend requested that I come and retrieve you," answered the loud man.

I moved out of the bed, wrapped the blanket around me and went to the door. Standing there in his uniform was the Major, alone. The familiar mental signatures of Laurel and Hardy, my silent sentinels, were nowhere to be found.

He lifted up his wrist, tapping on his silver watch. "Hurry my friend, we must go if we are to make this work."

I looked at him for a moment before it clicked.

He's the damn signal.

Letting him in, I moved to the bathroom and turned on the shower.

"No time," said the Major, "get dressed and let's go."

"Come on, I need a shower, you and your nose can tell that," I pointed out.

"Yes, and you can take one later," he said as he grabbed my black duster jacket and officer's hat, "but for now, we must go."

Turning off the water, I gave in and got dressed. We left the apartment about a minute later, walking nonchalantly out of the dormitory toward the car park next to it.

"Are we trying to move about unnoticed?" I asked the Major.

"Yes."

"Then please tell me that roadster isn't your car."

"Yes it is mine, who else here would drive such a beautiful machine?"

I pinched the bridge of my nose as we got closer to the beige sports car. "That's the problem, Major Welch. Everyone will be looking at the car."

"Call me Court, stop with the Major Welch business," he said as he got in the driver's seat. "I have the roof up, so trust me, no one will notice you."

This guy is going to get us caught, I thought as I reluctantly got in the passenger's seat. I felt our chances of being caught increase when the engine of the roadster purred to life. If it was loud on the inside, then it had to be deafening on the outside.

Welch had a lead foot and squealed the tires every chance he got as we sped through the base.

"You're going a little fast there," I said through gritted teeth as I grabbed something to hold on to.

"Yes, because we have an appointment to make," Court shouted over the hum of the engine. We weaved in and out of the traffic, almost running head on into an army truck twice.

Clear of traffic, he accelerated down the straight road that led to the entry gate. Outside, two guards watched us approach as we kept going faster and faster as we got closer.

"Court, you do see the guard post, right?" I pointed out.

He ignored me, accelerating toward the closed gate.

"Court!" I yelled, bracing myself for impact in a car with no seatbelt.

The car quickly decelerated as the demented Major downshifted and applied the brakes, bringing us to a gentle stop next to the guard shack.

"Relax Captain Walker," he said before rolling down his window. "Good morning gentleman."

"Good morning Major Welch. That's a fine car you have sir."

"Thank you, it was a gift from my wife Shasta," he said as he patted the wheel.

"Lucky man, I wish my wife knew cars," huffed the other guard.

Court leaned out the window. "Trust me gentlemen, I am aware of how lucky I am. Now, the Captain and I have an appointment in town that we need to make, could you..." he gestured to the lowered security gate.

"Yes Sir, Major Welch," said the first guard as they both moved to the gate and lifted the arm. They saluted the Major and myself before Court stomped on the gas and launched us forward like a slingshot.

"What did I tell you?" Court said as he shifted gears, "Those men only care about two things, fast cars and beautiful women. You could have been sitting in that passenger seat with a sign saying you were a human and they would not have noticed you."

I relaxed in my seat as the countryside scenery went by in a blur.

Maybe Court is smarter than he seems...

The forest started to thin out, replaced by fields of crops and pastures filled with strange looking cattle with four horns. We blew past a sign that read *Welcome to the Village of Gilmore,* and small houses began to come into view. This apparently was enough for Court to slow down-a little bit.

The Village of Gilmore was picturesque, and felt almost like it was plucked from a fairytale. Multi-floored timbered houses with flower boxes below each window lined the streets. Some had shops on their bottom floors where different wolf and foxkin could be seen coming and going. Every now and then, I swore I saw long skinny rabbit ears or big round mouse-like ears on some of the people, but they always ducked out of view before I could get a proper look.

It was a lively village, and everyone seemed cordial, waving as we drove past them.

"This is our first stop," Court announced as we parked in front of a tailor shop.

"What are you getting here?" I asked.

"Not me, you!" He chuckled as we got out of the car and entered the shop.

"Good morning," greeted the gentle voice of a short, elderly foxkin man with reddish gray ears and tail.

His shop smelled of textiles and leather. The walls were covered in dark wood panels with shelves of fabric surrounding headless mannequins that were displaying the style of suits that he specialized in. By where we entered was a counter with a register, with the shop's window behind it. On the opposite wall was a door to the back of the shop, and next to that a collection of mirrors, a changing room, and a dry bar.

"Good morning Stephan," replied Court to the elderly canid.

"Ahh, Archduke Welch, it is an honor to have you visit my humble store once again," said the shopkeeper with a bow.

I slowly turned my head to look at Court. "Archduke?"

It had been mentioned that Major Welch, Court, was of nobility, but if my memory serves me right, the archduke was up there with maybe one or two titles greater than that before you got to the King–Emperor.

Court gave me a nod before turning to the still bowing shopkeeper. "Stephan, I have been coming to you for more than five years, I have told you, bowing is unnecessary."

"Right you are my lord," Stephan said as he straightened himself out. "What can I do for you today?"

"Not me, my friend James," he said, slapping me on the back.

Stephan looked at me, sniffed the air, blinked and rubbed his eyes a few times before looking back to Court. "My lord, I might be seeing things, but this man seems to have deformed ears…and, no offense, he smells funny."

"I told you I needed to take a shower," I whispered to Court.

Court shook his head. "Stephan, my friend here is not deformed." The archduke pulled a money clip from his back pocket and stepped toward the shopkeeper, unfolding papers of currency with two zeros on them as he did. "But his being here needs to be kept a secret. What you see and what you hear is nothing more than a figment of your imagination."

Court held out five of the bills for Stephan, smiling at him as his eyes twinkled at the sight of the money. "I believe I understand what you are speaking of, my lord. Your friend will be taken care of and then forgotten once my business is done."

"Very good," Court said as the shopkeeper took the money.

"How am I supposed to pay for this?" I hissed at Court as Stephan led me to a platform in front of a set of three mirrors.

"Don't worry about it, Agent Reynolds has assured me that a line of credit is being established for you through her employer."

Because going into debt never hurts anyone...

The next few hours were spent with Stephan having me try on different styles and colors of shirts and suits while checking and marking the fit. I had never experienced anything like this before, and having the elder canid get as close to me as he was getting was a bit uncomfortable.

The cocktails Court mixed at the dry bar helped to alleviate some of the awkwardness.

"It's going to be the navy pinstripe for me," I told Stephan when it came time to make the final decision.

"Very good. I have your measurements, and will handle the accessories that go with it. Should I have the finished suit delivered to the base?"

"No," Court answered, "have it brought to my estate."

The man nodded as he moved to the front counter.

"Your estate?" I asked as we followed him.

Court nodded. "I understand you wanted to take the Agent out for dinner and drinks?"

It was my turn to nod.

"There is no better chef than my own, and no finer collection of spirits in the region than those I possess. My estate also provides privacy from gawking civilians who would be asking about your deformed ears."

After leaving the tailor to do his thing, we made our way out of the village and down a narrow two lane road back into the countryside. I took in the views of the countryside as they sped past me. Little was said between Court and I as he seemed to be more focused on driving than talking.

He eventually turned right through an already opened gate that had two armed men standing guard. We drove along the tree-lined private drive until a grand three-story estate came into view. White limestone walls had green creeping vines climbing the surface to the red terracotta roof that topped the palatial estate.

Four white columns supported the portico that pushed away from the front facade, providing a covered space for Court to bring the car to a stop under. Two white-gloved butlers, one a rabbit, the other a squirrel, quickly rushed to the sides of the car, opening the doors for us.

"Welcome home Sir," greeted the rabbitkin on Court's side.

"Welcome to *Summerview Manor*, honored guest," the squirrelkin on my side exclaimed as I climbed out of the roadster.

"Thank you," I said as I moved around the car, entering the estate behind the canid noble. "This is one hell of a house you got here, Court."

He chuckled before responding, "Yes, it is. It has been in my family for five generations."

We walked through an ornately decorated hallway where Court pointed out the paintings and tapestries of historic events in Crestia's history that his family was present for. I nodded along as he talked, feigning interest as we moved through his home. His surface thoughts showed that he was trying to impress me, but I had never been one for art...or history, so art of his family history was wasted on me.

"Court? Is that you?" called a voice from the room we were heading toward.

"Yes, my love," he replied as he turned a corner.

I followed him into a large parlor where a wolfkin woman was laid out on an ornate chaise lounge. She was reading a book and listening to soft jazz from a large record player on the back wall and didn't seem to be expecting guests. When she saw me, her ears perked up, and she quickly jumped to her feet, setting down the book while smoothing out her shirtwaist dress.

"Honey," she yelped excitedly as she flashed a fake smile and moved toward Court. "I thought you said your guest would be joining us for dinner."

"He will be," he replied, "but I told you I would be bringing him over before noon. This is Captain James Walker."

Her eyes narrowed as she side eyed him. Her mind was replaying their conversation from last night, but didn't seem to recall this conversation. Shaking her head, she turned to me. "Good afternoon, I am Court's wife Shasta..." She froze and turned back to her husband and stared at him.

I looked at both of them before I realized they were talking telepathically.

"...*what is a human?*" she asked.

"*They are a race from another world,*" replied Court.

"*There are people from another world? When were you going to tell me?*"

"*I was sworn to secrecy, my love. Ever since I met my first human, I was ordered to not tell anyone about their existence.*"

Her eyes went wide when he told her I was a secret, which surprised me because if humans were supposed to be a secret, why had he just driven me all over town?

"*If humans are supposed to be a secret, then why is he in our house?*"

She must be the smart one in the relationship, I thought.

He stared at her for a moment before turning to look at me. I moved around the room to the record player and pretended to study it so they didn't think I was listening in. "*You can't be serious, Shasta. Madeline spoke to you about this last night.*"

"*I remember that, she said she had some guy she wanted to bring over. The man who saved you. Wait...he's the guy?*"

83

I didn't hear a response, but I assume Court nodded his head.

"*She's going crazy over a guy who isn't even from our world?*"

I smiled, but once again didn't hear an answer.

"*Are you sure this is ok?*" she asked with a tone of concern.

"*It will be fine, my love,*" he replied, followed by the sound of a kiss. "James, let us try this again," he said, calling me over, "this is my alpha wife Shasta. Shasta, this is Captain James Walker."

Shasta stepped forward and gave me a gentle bow before rising to meet my eyes. "It is a pleasure to meet you, Captain, I understand I have you to thank for my husband still being alive?"

"Yes ma'am, I saved his tail," I said with a nod. "And please call me James."

"I will if you call me Shasta. Formality is so dull."

I nodded in agreement. "Do you mind if I ask what you meant when you introduced her as your alpha wife?" I asked Court.

He nodded and smiled. "Shasta is my first wife, and the leader of my women. She keeps them all in line so I do not have to."

"What do you mean by women?" I asked.

As if on cue, three other women walked in the room, greeting Court with embraces and kisses as they did. I noticed they were all wolfkin of varying height and fur color. The one thing they all seemed to have in common, other than being beautiful, was their slender bodies and busty chests. If these were Court's other wives, then he definitely had a type.

"Ladies," Court said after greeting the last one. "This is Captain James Walker, he is the man who saved my life. James, allow me to properly introduce my wives, Shasta you have met." She waved and was the tallest of the four. "Next are the twins, Luna and Lila." The short pair stepped forward and gave me a bow that was so well in unison, it almost felt practiced.

"And last but not least, Destiny." She stood taller than the twins, but also looked to be the younger of the four.

"Nice to meet you ladies," I said, trying to move my eyes around the group so none felt left out.

There was an awkward silence as I felt three pairs of eyes studying me, and their minds were starting to pile up questions I was not looking forward to answering. The younger one, Destiny, was the first to step forward.

"Captain Walker," she said in an accent that sounded more British than the Latin accents I had heard from the others, "it is nice to meet you, but what are you?"

The others nodded in agreement as Court and Shasta both rolled their eyes. We sat down in the parlor and I explained what and who I was. That was then followed up by a stern warning from Court that they were not to speak about me with anyone else. The girls voiced their agreement before they bombarded me with more personal questions.

The rabbit and squirrelkin butlers from earlier brought drinks to everyone before standing aside. Court's wives drilled me with questions about where I was brought up, how large my family was, if I had a wife or girlfriend, what type of women I fancied, and so on and so on. The questioning stopped once I asked if they were trying to set me up with one of their friends.

The girls giggled before Shasta answered me, "I'm sure they have a few friends they could introduce you to, but that would step on the toes of Madeline."

"Maddy has claimed him already?" Luna asked...or was that Lila?

"Yes," Shasta replied, "in fact the reason he is here is because our dear husband has offered our house up as the location for their first date."

"Awww," rang out a chorus of voices.

"Thank you, by the way," I said to Court, raising my glass.

"It's the least I could do. I told you I would show you Crestian hospitality."

All four nodded before the other twin, Lila-or Luna, spoke up, "What about after Maddy? You can't have just one wife."

I was mid sip of a glass of whiskey when she asked me this, so it gave me time to think of an appropriate response.

"Thank you for having an interest in my love life, but I don't plan on staying in your world any longer than I have to. Once the other humans return, I expect to be going back to earth with them."

Silence filled the room before Destiny spoke up, "There are other humans?"

Court nodded, his silence telling her not to ask anymore questions.

"What if you were to stay?" Shasta asked.

I looked over at her. I recalled Madeline saying she was friends with Shasta, and her mind told me she was concerned about the feelings of the foxkin.

"If I were to stay..." I said, pausing to gather my thoughts. "If I were to stay, I would definitely pursue a deeper relationship with Madeline. As for having more than one wife, I can see the appeal, but in my world, one is enough."

This caught the four of them off guard, because they then proceeded to bombard me with more questions. Each question they asked came with its own mental image that created a struggle for me to keep a straight face during.

"Why?"

"Are humans that poor?"

"Are the women of earth ugly?"

"Are there more men than women?"

"Oh, do multiple men share one woman?"

"I don't like that thought of that." Shasta shuddered.

"I personally don't think I would mind it," insisted one of the twins.

"Sister!" the other said, flicking her ear as a punishment for having such a thought.

"No, no, no," I said, getting the girls to calm down, "On earth we marry for love. We date that one girl who drives us wild. Fall in love, propose, get married, have kids and then grow old together."

The room fell silent for a moment before the youngest spoke up.

"I love my husband," Destiny said, the other girls agreeing with her.

A feeling of defiance rose from the girls, and I started to think of what I had to do to defuse this situation. "But what do I know? I'm twenty-five, single, and can't tell you what love is."

The four girls looked at each other and then nodded in a silent agreement.

"Don't you worry, Captain Walker. I'm sure you will find it sooner rather than later," Shasta declared with a confident smile.

CHAPTER
NINE

"HOW DOES THAT LOOK, MR WALKER?" asked Peter, the rabbitkin butler.

He held a mirror for me as I moved my head to the left and right. I hardly recognized the man looking back at me. My hair was slicked back with the sides trimmed to a fade, and my face was shaved smooth. Not only was Peter a veteran butler, but he was also a skilled barber.

"Not bad," I remarked, "you know, if this whole butler thing doesn't work out for you, you can always be a barber."

He grunted in acknowledgement

The navy pinstripe suit that had been custom made for me had been delivered around mid afternoon. It fit perfectly, and it along with my fresh cut and shave made me look like a new man. I felt like one of those movie stars who got to walk the red carpet at the big premier of their movie.

Now all I needed was my date.

I moved downstairs to the parlor and waited with Court and his wives. They were dressed up as well, but had assured me they would eat in a different dining room and let us have our privacy.

Of course they have more than one dining room.

But that shouldn't have come as a shock in an estate as big as Court's in a world with beast people and floating continents.

Madeline arrived shortly after I joined the others.

She wore a black grecian style draped gown with a belt covered in gold shells around the waste with black heels. Her white hair was pulled back with soft curls framing her neck. The ensemble of gold accents continued with a snake chain necklace and a gold loop around the base of her left ear.

Her makeup was simple, she had smokey black eyeliner that helped the red of her lips and eyes to pop perfectly.

"Wow...you look incredible."

"Thank you," she said as she pushed herself up on her toes to kiss me. "You look handsome yourself."

There was a clicking sound from beside us.

"That is going to be a great picture," Destiny exclaimed as she backed away, winding her camera for another picture.

"Don't mind her," Shasta said, "photography is her hobby, but you two do make a lovely couple."

"Thank you, Shasta," Madeline replied.

Before splitting to our separate dining room, Destiny directed us to pose for a few more pictures. The camera was passed to Court to take a picture of just the girls before he asked if I would take one of him and his wives. I hoped I did good, it was the first time I had ever operated a camera, but it seemed easy enough.

"You two enjoy your date," Court said as Peter the butler led us to another part of the estate.

"You kids have fun," Shasta shouted as the other girls made barking and howling noises behind us.

She's calling us kids?

Madeline laughed and moved closer to me. I took her hand as we walked in silence and enjoyed just being with each other.

Our dining room for that evening was a solarium that overlooked the large garden on the back of the estate. The sun was setting but it still cast warm light into the room through the many vine-framed windows. A small table with two chairs sat in the middle of the room with a slender vase and red roses at the center. Along the edges of the room were miniature tropical trees and plants that surely would not have survived the climate of this region without this room.

    We took our seats as Peter poured us each a glass of wine before leaving. I was about to take the first sip when the beautiful foxkin stopped me.

    "My mother always said it is bad luck not to say a toast before drinking red wine," she said.

    "I would hate to bring about bad luck," I remarked as I raised my glass. "To high winds and mermaids."

    "Hold on, that can't be it."

    I let out a chuckle. "That was my grandfather's favorite toast. My dad might have been a pilot, but his father had been a sailor."

    "Interesting," she deadpanned, "do you want to try again?"

    "Ok, ok. May the best of our past be the worst of our future."

    "I'll drink to that," she said as we clanked our glasses and took a sip. "Mmm, that's wonderful."

    The wine was dry but sweet and full bodied, so much better than the bottles we had purchased from the commissary.

    "It really is," I said, agreeing with her.

    We sat in silence as we sipped the wine. I turned in my seat and took in the scenery and admiring the room and the garden beyond the windows. Meanwhile, I noticed Madeline was admiring me out of the corner of my eye.

    "Do you like what you see?" I asked as I turned back to her.

    She turned as red as the wine when she discovered she had been caught.

    "James," she said when her blush faded away, "are you dead

set on going back to your world if the other humans will let you?"

I had to think about that. After spending the day visiting with Court's wives, and mainly Shasta, I had learned that Madeline was starting to fall head over heels for me. She wanted me to stay here with her.

"I do want to go, but I'm not as dead set as I was two days ago," I answered honestly.

"What has changed?"

"You know the answer to that, you. Every moment I spend with you makes me want to make this world my permanent home."

The beautiful foxkin's face lit up at my answer. If she had been trying to play it cool, she was failing.

"But," I said, interrupting her high, "there are reasons for me to go back to earth. The biggest being my father."

"I understand," she said, sitting back in her chair. "What about your mother?"

I looked away for a moment before answering, "She passed away when I was five."

"Oh no, I'm sorry to hear that," she said as she reached across the table to take my hand.

"Thank you, but it's ok. She had tuberculosis, and because of that, I don't have many good memories of her. In fact I kind of hated her before she passed. Now I wish I could have those moments back."

She squeezed my hand. "Why did you hate her?"

"She had told my father to keep me away from her because she didn't want me to get sick. My father had tried to explain that to me, but five year olds struggle at understanding the decisions our parents make out of love. It wasn't until I got older that it all made sense."

Madeline continued to hold my hand. It was comforting to

me, and helped me to take the deep breaths I needed to keep my composure.

"What was your mother like?" I asked, as Peter brought out what looked like Caesar salads for our first course.

She shrugged as she started eating. "My mother did what she could."

"I think she did a pretty good job. She raised a beautiful young woman while being married to your father."

"She wasn't married to my father," she said with a hushed tone.

I stopped and looked at her before it clicked in my head. "Do you blame her or him for that?"

"A bit of both. He knew better, so did she. Their relationship had to be kept a secret because of how taboo it was."

"Taboo?"

"Not that kind of taboo. More of a boss and employee relationship taboo."

"That makes sense."

The main course was brought out shortly after that.

"Beef tenderloin with mashed potatoes and asparagus," Peter announced as he set the plates down.

The table was silent save for the occasional moans of satisfaction as we both ate our meals. I cleared my plate off sooner than Madeline did, who seemed to be eating the vegetables quickly, but took some time when it came to eating the meat.

"I'm savoring it," she said as she took a drink of wine. "It's not my fault you scarfed yours down like a starving orphan."

The conversation became more light hearted from then on out. We took turns asking each other questions that had nothing to do with our parents, since it always seemed to hit a sore spot. By the time dessert was brought out, we were sharing what our favorite holiday was.

"My favorite holiday is Christmas," I said as I prepared to take a bite out of the creamy cheesecake that was brought out.

"What's Kriss-mass?"

"Christmas. It's a holiday at the end of the year where we give presents to our loved one and those we care about. Pine trees are cut down and brought inside to decorate, lots of green and red. Then there is Santa Claus."

"Santa...Claws?" she repeated.

"Yup," I said with a smile, "he's a man who comes down your chimney while you are sleeping and gives good kids toys and bad kids a lump of coal."

Madeline sat there staring at me like I had grown a third eye. "So your world has wizards?"

"What?" I asked with a laugh. "No, he's made up so kids will behave."

"Ok, I guess that makes more sense."

"Yeah, What's your favorite holiday?"

"The Festival of Flames!" she said excitedly as her tail wagged behind her.

"The Festival of Flames?"

"Yes! It's celebrated every six months, so at the new year and the mid year. We build wooden statues of the five gods, place wishes on paper that are nailed to the statues and then set on fire. Everyone dresses up in traditional clothing and dances, drinks, and gives gifts to their mates."

"So there is gift giving?" I asked.

She nodded, "At the new year, men give gifts to their mates, and at the mid year, the women give the gifts to their mates."

I imagined what it must look like, trying my best to compare it to other holidays on earth that I had heard of.

"When is the next one?" I asked.

"The New Year Festival of Flames is three months out, and I like red pearls," she said with a cheeky smile. "You know, just throwing that out there."

"I'll keep that in mind. How do you like your dessert?"

"It's delicious, but something is missing."

"Chocolate?" I asked with a smile.

"Mmm, yes, chocolate," she purred before she took her last bite.

"Maybe we should ask for some chocolate syrup?" I offered.

"But I just took my last bite of my cake."

"Oh sweety, I have such pleasures to show you."

We moved from the solarium to the guest bedroom that had been provided for us for the night. I was more than happy to let Madeline lead the way so I could follow behind and watch her sumptuous hips sway with every step she took. Her tail added to the show by swinging in time with her ass, giving a little flick at the tip as she moved. The view was at its best as we moved up the stairs.

"You are going to run into me if you don't focus on walking," she said, looking over her shoulder.

"I am focused," I said with a smirk.

As if to prove her point, she stopped abruptly in front of me. I amused her by running into her, as she said I would. She let out a yelp as I swung my arms behind her back and under her legs before lifting her off the ground. I held her tight as she laughed at the sudden change in her position.

"Oh James," she said softly as she wrapped her arms around my neck, nuzzling her face against my skin.

I carried her the last few feet to our room, setting her gently on the bed once we arrived.

She looked up at me with dancing eyes, biting her lower lip, her tail stiff behind her. I could tell she was nervous, though she was trying to act calm and cool.

Her hands shook as she reached out for my belt. I grabbed them and lifted them to my lips, kissing the backs of her fingers before pulling her up. "We don't have to do anything you aren't comfortable with," I said as I wrapped my arms around her.

She melted into my embrace and rubbed her cheek against my chest. "Thank you. But I'm not nervous about being intimate with you. I am nervous that I'll disappoint you...since it's my first time."

"Madeline, there's nothing you could do that would disappoint me," I whispered as I kissed the space between her ears.

She looked up at me and pushed herself up on her toes to kiss me-

A soft knock at the door stopped us.

"Yes? What is it?" I asked with annoyance.

There was no answer. I let go of Madeline and moved to the door, opening it to give whoever was there a piece of my mind, but no one was there. What greeted me was a silver tray on the floor, and on that tray was a glass syrup jar filled with chocolate.

Thanks Peter, I thought as I bent down to pick up the jar.

"Who is it?" Madeline called from behind me.

"Nobody," I replied as I turned around, "but this was left..."

The view before me took my breath away. A mound of clothing was at Madeline's feet, and she was bent over as she removed her sheer stockings. Red panties hugged her ass as her fluffy white tail swung slowly from side to side.

Her red eyes met mine as she looked back at me, her tush giving me a quick shake before she rose up. She reached back and unclasped the red bra, letting it fall off her shoulders and chest as she turned to face me.

"Is that the chocolate syrup?"

I nodded, still unable to speak as I soaked in every curve of her body, from the perfect pink nipples atop her perky breasts to the creamy smoothness of her supple thighs. My feet moved on their own toward her. I set the bottle on the bedside table as I went.

Her hands still shook as she moved in close and began removing my clothes, tossing them on the floor.

The last piece to join the others was my underwear. She let out a gasp as she saw my full size, then blushed, her hands covering her chest.

"Are you ok?" I asked.

"Yes, I...I'm just not sure what to do next," she said as her eyes met mine.

Her ears were laid flat against her head as she waited for me to say something.

"I'll show you."

I bent over and kissed her while my hands rested on her hips and slowly pushed her onto the bed. Our tongues played between our lips as I nudged on her more, causing her to lay on her back.

My lips broke from hers as I kissed along her neck to her collar bone, hands taking her round breasts into their grasp, squeezing and teasing her sensitive pink nubs. I licked and kissed my way to one, taking it between my lips and suckling on her tit as she gasped and moaned.

I reached over and grabbed the syrup dispenser, pouring the chocolate over her breasts before licking it up. It was rich and sweet. I poured some right on her nipples, watching as it coated the nubs and dripped down her breasts.

"You're going to make me sticky," she moaned as I cleaned away my delicious mess.

"Exactly," I said as I pressed my cock against the soft lace that covered her valley. Heat radiated through, and her wetness soaked the red fabric. The wetter she got, the more I could pick up that familiar scent I had smelled on my fingers from yesterday.

Chocolate laid out a trail for my tongue to follow down her stomach. I sat the bottle on the floor next to me as I crouched between her legs, kissing and teasing the insides of her thighs.

My lips and tongue would occasionally graze the fabric that hid her womanhood from me, drawing a whimper from her lips each time I did. Her legs and hips worked awkwardly to pull my head closer and closer to her pussy, but I fought them off easily and moved in at my own pace.

When I was ready, I pushed my face against the wet red fabric, licking at her sex through it. She moaned and writhed as I got my first taste of her. It was muted, but the smell was not. My nostrils widened as I got a strong whiff of her sweet scent, like the other day, it was musky and smelled of honey.

I need to taste her!

My hands went to her waist and hooked the top of her panties with my fingers, pulling them down past her feet in one smooth motion. Before me lay her wet pink pussy lips with a white tuft of soft downy hair at the top. Peeking out from below the hair was the pearl of her clit, which was doing its best to hide under its hood.

"Does it look...ok?" she asked, blushing.

I looked up and locked my eyes onto hers before licking my lips and moving in to kiss, then lick, her folds. My tongue darted out to sample the wet warmth that lay before me, drawing moans and gasps as her delicate folds were explored by my adventurous mouth. I did my best to pay attention to what movement did what to her, every moan, yip and shudder being noted so I could do it again.

Flicking her clit with the tip of my tongue made her breath fast, but sucking on it made her whimper. However, the best reaction I got was when I penetrated her as deep as I could with my tongue and wiggled it inside her quivering tunnel. She gripped my hands tight the first time I did it, so I locked my fingers with hers as I pushed my tongue as deep in her as I could a second time.

"Oh, b-by the Goddess, don't...don't stop!" she howled as she ground her soaking wet pussy on my face.

I did stop a few times, but only long enough to pour some chocolate on to her clit so it could run down her lips before I licked them clean.

I knew she needed to orgasm when her hands reached down and grabbed my head, pushing my face into her valley. She held the back of my head as I licked and sucked on her clit, catching breaths when I could, and ignoring the ache in my jaw.

Reaching up, I squeezed and kneaded her breasts as my tongue lapped at the sweet heat of her pussy, pushing her closer and closer to the edge. When she finally tipped over it, her thighs squeezed my head as she let out a long primal moan, spilling her juices on my face, and soaking me from mouth to chin. Her nectar was sweet and addicting, and I licked it all up, eliciting more moans and a few swear words from the mouth of the sexy vixen until she had to push my face away.

"That was amazing," she panted as I crawled up to lay next to her, "I-I have never felt anything like that."

"I'm glad you enjoyed it." I smiled as I leaned in and gave her a kiss.

She kissed back, but grabbed my face and licked my lips. "By the Goddess, you taste so good with me on your lips."

We continued to kiss, making out like there would be no tomorrow. I rolled onto my back and she climbed on top of me, stretching out to cover as much of me as she could with her lithe body.

"My turn," she said excitedly as she reached over the edge of the bed and grabbed the bottle of chocolate syrup.

She proceeded to make a mess of my chest and stomach, as well as her face as she poured and licked away at the chocolate. Her tail wagged behind her as her tongue moved quickly to lick up the chocolate, tickling me in some spots. I'd like to say she didn't let any get on the soft white sheets of the bed, but that would be a lie.

Laying my head back, I moaned or laughed, depending on where she was licking, but then there was a pause. I knew she had licked my hips last, and looked up to see her staring at my member. She had a curious look on her face as she gripped it in her hands and studied it. Her exploratory hands squeezed and tugged at the tip, shaft and balls.

It felt amazing, and then she started nuzzling my cock and balls, inhaling deeply as she did.

"You smell amazing!"

"Thanks...I guess?" I said between gasps.

The nuzzling eventually led to licking, which I preferred. Her tongue was soft, warm, and long. She licked me from base to tip, lapping up the bead of pre cum that waited for her at the top.

"Mmm, I want more of that."

"If you suck on it, I guarantee you'll get more."

"Like this?" she asked as she took the tip of my cock into her mouth and sucked on the head.

My eyes rolled back into my head as her lips and tongue swirled and bobbed up and down on my shaft. Her soft hands cradled my balls and gently stroked the base of my shaft. Looking down, I couldn't help but reach out and take her ear in my hand, rubbing the soft fur between my fingers as she worked my manhood. Her chocolate-smeared cheeks were flushed, and her eyes filled with lust when they met mine.

With a pop, she released my cock from her mouth, rubbing the sensitive tip against her lips as she brought the chocolate syrup over me. "You taste amazing baby, but I wonder how you taste covered in chocolate!"

I watched as she poured the cool syrup on my rock hard member, making sure every inch was coated with the sweet substance. The reasonable part of my mind said she poured too much, but I ignored it, because I didn't care.

Her tongue went to work, moving between long licks and

quick ones as she tried her best to clean up the mess she had made on me. The speed and pressure of her tongue was phenomenal, and as she got to the tip, I could feel my balls starting to tighten. I fought the urge to cum, grunting and breathing quickly as I gripped the sheets, trying hard to enjoy the pleasure longer.

"I'm going to suck the tip clean," she said with a husky tone to her voice. True to her word, she took the tip of my cock into her mouth and swirled her tongue around it, and I was done.

My dick swelled to blow, but she didn't stop. Our eyes met and she gave me a wink. I gripped her hair, forcing her face down on my cock as I erupted.

"Mmmm" she moaned as rope after rope of my seed filled the foxkin girl's mouth.

She eagerly bobbed her head as she milked me dry, drinking every drop as I laid back and relaxed with a goofy smile on my face.

"That was amazing," I said with a huff.

"I know! You and chocolate make a wonderful combination," she said with a smile before returning to licking.

There was still quite a bit of the chocolate syrup, and she was hellbent on licking my manhood clean. Though I was sensitive in her hands, it felt comforting to feel her warm tongue lap away at my resting cock. I did my best to not fall asleep as I relaxed and melted into her, the soft blankets of the bed below me.

"Look who came back out to play," she giggled as I grew harder in her hands. I had never been able to bounce back this fast, but I was not going to worry about it. If my dick said it could go again, then it was time to go again!

"Indeed, I think that means he likes you."

"Aww, well I like him," she said as she crawled up and gave me a kiss, "but I like you more."

I rubbed my thumb over her cheek to clean off a smear of chocolate, licking it off, "I like you a lot too, Madeline."

I wrapped my arms around her and pulled her onto me, holding her tight, "I'm happy I met you."

"Me too. I want to end every day like this."

"That would be nice."

"You know, if you stayed, it could be."

I smiled at her persistence. "Let's finish tonight before we worry about tomorrow. Now hand me the bottle, I'm still hungry."

CHAPTER
TEN

THE CAW OF A MOCKINGBIRD, or the Dione version of it, pulled me from my sleep. It seemed it didn't matter what planet you were on, there was always going to be some stupid bird that kept you from sleeping for too long.

Soft light was filtering into the bedroom around the edges of the curtains, and the air smelled of chocolate and sex, though that was the one thing we didn't actually do. Madeline wasn't ready, and I wasn't going to force her. Thinking of her, I reached over to where her warm body had been laying, looking forward to cuddling up against her fluffy tail, but the spot was vacant.

I reached further, thinking she might have scooted closer to the edge on her side, it was a huge bed afterall. Still nothing.

Opening my eyes, I finally saw that she wasn't there, and sitting up, I saw I was alone in a very opulent room.

It was the nicest bedroom I had been in. The walls were white with framed light blue panels outlined in gold and decorated with a few paintings of landscapes and different wolfkin people, who I assumed were ancient relatives of Court and his family. In the middle of the room was a massive bed that seemed far too large for just two people, with a night stand on both sides. Soft white sheets and pillows had covered the bed, along with a navy blue comforter, but the comforter was on the floor and the sheets were covered in chocolate stains.

Oops...

When I finally pulled myself out of the bed, I saw a note on the bedside table.

James

Sorry I am not there to give you a good morning kiss, but I needed to get back to work, and you looked like you needed your sleep. You are so cute when you sleep!

Yesterday was amazing! I never thought I would meet someone like you. I truly felt that we connected on a deeper level, and the next time I see you, I don't know if I will be able to keep my hands off you! Be careful sneaking back onto the base, and I'll see you later today when you get back.

Madeline
XOXO

PS: If you stayed, I would make sure every night was like last night.

I read the letter multiple times, and each time, my smile got bigger. She was something else, and like her, I couldn't wait to see her again. My mind started to think of all the things I wanted to do with her, like dancing, or going to see a movie. I could even take her up in a plane for her first flight. It wouldn't be in mine, no, the Mustang was a single seater, but maybe a two-seat trainer.

"My plane," I said to myself. I had not thought about it in a few days, and now started wondering if they had done anything to it.

A wave of panic washed over me as I worried about what some greasy mechanics could be doing to my plane.

"I need to check on my plane," I said to my reflection as I passed a mirror in the bathroom before turning on the shower. "I need to speak with Marshall Altros and ask him to let me do something more than sit around."

But how? What reason did he have to see me?

"I should have you both thrown in jail!" Marshall Altros shouted with his gravelly voice.

Turns out, getting to see him was easier than I thought, because he was looking for me when I arrived back on the base with Court. He had pulled the same loud sports car stunt as we came back on base, but this time there were multiple guards at the gate, and they had no interest in the Major's roadster. The guards took us both into custody, and one of them had a smile on his face as he got to drive the powerful automobile to some parking lot on the base.

We now stood before the Marshall in his office. It was a large room with pictures of him with other officials lining the wall, as well as a few plaques that honored his service. He was seated behind his desk in a large leather chair, staring at us both with contempt.

"What do you have to say for yourselves?"

Court and I traded glances before I spoke up, "It's my fault, I pressured the Major into getting me off the base."

The Marshall looked at Court, who nodded, before looking back at me. "Was I not clear that you were to stay sequestered in the room I assigned you?"

"Somewhat," I replied, "but you did seem to cave on allowing me out of that dorm room as long as I was escorted by a Crestia military official."

"I gave that permission to Agent Reynolds. Speaking of," he squinted his eyes, and I could vaguely make out his telepathic call for her.

A moment later there was a knock at the door.

"Come in," he grumbled.

Madeline came in and stood next to me, saluting the Marshall, "You called for me, sir?"

"Yes. Why was I not alerted about this human leaving my base?" he asked, glaring at her.

She looked at me before taking a deep breath, "To be honest sir, I did not think it that big of a deal."

"Come again?"

"He was with a Crestia Officer the entire time, was he not?"

"That is not the point," huffed the Marshall, "the point is I said *you* needed to be with him if he left his room. You were not to pass him off to some Major who lives off base and has more money than wits!"

Madeline froze, and in her silence, the Marshall continued.

"I am now starting to see why the Ministry of State Secrets sent you here. You have been here as long as he has," he pointed at me, "and caused me as much trouble as him. All those *gifts* and *noble blood* yet you can't follow simple instructions. You truly are worthless."

Madeline's shoulders and ears sagged as her eyes went distant.

"I think she's doing a damn good job," I said.

"Excuse me?" scoffed the Marshall.

I looked him in the eyes. "I said she's doing a damn good job, and if you want to point out someone who is being worthless, why don't you point at yourself."

"James," hissed Madeline, but I ignored her warning.

In for a penny, in for a pound.

Marshall Altros had pissed me off. I glared at him and then felt his mental barrier break before me. After that, my mind hit his subconsciousness, and before he or I knew what had happened, I felt him submit to me mentally. In doing so, his face relaxed as he stared at me with a distant look.

"James, what did you do?" I heard Madeline ask, but I was too focused on the Marshall to respond.

"You will apologize to Agent Reynolds, and Major Welch for what you said."

He nodded slowly, mumbling, "Apologize for what I said…"

I continued, my mind still gripping his, "You will overlook the fact that I left the base last night, and you will give me leeway to move freely while on the base."

He nodded again, "Overlook last night, you can move freely."

"That's a good boy," I said as I relaxed my mind.

Marshall Altros' eyes came back into focus, and he shook his head before looking around. "My apologies, I don't know what came over me."

He sat down in his big leather office chair and pulled a bottle of amber liquid from his desk drawer, pouring a glass and drinking it quickly.

"Major Welch, I am sorry I took that tone with you, any time you want to take Captain Walker off base, you have my permission."

"Thank you sir," Court replied with a surprised tone before saluting the Marshall.

"Agent Reynolds," Altros continued, "you are a valued member of this base, and I am glad to have you on my team. You also have permission to take Captain Walker where you deem necessary."

"Thank you sir," she said uneasily before giving him a salute as well.

"Captain Walker, have a nice day, enjoy the hospitality of the *Imperial Base Gilmore*."

"Thank you," I said with a nod.

"Now fuck off," he said, waving his hand before turning to look out the window behind him.

The three of us quickly ushered ourselves out the door, moving past his secretary and into the hall before Madeline pulled us aside.

"What the fuck was that, James?" she asked with a shocked look on her face.

"I have no idea," I replied.

"That was what you minders call *thought reformation*, correct?" asked Court.

"Yes," said Madeline before turning back to me, "You didn't tell me you could do that."

"I didn't know I could do that. I don't know what I did."

"You took control of the Marshall's mind and forced it to submit to you," Madeleine said as she covered her mouth with her hands. "Once a minder with the gift of thought control puts a subject into that state, they can force their target to do anything."

"Anything..." I said.

A cold chill ran down my spine as I thought of the implications of what that meant. I had just taken over someone's mind and forced them to do what I wanted. The thought of how I could use, or misuse this "gift" weighed heavily on me, and the worst part was that I had no idea how it happened.

I looked into her wide red eyes and thought back to what I had done, trying to replay what had happened. I had been angry, I had wanted to hit him, not just once, but multiple times, then I felt him submit to me. It felt like when a snarling dog realized who was in charge. I doubted I could do it again, unless...

"James?"

I looked at Madeline. "Sorry, I was thinking back on what happened."

"Are you ok?"

"I don't know," I said with a shrug, "I feel like I should be worried about this power I just demonstrated. How did I trigger it? How do I control it?"

Her hand caressed my cheek as she looked up at me. "You triggered and controlled it because you are special, and I will help you increase the strength of your gift."

"Thank you." I said

"No, thank you," she said as she hugged me, her tail wagging behind her. "You stood up for me, you have no idea how happy that makes me."

"Don't mention it. No one talks to my girl like that."

She squeezed me tighter, her tail wagging so fast it was creating its own wind current.

"I also want to thank you," Court said, "but mine can wait for another time. You two have a nice day."

"See you later," I said, gasping for air. "Madeline, I can't breathe!"

"Sorry," she said as she relaxed her grip. "Do you mean it? Am I your girl?"

"Why would I say it if I didn't mean it?"

She looked up with a blushing smile, giving me a lust-filled stare. "I need you!" she purred as she rubbed her body against mine.

"Really?"

"Really."

"Then let's go back to my quarters-"

"No, too far, I need you now!" she pouted.

I scanned the hallway. We were on the top floor of the administrative building I had been brought to a few days ago.

"I know a room downstairs," she said as she grabbed my hand. "It's a special equipment room, I have a key."

We quickly moved down the stairs and found the room in question. Madeline checked our surroundings before pulling out a key and opening the door. Before it was shut, she jumped at me, wrapping her arms and legs around me, kissing me wildly as I cupped her ass.

Heavy breathing filled the room as we hurried to pull each other's clothes off, stripping down quickly. I got a sniff of her scent once she removed her panties, and by now it was the most intoxicating thing I had ever smelled, hardening me instantly

"How do you want me?" she asked, kissing my chest as she reached over and stroked my stiff member.

"On your back, it's perfect for your first time."

She nodded and looked around the room. There were heavy duty crates on reinforced shelves that were covered in black blankets. She grabbed a few and pulled the blankets to the floor, making a makeshift bed before turning around and kissing me again. I wrapped my arms around her and slowly lowered her to the ground, laying her gently on the blankets.

I looked into her eyes, and I rubbed the tip of my cock against her already slick opening. "Are you ready?"

She nodded as she leaned in to kiss me.

Slowly I entered her, both of us gasping into each other's mouths as her folds spread to accept me. She was tight, but wet enough that my forward progress was smooth and pleasurable.

She let out a yelp and pulled her lips from mine. I watched her eyes as she brought her hand to her face, covering her mouth as she took quick deep breaths. She nodded again as she looked back at me, and I pressed forward.

Her eyes widened and fluttered as I finished inserting my full length inside her. We stayed that way for a moment, her soft warmth clenching down on my length as she adjusted to my size.

"I can feel your heart beating," she said softly.

"I can feel yours."

I leaned in and kissed her, withdrawing myself half way before thrusting back into her. She moaned into my mouth as I did it again and again, her hands holding the sides of my face as I made love to her. The pace was steady, and her warmth was amazing.

"*Faster,*" I heard her say in the back of my mind as our tongues intertwined.

I broke free of her lips and picked up the pace, thrusting my hips into her with more force. She moaned as I pulled out further, and rammed my cock back into her harder and harder with each thrust. At the speed I was going, we soon transitioned from love making, to fucking.

Her pussy was tight, almost too tight, but in a good way. If she hadn't been as wet as she was, the friction would most likely start a fire, but her slickness was the saving grace. I glided in and out on a cloud of euphoria, pumping my cock in and out of her slit as the smells and sounds of our sex filled the small room.

Grabbing her hands, I pulled them over head and held them there, watching in delight as her tits bounced every time I drove my cock into her slit. With every slap of my hips against her, a whimper and moan was drawn from her lips.

"Oh Goddess...Oh Goddess!" she howled, not caring if anyone heard us.

"You like that?"

"Yes! Don't stop!"

I didn't plan to. She felt amazing wrapped around my cock, and I was determined to last as long as I could. I wanted to soak in the pleasure and joy of this moment and not let it end, not yet.

Madeline pulled her hands from mine and wrapped her arms around my neck, pulling my face into her soft breasts. "I'm gonna cum, oh Goddess I'm gonna cuuuum."

I shook my head that I understood as I let her suffocate me between her soft pillowy mounds.

Her arms and legs wrapped around me tight as her pussy clenched down on my cock. Her body shook as she let out a deep howling moan. I felt her cum on my cock, her grip on my length as tight as I had ever felt, pushing me close to my own edge.

"I-I need to pull out," I said as I kept thrusting.

She held me tighter when she heard me say that, still moaning and pressing her soft body into mine.

"Madeline, I-I'm about to cum."

"Fill me," she whimpered, "I need to feel you inside me, make me yours!"

That did it. Her words, her wetness, her tightness, it all came together in a perfect storm that triggered my own orgasm. With a heavy thrust, my cock erupted inside her, filling her womanhood with spurt after spurt of my seed. I kept thrusting as the intoxicating bliss of my own orgasm shuddered over me before I collapsed on top of her.

I rolled off her as I worked to catch my breath. She curled up beside me and did the same. Her breathing eventually turned into sniffles that turned into the soft sounds of her crying.

"Madeline, are you ok?" I asked as I wrapped my arms around her.

She nodded and wiped her face before looking at me. "I'm ok, I'm just mad at myself."

"Why? Was it something I did?"

"No! You did nothing wrong. I am mad at myself for waiting so long to have sex with you," she said, looking at me with tear-filled eyes.

"Really?"

"Yes. I'm so happy that my first time was with you."

I pulled her to me, pressing her forehead to mine as I

reached up and rubbed her ears. "I'm happy I was your first, and if things keep going the way they are going, I hope I will be the only man to ever have sex with you."

She burst into more tears, and pulled herself in tighter, hugging me while I patted the back of her head, "Yes! I want that so much! I want to be yours and only yours!"

I smiled as I held her there, my eyes starting to look at the room around us. The lights were off, and the only ambient light was coming from the back wall where small windows let in the warm daylight. In that dim light, I focused on a design stenciled on the side of one of the wooden crates.

"Madeline...what is this?" I asked as I moved closer.

"What is what?" she asked as she adjusted in my arms.

I let her go and pressed my hand against the black paint, my eyes going wide as I made out what it was. I looked at the box above it, and the ones next to it. They had the same stenciled design. Jumping to my feet, I pulled blankets off the other crates, exposing them, and sure enough, it was there as well.

"Swastikas and black eagles..." I said under my breath.

"What was that?" Madeline asked as she waved away the dust in the air.

"Where did these crates come from?" I demanded as I pulled my clothes on.

She looked at them and back at me, "From the other humans. These are some of the supplies they trade with us."

"Are you being serious?" I asked, reaching out to stabilize myself as I felt my legs go weak.

I was breathing heavily as my heart pounded in my chest. My mind was spinning, making me feel dizzy as it started putting everything together.

"James, what's wrong?" she asked as she tried to help me.

"This is wrong," I said, gesturing to the stencil, "do you know who these people are?"

She looked at the symbol and back at me. "They are humans, like you."

"They are nothing like me!" I yelled. "They are genocidal psychopaths who are trying to take over the world."

"Please stop yelling," she asked, "and they aren't that bad."

"What?" I said, my head starting to spin, "I-I can't breath. I need to get out of here."

"James wait-"

I ignored her and opened the door, stepping into the hallway. I looked back to see her fall down in the mess of blankets as the door shut.

"Oof!" I grunted as I fell to the floor.

"I'm sorry, I was not paying attention," the man I had run into said as he extended his hand to help me to my feet.

"No, that's on me," I replied as I instinctively took his hand and climbed to my feet.

"Oh, you must be Captain Walker, it's nice to finally meet in person," the man said.

"How do you-" the blood drained from my face as waves of fear washed over me.

The man who had helped me to my feet wore a gray uniform with a black collar and pants. At his collar he wore a black iron cross outlined in silver, with another one hanging from his uniform's left coat pocket. The officer's cap bore the skull and bones of the *SS*, but what I couldn't stop staring at was the red armband on his left arm.

"Ah, I see you noticed my armband," the man said as he touched the red fabric. "I got this at my first party rally eleven years ago in Nuremberg. Would you like a closer look?"

He raised his arm and moved the black swastika toward me. I moved my feet to back away from him and bumped into someone again, only this time, I didn't fall down.

He looked at the person behind me. "Agent Reynolds! Good morning to you."

"Major-General Kampf," Madeline replied nervously. "I was not aware that you would be arriving today."

My heart dropped.

She knows him?

"I know. It was a bit of a challenge to get a hold of a transport that would bring me here from the installation site. However, the reports I was getting on Captain Walker made me want to meet him more and more," said the Nazi officer with a smile.

"What reports?" I asked, turning to look at Madeline.

"The reports I have been turning into the Ministry have also been given to our human allies."

"So this Nazi fuck knows everything about me?"

"Captain," Major General Kampf scoffed. "Why so hostile? I do not believe I have done anything to warrant this type of treatment."

I slowly turned to glare at him. "Are you kidding me? Our countries are at war with each other. I think that gives me more than enough reason."

Kampf shook his head. "Captain Walker, James, do you mind if I call you James?"

I said nothing, but I wanted to. I was trying hard to keep my emotions under control while I fought the urge to not see red, opening and closing my hands at my side.

He shrugged and continued. "Yes, my country and your country are at war with one another on Earth. As you can see, we are not on Earth, we are on Dione. We are the same, you and I, human to the core, and I believe that we humans should work together while on Dione."

"You and I are nothing alike." I spat.

"True, you do seem to have the mental abilities of these creatures, with the ability to read minds-"

"He also just learned to control minds," Madeline added.

"Why are you telling him that?" I snapped.

"Really?" the Major General asked. "Dr. Gerver will be excited to hear that. He has been chomping at the bit to examine you."

My ears perked up as well as normal human ears could. My eyes went wide with shock as I turned to look at the Nazi. "Dr. Gerver?"

"Yes, Dr. Volker Gerver, I am sure you have heard of him."

"The Mad Scientist of Strasburg? I heard he was dead."

Kampf shook his head. "No, he's very much alive and advancing his research here on Dione."

"Why me? Did he not find enough people to vivisect back on earth?"

Kampf shrugged. "You are a human with minder abilities, why wouldn't Dr. Volker want to examine you?" He then snapped his finger as his face lit up like he had a good idea. "If you come with me, I can make proper introductions."

I balked at his proposal. "I'm not going anywhere with you." I turned to walk away.

I need to get out of here.

"The doctor will be disappointed that you turned me down."

"Sucks for him," I said before flipping him the middle finger.

Kampf raised his voice, "It doesn't have to be this way. I'd rather you work with us freely than be forced."

I stopped, clenched my hands and turned to him, "You aren't going to force me to do shit!"

Madeline moved to stand beside me and placed her hand on my arm. I jerked it away from her, startling her. She backed away as I stared daggers at her.

"You don't have many options available to you, Captain Walker," Kampf said as he slowly walked toward me. "If you work with me and my men, I guarantee that this *foxkin* isn't the only beast that will warm your bed."

Madeline cringed when he referred to her the way he did. She then scowled at him when he brought up the idea of me being with other women.

"He's mine." She growled.

He moved past her as he closed the distance between us. "If you don't work with my men and I, then I'm afraid we will have to get creative. It will be less pleasurable than option one, and probably take more effort on our end, but it is what it is." He held his hands out with his palms up, as if he were weighing the proposals on a scale. "The choice is yours."

I stared at him. "How about option three?"

"What is option thr-"

My fist connected with his face. I jumped on him and delivered two or three more satisfying punches to his smug face once he hit the floor.

"James, stop!" shouted Madeline as she grabbed a hold of my arm.

I pushed her aside and gave the Nazi one more punch before jumping to my feet and taking off down the hallway.

I need to get out of here. I need to get to my plane.

Once I left the building, I ran toward the familiar sounds of the flight line, weaving between buildings as I cut across the base. While I ran, I checked over my shoulder and scanned the surrounding area with my minder abilities, but no one was giving chase.

The minds I read as I went by were more confused than worried. They watched me and wondered what could be so urgent. If only they knew, or maybe they did know, and like Madeline, they didn't care.

"You damn fool!" I growled to myself as I approached the hangers. I ran past planes that looked like the ones Court had been flying on the day I saved him, but I didn't see my Mustang. Mechanics and pilots looked at me strangely as I paused and scanned each hanger one by one.

There she is!

To my relief, my Mustang was still in one piece. To my horror, she was parked next to two Nazi Messerschmitt Bf-109s. *No wonder they wouldn't let me come see my plane.*

I moved into the hanger where my plane was waiting and gave her a closer visual inspection. The only surprise I found was when I rounded the tail and saw Madeline sitting on the wing. She slid off and looked at me with concerned eyes when I got close to her.

"What are you planning on doing, James?"

"I'm getting out of here."

I stepped up to the wing and leaned into the cockpit, powering on the instrument panel. *Seems they topped off her fuel for me.* Turning and jumping from the plane, I nudged Madeline out of the way as I ducked under the wing and pulled the parking blocks from the wheels. When I stood back up, she was there again, doing her best to corner me with her small frame.

"What are you doing?"

"I'm trying to get you to stop," she said as she extended her arms to block me.

"Why?"

"Because I don't want you to leave."

"I'm not staying."

"Not even for me?" she asked weakly, looking up at me, ears flat, and eyes filled with tears.

I met her eyes, then placed my hands on her shoulders. "Come with me."

"I can't."

"Why."

"It's complicated," she said as a tear ran down her cheek.

I shook my head. "It's really not, Madeline. The Nazis are not good people, and I will not stay here if your country is working with them."

Her bottom lip quivered as she dropped her arms and

wiped her face. "I-I understand. Can...can I get one more hug and kiss before you go?"

It's not her fault, she's just following orders. She doesn't know how evil they are. She doesn't know what they did on Earth.

"Of course," I said as I moved in to kiss her.

She wrapped her arms around me and squeezed while our lips pressed against one another. My insides were in a knot. I had truly come to care about Madeline over the last few days, so saying goodbye made my heart hurt. When we were done with our kiss, she rubbed her face against my chest as I scratched her behind her ear.

"I'm sorry, James."

A searing pain radiated from my side, like something had just been jabbed in me. I looked down as Madeline stepped back and pulled a syringe out of my lower abdomen. My hand instinctively clutched the puncture site, and my head started to spin.

"It's done," she called out.

The sounds of boots on the hanger floor and a soft clap got my attention. I turned to see Major-General Kampf entering the hangar, flanked by two armed guards. "Well done, White Rabbit, quite the performance," he said as continued to clap.

"Don't call me that," she growled.

I dropped to my knees as the effects of her betrayal felt like she had stabbed me in the heart instead of my side. "Madeline...wh-why?" I asked between labored breaths, struggling to look up at a woman I hardly knew anymore.

She lowered herself to her knees in front of me. "I can't lose you, James. I told you things are complicated, but you didn't want to listen. Now you will have time to think about how you were about to make the wrong choice."

My head began to spin faster as the edges of my sight started to blur. Madeline reached over to pull me to her, but I clumsily swatted away her hands. She finally succeeded when my arms went numb. She grabbed me and lowered my head to rest on her thighs.

"Shh, shh, shh, it's ok James, go to sleep," she whispered as she ran her fingers through my hair.

"You...you are fu-fucking crazy." I groaned as I fought to stay awake.

"No, I'm just in love with you," she replied as my eyes closed, and I slipped into unconsciousness.

CHAPTER
ELEVEN

I WAS RUNNING THROUGH A FOREST. It was dark, gloomy, and filled with fog. Every direction I looked faded into the same misty nothingness. I didn't know where I was running, but I knew I needed to get away from what was chasing me.

When I stopped and leaned against a tree, I asked, "What is chasing me?" The words didn't come from my lips. Instead they came from overhead in the tree. Was that a crow?

The sounds of rabid dogs came from behind me, and they were closing in fast.

"Run, run, run!" screamed my voice from the crow.

I took off running again, taking a look back to see how far they were, and then realized that they weren't dogs, they were *wolves*. These were the largest wolves I had ever seen, running as if they were made of water instead of flesh and bones, moving as a pack.

"Oh crap! Run faster you idiot!" I screamed through the crow as it flew overhead.

"I'm trying!" my lips finally answered.

The first wolf got close to me. It was black with blue eyes. It lunged at me, its paws materializing from the fluid as black razors. Just before it hit me, the crow dove toward the beast, wings open as it fired a hail of bullets from guns that materialized from within them.

"Stay away from me!" I yelled through the crow.

"Thanks buddy," I said with my mouth.

More wolves of different types showed up as I ran, all trying to lunge and get a hold of me with their claws and teeth. My crow wingman fought them off overhead as valiantly as he could. Each time he dove, it felt like I was the one in control of the bird, but I was also on the ground running.

Up ahead, a dusting of snow appeared and materialized into a white rabbit. It looked back at me with black eyes and gestured for me to follow it.

Hesitation filled my mind and then I heard footsteps behind me. I looked back and saw a new wolf running toward me. It was silver and had yellow eyes, but this one wasn't made of liquid. I could make out all of its form.

The wolf ran up and jumped over me, landing next to the rabbit, growling at it before turning to me and gesturing for me to follow it with a jerk of its head.

The sounds of the wolf pack to my rear howled back to life.

"Decide quickly you idiot!" I yelled down at myself from the crow.

Taking a step toward the rabbit, I apologized to the wolf, "Sorry." I built back up my speed as I followed the rabbit, leaving the wolf behind, where it let out a sad howl, and then vanished.

The white rabbit led me through the forest of fog at a breakneck speed. We dove under logs, leaped over streams, and barreled through bushes and underbrush that stood in our way. Up ahead a cave appeared. It looked so close, but seemed to pull away as I got closer.

The wolfpack behind me was bearing down on me when the silver wolf appeared again. It tried to push against me, to guide me away from the cave, but I didn't budge. I was going full speed into the cave and nothing could stop me.

The darkness of the cave enveloped me and everything faded away, except for the white rabbit. I eventually drew even with it as we ran through the void, and it looked at me and smiled, its eyes going from black to glowing red.

"I'm sorry, James!"

The rabbit began to transform while it ran next to me, its long bouncing hops replaced by the thumps of four large paws as its legs grew out into long sinewy limbs. Its bones cracked and stretched as it morphed while it moaned and groaned until the beast running next to me became a massive rabid white fox that looked like it hadn't eaten in days.

"I'm sorry James," it wailed from its drooling maw as it held a dagger over its head and brought it down in my gut.

"Ahhh....Ouch!" I shouted as I grabbed my head. The front of my skull had bounced off one of the bars of the bunk above me as I was jolted awake from the nightmare. I rubbed the throbbing spot just above my forehead and looked down to notice I was still in my clothes from the other day.

I scanned the room and came to the conclusion that I was in a jail cell. It was my first time in one so I couldn't comment on if it was nice or not. It was a corner cell, only two of my four walls were made up of bars, with another two cells to my left as I looked out from my bunk. Across from my cell were three others, just like mine, there were lights in the cells, but they were off, and the only light source was in the middle of the hall, casting an eerie glow into the cells. Next to my bunk was a toilet with a sink above it with no walls to provide any type of privacy.

My joints popped and my muscles ached as I stood up to relieve myself in the toilet. I was sore all over and felt the sudden need to never lay down again. I hadn't felt like this since I woke up in the infirmary after being shot down. I gazed out the bar-covered window and tried to make out what few buildings I could see around me in the dawn's early light.

I looked over at the neighboring cell and noticed someone was curled up in the bunk. Glancing over my shoulder, I scanned the other cells to see if there were any other prisoners, but saw that they were empty. It was me and my neighbor, all alone, except for the two guards in the other room, whose thought patterns I could pick up.

"Psst, excuse me," I whispered as I zipped up my pants.

Annoyance radiated off the mind of the sleeping individual as they woke up. The person lifted their head long enough to show that she was a woman. She stared at me with yellow eyes that glowed in the dim light of the cell before laying her head back down.

"Hey, come on, can you please tell me where we are?"

"Isn't it obvious?" replied a soft voice with a British-sounding accent.

"My bad, dumb question."

Her mind started to drift off again, but I had more questions.

"Sorry to bother you again, but how long have I been asleep?"

She let out a growl from under her blanket before answering me, "The guards brought you in two days ago."

"Two days...?"

I pulled off my coat and unbuttoned my shirt, examining my stomach. On my right side was a bruise where Madeline had injected me.

"I'm James by the way. James Walker," I said as I lowered my shirt.

She didn't say anything, so I turned and moved back toward my bunk.

"Hope Barnettt."

I turned to see her stand up from her bunk, put her hands over her head and lean backward, stretching her spine. She was a gray-furred wolfkin with silver hair that hung down to her shoulder in loose curls. A tan flight suit tightly hugged her lithe body, showing off the curves of her average-sized breasts and the fullness of her bubble butt. A gray tail with a white tip stuck out the back of her uniform.

She grabbed the blanket off her bunk and wrapped it around her shoulders like a cape before walking toward me, her bare feet padding softly on the floor. As she got closer, I could make out the details of her face. She had high cheekbones with a slender nose and pouty lips between them, her eyes were alert, even with bags under them. Though her fair skin was dirty, it did nothing to take away from how beautiful she was.

Is every woman on this planet gorgeous?

She stopped a few feet from the bars that divided us. Her gray and white ears were smaller than Madeline's, but they stood alert as she looked me up and down with her yellow eyes.

"What are you?" she asked.

"Excuse me?"

"What are you?" she repeated. "You have weird ears, no tail," she paused to sniff the air, "and a strange scent. So, what are you?"

"Oh, I'm a human."

She gave me a blank stare as her head tilted to the right and her ears twitched.

"I'm not from Dione, I'm from another world called Earth."

She backed away and looked at me cautiously. "You're from another world?"

"Correct."

She leaned forward and inspected me further. I peeked into her mind as she studied me, curious as to what she was thinking. Images of reptilian aliens fighting a tigerkin in a green suit came to her mind. The image shifted to some flame beings and then a weird slimy tentacle monster, all being fought back by this *Green Tiger* from a comic book she was obsessed with.

She thinks I'm a space alien!

"Oh boy..." I mumbled under my breath as I pinched the bridge of my nose.

"What was that?" she asked, her ears going alert again.

"Nothing."

She frowned, not liking being waved off, but she took a step closer to the bars. "So...how did you get here, Mr. Walker?"

"Please, call me James. I guess I got in here because I pissed off some Nazis."

Her head tilted to the left this time, and her ears twitched as she asked, "Who?"

"They're from my world, and all around bad people. The country I am from, the United States, is currently at war with them."

"Ok..."

"Yeah, so they wanted me to work with them, and I said no and punched their leader. I guess he then had the foxkin girl I was having a fling with inject me with some drug...and then I woke up in here."

"That explains the fox scent, but it doesn't answer my question."

I gave her a puzzled look. "Yes it does, you asked how I got here," I said as I pointed at the jail cell.

"No no no, how did you get to Dione? Did your spaceship crash land or something? Oh, was it those Nazis you said you are at war with? Did y'all have a big space battle and your ship had to land here for repairs?"

Her tail shook quickly behind her as she gripped the bars that separated us. She was so excited that she was getting to meet an alien, and I felt bad that I was about to crush her dreams.

"Miss Barnett, I am not an alien."

"But you said you were from another world," she stated as her tail stopped moving.

"I am from another world, but I did not come here on a spaceship. I think I was portaled here while I was flying my plane."

"You aren't from space?"

"No, I am not. In fact, the world I come from has very similar technology to yours."

She didn't say anything and was lost in thought that flitted across my mind. She was thinking through all the comic books she had read, but couldn't find anything like "people being teleported to another world." Eventually she shook her head and returned to the here and now. "So you are a pilot? What type of plane?"

"Fighters," I said with a smile.

"Me too!" she exclaimed, her tail starting to wag again.

"I assumed by the flight suit that you were a pilot, just didn't know you were a fighter pilot. How good are you?"

"I'm an ace," she said excitedly.

"I am also an ace. How many kills do you need on Dione to become an ace?"

"Five, how about on earth?"

"Five as well. I'm actually a double ace with thirteen kills," I noted smugly.

"That's cute, I'm a triple ace with sixteen, so…" She stuck her tongue out at me in order to hammer home the win.

I bowed my head to her as I accepted her win. "Miss Barnettt, do you mind if I ask you a personal question?"

"Sure." She shrugged. "As long as you stop with this *Miss Barnettt* nonsense. Please call me Hope."

"Ok, Hope, how long have you been locked up?"

"Almost a week, if you count the first day."

That was about how long I had been on Dione. Curious, I pushed on, "What did you do to end up in jail?"

Her smile faded as she sighed. "I was shot down."

I turned my head to the side. "They put you in jail because you were shot down? That sounds like a bit of an overreaction."

She didn't say anything but looked at me like I had three eyes before it hit me.

"You aren't from Crestia?" I asked.

"Nope, I am a pilot for Thurnmar," she said as she pulled down the blanket to show me a patch on her shoulder. It was white X over a purple circle with a yellow ring.

Purple and yellow...

"Did you say you were shot down a week ago?" I asked solemnly.

She leaned against the bars and fiddled with her fingers. "Yeah, my wingman and I were escorting a raid on the Empire that was launched from our carrier. We spotted two Crestia planes on intercept and moved in to cut them off. We got the upper hand and shot one of those red-tailed bastards down before being pounced on by a silver plane I've never seen before. My wingman was brought down before we knew he was there. I threw every trick in the book at that pilot before he got my engine when I went into a dive to outrun him. I ditched, but was picked up by one of the Empire's gyrocopters."

While she spoke, I watched her memories and saw my first moments in Dione from her perspective...

"Don't let him go Lone Wolf," her wingman said.

"Worry about yourself, Jackal, and take the shot when you get it," she shouted at the man as he toyed with the red plane in front of them.

"Shit! I'm hit! Where did that plane come from?" Jackal called out.

Hope craned her neck to get a view behind her.

"What type of plane is that?" she said to herself as she looked back at the sleek silver warbird that had ambushed them.

She looked back at Captain Hyde's plane just in time to see his left wing break apart from another volley of gunfire from the unknown fighter. His plane dropped, spinning out of control before, and then exploded.

"No!" she screamed.

She broke right, diving and pulling away, checking the mirror at the top of her canopy to see if *I* was pursuing her. Her breathing became panicked as her heart rate skyrocketed when the glint of light of my plane's sheet metal appeared.

She pulled up to the left. I was still there.

She inverted and pulled back on the yolk, causing the plane to speed down toward the ground, gaining momentum before leveling out. I was still there.

"Come on!" she cried as she flinched from the bullets striking her plane, her breathing rapid.

The wolfkin tried every defensive maneuver she knew while trying to get me off her tail, but nothing worked. My plane was behind her the entire time, peppering her plane with holes.

"Gotta run!" she told herself with a panicked tone. "No Imperial plane can keep up with us in a dive."

Hope pushed forward on the yolk and put the plane into the dive, racing toward the ocean below. She focused forward, her eyes occasionally checking her altimeter and speed indicator.

"Come on, go faster...Go faster!" she screamed.

She flinched and closed her eyes as gun fire shattered her canopy and impacted the armored plate behind her seat. When she opened her eyes, she saw that her instrument panel was shot to shit, and worse, her engine was on fire.

"Fuck fuck fuck!" she yelled as she pulled back on the yolk to level out the plane, but it didn't respond.

Hope was falling fast towards the water below.

Instinctually, she reached up and pushed away what remained of her canopy, then quickly released her harness. Wind rushed past her as she stood in the seat, put her boot on the edge of the cockpit and jumped up and away from the plane.

She fell for a second while she frantically searched for the rip cord of her parachute, finding the D-ring and pulling on it with all her strength.

For a moment, she didn't know if it was working, but then her body jerked downward as the parachute deployed overhead and slowed her down. She was safe...for now.

"Are you alright?" Hope asked.

I shook my head as I returned to my own head, my heart pounding as her memories stirred up my own repressed memories of being shot down.

"Yeah...I'm fine." I lied.

"Hey! Do you think that silver plane might have been one of those Nazis you mentioned? The plane had an emblem I had never seen before, a blue circle with a star in it, and white bars to the side."

I put my back to the bars and leaned against them, shaking my head. "That wasn't the Nazis, but I do know who the plane belonged to..."

"Oh? Are you going to tell me?" she asked.

I took a deep breath before answering her, "That belongs to the United States Army Air Forces."

She was silent for a moment, I couldn't see her face, but I was monitoring her thoughts as the words I had spoken registered in her mind.

Smack!

"Ow! What the hell?" I yelled, as I rubbed the back of my head.

"You!" she barked as I dodged a second punch from her. "You shot me down!"

"I'm sorry," I said as I backed out of the range of her reach.

"Motherfucker!" she shouted as she kicked the bars with her bare foot. She fell to the ground and shouted a tirade of swear words as she rubbed her quickly swelling toe.

The main door to the prison hall opened and a wolfkin guard stepped into the hall, flipping on the cell lights. He pulled a baton off his hip and smacked it against the bars a few times to get her attention.

"Keep it down, you mutt!" he spat at Hope, looking at her with disgust before turning his glare to me. "Look who finally decided to wake up."

"What's going on in there?" hollered another voice from the other side of the door.

"Nothing much, I think the human pissed off the Thurnmar mutt. Notify the Ministry and let them know he's finally awake. I'm tired of babysitting him," he said with disdain as he closed the door behind him.

"You're lucky there are bars between us," Hope hissed while still rubbing her foot.

"Hey, I said I was sorry-"

"Oh, you're sorry alright."

She then crawled into her bunk and curled up under her blanket, staring at the wall. I reached out to read her mind so I could see what she was thinking. Her thoughts were a jumble of confusion while fighting the urge not to cry. She was also repeating one word over and over again in her mind.

Why?

"They tricked me," I said, answering her unspoken question. "When I showed up in this world, I was confused and desperate to get a hold of anyone on my radio. They answered first and asked for help. I wasn't sure who to help, but I could sense what you and your partner were thinking, and it made me take pity on the Crestia pilot."

She looked over her shoulder at me, her eyes filled with anger. "Are you a fucking minder? This just keeps getting better!"

"I'm sorry, Hope."

"I don't need an apology from the man who killed me," she chided as she laid her head down.

"Don't be dramatic, I didn't kill you," I responded angrily. "Besides, you're a prisoner. It's against the rules of war to kill prisoners."

She sat up and looked at me. "Rules of war? We aren't in your world. There are no rules of war." She glowered as she continued, "You see these ears? I'm a wolfkin fighting against a canid supremacy nation. I have the blood of Crestia running through my veins. Years ago they called on all canids to return to the 'fatherland' and all those who didn't were fair game. Since I didn't go, I'm seen as a race traitor."

Her words bit at me, causing me to sit down on my bunk. Hope was a fighter pilot, so she knew the risks of fighting, but it wasn't right for them to execute her just because she didn't agree with their way of life.

"I'm sorry, Hope," I said as I held my face in my hands. "I know I'm not from this world, but it's not right for them to execute you for that."

"Thanks, but it's right to them, and as long as we're in this cell, that's all that matters."

CHAPTER
TWELVE

THE REST of the day crawled by at a snail's pace. By noon I had run out of things to do to keep my mind occupied. I had counted how many bars were in the walls, how many steps there were across the cell in both directions. I tried to nap but was too restless so I settled on working out in my cell instead, which drew peeking glances from the wolf girl who was trying to ignore me.

After finishing my fifth time through my routine of pushups, sit ups, air squats, jumping jacks and burpees, I stopped to catch my breath. As I awkwardly tried to get a drink of water from the sink, my ears caught the familiar sounds of a Rolls Royce Merlin engine. I looked out and saw my plane buzzing through the air with some of the Empire's fighters, as well as the two Messerschitt Bf-109s I had seen a few days earlier.

"God damn it!" I yelled out as I grabbed the bars of the window and attempted to shake them.

The Mustang had a few engineering aspects to it that the Nazi engineers hadn't thought of, and I didn't like that they and the Crestia engineers now had full access to her secrets. I pounded my right fist against the frame of the window until my anger subsided, only to be replaced by pain.

Smooth move, good thing you are left handed.

"Isn't that your plane?" Hope asked as she looked out the window of her cell at the planes flying overhead.

"Yes," I huffed, "and those pricks are going to use her to suit their needs. I just know it."

"That's a shame. It's a sweet looking plane, I wish Thurnmar had it."

"I'd gladly let your side study it if I had to choose between the two," I reassured her.

"If only we had had that thing you called a radio, right?"

I nodded. "If only."

That was the moment that began the mending of relations between Hope and I. We soon found ourselves sitting across from each other, talking about flying and comparing the rules of dog fighting between the two worlds. She knew a lot, but there were a few things I was able to explain to her that were new concepts to the skies of Dione. It seemed their understanding and development of planes lagged behind Earth's by maybe five years.

"Why would you need a plane with that much range?" she asked as she tore off a piece of the sandwich the guards had brought us for lunch. She was lounging on her side, laying on the mattress she had dragged off the top bunk of her cell. Her tail wagged slowly as she asked questions between bites, "Why not just deliver your fighter and bomber squads by carrier?"

"We do that, but carriers are large and expensive. We primarily use them in the Pacific Ocean, where it's almost five thousand miles between the United States and Japan."

"Japan?" she asked as her ears twitched. "I thought you were fighting the Nazis and Germany."

I nodded. "Japan is allied with the Nazis. In fact, they used a carrier attack on one of our bases to drag my country into the war."

She nodded as she chewed on her food.

"So how hard is it to launch a carrier strike on a country like Crestia?"

She tilted her head to the side and twitched her ears as she thought, something that was a Canid mannerism that I was starting to pick up on. "It's not that hard. The ship just has to get close enough while not being spotted."

"But that's just it. The land floats more than two miles over the water, any ship in the ocean would be easily spotted as it approaches."

"Why would a ship be in the water?" she asked, her ears twitching again.

"Because that's where ships are. They float in the water."

She held it in for a moment, but eventually burst into hysterical laughter, rolling onto her back. "That's the dumbest thing I've ever heard. Why would you put a ship in the water?"

"Because that's where ships go!"

She laid on her back and stared at me, realizing I was being serious. "Hold on. Ships float in the water on Earth?"

"Yes."

"Oh my Goddess, that's so dumb."

"Where else would they go?" I asked, getting annoyed with her tone.

She sat up and crossed her legs. "In the air, where ships belong."

Now it was my turn to laugh at her.

"Hey, stop laughing at me," she pouted, her bottom lip jutting out as she frowned and dropped her ears.

I fought the urge to bust her chops further, since she had laughed at me, and scanned her mind. I quickly realized she wasn't joking. "Wow, you're being serious?"

She nodded.

"I'm sorry, that was not very gentlemanly of me."

"Thank you."

While we sat in awkward silence, my mind thought of images of zeppelins, blimps, and footage I saw at the theater once of the Hindenburg bursting into flames. I imagined big gas bags holding warships overhead by large cables. None of that sounded safe.

"How do you protect the gas bags from being damaged during combat?"

"What?" she asked, furrowing her brow at me.

"How do you protect the gas bags that the ships hang from?" I asked again. "I would imagine that they are vulnerable to small arms fire, and would be targeted first."

She tried hard not to laugh, but failed.

"You're too funny! Why would we use gas bags to lift our ships when we can use greyosite?" she asked, as if the answer was obvious to me once she said it like that.

"Greyosite?" I repeated. "What's that?"

"It's a mineral that levitates. It's said to be the reason why the continents float the way they do."

"And you use this mineral to make ships float in the air?"

She nodded.

"How do you control the ships?"

"Hmm," she said as she thought. "I've never had to explain it before, but what we are taught in school is that greyosite reacts to electricity. With the right charge, you can manipulate the mineral to go in any direction you want. How does that work? I have no idea. I'm a pilot, not a greyosite scientist, but I think with greyosite alone, we can get ships up to thirty to forty knots."

"That's pretty fast for a ship," I said.

The ship I had been on when I went to England to join the

Royal Air Force had gone fifteen knots, which was about seventeen miles per hour. I could only imagine what it would be like to go twice that speed on a large airship.

"Not really," she said, "that's slow as far as warships are concerned."

I was taken aback. I might have been a ground-based pilot, but I had visited with carrier-based pilots from the Pacific theater, and they had told me that the carriers had to go at least thirty-three knots to launch planes.

"How do they go faster if the greyosite only goes forty knots?" I asked.

"Propellers."

"Propellers?"

"Yes, huge ones at the stern that can push the ships up to ninety knots. There are even some high-speed freighters that can exceed one hundred eighty knots. If you want to go any faster than that, you need a plane...James?"

I gawked at her through the bars as I tried to process those speeds. If I hadn't been able to see the images of these ships in her mind, I would have never believed her. However, if you had told me continents could float and girls with wolf or fox ears existed, I wouldn't have believed that until I saw it, either. So I took her word on that, just like she took my word that our ships floated on the ocean and our continents were in that same ocean, and not above it.

As we went back and forth, I was glad Hope didn't hold a grudge with me. I still felt she was a little angry, but she was coming around to it being a mistake, and not intentional.

The next day saw my first visitor that wasn't wearing a guards uniform.

"James," she said with a lustful tone.

I opened my eyes as the familiar voice called to me from the entrance to my cell.

"Wake up sleepy head."

Finally giving in, I rolled over in my bunk and saw the white-haired foxkin pressing herself against the bars.

"There he is! That's right baby, wake up!"

"What do you want?" I growled.

"To talk," Madeline said meekly in response to my tone.

"Then talk." I rolled back to face the wall.

"James! I don't want to talk to the back of your head. Please turn and face me."

Her voice had a whining tone to it that sounded more like an over-infatuated lover than that of the calm and cool Ministry of State Secrets agent I had met when I first arrived in Dione.

"Please talk to me. Please! Pretty Please! Please! Please! Please!"

"Oh my Goddess! Talk to her and make her shut up!" Hope shouted.

"Hey! No one was talking to you, mutt!" Madeline barked.

Hope threw her pillow at the bars. "Big talk from a weird-smelling fox."

"Bitch!"

"Whore!"

"Shut up!" I yelled as I finally sat up in my bunk and looked at the woman. "What do you want, White Rabbit?"

Out of the corner of my eye, I saw Hope's ears twitch. I had decided to use her codename over her given name, hoping she would pick up that I knew what she was and didn't trust her.

"Please don't call me by my work name. We are much closer than that," Madeline said, pouting and crossing her arms as she backed away from the bars.

I rubbed the sleep from my eyes, finally focusing on her. She wasn't wearing her military uniform, instead opting for something I guessed she thought would get my attention. She had on a tight white short-sleeved blouse with the top buttons open to show off her cleavage. Below that, a simple blue skirt that ended just above her knees, allowing me to see the smooth pale skin of her lower legs as they led to her small feet in red heels.

"What do you want, Madeline?" I demanded after we had been silent for too long.

"I want you to stop being all moody and to come to your senses," she pleaded as she grabbed the bars and pressed herself against them.

"And how would you propose I do that?" I asked sarcastically.

"By accepting to work with Major-General Kampf. If you do that, then we can be together," she said with a smile.

I shook my head. "Why would I want to be with you, Madeline?"

"Because you care about me?" she asked hopefully as her tail wagged.

"Please. The person I cared about was an act to deceive me. I don't even know who you are."

"It wasn't all an act..." she mumbled. "Listen, I know that I lied to you, and I can see how you don't like that, but I promise I won't ever do it again."

"Whatever," I said as I looked away from her.

"Please James! I just want to be with you, even if you only want to use me physically, that's fine. At least then I'll get to be with you."

I stared at her as I thought of what to say. My dad always told me to count to ten when I was angry, that way I wouldn't say anything I would regret.

I had counted to twenty by the time I responded to her.

"Madeline, I can't be with anyone who is working with the Nazis," I said.

"But why?"

"Because they're evil. They're systematically killing people on Earth because of their convictions. They've carried out atrocities on my world that are unforgivable. If the Empire is partnering with them, then I have to assume that those same actions are going on here. The sad part is that with every minute that goes by, I'm seeing nothing that proves me wrong."

"James, I told you, things are complicated," Madeline said.

I stared at her and shrugged. I didn't have anything else to say to her.

"Fine, be that way. Maybe a few more days here will change your mind. But if you find yourself feeling lonely and missing me..." She lifted up her skirt, exposing her black panties before pulling them aside and running her fingers through her slit. "Just let the guards know, and I'll help guide you home. All you have to do is call me."

She lowered her skirt and licked her fingers before turning to Hope. "Listen up, mutt. You better not think of stealing him from me. He's mine."

Hope raised her hands in surprise. "I don't even find him attractive!"

"Don't you know you can't lie to minders?"

Hope blushed. "Is everyone in this damn country a minder?"

Madeline huffed at her, then blew me a kiss as she left the jail.

I sat there in silence before Hope spoke up.

"I don't like you that way, but you are attractive...for an alien."

"Thank you, Hope," I said with a laugh, "you're also pretty attractive."

She blushed and looked away. "You know, we have a saying

in Thurnmar. *Don't sit on crazy.* I guess for you, the opposite applies."

I held my head in my hands and let out a soft laugh, "In my world, the saying is, *don't stick your dick in crazy.*"

"Well, you definitely stuck your dick in it."

It was later that afternoon when I received my next unwanted visitor. Hope and I were both looking out our cell windows, watching the planes fly overhead when our fun was interrupted by a human in gray uniform.

"Guten Tag Kapitan Walker" said the cheerful German as the guards brought him a chair, setting it up in the hall before leaving and shutting the door behind them.

Kampf sat down, but kept his hat on, which seemed odd. Sitting there smiling, he looked like the model Nazi citizen that was shown on propaganda posters—blonde hair, blue eyes, though one was black from where I had hit him, a strong chin, and the smile a door to door vacuum cleaner salesman would be proud of.

"Major Kampf, to what do I owe the displeasure?" I asked, sitting on my bunk and staring at the smiling Nazi.

"Major-General," he corrected before continuing, "I just wanted to see how my American friend was doing. Possibly see if the time we gave you to think was enough for you to come to a favorable conclusion for both of us."

"Geez, I didn't know we were friends," I quipped.

"We could be," he said as he relaxed in the chair. "Do you remember when we first talked, Kapitan Walker?"

"Sadly, yes I do."

"Do you recall the reward I promised you?"

I nodded.

"I am prepared to give it to you, and more, if you will work with me willingly. You have already enjoyed parts of it, delicious nights with a beautiful woman, a friendship with a powerful noble, and I am sure I could have this mutt thrown in as well, " he said, gesturing to Hope.

Hope growled in response.

"Ahh, you understand me?"

"My parents were from Crestia. They taught me the tongue."

I looked back and forth between them, trying to make sense of what they were talking about. Kampf nodded, then turned back to me to continue.

"Agent Reynolds assures me you have some of the Dionian mental abilities, as well as a natural mental block against their abilities. I believe she said you have the potential to be a Class A minder. We have not brought over a man yet who could even communicate telepathically with these beasts, let alone block their mind reading or mind controlling abilities, which is why we wear special hats like this one," he said, lifting his hat off his head and allowing his thoughts to be picked up.

"So you want to make me a lab-rat?" I asked, wincing at the polka music playing in my head.

"Not exactly. You see, lab-rats live in a cage, you would live in Crestia! You would be free to go where you want, as long as you would come when called by Dr. Gerver for more studies."

"And you think that this Dr. Gerver would be able to unlock the hidden mental abilities for your master race?"

This triggered images of Nazi parades to play across the German's mind as he continued to smile at me. "You would be surprised what Dr. Gerver and his team have accomplished since we found our way to this world," Kampf declared. "Experiments not thought possible on Earth are possible here thanks to new minerals, and the mental abilities of these Dionians."

I leaned back against the wall and crossed my arms. "And if I say no?"

The smile melted off of Kampf's face. "If you say no, then that is not the end of our business. We will be forced to carry out the good doctor's experiments on you by force. I am just here to try and give you options."

"What about option three?" I asked with a smile, "Can I choose that one again."

Kampf reached up and touched the swelling around his left eye, and I saw a quick flash of anger on his mind before he suppressed it. "You got me good on that one, Kapitan Walker, but option three was a one time action by you. It will not happen again."

I was starting to notice that if I asked him certain questions, it would help me to see his thoughts more clearly. At the moment, he was letting me see his thoughts by removing that special hat, and he felt he could control what I saw. Kampf believed that since he had been around Imperial minders for eight years, he could dictate what my untrained mind could see.

"So is science the only reason the Third Reich is on Dione? Or is there more?" I asked as I leaned forward, expanding my consciousness to dive into his.

"Science is a part, but the exchange of goods and ideas is another. They get new technology, like planes and wonder weapons. We receive resources in the forms of petroleum and rare minerals. We also get a vacation destination in another world to a country that shares much of the same ideals as we do."

I could see that list of goods going back and forth, and saw for a moment how they were going back and forth between our worlds. It seemed they had found something related to the lost city of Atlantis and a portal in the Caribbean. But all that went away when he mentioned the "same ideals."

"Same ideals?" I asked. The Major-General's mind went dark, and not as in black.

"Yes," Kampf replied. "This war on Dione is about more than Crestia Territorial expansion. This is about the Canids cleansing Dione of the lesser races that have done nothing for this world except waste its resources and time."

Images of non-canid beastkin being rounded up and sent to camps came across my mind. They were used for servants, manual labor...and experiments.

What the fuck? I have to stop this.

"What are you doing?"

I didn't answer him, I just continued to stare at him, trying my best to take over his mind like I had done to Marshall Altros a few days earlier. If I could use what Court had called *thought reformation* on this asshole, then I could possibly save millions of lives.

But first, I had to get control of his mind.

"What are you doing, Kapitan Walker?" asked the Major General.

He stared at me for a moment before his eyes went wide, he quickly grabbed his hat and moved to place it on his head.

Shit, come on, James!

He stopped. The hand shook as his hat was half on his head. I could tell I didn't have full control. I had some, but the hat was interfering with my ability.

"Clever, Kaptain Walker," he spat at me through gritted teeth as he struggled to put the hat on all the way. "I have not had a minder try and take control of my mind in years. I was lucky I knew what to look for."

I pressed my mind toward his with everything I had, my face locked in a scowl as beads of sweat ran down my face. My mind swam through his, looking for anything I could do to win full control over his mind, and then I saw it.

A thread appeared in front of my mind, and I followed it. As the thread pulled me deeper into his mind, I noticed that his hat started to move off his head. I was doing it, I was winning!

"What?" Kampf yelled as he felt himself lose more and more control, "No! I will not let you control me!"

There was a desperate push from him and the scene in his mind shifted to bombard me with images that terrified me. Images of death and destruction, and subjugation at the hands of those wearing that damn swastika.

This made me lose the thread I had been following, and as I struggled to find it again, I became distracted by what the Nazis had planned for Dione.

They planned to wait for the Dionians to kill themselves off on both sides, aiding the Empire to help them win. Then, once the Empire had exhausted its forces in conquering this world, the Nazis would bring their troops over to conquer the Empire. They planned to subjugate the Dionians and use them as slaves and living experiments.

"Do you see?" Kampf asked with a wicked cackle. "Do you see now what we have planned for this world?"

The images became darker and darker, pushing me to a point where my mind and stomach couldn't take anymore. I felt an acidic burn in the back of my throat as bile started to push its way up. I let go of his mind and turned to run to the toilet, making it just in time to see my lunch come back up.

"Are you ok?" Hope asked from her cell.

"Was that too much for you, Kapitan?" Kampf laughed as he wiped the sweat from his forehead. He then put on his hat, ending the slideshow of planned horrors.

"They don't know," I coughed. "They don't know that they made a deal with the devil." I spit as I rose from the toilet.

"They know what they need to know, not that you can do anything to stop them. All you can do is choose how you will aid us."

"I'd rather die than help you psychopaths."

"It is going to be a long time until you die, Kapitan Walker. Your brain is too valuable to us, but luckily for you, we do not need it yet. I want you to come willingly, so how about I give you more incentives?"

"There is nothing you could say that would make me willingly help you."

"What about her?" he asked, pointing over at Hope. "In two days she is to be publicly executed. You can spare her life by making her your slave when you choose to work with us willingly."

I opened my mouth to say something, but had nothing left to say.

"Ahh, I guess Agent Reynolds is right to be worried." He stood up and chuckled. "I will return in two days for your decision. Remember, you cannot save this world, but you can save her."

"He doesn't need to save me, I'd rather die than be someone's slave," Hope said to Kampf.

"Just so, we will see how your tune changes as we get closer to your execution day. You two enjoy the next two days, I am sure they will be relaxing."

With that, Kampf exited the jail hall, leaving the two of us alone.

I moved to my bunk and collapsed once I was sure he was gone. Our battle had exhausted me mentally and physically. I closed my eyes and felt myself starting to drift off to sleep.

"So that was a Nazi?" Hope asked.

"Yes. That was a Nazi."

"What did you see?"

I didn't want to remember the images I had seen in the Major General's mind, but I powered through and explained what they had planned. They didn't care about the Empire, they were just using them so they could conquer this world.

"We can't let them do that," she said, sitting with her back against the bars as I sat on my bunk.

"Nothing we can do about it, Hope. We're stuck here."

"What if we could escape?" Hope asked after a few moments of silence.

"Ya, wouldn't that be nice?"

"No, I'm serious!" she said, jumping to her feet, "we could do it, and we have the perfect bait to make it happen."

CHAPTER
THIRTEEN

"COME ON JAMES, you have to make this link or the plan won't work."

Hope sat cross legged at the bars of her cell, her yellow eyes watching me pace my own. We had been trying to establish a telepathic link between the two of us for the past hour, and I was starting to get a headache.

"I'm not even sure I can do it. Kampf said no human has ever been able to."

"True, but no other human was a minder. You said Major Welch was able to reach out and talk to you without you two ever seeing each other, and you've been able to receive my projections. Let's keep trying," she said with a patient voice.

I let out a sigh and returned to where I had been sitting in front of her. I crossed my legs and closed my eyes as I cleared my mind. When I was ready, I opened them again and focused on the beautiful face across from me.

"*You can do it. Focus on my voice,*" she said in my mind.

I tried to grab ahold of the source of her voice, but it felt like trying to grab at water with a net. Madeline had told me that all Dionians had telepathic abilities and went through this process on the day they turned fifteen. Telepathy was a game changer in the world of military tactics, it allowed them to move troops, planes and ships without worry of the signal being intercepted. This eliminated the need for radios all together.

I needed to do this. I kept focusing on her mental signal, gritting my teeth and squishing my face before I let out a hushed roar. "Grrr...I can't!"

"Please stop using your mouth and use your mind."

Easy for you to say.

I closed my eyes, again, and took a few deep breaths as I squeezed the bridge of my nose.

How could I make this work?

It was like when my dad and I had to fix the radio for his plane. It was able to pick up calls, but wasn't able to answer. In the end, the fix had been to clean some dirt build up out of the radio housing, and it started to work just fine. What if there was just some mental dust blocking this connection?

"James, please focus on me."

My eyes opened and I focused on her.

"Let's try a different approach. This is one my mother tried with me that was successful. I want you to think of anything you want to tell me, and say it to my mind."

I nodded and took a deep breath after I figured out what I wanted to tell her. I pushed it out there and for a moment, I swore I could sense the thread, the mental wire that called for me to grab it in order to make the connection. I reached out for it with my mind, but it faded away before I could grab it. My face contorted in frustration, and then I felt a soft hand on mine.

"Hey, relax."

Her calmness flowed into me, and my stress over making the connection faded away. I opened my eyes as I saw Hope's mind. Her desire for this to succeed and to connect with me was mesmerizing. She had faith in me that I could do this, and I did not want to let her down. I stared into her eyes, studying the many hues of yellow that had been used to paint her iris, and that's when I decided to tell her something else...

"You have beautiful eyes."

"W-What?"

The wolf girl's face turned a bright crimson as she pulled her hands back to cover her mouth.

"Wait, did you hear that?" I asked, missing the quickness of her hand darting through the bars and flicking me on my nose.

"Stop using your mouth."

I rubbed my nose but smiled. I had done it, but how? I searched my mind and saw the strand again, my mind grabbed for the link as I began to hyper fixate on the details of her face again. I studied her lips, nose, cheeks, and finally, her ears. They were forward and alert on the top of her head, covered in fur that looked so soft to the touch.

"I'd really love to touch your ears," I projected as my mind grabbed the connection and didn't let go.

"James!"

"A-am I doing it?"

Hope blushed the darkest shade of red I had ever seen as she turned away from me, covering her ears with her hands.

"Hope? Can you hear me?"

"Yes! But for the love of the Goddess, stop talking like that!"

I thrust my arms into the air and let out a celebratory laugh before apologizing to the flustered wolfkin. I had learned it was uncouth to talk about a woman's ears.

"I'm sorry Hope, this is new and weird to me. Hard to control what comes out."

"I understand. After my fifteenth birthday, I accidentally connected with a boy in class who was picking on one of my friends."

"Oof, what did he do?"

"He ran off screaming that I was going to eat him."

I smiled at her once she turned back to me and straightened up.

"That sounds embarrassing, what did you say?"

"Um, something about how I had sharp teeth and was not afraid to use them. In retrospect, it's easy to see how a rabbitkin would get scared."

The image of the big bad wolf intimidating a little rabbit made me chuckle before I regained my composure to ask her another question. *"Just curious, how many years has it been since that happened?"*

"James, If you want to know my age, just ask."

The sun started to set the following day as I broke down and called on the guards to notify Madeline that I wanted to talk to her. They moved quickly to get a hold of her, mentioning how they didn't want to piss off the White Rabbit.

"Remember to keep your cool. Don't let her win easily," Hope projected while I waited.

"Don't let her win easily? Do you not remember how she behaved yesterday?"

"I do, I just don't want her to get suspicious. I know I would be suspicious if you talked to me the way you did one day, then pulled a full one-eighty the next. However..."

"However?" I pressed as her thought trailed off.

"However, she might be the craziest woman on the planet."

"Oh, without a doubt."

The door to the cells burst open sooner than I expected as hurricane Madeline rushed to my cell wearing the same outfit as yesterday.

"James! I'm here for you!" she proclaimed as she pressed her breasts between the bars, causing the fabric of her top to strain against her luscious mounds.

"Madeline!" I said, stepping toward her.

She reached through the bars and pulled me to her,

hugging me through the bars. "I wish these bars were not in the way."

"I do too," I said as I returned the awkward hug.

"James? I don't want to make assumptions, but have you changed your mind? Do you want to be with me?"

"Yes," I said as I looked down at her. "I'm sorry Madeline, I was only thinking of myself and never stopped to think about us."

"Truly?" she asked, her eyes wide with hope as she looked up at me. "You have been thinking about us?"

"Go on, tell her what you have been thinking," Hope mentally teased.

I channeled my inner Clark Gable and let her have it. "I don't want to die because of my pride, Madeline. And I would never be able to forgive myself knowing I took your feelings for granted. Please, help me, Madeline!"

I dropped my head against the bars and forced out a sniffle and single lonely tear.

"You are way too good at this."

"You know it's not polite to talk during a performance."

"Guard! Come open this cell at once!" Madeline shouted.

The guards came into the room to protest, but all that did was anger her further, and got the one closest to her a broken nose.

"Question me again and I will see that you spend the rest of your lives in the mines!"

"Don't be too harsh, they are just innocent men, following orders the best they can," I said as the guard with the busted nose fumbled with his keys.

"Shush my love. I will not let anyone question our need to be with each other!"

"Her love?" Hope snickered in my mind.

The guard fiddled with his keys before finding the one for my cell. The door clanked open, and Madeline rushed past the guard, leaping into my arms and covering me with kisses. I was able to catch her before we fell to the ground, but I wasn't able to keep up with her lips as she kissed down my cheek to my neck.

"Oh, James! I've missed you so much," she whimpered as she started unbuttoning my shirt. "I am afraid I have a fever, and the only thing that can cure it is more of you. I need you James, I need you now!"

"Damn! What did you do to her?" Hope asked.

"Here? Now? In front of the mutt and the guards?" I asked as I lowered her to the ground and gestured toward the two wolfkin guards who were gawking at us.

"You're right, I can't have other men looking at me if I am to belong to you." She snapped her finger at the two men while never taking her eyes off me. "You two get lost, I want to be alone with my man."

"But Agent Reynolds-"

"That's it, to the mines with the both of you!" she yelled as she turned around, but the door quickly slammed shut as both men vanished.

"Maddy, you aren't really going to send them to the mines are you?"

"Not unless you want me to."

I shook my head. "Don't worry about them anymore, they're gone. But what about the mutt?"

Madeline looked over at Hope, who was sitting on the end of her bunk, elbows on her knees as she looked at us. "Let her watch. It would do her some good to see what she can't have."

"You're bad," I growled as I moved in to kiss her.

My hands cupped her face as our tongues danced between our lips. Though we had kissed many times over the past week, there was something about kissing her that always felt like it was the first time. If you had told me we were high school sweethearts, I would have believed it by the way that we kissed.

I moved my hands down from her cheeks to her neck and over her full chest, kneading her perfect mounds once my hands got there. She let out a groan as I pinched her nipples through the fabric, reaching down to unbutton her shirt, and throwing it on the floor.

Licking my lips, I kissed down her neck and used my body weight to push her back against the bars.

"Oh! I like when you are forceful," she moaned into my ear as I kissed and licked along her collar bone.

Her hands grabbed my shirt and began working the buttons, but I grabbed them and put them up above her. "Not yet my love, let me take care of you first," I demanded, rising up to kiss her again, biting and tugging on her lip as I pulled away.

She whimpered as I held her hands above her, but kept them there when I brought mine down her arms, gently caressing her sensitive pale skin. I bypassed her chest and kissed down her stomach, my fingers working to unbutton her skirt, before it fell to the ground. She now stood before me, fully exposed with her hands still over her head, breathing heavily in her black lace underwear.

"Are you ready?" I asked.

She nodded.

"Good, be sure to keep your hands over your head."

I leaned in and caressed the top of her thighs, lifting up her left leg and kissing the inside as I moved closer to her satin covered pussy. She whimpered and groaned as I teased her slit, causing her pussy lips to swell, and the fabric to wetten. Her sweet musky scent filled my nostrils, and I so badly wanted to pull down her panties and lick up her honey, but I had to focus.

Keep your eye on the mission!

I grabbed a strip of fabric off the ground, and balled it up in my hands as I worked my way back up her soft body.

"You aren't going to eat me out?" she whined.

"No," I whispered as I peppered her chest and neck with

kisses, "in time. First I need you to close your eyes, open your mouth and say *ahhh*."

She giggled as she complied with my order, and that gave Hope the window she needed to bring a strip of fabric over her mouth, gagging her as she quickly tied her head to the bar behind her.

A muffled "what the fuck" could be heard as her eyes flew open. She attempted to bring her hands down to grab at the gag, but I was already there. I held her wrists together over her head while Hope grabbed the fabric strip from my hands and bound her to the bar.

Madeline screamed and pulled against the restraints, kicking out as I pushed against her body and wrangled in her legs. Once again, Hope was quick with her knot tying, and we soon had her arms, legs and head restrained to the same bar.

"What are you doing?" she called out to me telepathically.

"We are getting out of here," I said as Hope and I tightened my belt around her waist, restraining her stomach to the bar as well.

"Why? I thought you wanted to be with me?"

"I want to be free. I gave you a chance to leave, but you chose Kampf and the Nazis over me."

"Babe!" she pleaded, *"I told you it was complicated."*

"I know what you said," I replied as I grabbed her clothes and passed them through to Hope.

"Thank you," Hope said as she took it and started changing.

"Hold on," she cried as she tried to turn to look behind her, *"don't you let that mutt wear my clothes!"*

"Fuck off bitch." Hope growled.

I leaned to the side just as Hope's lithe body stepped out of her flight suit. Her lush ass and overly fluffy tail were pointed at me as she bent over to pick up the top. My mouth dropped as she straightened out her supple back, showing off the dimples above her heart shaped bottom.

"*Stop looking at her like that!*"

Hope turned to smile at me as I looked away, blushing that I was caught. "Aww, is the little vixen mad that her boyfriend likes wolves more than foxes?"

"I'm not her boyfriend."

Madeline got quiet and stopped moving, her eyes welling up with tears as she stared at me, her breathing heavy. "*You won't get away, I'll call for help.*"

I leaned towards her and stared into her eyes, my hands resting on the bars on both sides of her, "No you won't. I'm not going to let you."

"*You think you can stop me?*" she asked, "*I am a Class-A minder for the Ministry of State Secrets. It would take you years to break me!*"

I narrowed my eyes as I glared at her and focused on pushing my consciousness out toward hers. Her barrier was up, and it was strong, but I could see cracks in its foundation. Sticking from one of those was the thread, similar to what I saw when working with Hope. I pulled on it and a tunnel opened for me in her barrier, which I quickly dove into.

She fought against me, and as she did, the opening tightened and constricted around me. I struggled to fight back, but as she had pointed out, she was a Class-A minder.

"I thought you said you were mine, Madeline?" I asked through gritted teeth to distract her.

Madeline's eyes went wide before going distant. The tunnel she had been squeezing me in widened, and allowed me through. I followed the thread deeper into her mind until the thread led me to the spot where I now had full control of her mind.

"*No...how?...This shouldn't be possible,*" she whimpered once she realized what was happening, her body going lax.

"That's not important. What is important is you aren't going to call for help, well, not until I tell you to, is that understood?"

"I am not going to call for help until you tell me to," she repeated back to me with a defeated tone.

A terrifying thought then crossed my mind, "I could easily reform your mind to make you come with me, couldn't I?"

"Yes. You could make me do anything..."

"That's appealing, but I don't want to abuse this power, or gift, as you call it," I said, looking away and releasing the hold that I had on her mind. I felt myself pull out, but could still feel that I had a small presence in her mind.

"Hope and I are going to be leaving now. I truly wanted to take you with me, Madeline, but we have to live with our choices."

She shook her head and screamed into the gag tied around her mouth. *"No James, please don't go. Please don't leave me!"*

Hope covered her ears, though it did nothing to stop the telepathic temper tantrum. "Are you sure we can't go with my idea and just kill her?"

"What?" Madeline screamed.

"No, we have wasted enough time," I said before turning back to our captive. "Now Maddy, would you be a good girl and call for the guards?"

CHAPTER
FOURTEEN

"AGENT REYNOLDS, YOU CALLED?" the guard asked as he entered the hall.

He froze when he saw her tied up to the bars of the jail cell, not looking anywhere else as he stepped toward her and started to draw his baton. Before he could take another step, I moved in behind him, grabbed his head, and gave it a quick twist to the side, snapping his neck.

I stepped back as his body dropped to the floor and waited for the second guard. After a minute of waiting, I poked my head in the office that was attached to the jail cells and saw it was empty. I returned and grabbed the keys off the dead guard's belt before going over to let Hope out.

"Where's the other guard?" she asked as I opened her cell door.

I shrugged, but upon further examination of the dead guard, I noticed he was not the one with a busted up nose. The other guy had probably run off to the infirmary or something.

"It seems pissing you off saved the other guards life," I said to Madeline as Hope and I started removing his uniform.

"*Whatever,*" Madeline pouted as she watched us.

After my wardrobe change, Hope and I gave each other a

quick once over to make sure everything looked right. The blouse and skirt outfit Madeline had been wearing to impress me fit Hope well. She was taller than Madeline, so the skirt showed off more of her long legs, and the wedge heels on her feet accented them perfectly.

As I stared at her, Hope was dusting off and straightening out the uniform I was wearing, her hands lingering over my chest and shoulders. A few stray thoughts crossed her mind as she did, and she pursed her lips to hide her blushing smile.

"Stop looking at each other like that," Madeline barked.

Hope and I made eye contact before looking away from each other, blushing.

"You aren't as pretty as me," Madeline spat.

"Does she ever stop talking?" Hope asked as she crossed her arms under her chest.

"Are you trying to make your boobs look bigger?" the tied up foxkin asked with a laugh. *"My shirt looks deflated on you. Aww, look, she's going to cry."*

I was about to say something, but Hope stepped up to me and pulled the guard's service knife from my belt, and lunged at Madeline.

"James!"

I grabbed Hope by the waist before she got close enough to do any damage, and lifted her up off the ground. "Woah! Easy there."

"Just let me cut her, just a little bit," Hope pleaded.

"No!"

"Ughh! Fine," she sighed as I sat her on the ground. She then turned to the guard's body, grabbed his tail and with a few sawing motions at the base, freed it from his body.

"Turn around," she ordered when she turned back to me.

Not wanting to piss off a woman with a knife, I did what she said and felt her messing with the back of my pants.

"There! Now you look like a wolfkin."

I grimaced as I looked back and saw the guard's tail hanging from the back of my pants. "Ew, I can feel the blood soaking through."

"It's that, or explain to anyone we see why you're missing a tail."

"They are going to notice the ears," Madeline pointed out.

Hope nodded and turned back to the dead guard.

"Hold on, I'll just wear the helmet," I said, stopping her from hacking more body parts from the corpse.

She shrugged and handed the knife back to me.

"Goodbye Madeline," I said for the last time as we stepped through the door into the guard house.

"No, James, please don't go!" she sobbed as we moved through the building. *"They are going to kill me if you leave, please, don't do that to me!"*

I looked over my shoulder at Hope. "Would they actually kill her?"

"Does it matter?" She shrugged. "Besides, she's just being dramatic. Minders are too valuable."

She had a point.

We stepped out into the night air and began to move through the shadows of Gilmore Military airfield.

"Be sure to keep your helmet on," Hope said as we moved through the shadows, avoiding light as we weaved in the direction of the airfield.

"Thanks, Captain Obvious."

"You mean Captain Barnettt? Did you really forget my name?"

I chuckled and was going to tell her it was a joke, but decided against it as I could feel her yellow eyes glaring at me.

We reached the last building before the pavement opened up to the flight line. About one hundred meters ahead of us, my plane and the two Bf-109s sat in the same hangar as the other day. The place appeared to be desolate, but as we got closer, we noticed there was a mechanic still working. He was busy tinkering with something under the wings of one of the German fighters.

"Come on babe, I'll show you the planes real quick!" I said as I stepped up next to Hope and pulled her tight to my side. She quickly picked up on my idea and wrapped her arm around my waist as we strolled into the hanger.

"Here they are, sugarplum." I said, as we got closer to the planes and drew the attention of the mechanic.

"Wow!" she said, stepping forward and running her hands along the body of the Mustang. "It's so shiny! Do you think I could get in the seat?"

"Hey bud," I shouted to the grease-covered wolfkin, "do you mind if she hops in the seat?"

He looked back and forth at the both of us before approaching. "You shouldn't be here," he hissed once he got next to me.

Thankfully it was dark, so he couldn't see my human ears, though I felt him double check before I drew his attention to Hope. "Come on man! Look at her! She said she'd give me a special surprise if I showed her the planes."

The mechanic leered at Hope as she leaned over the wing and wiggled her ass and tail at us. I picked up the thoughts of the man, and wanted to punch him square in the jaw, but reminded myself that this was part of the plan. He connected the dots that we were putting out there, but he still feared getting in trouble.

"Come on brother," I begged as I felt around the pockets of the uniform before feeling what felt like a money clip. "Here, will...five, ten, twenty crowns do it?"

He looked at the money in my hand before taking the bills and stashing them in his back pocket. "Let me get that canopy open for you, ma'am."

Hope awkwardly crawled into the cockpit after the mechanic had it open.

"Wow! So nice!"

She grabbed the stick and put her feet on the paddles, moving the flaps around while making engine noises with her mouth. She even made a show out of asking the mechanic what some of the gauges on the control panel did, before finding out that the plane was fully fueled.

"What about that one?" she asked as she pointed at the Messerschmitt that wasn't being worked on.

"How about it, bud?" I asked the mechanic.

He rubbed his fingers together in the universal sign for "more money." I slapped another twenty crowns in his hand before he took her over to see the German plane.

Hope put on the same show with the Bf-109, going as far as getting the mechanic to show her how to start the plane. As she did, I noticed the planes had drop tanks added under their wings.

"What's with those bombs under the wings?" I asked absently as he and I climbed down from the plane.

"Those aren't bombs," he snorted, "they are extra fuel tanks that should double the range of these planes, which is crazy because they already have ridiculous range when compared to our current front line fighters," he growled as he shook his head. "But the top brass think they might be able to reach continent to continent."

"Continent to continent, that would be impressive," I added as he took a breath.

"Yes, it would. The range test is going to take place tomorrow morning. These two are ready," he continued as he gestured to the plane Hope was pretending to fly, and then my Mustang. "That one that I was working on has a leak in the tank seals, gotta get her fixed before the morning."

"I see, but these two are good to go?"

"Yes, they are."

"That's what I wanted to hear, thanks man, you're a life-saver," I said before smacking him across the back of his head with the guards club. He fell to the ground like a sack of potatoes.

"You remember how he said to start it, Hope?" I called out as I jumped back on the wing and looked in the cockpit.

"Yeah. It's a little more complicated than the Hak-17 I fly back home, but I got it," she said as she flashed me a big smile and a thumbs up before I jumped off the wing and removed the parking blocks from the wheels of her plane. I scurried over to my Mustang and began carrying out the familiar steps needed to get her ready to fly. Thankfully, both engines roared to life around the same time.

However, this alerted the airfield to what we were doing.

"I'm good to go," I projected to Hope.

"Same. When we get in the air, head west."

Small arms fire bounced off the side of the fuselage as we lifted into the darkness of the early morning air. This would be their only chance to stop us, and those small rounds weren't going to cut it. Once we were in the air, we pointed our planes to the west and flew as fast as we could to get off the continent.

"What are those blinking red lights out in front of us?" I asked as we were three hours into our flight to freedom.

"Those are the edge markers," Hope replied, "they're there to warn ships and planes about where the edge of the continent is."

The sun was slowly rising behind us, and the blinking lights formed a strange outline that separated the soft darkness of the land from the absolute darkness that led to the ocean below. It felt odd to know that we would soon be transitioning from flying over ground that had been three hundred feet below us, to the two miles of darkness that led to the ocean below.

"Targets in sight, open fire!"

A series of flashes out ahead of us pulled my attention away from the edge of the continent, and I instinctively pulled up.

"*Fighters!*" Hope shouted.

"*I see them.*"

I was suddenly more aware of the active minds around us, and I counted six in total. Banking right, I looked back to see the planes that were pursuing us were the same as the ones I had seen Court flying on my first day in Dione. Instinctively, I checked my six magazine counters and smiled. The counters had been reset.

"*Hope,*" I called out, "*we should be able to outrun them, or we can fight. I don't know about you, but the Empire was nice enough to reload my magazines, and I feel like taking out some aggression.*"

"*Sounds like a plan. This bird is loaded as well.*"

"*I believe your plane has two machine guns and a 30mm autocannon.*"

"*Sounds like fun,*" she exclaimed as she brought her plane around. "*Just give me a second to get used to how this bad girl handles.*"

I laughed to myself as I continued my turn and saw the silhouette of a Crestia fighter enter my line of sight. The pilot stayed calm for a moment, then started to panic when he realized he couldn't shake me. His panic ended when I lined up my gun sights with his cockpit and watched as the glass shattered before the plane dove from the sky.

"*One down,*" I said to Hope while working to gain position on a second plane. Its right wing exploded as my rounds hit where the wing met body. "*Two down.*"

"*Not fair! You know how to fly your plane,*" Hope protested.

She was flying the German plane awkwardly as she closed in on the tail of an enemy fighter. A flash came from the nose of her propeller, and the 30mm autocannon shredded her target.

"*One!*" she shouted.

"*Three!*" I countered as I intercepted a fighter that was trying to get on her tail. *"You're gonna have to work harder than that, Miss triple ace."*

She growled at me out of annoyance, but blew up another plane shortly after. *"Two!"*

I saw the last plane to my right as it dove toward the ground to speed away from us. It was the squad commander. I could tell because he was screaming out prayers to any God or Goddess that was listening, hoping we didn't do to him what we had done to his squad.

"Do you want to chase him?" I asked the excited wolfkin.

"No, but let me try something..."

She had already oriented her plane to point in the direction of the fleeing combatant. I peered into her mind and saw she was focusing on lining up a shot with her fighter's sights. She pulled the trigger and the autocannon in the nose fired for a little more than a second.

Out in the distance, the remaining plane exploded into pieces, *"I love this autocannon! Did you see that?"*

"I did. Nice shot!"

"Thank you, and with that I have nineteen kills, and I am one away from being a four time ace!"

"Nice," I said, congratulating her, *"with my three kills, I am now a triple ace."*

"Way to go, but you are still three behind me, right?"

"Only one if I count our first meeting."

She got quiet, but I felt her scowling at me as we fell into formation.

"Don't worry, I won't count shooting you and your wingman down into my total."

"Thank you," she said, her mind feeling more at ease. *"Let's get out of here."*

We pointed our planes west again and flew out beyond the border of the Empire, flying into the void that lay beyond the continent.

"Hey Hope, how's your fuel looking?" I asked a few minutes later, tapping on my fuel gauge.

"Pretty good. I have maybe used a third of my vuel. What about you?"

"I'm seeing the same," I said with a bit of confusion.

"Is everything ok?" she asked, catching the tone in my response.

I had to think about that, with drop tanks, the Mustang could fly for almost six hours. Knowing this, my tank gauges should have been past the halfway point, but what I was seeing didn't add up. Maybe their version of "fuel" burned differently from the standard Grade 150 aviation fuel used on Earth.

"I'm not sure if everything is ok, but I'm guessing my plane has maybe four hours of flight left in the tank. That's just under fifteen hundred miles, if we get lucky. How far to Thurnmar?"

"Right now we are crossing the Primal Expanse, so...two thousand miles."

I must not have heard her right. "Hope, you didn't just say two thousand miles, did you?"

"That's what I said."

"So we are screwed," I projected with a flat tone.

"Not exactly."

I looked to her on my right. "Just an FYI, I have a bad history with having to ditch planes in the water," I informed her as memories of nearly freezing to death in the winter waters of the North Sea danced across my awareness.

"We won't be ditching our planes. We have two options, it was three, but I also don't want to ditch in the water...again. Option one, when fuel gets low, we drift down to the ocean below and look for an airstrip on one of the core lands, convince them to give us more fuel and get back in the air."

"Core lands?" I projected at her. "What is a core land?"

"A core land is land in the middle of the ocean. There are quite a *few scattered around, so we should get lucky. Most have landing strips."*

I reached out to her mind and saw the image of sandy beaches surrounded by water with palm trees. She was thinking of islands. I laughed to myself, my Dione vocabulary was growing by the minute. *"What's option two?"*

"Option two is we get lucky and come across a Thurnmar carrier squad patrolling the Expanse and land on their ship."

I didn't like that idea. I'd never performed a ship landing, and knew that planes needed special tail hooks to attempt them.

"Is now a good time to tell you I've never landed on a carrier?"

"Not a problem," she projected smugly. *"It's easy."*

"Says the girl who's done it multiple times," I said into the stillness of the cockpit.

I didn't send that to her, she had already shown she could give as well as she could take when it came to talking shit. She wasn't like your normal woman, she had a playful yet no bullshit tomboyish personality. Hope reminded me of my best friend's little sister. When we were kids, she wanted to run with us boys, getting dirty and roughhousing with the best of us. Last time I was home I ran into her. I didn't recognize her at first because that tough blonde with big ears had turned into a bombshell of a woman.

The hours ticked by, and I found myself watching my fuel gauge as the sky lit up around us. In the back of my mind, I could hear Hope calling out to any Thurnmar planes of ships in the area. I decided that her working to save us was more important than my boredom, so I went back to watching my fuel gauge.

With maybe an hour of fuel left, Hope screamed into my thoughts, *"I got a hold of a carrier!"* Her mind jumped for joy.

"That's great news! Now how do we find it?" I asked, shaking my head from her loud outburst.

"The air controller is directing planes to us, to check that we aren't hostile, and they'll escort us in. We're maybe thirty minutes away from them. Follow me."

Fifteen minutes later, we came across the Thurnmar patrol, two planes that I recognized from my first day on Dione.

"This is Captain Hills of the TNS Longbow, please identify yourself."

"I am Captain Hope Barnettt of the TNS Twilight," she said as she rocked her wings, *"call sign Lone Wolf."*

"How is the tea in Thurnmar?" Captain Hills asked.

"As good as coffee in the morning," Hope replied.

"Welcome Captain Barnett, who is your friend?"

"This is Captain James Walker, he's...special."

There was a pregnant pause before Hills spoke again, *"Very well, stay on your current heading. Do not deviate."*

Both pilots fell in line behind us, their minds showing that they were ready to open fire if we didn't do as we were told.

"Unknown fighter, this is the air traffic controller for the TNS Longbow, do you copy?"

I tried reaching out to the woman's voice in my head, but without seeing her face, I wasn't able to.

"Hope. I can't answer her, I'm trying, but I can't connect."

"It's ok, I'll let her know." Hope assured me.

In the distance, I could make out a small dot suspended in the air. It grew larger and larger the closer we got, and as it filled my forward windshield, I knew no one on Earth would ever believe what I saw. The dot was a huge floating carrier, much larger than the one I'd seen in the New York City harbor in 1942.

The *Longbow* was about the same length as a US Navy carrier, but over three times its width as the flight deck sat upon two long cylinders that stuck out past the flight deck on her bow and stern. The front of the cylindrical hulls looked like the bow of a World War One era battleship, while the stern had two contra-rotating fans that were pushing the carrier through the air. The command tower sat over the starboard hull, and her sides were covered in anti-aircraft gun turrets that turned to track us as we got closer.

The deck had three runways running along the length of the port side, with the planes being raised and lowered by four elevators in the middle. There were a few planes staged on the starboard side of the deck, as well as two crafts like nothing I had seen before with massive propeller blades sticking out of the top instead of the front.

"Alright," Hope said, "*here is what is about to happen. As you come in to land, a powerful telekinetic minder is going to grab a hold of your plane and help land it on the deck. All you have to do is land like you would on the ground.*"

"You make it sound so easy," I said with a mocking tone.

"*It really is. The landing officer will make sure you don't crash as long as you don't do something stupid. Just remember you're landing on a moving surface.*"

She said it calmly, like it was something so easy that even a caveman could do it.

She went first so I could watch. She lined up her plane and made her approach on the moving surface. Her plane put down its landing gear, and was moving slowly; she probably had it just above its stall speed as it headed for the deck. When she was about 100 yards out, her plane stabilized, and no longer looked like it was bothered by the turbulence created by the ship. The touchdown was smooth, and by the time she reached the midpoint of the deck, she had come to a stop.

"*That actually did look easy,*" I projected to her.

"*It really is, now listen for the air traffic controller and do as she says.*"

"Unknown fighter, move one mile out and begin your approach," the calm voice of the controller ordered. "Come in at a steady angle and decrease your speed to just above stall."

Here goes nothing! I moved my plane into position and began to approach the deck. I aimed my nose toward the front of the deck, hoping that would help.

"Good angle, pilot. Continue to decrease air speed."

I throttled back on the engine and opened my landing gear doors. I checked the speed indicator, one hundred ten miles per hour, the proper ground landing speed. As I got closer, the turbulence given off by the ship started to shake the plane. I worked the stick and throttle to keep her steady.

"Easy girl, we can do this!"

When I got within three hundred feet, all the shaking stopped and the air calmed down.

"Good job pilot, the landing officer will set you down from here. Fully decelerate once your wheels touch down."

The plane moved toward the deck like someone was holding me. I wasn't even sure if I was still flying at that point. When the wheels made contact, I cut back all power to the engine and felt an invisible force push on the plane to slow it down. I came to a stop in the middle of the deck, just like Hope had, and waited for my next order.

"Taxi to your right and come to a stop where the flight deck officer is motioning. Welcome aboard the Longbow."

Up ahead, a person in a bright orange vest with two flags was waving for me. I moved my plane over and parked where I was instructed, next to Hope's stolen plane. They then made an X shape with their arms, which back home meant to cut engines, so I did.

I don't know what kind of reception I was expecting when I got out of my plane, but being surrounded by armed MPs and told to get on the ground with my hands behind my head felt like a bit of overkill. Hope was irritated by it as well, since she was being ordered to the ground next to me.

Within minutes we were both in a jail cell in the ship's brig and being searched for any hidden contraband. It didn't take long for them to notice I wasn't from Dione, which caused some strange whispers amongst the MPs. They took the Crestia soldiers uniform I had been wearing and locked the door, leaving me in just my underwear and white undershirt.

One thing was certain: The jail cell wasn't as nice as the one I had escaped a few hours earlier. It was smaller, didn't have windows, had a dusty blanket and mattress pad, and stagnant air that smelled of mothballs and oil.

"At least there aren't Nazis," I said as I layed down and closed my eyes, quickly drifting off to sleep after a long night.

INTERLUDE 1: HOPE & MADELINE

AN HOUR after their arrival on the *Longbow,* an officer in a tan uniform came to retrieve Hope from her cell. The officer was escorted by MPs, both female horsekin who prided themselves on having more muscles than brains.

James waved to her as she left the brig.

"Don't worry, I'll get you out," she said as she waved back to him.

"You know where to find me if you do," he said nonchalantly.

She shook her head. He was still in his underwear and undershirt, they had yet to give him clothes to wear, but it didn't seem to bother him, and it definitely didn't bother her.

"So...where are we going?" she asked her escorts as they wound their way through the corridors of the ship.

She crossed her arms and let out a huff when they didn't answer, growing more and more annoyed with how she was treated. There were procedures in place for landing on a carrier you didn't launch from, and she had followed them to the T. She had even given them the proper friend or foe code when Captain Hills intercepted James and herself.

Granted, she could understand why they did what they did.

She was in a skirt and blouse instead of her Thurnmar flight suit; it had to be left behind in the cell in Crestia. James was with her, and he was a strange-looking person from another world who flew a strange plane that no one had seen before. Then there was the fact that she herself was also flying a strange plane that no one had ever seen before.

In the end, she hoped that they had authenticated her from her military ID tags that she wore on a bracelet on her wrist. If that were the case, everything would soon be cleared up.

Their destination was one of the squad ready rooms toward the front of the ship. She sat down on the front row, in the seat usually reserved for a squad commander. She figured it was okay this time since the room was empty.

The door to her left opened and in walked a tall horsekin with gray hair and tawny fur wearing the tan uniform with the shoulder tassels that distinguished him as a Commodore. Behind him was a birdkin woman carrying a leather briefcase and wearing the olive green uniform of the Thurnmar Intelligence Agency, TIA for short. She was pretty, with sharp yellow eyes, shoulder length brown feather-like hair that all birdkin possessed, and a pair of brown wings on her back.

Hope quickly jumped to her feet and saluted the Commodore. "Good afternoon, Sir."

"At ease, Flight Captain," he said with a grizzled voice. "I am Commodore Aldo Jacobs, commander of the 28th strike group. This is TIA officer Priya Lowe." He gestured to the birdkin woman. "We have authenticated your ID with the Citadel and verified your identity. Welcome back, Flight Captain Barnett."

"Thank you sir, it's good to be back."

The Commodore smiled at her excitement, but it faded before he continued, "Captain, you have made my life more difficult than I thought could be possible when I woke up this morning. Not only have you returned to Thurnmar with two strange planes that have never been seen before, but you also are accompanied by an equally strange man. To say you have caught the attention of the TIA would be an understatement. Because of that attention, I have been ordered by those above me to hand over all questioning to Agent Lowe and to bring you, the man, and the two planes to the Citadel as soon as possible. Once Agent Lowe is done with you, you will have full access to the ship as befitting your rank. However you are grounded from flight until further notice. Is that understood?"

"Yes sir," Hope nodded.

"Very well, you girls play nice," the Commodore said as he exited the room, leaving Hope alone with the birdkin intelligence officer.

Agent Lowe walked to Hope and sat down next to her. "Hello Captain Barnettt," she said with a melodic voice, "my name is Agent Lowe, it is nice to meet you."

"Likewise," Hope replied as she watched her pull a portfolio out of her briefcase.

The birdkin flashed a dimpled smile before continuing, "This is your official debriefing of all events since you left the *Twilight* over a week ago. Please recap everything that happened to you, up until you arrived on this ship, with as much detail as possible."

Hope took a deep breath and started telling her story, as she did, Agent Lowe took notes. Where she was held, what they asked during her interrogation, meeting James, getting to know him and learning about humans, meeting Madeline, AKA, the White Rabbit, and a Nazi named Kampf.

"Time out!" interrupted Agent Lowe, "You mean to tell me you saw a woman who identified herself as the White Rabbit?"

"Saw her? We tied her up to a bar so we could escape. I'm wearing her clothes."

The TIA agent had a shocked look on her face, but after a moment, her expression settled into her dimpled smile. "I can see you are being serious."

"Did you just read my mind?" Hope asked.

Agent Lowe nodded. Hope's ears went flat along her head as she shuddered and thought about all the things the TIA Agent could pull from her mind. She knew there was nothing she could do to stop a well-trained minder like Agent Lowe, but knowing it was happening as she sat there made her feel exposed.

"Please, I didn't dig deep enough to see anything you should be embarrassed by," Agent Lowe said.

Hope cringed. "Please don't respond to my thoughts."

The birdkin nodded, then continued, "So you tied up the White Rabbit? How?"

"I think you already know-"

"But I'd like you to tell me."

Hope let out a sigh and continued, "You see, Madeline is infatuated with James, Captain Walker, so we made a plan for him to seduce her so we could subdue her." Hope paused, looking at the TIA agent.

"Go on."

Hope squeezed her thighs together as she retold how James had seduced and undressed the white-furred fox girl. She poured in more detail than was probably necessary, getting carried away in remembering what had happened just a few hours ago. Agent Lowe's eyes were wide, her mouth hanging open, her precise note taking interrupted by Hope's story.

"Woah," said the birdkin as she undid the top button of her uniform and fanned herself off.

"Ya, it was kind of hot," Hope recalled, closing her eyes as she imagined herself in Madeline's place. James' strong hands held her own above her head as he tied her up to the cold bars of the cell. He removed her clothes and admired her body, kissing her lips as he had his way with her. She bit her bottom lip as she opened her eyes, seeing Agent Lowe blushing and breathing heavily.

"A-and you just left her there...?" she asked as she regained her composure.

"Yes," Hope answered as she took a few deep breaths to calm down.

"Why didn't she call for help?"

"She was gagged."

"I mean, why didn't she call out for help telepathically?" asked the Agent.

"James stopped her. He was able to overpower her will and training to make her only call for help when he told her too."

Agent Lowe looked perplexed. "Captain Barnettt, you have told me twice that Captain Walker has used mind control, and the second time he used it on a highly trained Ministry minder, and it worked?"

Hope nodded. She had a loose understanding of the minder class rankings, but she knew Madeline had touted she was Class-A before James overpowered her mind.

"What happened after you two left the tied up White Rabbit?"

"Not much else other than getting lucky that both the planes were being prepared for long range flight testing and armed. We got them up, flew west as fast as we could and hoped to come across a carrier. We did have a tussle with planes sent to intercept us, but we made quick work of them."

Agent Lowe bobbed her head as she got back to taking notes before asking her next question, "What can you tell me about these Nazis?"

Dr. Volker Gerver looked closely at the strangulation wounds around the neck of the naked corpse that was lying on his examination table. The body belonged to Madeline Reynolds, one of their assets in this world. She was one of his most successful experiments, and the speed at which Major-General Kampf was able to get her body back to their facility was impressive.

As the scientist recorded his notes, his eyes were drawn to the curves of the dead foxkin. She had a lovely body, and though the Major-General found the Dionians disgusting, Volker found them to be delectable, having had his way with a few of the test subjects that the Empire had given them.

The doctor set down his clipboard and moved his hands toward the firm breasts of the dead woman-

"I'd appreciate it if you didn't do that," said a woman's voice as she walked up behind him.

The doctor pulled back his hands. "Sorry Agent Reynolds."

Madeline moved closer to the examination table and inspected her dead body. She was wearing a white bathrobe that was littered with blue stains. A towel was wrapped around the top of her head to finish drying her hair.

She reached out and touched the bruising around her dead body's neck before touching her own. The memory was fresh on her mind, and sent a shiver down her spine. This was her fourth reawakening, and each time, the way she died was the hardest memory for her to suppress. It was enough to drive her insane, but she felt she had that under control.

"How was your shower?" asked the Nazi scientist.

"Irritating. Do you know how long it takes to get that blue sludge you use out of my fur and hair? And then there is the taste, blah! Could you please do something about the taste?" she asked as she undid the towel around her head, letting her long damp hair fall down her back, and two long white ears stand up. "And I need to get my hair cut, again."

"You also need to fix your ears," Gurver said as he pointed to the top of her head, "and that little cottontail."

"I will, I just want to relax for a moment before I do. Do you know how much concentration it takes to constantly hold a foxkin form?"

"You are a shifter, it should be easy."

"I just want to take a break before I have to do everything to make myself look like me again," Madeline whined.

"If you don't like it, we could always pull the plug on the program and destroy your collection of clones," snorted the mad man.

Madeline grit her teeth.

These humans owned her.

She looked at the body she had previously been using and closed her eyes. Anger boiled in her chest as she remembered how she had ended up in Project Lazarus...

Two years prior, Madeline was looking at herself. Her clone was floating in a blue gel, connected to hoses and IV's to keep it alive. She made faces at herself as she moved around the tube, examining Dr. Gerver's handy work. This was the first clone he had successfully made, and because of her father's funding, she was the first person on Dione to be cloned.

"Why can't you make my clones foxkin?" she asked as her reflection lined up with the face of the clone. She looked to the top of her head where the long ears of her true rabbitkin form clashed with the reflection of her luxurious foxkin ears.

"It is a clone," Gerver replied. "You are a rabbitkin who pretends to be a foxkin, therefore your clone will always be a rabbitkin. If I messed with your genetics, you might lose some of those gifts you cling to so tightly."

Madeline glared at the human before asking her next question, "Is it-she alive?"

"Define alive," asked the German as he moved to stand next

to her, looking back and forth between the original and the clone.

"Like, if I were to break the glass, would I be able to talk to her? Have a conversation with...myself?"

The doctor shook his head, "I am afraid not. She is soulless. You might have two bodies, but you only have one soul."

"So she's just a shell?"

"Yes."

"And your soul reader will transfer my soul to her if I..." she trailed off her sentence, but made a throat cutting gesture while sticking her tongue out.

"It should."

She let out a nervous laugh. "It should? Well how do you find out if it will work or not?"

"Through a final test."

Bang!

Moments later, Madeline fell forward onto her hands and knees, coughing up the blue sludge she was covered in. She blinked as her eyes slowly came into focus on the object in front of her. Once she realized what she was looking at, her eyes went wide as she screamed, "What the fuck!"

In front of her was her, except this one had the top of her head missing from the gunshot wound.

She panicked and tried to crawl backward, slipping on the blue sludge. Breathing heavily, her heart was racing, head pounding, and stomach turning to the point she rolled to the side and retched up more of the nasty blue liquid.

"Calm down, Fraulein," said the Doctor, draping a towel over her shoulders.

"You fucking shot me!"

"And you reawakened. A success!"

"And what if it had failed?" she protested.

"Don't focus on that. The good news is it was a success!"

"White Rabbit. White Rabbit!" shouted the man who had just entered the lab.

She snapped out of the flashback thanks to the annoying voice of Major-General Kampf. Shaking away the fog, she finally addressed him, "Yes, how can I help you, Major Kampf?"

"It's Major-General!" he snapped back.

She smiled. The small victories to annoy these humans were what helped her keep what was left of her sanity.

"You failed, Frau Reynolds. Your relaxed attitude allowed the American and the Thurnmarian to escape," Kampf declared.

"Yes, I know, I watched it happen." She sighed with annoyance. "Then I remember seeing some human asshole find me tied up to the bars of the jail cell, and instead of freeing me, he strangled me to death!"

"A lesson needed to be learned," Kampf noted.

Madeline gritted her teeth. "Next time you want to kill me, make it quick. I can still see your creepy smile when I close my eyes."

"Next time I kill you, I may make sure you do not revive at all."

The rabbitkin held her tongue. She liked to play things loose with other people, knowing that death was not her final destination. But these humans were the ones who controlled whether she would wake after dying. She rubbed her neck again as her long ears dropped forward, covering her face.

"Now that you have learned your lesson, we must continue with the mission. Do you remember what the mission is, White Rabbit?"

"Yes," she said as she looked at him from behind her ears. "My mission is to convince the American pilot to stay in Crestia and work with you."

"Convince? No! You were to seduce him!" Kampf spat. "You convince your mother to give you strudel before dinner, you convince your father to let you drink beer when you are a child. You seduce a man so he will do as you say and become putty in your hands. Instead, I would go as far as to say he seduced you."

He wasn't wrong. James had had an effect on her, but right now she just needed to let the angry human vent.

"You will rectify this," Kampf said calmly. "You will go to Thurnmar and bring him back to us. Prove your value to us and your father, or we turn off the machine and let your next death be your last."

His words gave her goosebumps as they passed over her. The dying part wasn't what triggered the reaction. No, it was the thought of her disappointing her father...again.

"I'll go, even though I hate that country," she groaned, "but on the bright side, at least James will be there."

"Foolish girl, of course you will go, you don't have an option. And there are only two ways back!" He said as he pulled her ears away from her face and held his hand in front of her. "With the American, or through the reawakening. Is that understood?"

She looked at his hand with its thumb and index finger extended. She hated the way the Germans counted on their fingers. She wanted to say something about it, but the man had threatened to actually kill her, so she settled on rolling her eyes and leaving the lab without saying a thing.

"White Rabbit, your appearance," Dr. Gerver said before she reached the door.

She stopped, realizing she almost walked out into a facility filled with Canids while still looking like a lowly rabbitkin. She closed her eyes and focused on the foxkin persona she had created for herself.

Her ears shortened and widened, the fur growing thicker.

Her cotton-covered scut grew longer under her robe, filling out into the large fluffy fox tail she treasured. It was a complicated transformation that few shifters could do, but she had perfected the gift and learned to hold it for days at a time.

"Do not let us down, White Rabbit," Kampf said.

"I won't, Major Kampf," she said with a smile as she left the lab.

CHAPTER FIFTEEN

IT WAS hard to tell if it was day or night in a cell deep in the belly of an aircraft carrier. The guards didn't like to talk, were trained in the art of brick wall mental defense, and ignored me completely when I tried to visit with them. I could pick up trace thoughts from different members of the crew, but they were random and useless. If I tried, I could focus on one, but not knowing exactly where they were would lead to me losing them if they were moving.

"*James! Can you hear me?*"

I jumped in my bunk, startled by Hope's voice. Since I was still getting used to telepathy, communications without warning sometimes felt like a ghost calling out from behind you in a dark empty room. "Yes, I can hear you. Could you tone it down next time? You scared me half to death!"

"Sorry. Did you hit your head again?"

"No."

"Good! So I just finished my debriefing. Has anyone told you what's going on?"

"Nope," I responded as I laid down on my back. "These guards are no fun. I'm trying to work my country boy charm on them, but they keep ignoring me."

"That sounds about right. The Thurnmar Marines are well disciplined."

I looked over at the back of the horsekin woman who was guarding my cell. She looked like she had a strong physique under her uniform while standing two inches taller than me. If I hadn't seen her shoulders rise and fall with her breathing, I would have mistaken her for a statue.

"So, since they won't tell me anything, will you?" I asked her.

"Of course! I told the TIA agent-"

"TIA?" I asked as I interrupted her.

"The Thurnmar Intelligence Agency."

"Got it."

"I told the agent the story of our escape. She's impressed we were able to subdue Madeline, aka, the White Rabbit. She's a notorious spy for the Empire. A femme fatale type. Her accomplishments were known, but no one knew for sure what she looked like. Now they do, thanks to us! This is a small victory for Thurnmar."

"Glad I could do my part," I noted.

"After that, she asked about the Nazis. She wasn't fazed by what I told her, and it seems the TIA was aware of them."

"Does that mean they know how bad they are?"

"I don't think they are aware of how evil they are back in your world. As far as the TIA is concerned, all humans are bad because the only humans they have seen are aiding the Empire."

The way she said that didn't go over my head. The TIA thought all humans were their enemy, and that included me.

"What does that mean for me?" I asked, though I could figure out the answer, and it looked similar to my current surroundings.

"I'm not sure. I've been granted full liberty of the ship based on my rank, but I'm not able to fly. Meanwhile, they are going to keep you locked up until we reach the Citadel," she said with a guilty tone.

"What's the Citadel?"

"It's a military installation in the Scarlet Highlands, it serves as the headquarters for the TIA and Thurnmar Republic Military," she exclaimed while her mind showed a fog-covered base that no one had access to. "It's also where they develop and test new military technology."

"I see, so taking us there serves two purposes. They'll get to interrogate me while studying my plane and the Nazi one you brought them."

I could sense her nodding along with my assumption. I focused on her mind and for a brief moment I could pin down where she was. Once I had a better grasp, I could feel what she felt. The smell of fresh air, the wind blowing through her hair, and the sight of land starting to form out in the distance above the horizon.

"Where are you?" I asked as I peered through her eyes.

"I'm at the bow of the ship on the hangar deck. It's the best place to stand and think while having a mental conversation with someone." The imagery shifted in a haze as she looked over her shoulder at the cavern behind her where mechanics were working on planes.

"That's a big hangar. This ship is massive."

"You can see that?" Hope asked with a surprised tone.

"Kind of. It's not clear, but I can feel your senses. Sorry, I should have asked."

"No, it's ok. You can use me to help your mind leave that cell."

"Thank you, Hope," I replied as I felt her blush. "So how long will it take to reach this Citadel?"

"We're moving at a fast cruising speed. Too fast to launch or receive fighters. The ship was ordered to go there immediately once the higher ups learned we were on board. If I had to guess, almost three days? Which is good with the full moon approaching."

"Why? Are you superstitious about the full moon?" I asked.

"No, not at all, it's just..." she trailed off. I could tell she was thinking of how to explain what was on her mind. "*All military actions are suspended during a full moon.*"

"Why? What's so special about the full moon?"

I felt she was embarrassed by how to explain what was going to happen, so she simply projected an image of a wolf staring at me. That's when it clicked, something I had been told on my first day of arriving in Dione by Madeline during my Dione history crash course.

"Ohhh, everything is suspended because everyone transforms into their animal form during the full moon."

"Yeah," she agreed bashfully.

"Makes sense. When does the transformation start?"

"*Just before sunset, and lasts until the break of dawn.*"

"Interesting," I thought absently, "*that would be cool to see—*"

"*No!*" Hope screamed in my head. "*It's embarrassing! We have to undress before we change or we could rip our clothes. Then there's the problem of not knowing where you'll be when you change back! I had to walk a mile naked once. It was so embarrassing!*"

"Well, now I really *want* to see this!" I chuckled.

I was pretty sure she rolled her eyes, but then she took a somber tone. "*It also could be dangerous for you, James.*"

"How so?"

"*When we change, we don't have full control over our minds and bodies. We revert to our most primal instincts. For predators like myself, we try our best to eat as much as we can before the change, but some predators get overwhelmed by the need to hunt and, well...*"

I thought about the different predatory types of races there were. My mind ran through images of me being ripped apart by a swarm of lions, tigers, or wolves. She was right. I didn't need to see her naked that bad. On that night, a little jail cell would probably be the safest place for me.

A small flash of pain ran across her mind, causing me to wince. "What was that?" I asked.

"Sorry! Hunger pains, I haven't had anything to eat since last night. I'm going to go get lunch. I'll talk to you later."

"Sure thing, you know where to find me."

I sensed sadness wash across her mind as I pulled away from her. She felt guilty for being able to move about freely while I was stuck in the brig. I hated the idea of a beautiful woman like her being sad on my account.

"Hope," I called out.

"Yes James?"

"Don't be sad that I'm locked up. You've helped me so much over the past few days, and I'm thankful that I'm here with you instead of that cell back in Crestia."

"Really?"

"Yes, I'm happy as long as I can talk with you. Trust me, I'll be alright."

It was quiet while I waited for her response, I thought to reach out for her mind again, but didn't have to.

"I'm happy when I talk with you as well."

The next three days dragged by at a snail's pace. Hope accepted that my being locked up was not her fault, and stopped feeling guilty about it. However that guilt was soon replaced by sadness, sadness that could only be cured by gaining my freedom. With no cure in sight, I did my best to visit with her to show that I was in good spirits for being locked up.

She didn't feel the need to socialize with any of the ship's crew members, who were giving her the cold shoulder to begin with, so that gave us lots of free time to visit with each other. I wanted to learn as much about Hope as I could, and luckily for me, she was interested in learning as much as she could about the strange human man from Earth. A win-win for both of us.

She spent long hours taking walks around the ship, or

watching the landscape go by under the ship while I used her eyes. One day she pointed out the town she was born and raised in as we passed over it, which led to conversations about our childhoods and parents.

"I bet your parents will be thrilled when they learn you are still alive," I said cheerfully.

She didn't share my optimism as I felt her emotions shift. "I'm sure they would be, but they died when I was thirteen, during the first year of the war."

"Hope, I'm sorry."

"It's not your fault," she said as she shook her head. "The Empire had carried out a bombardment raid, and our house collapsed on them. They were found in each other's arms, so I'm glad they were together when they passed."

I wished I could give her a hug, but sharing my sympathies was the best I could do.

"I know what it's like to lose your parents. My mother passed away when I was five."

"Oh no," she gasped, "I'm so sorry, what happened?"

"She was sick. Caught a disease called tuberculosis."

"That's terrible, I'm sorry. What about your father?" she asked.

"He's still alive," I said as I pushed past sad memories to happy ones. "He's the reason I got into flying. He was a fighter pilot and continued flying after the Great War. He raised me on an airfield, so it was inevitable that I learned how to fly."

"That sounds like fun."

"It was. Some dads taught their sons how to ride a bike or throw a ball, my dad taught me how to take apart a radial engine and how to pull a barrel roll."

"I am officially jealous of your childhood," Hope remarked.

"It was pretty cool. So what made you want to be a pilot?" I asked.

I felt her cheeks blushing through our connection, "My reasons aren't as cool as yours."

"It's not about who had the cooler path to becoming a pilot, I just want to know why you became one."

She took a deep breath. *"Addison Harris."*

"Who?" I asked.

"She's an actress who became a fighter pilot. I looked to her as a role model while growing up and figured that if she could do it, I could do it."

"Hope, that's actually pretty cool,"

"No it's not. It's dumb. Who becomes a pilot just because some actress they idolized did it?"

"Who becomes a pilot just because their dad did it?" I retorted.

The view tilted to the side as she considered my point. *"You're right. It really doesn't matter why we got into it, as long as we enjoy it,"* she said.

"And do you enjoy it?" I asked.

"I love it," she said with a laugh, *"flying is definitely the most fun you can have without taking your clothes off."*

I burst into laughter in my jail cell, which caused the stoic guards to look over their shoulders at me for the first time.

"I'm going to have to agree with you," I said once I settled down. *"My dad always said to do what you love, and love what you do."*

"Wise, you know what will make me love it more?" she asked.

"What's that?"

"I'll love it more if they can put an autocannon on my plane!" she said with a laugh that started innocent, but became more and more maniacal as it went on. She had gotten a taste of the powerful Messerschmidt autocannon, and she was not going back.

On the third day, I felt the ship decelerate, followed by the unnerving feeling you get in an elevator as it goes down faster than you expected it to. The minutes ticked by as the descent feeling came to a stop, then a booming shake ran through the ship, followed by clicking sounds below my feet.

"*Hope? Is everything ok?*" I asked as I reached out to her.

"*Of course. We just docked in the ship saddle at the Citadel.*"

Ship saddle? Well that made my mind wander as I imagined what that could be. My Texan roots kept trying to envision the ship with a large saddle on its back.

"So stupid." I said to no one in particular.

A sudden feeling of dizziness and nausea washed over me as I rose to my feet to stretch. My equilibrium felt off, and I quickly moved over to the toilet and held myself over it, hands on the toilet seat while I waited for the oatmeal I had been given for breakfast to come up. I stood there, hunched over, dry heaving and spitting, but nothing came up. Gingerly, I moved back to the bunk and sat down, holding my head in my hands.

"Land sickness," said the horsekin marine who was guarding me. She had taken multiple rotations while guarding me, but this was the first time the muscular brunette had said anything to me.

"Land sickness?" I asked, "What the hell is land sickness?"

She looked over her shoulder at me and grinned. "It's when you get so used to the swaying of the ship in the air, that when the ship saddles on solid ground, your mind struggles to adjust and makes you feel like you are still swaying with the air."

"Awesome," I said with a miserable groan.

I sat there taking deep breaths, trying to get my mind under control when two new marines came to get me. They placed handcuffs around my wrists, allowing me to keep my hands in front of me this time before we left the cell.

We worked our way through the maze of the ship until we exited into the bright light of the day. I shaded my eyes awkwardly with my cuffed hands as we made our way down the gangway. As my eyes adjusted to the light, I was able to look around and see the ship behind me sitting on dozens of large curved blocks that matched the underside of the ship.

Those must be the saddles.

Scanning my surroundings, ahead was a short tower that the gangway was attached to, and beyond that were a few buildings, none of which were taller than three stories. I could see a tall control tower next to rows of hangars further off, with a wall of mountains behind them. In fact, mountains made up the background of every direction I looked.

An olive green military car was waiting for us when we exited the bottom of the tower that the crew was using to exit the ship. Two new guards took possession of me, saluting the marines who had brought me to them before guiding me into the car and sitting to my left and right in the cramped back seat.

The two guards on both sides of me were men, one horsekin, while the other was...a zebrakin? He had black and white ears and stripes on his exposed arms. They were both impressively muscular and tall, just like the brunette horsekin on the ship. I hadn't met enough of their kind to know if their size was because of military training or genetics, but I was leaning toward genetics.

The driver who was skillfully speeding us around the base was the biggest rabbitkin I had seen so far, so maybe he was a harekin. I think I remember someone telling me in school that hares were bigger than rabbits. I wasn't sure, and he didn't seem like he would be interested in answering that question.

After a few minutes of driving along the inner edge of the base's perimeter fence, we stopped in front of a solitary building that gave off all the vibes of a jail. There were bars over the windows, and a fenced area in the back where a few inmates in striped jumpsuits were playing some game with a small ball.

"Hope, they're taking me to another jail."

I waited for a moment for her reply, but got nothing back. A chill ran down my spine as I followed the guards into this new jail complex.

"Hope! Hope! Come on girl, answer me!" I cried out.

Nothing. Either she was ignoring me, or she was out of range. We had driven quite a distance from where the *Longbow* had set down. This wasn't good. The only person who was on my side was now out of range for me to communicate with. I looked around and reached out with my minder powers to the guards who were with me and ran into brick walls.

The next hour was spent getting me "processed" into the jail. This included them taking my mugshot, then forcing me to strip so they could hit me with delousing powder that burned like hell before allowing me to shower. I was given new clothes, led to a cell and left alone with my thoughts.

The cell was smaller than the one in Crestia, but bigger than the one on the ship. It had a window that looked out to the mountains in the distance, a single bed and a toilet. No need to be fancy, I guessed. My stomach still felt a little uneasy from the land sickness, so I laid down, closed my eyes, and tried to doze off.

CHAPTER
SIXTEEN

THE HOWL of a wolf off in the distance jerked me out of a dead sleep. I quickly looked around to see where I was, remembering what Hope had told me about the predators and the full moon. I calmed down when I was satisfied I was safely locked up in my jail cell that was lit by the soft glow of the full moon filtering in through the window.

In the dim light I noticed that dinner had been left for me on the floor of my cell. My stomach growled, letting me know that I needed to eat, and I was glad I did. It was the best meal I'd had since being locked up. Grilled hamburger steak with a mushroom gravy, mashed potatoes and a dinner roll. It was cold, but that didn't mean it wasn't delicious. A big meal like that sat well enough on my stomach that I was ready to drift back to sleep.

I laid down to let the food coma set in, when I was interrupted by another howl, this time from outside my window. I tried to ignore it, but the beast making the ruckus howled again. I climbed to my feet, went to the window and looked outside, letting my eyes adjust to what was in the darkness.

"Holy shit!" I yelled as my eyes focused on the pair of yellow eyes looking back at me.

Once the shock wore off, I moved closer to the window and saw the largest wolf I had ever seen standing on the other side. The beast was covered in silver fur that shimmered in the moonlight.

When it saw me, it started to whimper, bark, and jump around, as though it wanted me to come outside and play with it. I tried to feel for its thoughts but found nothing. No surprise, I had never been able to pick up the thoughts of animals, though that would have been cool.

"Sorry pup. No can do. Besides, you might try to eat me," I said to the beast.

The wolf rolled around and jumped up against the wall, making playful noises at me. I watched it with a smile, and as I did, I realized that the ears, white-tipped tail and golden eyes started to feel more and more familiar...

"Hope?"

The wolf barked at me and wagged her silver tail at the sound of her name.

"Wow, look at you. You're so big and beautiful. Who's a pretty girl? Who's a pretty girl?" I said as I let my love for dogs rise to the surface. "If I wasn't locked up I'd come out there and play fetch with you, or scratch those ears and give you belly rubs!"

Another bark let me know she liked that idea. At least, that's what I thought it meant.

"I'm going to go back to sleep. I'll talk to you in the morning, ok?"

Hope let out a whimper, laying her ears flat while staring at me.

"Don't you give me that look, I'm tired," I said to the pouting wolf.

She eventually let out a big yawn, showing off her large and sharp teeth, before laying down and curling into a ball, her head and eyes pointed in my direction.

"Are you going to keep watch over me all night?"

She raised her head and let out a long howl in reply before resting it back on her tail.

"Thank you, Hope. You're a good girl."

She let out another bark, followed by another big yawn before resting her head and closing her eyes. I decided to lay down and do the same. It felt comforting to know that Hope was out there, even though she was in the form of a massive wolf, and I was in a jail cell. Still, her presence made it easy for me to go back to sleep.

The first rays of light shone through my cell window as I gradually stirred. I stretched and did my morning bathroom routine before I decided to look out and see if Hope was still there. I figured she would have already been up and left the spot she had settled down in, but was not disappointed when I looked out the window.

Hope was still laying there, curled up on her side and hugging her tail in all her sweet beautiful naked glory. I felt guilty for looking at her as long as I did, but I had to appreciate how beautiful of a woman she was. Her skin had freckles on her shoulders and chest, and looked soft and slightly tan, and her breasts, oh her breasts were perfect. Her perky mounds had small pink nipples that were hard in the cool morning air, and weren't too big, or too small. They were just right.

After I was satisfied that I had stored her curves to memory, I decided it would be a good time to wake her up.

"Psst, Hope!" I said as I tapped on the window.

This caused her ears to twitch, but nothing more.

"Hope!" I said a little louder.

Still nothing.

I reached out my mind and found her thoughts were there. I grabbed a hold of the mental tether and saw images of her dreams. One was her flying her plane against a dragon, another was of her running after a giant T Bone steak with a pack of wolves, and the last was...wait a second, was that me?

I couldn't help myself as I dove deeper into this dream she was having of me...

"*Can I pet that dog?*" asked a faceless human woman as she stopped the dream version of me on the sidewalk.

"*I would appreciate it if you didn't*" dream James said as he stepped between Hope and the lady.

Hope nuzzled up against the hand of the dream version of myself. She was in her wolf form, but she wasn't as large as she had been when I saw her last night. Dream James was holding a leash that was attached to a collar around her neck. It had a small bone shaped dog tag around it with her name on.

"*Come on girl,*" dream James called out as he tugged on the lead.

Hope quickly fell into step next to him, looking closely at those around them, doing her best to protect the dream version of myself.

I followed them as they walked down the sidewalk. They looked like a normal man and dog who were out for a walk, however both were protecting each other. Every time someone got close, Hope would stand between them and the dream version of myself, and if anyone asked to pet Hope, dream James declined them.

They still drew the attention of everyone around them, but not in a bad way, in fact they all had nothing but good things to say about her.

"*She's such a beautiful dog.*"
"*Her fur looks so shiny and soft.*"
"*She's so well behaved.*"

Every compliment made Hope strut with her head a little higher while her tail wagged a little faster.

"*Does she know any tricks?*" asked a faceless little boy.

"*She does,*" dream James said before turning to Hope. "*Do you want to show them the tricks you can do?*"

Hope barked and jumped up to lick dream James in the face.

"*I'll take that as a yes!*"

A small crowd quickly formed around them as they got their performance underway. I squeezed in so I could get a good look, but didn't get close enough for her to notice me.

"*Hope, sit,*" dream James commanded.

She sat, flashing her wolf smile as her tongue hung out of her mouth.

"*Good girl. Now lay down.*"

With a grunt, she lay down on the ground as a few faceless kids clapped and laughed. But no matter what happened, Hope never took her eyes off the image of me she had created.

"*Now roll over.*"

She rolled over onto her back, continuing the motion until her paws were back under her. She gave a playful bark to the dream version of me as the crowd started to clap.

"*Ok Hope, now sit pretty,*" dream James said.

Hope returned to a seated position, and then lifted her front paws off the ground, holding them as high as she could in her wolf form. The crowd clapped and marveled at how well she was doing, but Hope paid them no mind. She just continued looking at the smiling version of myself who was giving her orders.

Dream James then made the hand gesture for a gun before shouting, "*Bang!*"

Hope yelped and fell onto her back, holding her legs in the air as she turned her head to the side and let her tongue hang out. A textbook definition of playing dead.

The crowd burst into cheers and applause at her performance, which caused the wolf to roll back onto her paws and move to stand in front of her vision of me.

"*Good girl,*" dream James said as he reached into his pocket and pulled out a small strip of bacon to give to her. He gave her head pats as she chewed on the meat, and repeated the words "good girl" over and over.

Is this what beast girls dream of? I asked myself as I smiled and backed out of her mind.

"Hope," I shouted once I returned to myself. "Hope, wake up!"

Still nothing.

I switched to telepathy and projected right into her mind, "*Hope! Wake up!*"

She jerked out of her sleep, screaming and holding her head as she rolled around on the patch of grass she was laying on.

"*It's about time,*" I said with a flat tone.

She sat up and rubbed her head, down to her face. "*That was mean, James! Why did you wake me up like that?*"

"*I'm sorry, would you rather I let you sleep out where everyone can see you?*" I asked as I tapped on the window to get her attention.

She looked at me, her eyes still sleepy.

"Hello," I said with a wave

She waved back, but then her eyes went wide as she looked down and realized how exposed she was.

She screamed as she jumped to her feet, grabbing her tail and using it and her arms to cover herself.

"*We'll talk about this later!*" she cried as she took off in a dead sprint in the direction of the rest of the base, her ass shaking as she ran away.

"*I'm sure we will, thank you for being a good girl and protecting me last night.*"

"*Shut up!*"

Breakfast wasn't brought to me until it was almost noon. I assumed it was because it took a while for everyone to get back to their stations after running around in their animal forms last night. The harekin guard that drove me to the jail was the one who brought it to me, and he looked exhausted.

"Have fun last night?" I asked as he opened the small latch and slid the tray in.

"Don't even get me started," he sighed. "I spent all night chasing some of the rabbit girls."

"Sounds exciting. Have any success?"

He shook his head. "No, right when I was about to mount one, that damn wolf girl started howling and scared everyone into hiding."

Oops, that was partially my fault, I thought as I scratched the back of my head. "Sorry about that."

"Don't be, it's not your fault," he said with a shrug. "They say your kind don't transform."

"No, we don't," I confirmed as I took the tray and sat down so he could move on.

I looked at the food before me, biscuits and gravy with two strips of bacon. Well damn, being in jail in Thurnmar was starting to have its perks.

By mid afternoon I was brought to one of the larger buildings in the middle of the installation that was titled *Annex C*. I was ushered up two flights of stairs to the third floor and sat down in what appeared to be a proper interrogation room. The guards were nice enough to uncuff me before leaving me sitting there alone.

The room was about the size of a small bedroom, and had a metal table in the middle with four chairs around it, two on each side. The wall I was facing had a mirror on it, but I assumed it was one of those two-way mirrors. On the wall behind me was a cork board with a few push pins, but nothing on it. To my right was a window with the shades open. Out of it

I could see the *Longbow* sitting in the saddle as crews moved around to resupply the ship.

The door opened to my left and in walked two men and a small woman. The first was a lionkin that looked to be in his fifties. He had thick golden hair, brown eyes and carried himself like he was one the strongest men on the base. His tan uniform had a few service ribbons on his left chest, a name badge on the right that read *Gill*. On his shoulders were epaulets that had two stars on them, which must have meant he was important.

The second man was a birdkin with brown feathery hair, piercing yellow eyes, a sharp nose and a large pair of brown wings on his back. He wore an olive green suit that was pretty plain in comparison to the "Gill" fellow's uniform. The woman was a blonde rabbitkin that wore a blue sundress. She avoided eye contact with me and sat down in the back with a stenographer's typewriter while both men sat across from me. They placed the portfolios they were carrying in front of them, opened them and got the meeting underway.

"Good afternoon Captain Walker," said the lionkin in a deep voice, "I am Grand Marshall Keanu Gill of the Thurnmar Republic Military, the supreme commander of all Thurnmar forces."

"And I am Director Sonny Warren of the Thurnmar Intelligence Agency," said the birdkin with a flat but confident tone.

"Good afternoon gentleman, ma'am," I said as I returned the greeting. "I'm Captain James Walker of the United States Army Air Force."

As we introduced ourselves, the rabbit girl clicked away on her machine, recording everything that was said. She continued to avoid eye contact with me, but her memories were the only ones I was able to pick up in the room. She was annoyed and hoped this would be done quickly because she had a date with...was that the prison guard from this morning? Good for him.

A few other stray thoughts crossed my mind from people who I assumed were behind the two-way mirror. Their thoughts ranged from my strange looks to studying my body language and speaking habits. I was also pretty sure a minder was in there as well, but I wouldn't be able to get anything off them unless they let me.

"I must be really important if I'm being questioned by the Grand Marshall of Thurnmar and the Director of the TIA?" I asked with curiosity. "In Crestia, they let a spy and some Third Marshall conduct the questioning."

The Grand Marshall chuckled at my question, but director Warren was not amused. He looked at me with indifference, his eyes piercing my soul.

"The Empire has a history with your kind, you are not the first human they had met. However, my people tell me you were important to the Empire," remarked the TIA Director. "Therefore, I believe you will be important to us."

I looked over at the Grand Marshall, who shrugged before saying, "Don't look at me, I'm just here because I wanted to meet a human."

"Before I can dive into what I really want to know, let's go over your story," Director Warren said. "Starting at the beginning, it seems the first thing you did when you arrived in Dione was to shoot down two of our planes, is this correct?"

I made a bitter face at the question. It was true, I had shot down two of their fighters, one of them being Hope, but now I had to explain my reasoning. I told my side of the story, answering his question, along with the many others that Director Warren had. His questions were detailed and thorough, showing me just how deep some of his informants and operatives were within the Empire.

"You and Captain Barnettt restrained this Madeline Reynolds, who you both identified as the White Rabbit?"

"Absolutely. We tied her hands and feet to the bars and gagged her. We then used her to call for a guard, who I killed. I then put on his uniform and we ran out to the planes to take off."

The stenographer's fingers kept pace with our back and forth the whole time.

"Seems pretty lucky that you found your plane and one of their prototypes being loaded with fuel pods for long distance flight right when you escaped," the director stated.

"Yeah, that was a lucky coincidence."

"Coincidence? That's an explanation used by fools and liars."

"Are you calling me a fool, or a liar, Director Warren?" I asked with a flat tone. I was starting to believe that the Director didn't like me.

"I guess we will soon find out," remarked the director before continuing. "Tell me about this Nazi human. You said you bumped into one in a hallway before punching him, then he came to visit you while you were in jail. You then tried to convince Captain Barnett that this man and his country were your mortal enemies back on earth."

I shook my head at his wording before telling them everything I knew from the newsreels and what I had heard from those in the know. Their rise to power, territorial expansion by annexing territory lost during the previous wars, their brutal war tactics and finally the rumors of treatment of civilian prisoners. I told them I had shot down thirteen Nazi pilots while defending England and I would have never tried to help the Empire if I had known they were in league with the Nazis.

The two men said nothing, watching me as I kept going, making the occasional note in the collection of papers before them. The only other sound in the room was the hammering of the keys of the stenographer.

I told them about Major-General Kampf and the plans I had forced him to show me. Plans for not just Crestia, but all of Dione, and how I thought he was a lunatic and was probably the most vile person on the planet at the moment.

Director Warren nodded along before interrupting me, "You seem to know a lot about the Nazis for being their enemy."

"My commanding officer in England had a quote from Sun Tzu painted on the wall of our barracks" I paused to take a breath. "He was an ancient general and tactician back on Earth. *To know your enemy, you must become your enemy.*"

The director chortled before asking me his next question. "That quote leads perfectly into my next question. James Walker, how can you prove that you are not a Nazi?"

INTERLUDE 2: HOPE

HOPE SUCCESSFULLY SCAMPERED BACK to the quarters she was staying in without too many people seeing her in her birthday suit, mainly because most of those she came across were doing the same. They shared little nods and guilty smiles as they ran past each other while they were trying to find clothes. Most towns and cities set out blankets beforehand at central locations so those waking up after the full moon could cover themselves as they went home, but she had yet to come across one at the Citadel.

Once she made it back to her quarters, she quickly got dressed in her tan officers uniform, minus the tie, slipped on her boots, and then pulled on her new leather flight jacket before setting her side cap on her head.

"Don't you look cute?" she asked herself as she looked in the mirror of the barracks bathroom. The uniform would have looked better with her proper officers service hat, but that was with her personal belongings back on her old carrier, the *Twilight*.

As she made her way to the mess hall for breakfast, she waved her arms around, flexing them in order to break in her new jacket. The leather was stiff, making her movements awkward, so the sooner she broke it in, the better. She sat alone in the mess hall as she ate, thinking of what she could do that day, making a mental note that she needed to make her way over to the jail house on the opposite side of the Citadel so she could visit with James.

They had rushed him away so quickly the previous day that she hadn't had much time to visit with him, and she had grown accustomed to their talks. The image of how he was looking at her when she woke up played across her mind, causing her heart to flutter and her cheeks to turn pink. She then recalled the dream she had been having when he woke her, turning her face an even darker shade of red.

"Oh Goddess, did he see that entire dream?" she said to herself as she pushed her tray forward and laid her head on the table, wrapping her arms over her ears to hide her blush from anyone who might be looking. Thankfully the mess hall was empty due to the fact that most of the Citadels inhabitants were probably still outside running around naked after waking up where they had passed out during the full moon.

Hope spent the rest of the day moping around. She didn't have any new orders, so she was in limbo. She couldn't leave, yet she had nothing to do, so she decided to explore the Citadel. It was a top secret facility, and even though everyone knew about it, only those who were allowed were let in. Her mind made up, she went around taking in the sights of the intelligence and research facility, and the Scarlet Highlands that the facility was tucked inside of.

She got a few strange looks as she roamed around, looks that she was used to getting since she was one of the few wolfkin that still lived in Thurnmar. She sometimes wondered if it would have been easier to pick up and leave Thurnmar for Crestia when the call for all Canids to return to the Land of the Goddess went out eight years ago, but she was thirteen at the time, and her parents chose to stay because "Thurnmar is our home."

Besides, she owed nothing to the country of Crestia.

Hope had been born and raised in Thurnmar by parents that had immigrated here when they themselves were kids during the The Lupida Fog Famine over forty years ago. To Hope, leaving to live in Crestia made no sense. But then she remembered her childhood friend, Destiny, a black-haired wolfkin, her family had decided to return, and had pleaded with Hope's parents to do the same, but they didn't, and now Destiny was her enemy.

"I hope she's doing ok," Hope thought out loud.

Then there were the ideals of the Canid supremacy nation, none of which Hope agreed with. Growing up, her parents had encouraged her to make friends outside of other canids, and she did. Her best friends growing up had been a pair of girls who were her neighbors, one a zebrakin, while the other a rabbitkin. She never thought she needed to date and marry only other canids, like the Empire preached, instead, she kept her eyes open for any man who treated her right and made her feel...different.

James did all that. Yes, he had shot her down, but they had moved past that, and he was making a conscious effort to get to know her and to be her friend...and maybe more. That meant a lot to her. She had friends back on the *Twilight,* but she didn't know when or if she would ever see any of them again.

Since being shot down, she had spent a week alone as a prisoner of war before escaping with James. At the moment, he was the closest thing to a friend she had at the Citadel, not for lack of trying, it just seemed no one wanted to get to know the wolfkin that miraculously escaped Crestia.

As she was lost in thought, she found herself heading out to talk to James. She was walking along the perimeter road around the air strip that headed out towards the Citadel's jail house. She felt the need to talk with him, and she wanted to explain the previous night to him. Sure, she told him she couldn't control her animal form, but that didn't mean she couldn't remember what happened, and she had sought him out and then laid there to keep watch over him, like he belonged to her.

As she walked, she thought about the dream again. She had protected him, while he had made sure no one but himself touched her. Then they performed tricks, and at the end, he gave her head pats and a treat while praising her with the words she loved to hear.

"I am a good girl," she muttered to herself as she daydreamed and walked at the same time.

Hope was so deep in her thoughts that she didn't hear the woman's voice trying to get her attention in the car next to her.

"Captain Barnett...Captain Barnett!...Hope!" shouted the woman, honking the horn while she yelled.

Hope snapped back to reality and looked to her right at the birdkin leaning out the drivers side of the olive green army car.

"A-agent Lowe? What are you doing here?"

"Looking for you, wolf girl," said the TIA agent.

Hope pointed at herself. "Me?"

"No, some other wolf girl. Yes you! Get in!"

Hope hurried around the car and jumped into the passenger seat. Agent Lowe turned the car around, and sped back toward the main buildings of the military installation.

"By the Goddess, Agent Lowe, what's the rush?" Hope asked as she put on the seatbelt.

"Your human is being interrogated by Director Warren and Grand Marshall Gill, and let's just say it's not going too well for him."

"He's not my human," Hope murmured as her face reddened.

"Sure he isn't. You were just walking around the perimeter

toward the jail for the exercise?" the agent asked as she looked over at her, taking her eyes off the road, but still not missing a turn.

"Whatever. What does this have to do with me?"

"He needs your help with the Director."

"My help? What can I do?"

"You can speak to his character," insisted the birdkin as she cut off a supply truck. "He needs someone in his corner, and no one here has spent more time with him than you."

"I haven't spent that much time-"

"You do know I'm a minder, right?" Agent Lowe asked as she tapped the side of her head. "And while I can't read him for some reason, I can read you. I also might have listened in on your conversations while on the *Longbow*."

"How rude!" Hope protested.

"I know, I know. So will you help him?" she asked as she brought the car to a skidding stop in front of *Annex C*.

Hope bit her lip, looking at the building and then back at Agent Lowe, "I'll try, but why are you asking me to get in your boss's way?"

"Because he's a prick, and I owe a certain Grand Marshall a favor."

CHAPTER
SEVENTEEN

I GLOWERED at Director Warren as he sat across from me. The room had been quiet for a few minutes, and Warren was the first to break the silence.

"How can you prove you are not a Nazi, Mr. Walker?"

"I heard you the first time," I said as I kept my eyes on the sly birdkin.

"Do you have an answer for the question?"

"Other than my word, no."

Warren chuckled. "Not everyone's word is worth being taken seriously."

"Mine is," I said, "and where I come from, an honest man's word is his bond."

"Are you being honest?"

"Oh fuck off," I snapped. "Everything I told you was the truth, do I need to repeat it? Or should we ask your stenographer to read it back. Let me sum it up, I hate the Nazis. My country is at war with them, and I would never work with them," I exclaimed, jabbing my finger down on the table to prove my point.

"Except for when they convinced you to shoot down two of our-"

"For the love of Christ! That was a mistake!" I groaned, interrupting him before he could finish.

Director Warren took a deep breath. "Captain Walker, there is no need to ask the young woman behind me to read back anything. I listened to what you had to say, and it sounds like a good story, but on my side of the table, it sounds just like that, a story. How are we to verify this?"

"How do you verify anything?" I asked.

"Minders," Director Warren said coldly, "very powerful and well-trained Class-S minders, two of which have been trying to read and verify your memories for the past hour, to no avail."

I cringed in my seat. *All this could have been avoided if I didn't have that natural block!*

"I see I struck a nerve," the intelligence director said with a cheesy smile. "It's your mental block isn't it? It is very strong and has no cracks. If you dropped it, we would be able to verify everything in five minutes, tops."

"If only it was that easy," I sighed. "I can't drop it because I don't know how I am doing it. Even physical touch didn't do the trick."

"Isn't that convenient," Warren mumbled.

"Whatever man, do your job as an intelligence officer and use your eyes. For example, compare my plane to the prototype Hope, I mean Captain Barnettt, flew out of Crestia. I shot down twelve of those planes over England. You'll see the technology is nowhere near the same."

"Trust me, our best engineers and mechanics are already doing that," the Grand Marshall said with a calm voice.

"And on top of that," I continued, "if, did you hear that, *if* I was a Nazi, which I am not, but if I was, I wouldn't be a very good one if I was bringing the enemy of my allies two advanced fighters."

Now it was Warren's turn to glower at me. He didn't have a retort for that one.

"You may be right, yet we still have no way of verifying it. Let's try something new, let's lay out the evidence as we know it. You are a human. You come from a planet known as Earth. You came through a portal from Earth to Dione that is controlled by humans. All the humans we have spotted on Dione work with the Empire, so why should I believe that you, a human, are not in league with the Nazis and the Empire?"

"Because I'm not!" I groaned again as I dropped my head onto the table with a hard thud.

"Director, move on," the Grand Marshall ordered.

"Yes sir." Warren sighed as he dragged his briefcase onto the table.

I lifted up my head and watched as he pulled out the contents. He laid out multiple dossiers on the Nazis that were present in Dione. Major-General Kampf was at the top, I recognized his slicked-back blonde hair, his droopy eyes and his door to door vacuum cleaner salesman smile.

"Is this Major-General Kampf?" Warren asked as he pointed at the picture.

"Yes, and that man is a lunatic."

Warren proceeded to pull out the next file, this one had an older man that was bald and wearing thick glasses and a lab coat. He was talking with Kampf in the picture attached to his file. "Doctor Volker Gerver, have you seen him?"

"Haven't seen him, but I have heard of him. He was a mad scientist back on Earth, I can only guess about what kind of crazy shit he's concocting here," I offered as I looked at the man.

"This is the other man of interest," he said as he pulled out another file with a face I had never seen. He had blonde hair sticking out from under his cap with light eyes. His face had an air of indifference about it, someone you would hate to have to face during a game of poker.

"Who is he?" I asked, looking at the intelligence director.

WINGS AND TAILS

"He is Colonel Alric Stumpf, he is probably most angry with you at the moment, since he is the lead engineer for the team that is here. The rest of these pictures are soldiers that guard their facility. They are said to be mean, short tempered, and very well trained."

"Sounds about right for the SS."

"SS?" Director Warren asked.

I smiled as I learned that his informants didn't know everything. "That's what the skull and bones represent on their hats, as well as the lightning bolts on their collars. They are the elite soldiers of the Nazis."

"You do know your *enemy* well," Director Warren popped off, making air quotes with his fingers when he said the word *enemy*.

"Still with that crap," I murmured, my patience starting to wear thin with this bird brain.

Every time he accused me of being a Nazi drew me closer and closer to smacking him. For the first time in over a week, I felt the need for a cigarette, but since those were nowhere around, counting to ten would have to suffice. I got to twenty and was still thinking of doing something reckless when our attention was drawn to a commotion in the hallway.

"Is James Walker in there? The human?" a familiar voice demanded.

"Captain, I can't answer that," a less familiar voice that probably belonged to the guard responded.

"Can't, or won't?"

"Can't!" the guard replied.

"James? Are you in there?" Hope projected to me.

"I'm here, why are you here?"

"I'm here to help...if you need it."

I smiled. I could feel that she really meant it. *"Only if you can convince them I'm not a Nazi."*

We then heard the sound of a smack, followed by someone

falling to the floor. The door opened and Hope walked in, shaking her right hand but smiling once she saw me.

"James, I'm glad I-" Hope yelped as two guards ran into the room and tackled her to the ground.

Director Warren jumped to his feet in anger while Grand Marshall Gill stayed in his seat and tried not to laugh. The stenographer, who I had forgotten was in the room, was almost taken out by their actions, but to her credit, she kept tapping away at those keys.

"Oww!" Hope cried from the ground as the two guards forcefully handcuffed her hands behind her back.

"Captain Barnettt, what in the Gods' names are you doing?" Director Warren demanded.

"I'm here to help him!" she said, gesturing her head toward me as guards lifted her up.

"Ugh, get this wolf out of here," Warren sneered.

"Hold up," Grand Marshall Gill ordered. "I want to hear what she has to say."

"What?" Director Warren squawked. "You can't be serious."

The Grand Marshall ignored his intelligence director and looked at the guards. "Uncuff her and leave. Captain Barnett, have a seat."

The guards did as they were ordered, leaving Hope standing there rubbing her wrist. I reached over and pulled the seat next to me out as she got closer, earning me a nice smile as she sat down.

Director Warren quickly grabbed up all the papers he had laid out on the Nazis and put them away, shooting a glare at Hope. It was one thing to be skeptical of me, but treating her like she was a spy for Crestia was ridiculous.

"So, Captain Barnett," the Grand Marshall said in his deep voice, "you say you are here to help Mr. Walker? How do you plan to do that?"

She looked down at her hands as she collected her thoughts

before answering him, "I'm not really sure. I was told you were accusing him of being a Nazi, and after spending the time with him that I have, I can confirm that he's not one of them."

"What qualifies you to make that decision?" Warren demanded as he continued to sneer at Hope.

"First, he subdued one of their agents, Madeline Reynolds, or as you know her, White Rabbit. I know you can't search his mind to prove it, but you can look into mine. Second, I have met one of them in person, that Kampf guy, and the vibes he gave off were of someone who has never done anything good in their life. Meanwhile, James is a good man, I can feel it," she said as she looked at me and smiled.

"Even though he shot you down?" the Grand Marshall asked.

"Yes sir, even though he shot me down...which is another reason we need him," she said as her ears perked up.

"We need him?" the Grand Marshall asked as the birdkin next to him scoffed.

"Yes, he's a skilled pilot. I've seen him fly in combat on two occasions now, and we talked in depth about fighter tactics while we were together. He knows his stuff, and he can help us the same way the Nazis are helping the Empire."

"Both planes that you brought to us are more advanced than anything we are using, according to the initial inspection by Chief Murphy," the Grand Marshall acknowledged as he scratched at his chin.

"Marshall Gill, you can't be serious about trusting this wolfkin."

"Why not, Director Warren? Has she given us any reason to not trust her?"

All three of us looked at the TIA Director, waiting to see what he would say.

"I have a few," he declared. "One, she is a wolfkin and our enemy is a canid supremacist country. Two, she just escaped from a Crestia jail cell and looming execution in a manner that seems too good to be true. Three, both her parents were born in Crestia-"

"Does your intelligence explain how my parents died?" Hope asked, cutting off the Director. "They were killed in one of the early bombardment raids on the city of Tretshire. This happened while I was away at boarding school in the Northlands and living with my aunt, who is also a wolfkin."

"She is a triple ace," the Grand Marshall added, "with sixteen kills to her name-"

"Nineteen," Hope blurted out, interrupting the man. "It's nineteen kills now...sir."

Grand Marshall Gill nodded before continuing, "Nineteen kills. She is a born and raised citizen of this country, and many Thurnmarians have placed trust in *her* over the past three years."

Warren took a deep breath, letting it out as an over exaggerated sigh. "I know how good Captain Barnett is," he said to the Grand Marshall, before turning to look at Hope. "I am also well aware of your history. You did well at the boarding school in the Northlands by the way. Finished top ten in your class? Well done." He then turned to me. "However, I am not fully convinced about the human."

"Oh come on," I protested as I leaned back in my chair.

"Tell me, Director Warren, what would the TIA like to do with him?" the Grand Marshall asked.

"Let me see...We would prefer he be sent to a prison camp for the remainder of the war with the other war prisoners. We would also like to be able to call on him when we have questions about his otherworldly technology."

"Interesting," Grand Marshall Gill said.

"That sounds horrible," Hope added

"Just shoot me now if that's what you are going to do with

me," I said, drawing odd stares from the three of them. "Kidding! I was just kidding."

"Though you may not like it, it is the most logical plan." Grand Marshall Gill shrugged. "You are a human with minder abilities who has valuable knowledge on our enemy. Keeping you close for questioning is something we need to consider, although, I would propose we keep you closer than a prison camp."

"Then what? Lock me up in some private quarters with a posted guard at all hours?" I asked.

The Grand Marshall smiled. "That's exactly what I was thinking."

"I can agree to that." Director Warren nodded in agreement. "This way we can monitor him and keep track of his movements until we are sure if he is, or is not a Nazi."

"You know what, fuck you," I said as I rose to my feet, pointing a finger at the birdkin intelligence director. "I don't want to be locked up again, and I don't want to be sidelined from combat. I'm a fighter pilot, that means I want to fly, and I want to fight. You want me to prove I'm not a Nazi? Put me in a plane and I'll go out there and kill fifty of those Imperial bastards."

"Fifty? What would that prove?" asked the birdkin.

I clenched my fists. "Fine then, make it sixty, or seventy. Hell, let's go crazy and say one hundred! One hundred kills to prove I'm not a Nazi."

The two men sat there staring at me while Hope held up her hands and counted on her fingers as she did the math on how long that would take.

"And what if you die?" Grand Marshall Gill asked. "We would then lose all your valuable information."

I let out a laugh as I sat back down. "What information? The only thing I know about the Nazis is how to shoot them down. You can get more information about them by pulling apart their plane."

Everyone sat in silence for a moment before Grand Marshall Gill spoke up, "If fighting is all you say you are good for, then I can definitely use you as a pilot."

"But Sir," Director Warren whined in protest, "what about his plane?"

"Study it," I said. "Hell, make copies of it and use them against the Empire. I guarantee it'll fly circles around what they're making."

"What about your one hundred kill guarantee?" Warren asked.

"Don't worry, Daffy Duck, I'll get those numbers with your current front line fighter, that is until you return mine," I said with a smile. "Then I'll help train your pilots in how to fly your copies of the Mustang."

"You think you are so good that you can succeed in any plane?" the birdkin asked.

I nodded. "I do. My father told me that 'It's not the plane that makes the pilot, it's the pilot that makes the plane.'"

The TIA director glowered at me before turning to the Grand Marshall. "I would like assurances. We need guarantees that he will follow through with his promises."

"Sounds like you want him to have a cosigner," the lionkin said as he rubbed his chin. "You want someone who will assume his debt in case he runs off?"

"Exactly."

"My debt?" I asked with a confused tone.

"A life debt," Director Warren replied. "If you run off without fulfilling your promise of one hundred kills and don't train our pilots on how to fly your plane, then your cosigner will be executed in your place."

"Why would anyone-"

"I'll do it," Hope said, rising from her seat.

"Hope, no," I said as I looked up at her. "I can't ask you to take on that responsibility."

"Are you planning on running away?" she asked.

"No, but-"

"Do you want to be locked up in a jail cell for the rest of the war?" she asked, leaning over me.

"Obviously not-"

"Do you want to fuck over the Nazis?" she asked, hands clenched tight as fists in front of her.

"You bet your ass I do," I said with a smile as I stood up. "I, James Walker of the United States, will kill one hundred enemy fighters and will help train your pilots in how to fly the copies you make of my plane."

"And I, Hope Barnett, Captain in the Thurnmar Air Force will cosign for James Walker."

"Fantastic," the Grand Marshall said as he stood up. "Then I, Grand Marshall Gill, as Supreme Commander of all Thurnmar forces do accept James Walker into our forces, and accept Hope Barnett as his cosigner."

We shook hands and then turned to look at Director Warren, who looked annoyed. He was leaning back in his chair with his arms crossed before he spoke up, "FYI, all you had to do was sign a few papers. The whole grand declaration thing was so unnecessary."

CHAPTER EIGHTEEN

THE NEXT FEW hours were spent with Hope and I filling out the appropriate paperwork that was necessary for me to join the Thurnmar military. Oaths were said and contracts were signed, with ink and blood, before the final salute and handshake with Grand Marshall Gill could take place. Director Warren left without so much as a goodbye once Hope had signed her cosigner agreement.

The Grand Marshall then gestured for us to follow him. He led us out the door and toward the building's elevator. As we walked, he talked.

"Mr. Walker, I am going to grant you the rank of Flight Captain within our Air Force, which I believe is similar to the rank you had back in your world."

"Thank you, sir,"

"I will see to it that you and Captain Barnettt are in the same squadron, at least until your contract is completed," he added.

"Understood, sir," I said as I reached over and took Hope's hand. She squeezed it back as her cheeks slowly turned red.

He chuckled before continuing, "We are now on our way to meet Chief Murphy, our country's leading flight engineer. I am sure she will have questions for you and Captain Barnett concerning your two planes."

We exited the elevator and continued to follow him out the building to a waiting car, another olive green sedan. The driver drove us across the complex toward the large hangars of the airstrip with the Grand Marshall in the front and Hope and I in the back.

During the drive, Grand Marshall Gill turned and continued, "Captain Walker, you will be given private quarters to stay in during the remainder of your time here at the Citadel. As far as pay goes, you will receive the pay befitting your rank as an officer, and you will get an immediate sign on bonus that all Thurnmar citizens get when they join the military."

"Thank you sir," I said with a smile, happy to know I would have my own money.

"Sir," Hope began, "I know it's presumptuous of me to ask, but is there any chance I could get the recommendation bonus for bringing Captain Walker to the military?"

Hope smiled at the Grand Marshall as he thought about her proposal. I peered into her mind to see how much this *recommendation bonus* was and was taken aback when I saw it was equal to my sign on bonus.

Two hundred trade bills, I wonder how much that is in US dollars...

"Captain Barnett, you will receive a recommendation bonus once you have shown Captain Walker how to behave and act as an officer in the Thurnmar Military. You will also show him how to fly our planes, as well as how to fight as a member of our fighter squadrons. Is that understood?"

"Yes sir," she said, happy to be making the extra money.

He then looked at me. "Do you understand, Captain Walker?"

"Yes sir. I doubt it will take long." I assured him.

"Good, because the sooner I can get you in the air, the sooner we can officially announce the existence of humans."

"Are you only going to use me for publicity?" I asked, having flashbacks to my time as the war bonds poster boy for the US war machine after I returned from England.

"Yes, but I won't keep you from combat. We have quite a few celebrity pilots who fight, most popular of all is Lieutenant Colonel Harris. If you don't know who she is, ask your giddy wolf girl," he said, pointing at Hope.

I looked at Hope, even though I didn't have to, I had felt her emotions perk up at the mentioning of her role model's name. She was starry eyed and her tail wagged energetically.

"If you are going to use James for photo shoots and movie footage, is there a chance we could meet Lieutenant Colonel Harris?" she asked.

"I don't see why not." He shrugged.

Hope let out a squeal of excitement as she bounced in her seat.

"I know you are a fan, but I would expect your boyfriend here to become more popular than her," Gill said as he nodded to me. "We have worked hard to keep the existence of humans a secret from the general public, even though we have been aware of your kind ever since the first humans showed up in Crestia and started giving the young Emperor aid. However, now that you are working for us, I can't keep it quiet for too much longer."

"I understand," I said.

"I hope you do," he said as focused on me. "The entire crew of the *Longbow* knows you were on there, as well as what you are, keeping almost three thousand mouths closed about a round eared other-worlder will prove nearly impossible. Therefore, the longer it takes for you to show your value, the bigger of a thorn you will become in my side!"

The car pulled to a stop at the closed doors to one of the

hangars on the flight line to the airstrip. When we got out, I noticed the guard presence in the area around the hangar was higher here than anywhere else on the base. On top of that, two officers stood guard at the personnel entrance to this hanger.

The two guards were both women, one a tigerkin, and the other a horsekin. They weren't as well built as the marine guards I had encountered on the ship but still looked pretty stout. They saluted us as we entered the hangar and transitioned from the bright light of the day to the dimmer lighting of the hangar.

Once my eyes adjusted, I noticed a flurry of activity surrounding what had once been the Messerschmitt Bf 109 Hope had flown out of the Empire. Most of the mechanics and engineers moving around the parts of the plane were women, with a few men here and there.

It's true, there are more women than men in Thurnmar, I thought as I recalled what Madeline had told me.

On closer inspection, I noticed that all the mechanics had little cotton tails and long rabbit ears. They moved quickly, pulling parts away from the German warbird at a feverish pace, while documenting everything with meticulous detail.

I held my breath as I turned my attention to my Mustang sitting a few feet away from the disassembled Messerschmitt.

Please be ok, please be ok...

I let out a sigh of relief when I saw that she was still in one piece, though there was someone sitting in the cockpit.

"Chief Murphy! Get over here, I have someone you have been dying to meet," Grand Marshall Gill shouted.

The round ears of the person in the cockpit of my plane perked up at the mentioning of their name and raised their head. Chief Murphy was the first woman I had seen in Dione that was not attractive. She had messy brown hair that was held back by a red bandana that sat just in front of her ears. Her pale masculine face was smudged and dirty as she peered at us through a pair of goggles that had different lens attachments pulled down, which made her red eyes seem comically large.

"Oi! Grand Marshall Gill! Good to see you," the woman shouted as she climbed out of the cockpit of my plane. Her blue coveralls were covered in grease stains and hung loosely to her scrawny frame. Hanging out the back of the coveralls was a long hairless tail with a red bow on the tip, the only sign of femininity on the woman.

As she approached, she pulled her goggles up to her forehead, and the pale clean skin around her eyes gave the reverse effect of a raccoon's mask.

"James, Hope, this is the lead engineer of research in flight for the Thurnmar Republic Military, Chief Charlotta Murphy. Chief Murphy, this is Captain Hope Barnettt, and Captain James Walker, the human from Earth and pilot of the silver plane."

"So you're a human?" she asked as she eyed me up and down.

"Yes, and you are a..."

"Ratkin!" she said proudly as she extended a bony hand. "I'm Chief Murphy."

"Captain Walker," I said as we shook hands.

She looked beside me and quickly let go, sliding over to Hope. "And you must be Captain Barnett," the messy ratkin said as she took Hope's hand. "I'm Charlie, Charlie Murphy. It's an honor to be in the presence of such a noble and beautiful wolfkin," she added as she tried to kiss the back of Hope's hand.

"N-nice to meet you too," Hope said as she struggled to pull her hand free from the fawning rat girl.

"Charlie, cut it out," Grand Marshall Gill snapped, pinching the bridge of his nose.

"Yes sir," the woman replied, giving one last wink to Hope before turning her attention back to me. "Does this silver beauty belong to you?"

"Not yet, but I think we are getting there," I said as I put my arm around the wolfkins shoulder and pulled her tight to me. Hope returned the embrace by wrapping her arms around my waist and giving me a quick kiss on the cheek, making me flush.

"I was talking about the plane," Chief Murphy said with furrowed brows.

"Oh, of course you were. Yeah, she's mine," I said as my cheeks turned red. I pulled away from Hope, her arms slowly letting go. "This is the North American P51D Mustang. Probably the best plane in the sky in my world."

"Just from initial glances, I would have to agree with you. That maroon plane you two brought is more advanced than anything we're flying, but this Mustang, well it's leagues ahead of it. The shape of the wings, the bubble canopy, that engine under the hood, and just her overall shape. She's the second most beautiful thing in the hangar at the moment, second only to Captain Barnett."

She shot a wink to Hope who cringed.

"Chief Murphy," I growled, getting the randy engineer's attention.

"Sorry, and please, call me Charlie. What more can you tell me about the plane?" she asked as she pulled out a pad and pencil.

I spent the next few minutes filling her in on the specifics of the plane. I didn't know all the small details about the P-51, but as the pilot, I knew quite a bit. This included top speed, service ceiling, range and anything else I thought she needed to know. As I enlightened the energetic rat girl about my plane, Hope wandered around it, studying it closely while a few of the engineers who worked for Charlie made their way over to my plane, tools in hand.

"That's about it," I concluded as I scratched the back of my neck.

"Thanks Captain Walker," she said as she finished up her notes. "Before we get started, I want to let you know that you can trust me and my team to take good care of her while we study her. Once she's fully documented, we will put her back together like she's brand new!"

"Glad to know–wait, did you say put her back together?"

Charlie gave a whistle and the waiting engineers and mechanics pounced on the plane, quickly documenting and removing parts as they did. I tried to protest, but all that came out was a sad groan as I watched my plane being disassembled in front of me.

Grand Marshall Gill moved to my side and put his hand on my shoulder as he led me away. "Don't you worry, Captain. Charlie and her team are the best aviation engineers we have in Thurnmar. Her team are the ones who developed the Hak-17, the plane you are scheduled to start training on."

We left the hangar and moved to the flight line to examine the primary fighter planes of the Thurnmar Air Force. They were a short monoplane with gull wings and contra rotating propellers attached to a radial engine. Now that I was seeing them up close, I could see that it really was a beefy version of the Brewster Buffalo's I had flown in my first month in England.

"Captain Barnettt, please fill Captain Walker in on the details of the Hak-17," the Grand Marshall Ordered.

"Yes sir," she said as she stepped up to the plane closest to us. "This is the Hak-17 Thunderdrum. It has four 12.7mm machine guns, two in the nose and one in each wing, but no autocannon," she added with a frown.

"What?" Grand Marshall Gill asked.

"Nothing," she said, shaking her head. "The plane has a one thousand horsepower engine with a max speed around three hundred fifty miles per hour. They are fast in a dive, highly maneuverable, and that's about it," she said with a shrug. "You flew against me when you first arrived, you probably learned more from that encounter than from anything I just told you."

"I see. It looks similar to a plane I flew back on Earth, just with more guns and a slightly higher speed," I said as I leaned against the leading edge of the wing.

"Is that so?" asked the Grand Marshall. "Then it shouldn't take long to get you up to speed on how to fly one of these."

"I believe so, especially with Hope-I mean, Captain Barnett helping me."

The wolfkin beauty chortled at my confidence in her, or was it in how I kept forgetting to use her title now that I was in the same military as her? I wasn't sure, but I could tell she was excited. I also picked up a few stray thoughts off her mind that showed she wanted to fly with me so she could get revenge for shooting her down.

"Very well, you two will start tomorrow," the Grand Marshall said to the both of us before turning to Hope. "Captain Barnettt, be diligent in getting him trained up, but also be thorough. I don't want him to be seen as a burden for the squadron we assign the two of you to."

"Yes sir!" Hope said with a salute.

I did the same before Grand Marshall Gill left us.

Once the Grand Marshall was gone, I turned to Hope. "You better stop thinking about shooting me down."

"I'm sure I have no idea what you're talking about," Hope responded with a playful tone.

"Oh really? Don't forget I can see what's in your mind."

"I didn't forget, maybe I want you to think I am going to shoot you down," she said with a wink as she walked past me. "Besides, I might be doing myself and Director Warren a favor if I did shoot you down."

"It's a good thing I know you're joking."

She looked back at me with a smile. "Am I?"

"Don't toy with me. I already showed you who the better pilot was."

"Hold up, that wasn't a fair fight," she said as she held up her hand. "You ambushed us and had a better plane!"

"You heard what I said to Director Warren, it's the pilot that makes the plane, not the plane that makes the pilot."

"It's not that original, we say it too," she fired back as she turned to me and placed her hands on her hips. "Do you really think you're a better pilot than me?"

"I do," I replied confidently, crossing my arms.

"Then let's put a bet on it. Once you feel confident enough with the Hak-17, I'll take you on in a one on one duel. Winner takes all! The plane with the least damage wins."

"Hold up…you want to do this with live rounds?"

She nodded her head proudly, her ears bobbing with her nods.

"Y'all are insane! No deal."

"Awww, are humans related to chickens?" she asked with a laugh as she put her thumbs under her armpits and flapped her arms while clucking.

"No, I'm not a chicken, but I'm also not willing to die to prove who the better pilot is between the two of us," I said with a wave before turning and walking in the direction of the residential area.

"Who said anything about dying!" she shouted as she jogged to catch up with me. "We don't use war rounds, don't be silly."

I looked over at her as we walked, waving my hand for her to continue.

"Ughh! We use paint rounds. The bullets are made out of glass and filled with paint. They break apart harmlessly on the plane. We don't do them that often because the pilots are the ones that have to clean the paint off their own plane after a duel because it's really sticky."

"Why don't the ground crews do it?" I asked.

"They used to do them a lot," she pointed out, "but the ground crews whined about how long it took to clean the planes. They said that they have to clean out the guns, which takes longer, so it's the least the pilots could do."

"Interesting," I said as we walked. Having rounds like that would have made air combat training more accurate back on earth.

"Should we make it more interesting by placing stakes on the outcome?" I asked, raising my eyebrow to her.

"Sure, what do you want if you win?" she inquired.

"Hmmm," I wondered out loud as I rubbed my chin. "When I win-"

"When you win?" she asked.

"Don't be rude. When I win, I want to pet and rub your tail any time I want for a week."

"Fine, you pervert," she said as she blushed and grabbed her tail. She acted like she hated it, but I knew better. "Well when *I* win, I want you to buy me a gift."

"A gift?" I asked.

"Yes, a gift," she repeated. "More specifically, jewelry. I want you to buy me something that will make me look beautiful."

"Hope, you're already beautiful."

She smiled up at me as her cheeks turned a darker shade of red than they already were. "Thank you, James."

"You don't have to thank me for being honest."

"Damn, now I feel bad for calling you a pervert."

"So jewelry is what you want *if* you win?" I asked as I looked down at her.

She nodded.

"Then it looks like we have a deal," I said as I extended my hand.

She shook my hand and we continued walking.

"I can't wait to see what jewelry you get me." She chuckled.

"I can't wait to see how soft your tail is," I said in response. "Silly man, you didn't need to make a bet to find out."

CHAPTER
NINETEEN

"ARE *you sure you're ready for this?"* Hope asked as we climbed into the air.

"Absolutely," I answered as I kept her plane off my right wing tip. It had only been two days since our agreement to the duel, and I was more than confident that I was ready for her.

My assumptions about the Hak-17 had been spot on, it was almost exactly like the Brewster Buffalo I had flown in my early days with the Royal Air Force. Yes, it was bigger, faster, had more guns and was much smoother in its maneuverability, but it still felt very familiar. It was a fine plane to fly, but when compared to my Mustang, I felt like I was riding a donkey while the P-51 was a race horse.

That familiar feeling was what gave me my confidence to duel. After zooming around the skies over the Citadel for a day, I felt like I had tried on a pair of boots I hadn't worn in a while. It took me a second to get used to them again, but after a few steps, it was like I had never stopped wearing them.

"What are the rules of the dog fight for Thurnmar pilots?" I asked as our gray planes cut through the air. Since we were at the Citadel, they had issued us the latest variant of the Hak-17,

and as they were the Citadel's planes, they had a purple and yellow checkerboard design on the wings.

"Dog fight? What do dogs have to do with this?" Hope asked with an air of confusion.

"That's right, you call them duels. My bad," I replied while I laughed to myself. This world had dogs similar to the ones back on Earth, but Hope didn't like them. "So what are the rules of the duel?"

"Simple, really. We'll start by flying toward each other and passing on our right. Once we pass, the timer starts, and the duel begins. We fly for ten minutes or until we both run out of ammunition, whichever comes first."

"And the winner is decided on the ground?" I asked as I wondered if the paint would stay on long enough to withstand 350+ mph speeds and maneuvers. "How does the paint keep from coming off while we fly? What is to stop me from barrel rolling to fling the paint off my plane before landing?"

"Already thinking of how to cheat?" she asked with a smile I couldn't see, but I sensed through our connection.

"Not at all, I want to make sure you don't do anything to ruin my victory."

She projected an obnoxious, over the top laugh. "Remember, how I told you the paint is very sticky? Trust me, this stuff is only going to come off once we scrub it off."

"I see. Good to know."

I checked the control panel and saw that we were now going over twenty one thousand feet, putting us four miles over the planet's ocean surface but only two miles over the ground that was Thurnmar. We had flown south from the Citadel to a valley that was part of the testing grounds for the Thurnmar Air force.

I snapped my oxygen mask on and made the last adjustments to my helmet and goggles, getting everything as comfortable as I could.

"This is high enough, are you sure you're ready?" she asked.

"I'm as ready as I need to be."

"Ok then." She paused for a moment before coming back across our link, "Control Control, this is Lone Wolf of Flight 345-B1. I am accompanied by Rounder, do you copy?"

"Flight 345-B1, this is control. What can I do for you?" asked the new calm female voice in my head.

"Lone Wolf and Rounder will be taking part in a standard duel. Would you please keep the time for us."

"Copy that. Flight 345-B1 will be taking part in a standard duel. Time will be kept by control. The clock will start on your mark."

I waited a moment after control's last broadcast to address my new call sign in the Thurnmar Air Force. "Rounder? Why Rounder?"

"It's short for Round Ears."

"Wow..."

"What?" Hope asked. "You don't like it?"

"Why not use my call sign from back on Earth? Yellow Rose?"

"Because you aren't on Earth anymore, you're in a new world. New world, new name!"

"Yeah, yeah." There was no point in arguing over call signs. Once you got them, you had to wear them like a badge of honor, and if you complained too much, it usually got replaced with a new one that was far worse. As I sulked, I felt her eyes on me and looked to my right.

"Are you ready?" she asked.

"Ready when you are," I replied.

"Ok, I'll bank right, you bank left. Continue your turn till you spot me, then fly toward me for a right wing pass."

"Roger that," I said, breathing deeply and slowly to keep my calm.

"Break in three, two, one."

We both banked away from each other. I put my plane into a slow and drawn out counter clockwise turn, leveling out once

Hope's plane was in front of me. I pushed up on the throttle to increase air speed as we hurtled toward each other, and within seconds, her plane went from being a spot in the distance to a roaring blur zipping past my right wing.

"Control, start the timer."

I banked to my right, looking up to see if I could spot her, and soon I did. She had turned to her left, putting us in a one circle flow, turning back toward each other with each rotation.

After the first and second pass, I pulled up to climb and gain altitude, diving back down on her as the circles merged again. As I dove on her plane, I let off a half second round of fire, hoping a few rounds of blue paint had found their way on to her plane. As I pulled out of the dive, I banked away from the flow and used my speed to race low above the valley floor. As I raced away, I swung my plane left to right, craning my neck to find out where she was behind me.

She had reacted to my cut and run by pitching her plane up, climbing and then entering a dive behind me, and the most concerning part was that she was catching up to me. As she drew closer, I saw the flash of her guns as she tried to match my weave, then heard the ting of rounds hitting the plane, splotches of red sticking to the checker pattern on my wings.

I had to react quickly to get her off my tail.

I pulled up into a sharp climb, nosing the plane up into a maneuver known as an Immelmann turn back on Earth, rolling the plane over once I was going the opposite direction. Behind me, Hope was pulling up and climbing into a long drawn out loop. She was working to gain altitude, something I was also trying to do.

I spiraled up toward her as she matched the direction of my spiral, putting us into a two circle flow engagement. We spent the next few moments pitching and slicing through the air as we tried to get a shot on eachother, but with every move I tried offensively, I soon found Hope behind me on my six, peppering my plane with red paint.

It was infuriating.

We were in the same plane, and I could even sense her moves before she made them, but she was able to make slight adjustments in her plane's flight path that I didn't feel comfortable making myself. That difference in confidence was the difference maker in the air on this day.

As I flew defensively, I realized I had been overzealous in proving my abilities to Hope. My hubris had gotten in the way of logic, and now I had to pay the price as she turned my gray plane with purple and yellow checkerboard wings into an abstract work of art, and red was her medium.

In my defense, she didn't fully dominate the dog fight. I knew I landed a few good shots on her, the blue did contrast well with the gray, purple and yellow of her plane, and I could see a few spots on her fuselage when I maneuvered into a good offensive position, though those moments didn't last long.

The wolfkin fighter pilot from Thurnmar was out for blood, and with every shot she landed on my plane, I felt the confidence she had lost on the day I had shot her down slowly return to her.

As the fight drew on, I realized this duel wasn't for me to prove how good I was to Hope, it was so she could prove how good she was to not just me, but to herself.

Before the time ended, her guns went silent, and I didn't have to search her mind to know what that meant. With her magazines empty, I could have taken this opportunity to go on the offensive, knowing she couldn't counter attack me, but I didn't. Instead, I decided to just fly with her. She eventually picked up on my intentions and the two of us moved into formation with each other as we flew over the valley.

"Control to Flight 345-B1, the timer on the duel between Lone Wolf and Rounder has come to an end."

"Lone Wolf to Control, acknowledged. Thank you," Hope replied

"Control to Flight 345-B1, we have a few members of the control room who want to know the results of the duel...for monetary reasons."

"We will have to-"

"You clearly won by a landslide, go ahead and tell them," I said, interrupting Hope's attempt at humility. I would have told them myself, but I still didn't know how to connect with random people I had yet to meet.

"Rounder has conceded that I won the duel."

"Is that so? Way to go Lone Wolf! You made this girl a pretty sum of money."

"Glad to hear it, Control," Hope said with a chuckle.

"Meet me in the officers lounge tonight and all your drinks will be on me to celebrate!" the air traffic controller declared with a jubilant tone.

"I'll see. Flight 345-B1 returning to the Citadel."

We flew in silence for a good few minutes as we made our way back to the airfield. As the structures of the base came into view, I was the one who broke the silence.

"You are one hell of a pilot, Hope. Better than me."

"Oh come on, I just know how to fly a Thunderdrum better than you. I'm sure if we were in matching versions of your Mustang, my plane would be dripping blue paint."

"I'm not so sure about that," I said as we approached the runway.

"Did you even try?" the rabbitkin mechanic asked as he removed the guns from my plane's wings to clean. As he lifted the access panels on the top side of the wings, the sticky red paint dripped into the opening and onto the machine gun and its ammo belt. He grit his teeth and swore under his breath as one of the female mechanics came toward us.

"That's what you get for betting against the Lone Wolf," she informed the young mechanic on my plane's wing. "Maybe next time you gamble, don't place a bet for someone just because they have the same junk between their legs as you."

"She's got a point," I said as I ran a soapy sponge over the top of the plane's nose. The glare and emotions I got in return said I had betrayed him and that he thought I had lost on purpose to get Hope to want to sleep with me. I just shook my head and ignored him as I kept scrubbing.

After an hour of scrubbing, Hope came over to my plane from hers.

"How's it going?" she asked.

"Good," I said as I wiped sweat from my forehead with the back of my hand. "The fuselage is clean, now I need to get the wings."

"Good, because I was about to say that you missed a spot," she said as she walked over and pointed at the paint-covered wing.

She was wearing her tan chino pants and a white tank top that fit tight to her body. Her silver hair was pulled back in a loose ponytail, and her skin had a slight shimmer to it in the light of the sun from the sheen of sweat that had built up while she was working.

"How's it going on your plane?" I asked as I tried not to stare at her for too long, my mind wondering what it would be like to scrub her clean.

"I'm done, but I wanted to see if you needed any help."

Before I could answer, she grabbed a sponge and dipped it in the soapy bucket before stepping up on the wing and proceeding to scrub off the red paint she had deposited there. I began to say something about her not needing to help me, but could tell she was going to help whether I liked it.

With her help, the wings and underbelly of my plane were nice and clean after another good hour of scrubbing.

"Thank you," I said while trying to ignore the red paint that was smeared across her cleavage.

"No problem, I helped make the mess, it's only polite to clean up after yourself."

"That it is, what about the paint you got on yourself?" I asked as I pointed to her exposed arms.

"Yeah…that's going to take some time. I even got some on my tail," she said as she grabbed the big fluff of fur and showed me the smears of blue and red in her silver coat.

I examined her tail before my eyes ran up her sleek body to the large pair of ears on her head. "You got paint on your ears as well," I pointed out with a nod.

"Really?" she asked as she felt her ears and pulled down one hand covered in red and the other in blue. "Wow, one of each color."

"At least it's balanced," I said with a smirk.

"This is going to be a pain to get out, especially since the hot water is out in my building," she said with a shiver as she imagined herself showering under a stream of freezing water.

"Then why don't you come by my apartment?" I offered. "I think they put me in a building by myself, so there should be plenty of hot water, and I could lend you a helping hand at getting that paint out of your fur, if you wanted it."

She bit her lip as she thought it over before smiling at me. "Ok, but I need to eat first. I perform better on a full stomach than an empty one. Care to join me?"

"I'll have to take a rain check on dinner," I said as I turned down her offer. She pouted at me as I continued, "I have an errand to run that may or may not have to do with losing the bet."

Her expression changed as she flashed me a mischievous

smile. "Then I'll forgive you this time, since you have to go get prepared."

She gave me a kiss on the cheek as we parted ways, but not before promising to meet at my apartment in an hour. I watched her walk away before turning to one of the mechanics and asking them where I could find jewelry on the base.

CHAPTER
TWENTY

"YOU KNOW it's not good to keep a girl waiting," Hope said as I approached the door to my apartment.

It was forty five minutes past the agreed upon meeting time, and I was surprised that she was still waiting for me. I had prepared myself to have to walk to her apartment and drop to my knees to beg for her forgiveness. Luckily, she had waited.

"Hope, I'm so sorry," I said as I fished the key to the apartment out of my pocket. "The errand I was running took longer than I thought it would."

I was munching on a sandwich that I had grabbed on my way out of the Citadels commissary, it was in my left hand. In my other was a package wrapped in parchment paper and twine. Hope stared at the package as she stood up.

"Is that mine?" she asked.

"Maybe," I said, "but I won't give it to you unless you forgive me-"

"I forgive you!" she shouted quickly as she reached for the package.

I pulled it away before she could reach it to an audible protest from the wolf girl. "You also have to get yourself clean before I can give it to you."

"That's fair," she groaned as I unlocked the door and let her in.

I turned on the lights once we were both in, and Hope let out another groan.

"Not fair! How is your apartment so much nicer than mine?" she asked as she explored the small studio apartment I was being housed in.

It came furnished. The layout was one large open room with a small card table and two chairs to the left of the door under the apartment's only window. A queen size mattress with a brown comforter, white sheets and two overstuffed pillows sat on the far side of the room. On both sides of the bed were night tables, both with lamps, but the one closest to the door had a black telephone that had yet to ring once since I had moved in.

Next to the bed was the wall that enclosed the bathroom. The soft brown carpet gave way to the white tile of the kitchenette on the right and the door to the bathroom on the left. The kitchenette had a small sink, a two burner electric hotplate, and an electric toaster with two cupboards overhead. One was filled with a few plates, bowls, glasses and mugs, and a coffee pot, while the other had a few tins of cookies, a loaf of bread, and a large red tin of instant coffee.

The bathroom was nothing fancy. It had a bathtub that could also be used as a shower. There was a toilet and a sink with quite a bit of counter space and a clean mirror centered over it.

Beyond the kitchenette, was a small closet that I hung our jackets up in. Past that was a five-drawer chest dresser that sat partially empty, save for a few extra pairs of clothes that I had sitting in them. Next to that was a desk without a chair with a record player, similar to ones I had seen back home.

The walls were painted some hue of off white, and over their paint were prints of what I assumed were paintings by famous artists around Dione, as well as a map of the area. It was a comfortable room, and definitely better than the dorm I had been housed in back in Crestia.

Hope sat the backpack she was carrying on the small card table, made sure the curtains were drawn tightly, and started pulling out two different bottles of shampoo, a toiletry bag, and a fresh pair of clothes.

As she got situated, I went over and started making a pot of coffee. "I'll put a pot of coffee on the burner for when you get out of the shower."

"Thank you," she said, "do you know how long it's been since I took a hot shower in a private bathroom? I think they intentionally put me in a building that didn't have hot water. Because of that, I've been showering in the barracks with the enlisted soldiers."

"I'm sorry to hear," I said as I turned in time to see her bend over and slide her paint-covered chinos down her athletic legs.

Her ass and tail were pointed toward me, so I took the moment to admire the fair skin of her ass as it was wrapped in the tight green fabric of her panties. Women on Earth would never wear undergarments that covered so little, much less something so tight, but that difference between Earth and Dione women was something I was starting to appreciate.

Hope rose up once her feet were free of the pants, straightening her freckled back as she pulled her dirty tank top up and over her head, revealing a matching green bra.

"You better not be gawking at me," she warned.

She said that, but her mind wanted me to look, and who was I to disappoint a beautiful woman like her?

"I wouldn't call it gawking. More like appreciating."

She looked over her shoulder and gave me a playful smile before grabbing her shampoos and toiletry bag and walking past me into the bathroom.

"Need any help?" I offered as she shut the door behind her.

"Not yet," she said through the door. "You just make sure the coffee doesn't burn," she added before turning on the water.

I sat in my boxers and undershirt for nearly half an hour, listening to music on the record player before the water cut off and the door opened with a cloud of steam bellowing out. She stepped out with a towel wrapped tightly around her lithe body, and another wrapped around her head where a few strands of silver hair were loose and sticking to her glistening skin.

Her cheeks were wonderfully red from the heat, and she fanned herself off with her hand as she panted. She then flashed me a satisfied smile before plopping down onto my bed as the smell of her shampoo filled the air with the scent of vanilla.

"That hit the spot!"

"I'm glad to hear it. I'm curious, did you leave any hot water for anyone else?" I asked as my eyes ran up the base of her legs to her peach of an ass and the damp tail hiding the valley between her cheeks.

"You could probably use a cold shower," she giggled as she nodded to the tent slowly rising in my underwear.

"Do you want your reward now, or after I shower?" I offered as I ignored her teasing. I knew what was going on between my legs, and I wasn't embarrassed for her to see it.

"Hmm, I want you to be clean," Hope replied with a wink as she rolled onto her side to face me. "I don't want to get any more paint on me after I claim my prize."

Our eyes locked, and I didn't need to be a minder to read the thoughts that were playing openly across her yellow eyes. I nodded, got to my feet and entered the sauna she had created during her lengthy shower. I promised not to take any longer to get clean than I needed to so I could quickly join her in bed.

The paint turned out to be harder to get off my skin than I had expected, but it didn't take me thirty minutes to get scrubbed clean like it had taken Hope. As I was finishing, I was hit by a wave of excitement from the mind of the wolfkin in the other room. I thought to explore it further, but smiled to myself as I had a good idea of what she had done.

I exited the bathroom, towel around my waist, and turned the corner into the bedroom to find Hope waiting for me on the bed. She was sitting on her knees, towel still wrapped around her body, hair damp and tail wagging energetically with a guilty smile on her face. On the floor was torn up parchment paper and the destroyed box that had previously held the she-wolf's prize.

"Hope? What did you do?" I asked with a stern yet playful voice.

"Well...you see, I was waiting patiently, but then I got antsy because you were taking too long, so I grabbed the package and shook and sniffed it," she said as she reenacted the motions. "Then I sat it down and waited, but it taunted me, so I grabbed it again, and then there was a flurry of action and..." she pointed at the ground as she trailed off.

"So you admit that you were a bad girl?" I asked as I stepped up to her and grabbed the new leather collar around the base of her neck, pulling her to me.

Hope let out a subtle moan as I used her prize to control her. "Yes...I-I was a bad girl."

Her breaths were deep as she looked up at me with longing eyes, her tail still wagging, and her face flushed. Around her neck was a brown soft leather collar with paisley design down its length, held snug by a silver buckle at the back. In the front was a silver D-ring with a bone-shaped dog tag with the word "HOPE" engraved in capital letters.

"I take it you like your prize?"

"I-I love it!"

When the elderly clerk at the commissary first suggested the collar to me as a gift for Hope, I scoffed at the idea. But then the old rabbitkin explained to me that it was a traditional wolfkin fashion accessory that they wore with pride when given to them by someone they truly cared about. He promised me some of the finest jewelry he had if he was wrong, so I took him up on his offer, because if he had been full of shit, I would be able to get her something I couldn't afford with my pay.

There was also evidence that Hope wanted one based on the dream I had looked in on following the full moon. Now that I was seeing the effect it had on her, I knew the old rabbit knew his stuff, and that her dream was more desire than fantasy.

"I'm sorry, I couldn't wait...I-I've never been good at being patient when it comes to gifts," she said meekly.

"I see," I whispered as my lips moved close to her. "How does it look when it's the only thing you have on?"

She licked her lips and tried to kiss me, but my grip on her collar held her in place.

"I wanted us to find out together," she finally replied.

I relaxed my hold on her collar, allowing her to close the distance between us as she pressed her lips to mine. Her tongue eagerly gilded between my lips and found mine, coaxing it to join her as she grabbed the back of my head and kissed me with a feverish passion. Seconds turned to minutes as we held each other, lips locked as we pressed our bodies into one another as my cock hardened and throbbed against the soft towel around my hips.

She whined when I pulled away from her soft lips.

"Don't whine, I thought you had something you wanted to show me," I reminded her.

Her pouting lips quickly morphed into a smile as she bounded to the floor, took my hand and motioned for me to have a seat on the edge of the bed.

She stood in front of me and began swaying her sumptuous

hips to a song only she could hear. Her hands traced the outline of her curves as they ran down the towel she had wrapped around her body. Gripping the bottom, she slowly slid up the bottom, allowing me to see more and more of her creamy thighs.

She stopped maybe an inch from showing me her womanhood, instead letting the bottom of the towel fall into place, releasing a playful laugh as she watched my face.

"Not yet," she cooed, turning around and leaning forward to playfully wag her tail in my face.

The silver fur of her tail was damp and cool against my flushed skin as it brushed against my face, neck and chest. I inhaled the vanilla scented air that drifted across me, created by the rhythmic swaying of her tail.

She then pulled her tail away from me before standing up straight and slowly untying the towel. Grabbing both ends, she spread her arms wide and held the towel open like a superhero, but lifting it high enough for me to finally get a peak at her luxurious rump.

When she dropped the towel, my jaw dropped with it.

Her gyrations continued as I took in the luxurious splendor of her exposed back. I pried my eyes from the hypnotic combination of her ass and tail, moving my lustful stare to the perfect dimples at the base, and up her lithe form.

She danced back toward me, getting close enough for me to touch her before spinning around to show up the goods she had been hiding up front.

"How does it look?" she asked as she lifted her chin and placed her hands behind her back, exposing herself to my hungry eyes while her tail slowly swayed.

This wasn't the first time I'd seen her naked, but this was the first time she had wanted me to see her, and see her I did.

Her body was well toned, and her freckled fair skin showed it well. Perky breasts with hard creamy pink nipples were on full display as my eyes moved from her chest, down her fit stomach to her wide hips, which gave her a subtle hourglass figure.

Between her strong thighs lay a patch of silver downy fur sitting above a sweet valley, where the pink hood of her clit slightly peeked out to say hello. The lips of her pussy were already glistening with her wetness as a small trail of honey ran down the inside of her creamy thighs. Hope was beyond excited, and the more time I spent admiring her beauty, the less time I had to explore her body.

"You look stunning," I commented after my eyes had stored everything about her to my memory. "Do you plan to stand there all night? Or do you want me to show you how you can be a good girl?"

Hope's ears laid flat against the top of her head as she dipped her chin and leaned toward me. She reached down and pulled aside my towel, freeing my hard cock from the soft prison. She bit her lip as she looked down at it before pushing me back and leaning over while taking me in her soft grasp.

"I can't lie, I've wanted to get my hands on you ever since I saw how you handled that crazy bitch back in Crestia," she cooed with slow steady strokes of my shaft. "But that was for lust. Now I want you for different reasons. Lust still being one of them," she added with a smile.

"And what are the others?" I asked between moans as I leaned on my elbows and looked down at her hands as they caressed my length and cradled my balls.

"I want you for lust, passion, and love," she whispered as she crawled on top of me and hovered her body over mine.

A guttural moan rose from my core as she ground her sex against mine, coating it in her slick fluids. She then muffled my moans with her mouth as she licked and nibbled playfully on my lower lip. The lips of her warm pussy gripped my shaft as she continued to grind her clit into the length of my cock. I was overwhelmed with pleasure, but found my wits and wrapped my arms around her back, pulling her down on top of me so nothing, not even air, stood between us.

Our kissing evolved from sweet and playful to sloppy and driven by lust. We breathed heavily as her hips flicked back and forth, her heavenly womanhood massaging my cock.

The more she ground and teased at my length, the closer I moved towards cumming, and it felt great. If she didn't stop what she was doing, I was going to burst, and I wasn't ready for that. I still had much I wanted to do with her before I had my first orgasm.

With a thrust of my hip and the push of my leg, I flipped her off of me and landed on top of her. She let out a yelp as I made my move, but wasn't bothered by my new position on top of her.

"Let's play a game called *Good Girl*," I said as I grabbed her wrists and pulled them over her head to the bars at the top of the bed. "As long as you hold onto these bars above your head, I'll play with you, and make love to you. However, if you let go, I'm going to stop, and believe me, I do not want to stop. Is that understood?"

She bit her lip as she smiled, nodding.

"Are you going to be a good girl and let me make love to you?"

She nodded again.

"I'm sorry, I'm going to need to hear you say it."

"Yes, I'll be your good giiiirll-oh my Goddess!"

Before she could finish, my fingers pressed down on her clit, then split her pussy lips and curled inside her. Her juices coated my fingers as I rubbed her g-spot, and the noises she made made me work even harder. Leaning forward, I kissed and licked her neck down to her collar bone before I moved down her chest to her nipples.

I took my time giving her hard pink nipples the attention

they deserved, and if I spent too long on one, Hope did her best to direct my attention to the other. She did this by twisting her body so she was moving her chest as she held the bars, making sure both nipples received equal amounts of time between my lips.

As I sucked on her tits, my fingers didn't stop their assault on her depths, and soon my lips were working their way down her stomach, finding the ticklish spots above her hip bones that caused her to break into a lust-filled giggle. She was doing her best to be a good girl until I used my tongue to tease the hood that hid the pearl of her clit. Two hands gripped my hair, which caused me to stop and look up at her.

"What...oh! Sorry!" she said as she realized her mistake and grabbed the bars above her head. I let out a laugh as I shook my head and went back to exploring her soft pussy.

Her nectar had a sweet warm taste to it that reminded me of vanilla, and her scent was heavy and pleasing as the pheromones worked their way into my brain. She squirmed and writhed as I buried my face between her legs, and the words of my playboy uncle came to mind as I licked away at her: "If your eyelids aren't sticky, then you didn't do it right!"

"Oh baby! That's the spot! Nyaah-right there. Oh fuck!" She whined, and I listened, pressing my tongue against her clit and flicking it vigorously. Her breath caught in her throat as I flicked her pearl with my tongue, lashing at it until my jaw hurt.

She whimpered and moaned, tightening her thighs around my head as she shook. Her back arched, and her chest heaved in the air. She howled as she gushed on my face. I lapped up her sweet vanilla nectar like it was ice cream melting on a hot summer's day, making sure none of it escaped my enjoyment. And to Hope's credit, she didn't let go of the bars.

"Good girl," I praised as I crawled back on top of her,

kissing her cheek as she panted in the aftershock of her orgasm. "Are you ready to see what good girls get for rewards?"

"Yes please," she answered between breaths.

I reached down and pressed the head of my cock to her wet valley before splitting her with my length. Her eyes widened, and her face froze with her lips forming an "O." Her head tilted back and broken moans rose from her throat as I inserted inch after inch into her. She shuddered once I had fully sheathed my cock, and I held it there so she could get used to it.

"How's my girl doing?" I asked, checking to make sure I wasn't hurting her.

"I-I'm good, oh Goddess, I'm so good. Just please take it slow."

I smiled as I pulled back and pushed in again, sinking as deep as I could into her sticky honey pot with every thrust. She was stretched tight around me, creating a cozy wet home for me every time I bottomed out in her slick tunnel. When I withdrew, I could feel the pressure of her trying to hold on to me, not wanting me to let me go before I returned my cock to its new home again and again.

Hope adjusted to my size like a champ as she pushed her hips up to match my thrusting motion. Her moans became wild, and her golden eyes glowed as a primal smile spread across her face as we found our rhythm. We kissed, bit and licked each other from mouth to chest as our bodies made their best attempts to merge with one another.

Our connection gave me full access to her mind, and I could feel her orgasm build with every thrust of my cock, nibble on her neck, and pinch of her nipples.

"Harder! Nyaah-give it to me harder!" she barked at me as she kept her hands above her head. "Fuck your good girl harder!"

I could tell she was almost there and needed what she was demanding. Rising to my knees, I reached under her ass and lifted up her hips so I was able to thrust harder and faster into tightening folds. Sweat bounced off her breasts as they jiggled with each thrust like two wet buoys bobbing in the ocean of her glistening skin.

I didn't punish her by stopping when she finally let go of the bars so she could cover her mouth as her back arched for her building orgasm. I was lost in the euphoria created by the slick grip of her delicious pussy.

"Yes baby, yes-yes!" she howled between her fingers as her pussy clamped tight on my cock like a slick vice.

I couldn't take it anymore as my own limits grew near. I grabbed her collar and pulled on it, lifting her body off the bed as I rammed my cock home, releasing rope after rope of cum inside her. Hope shuddered in my grasp as my dick twitched inside her with every release, her pussy trying to milk me of every drop.

I gave her two more hard thrusts as I held onto her collar before I finally let go. She collapsed back onto the bed like a rag doll as she wheezed for air.

"That...was...incredible!" she exclaimed between gasps of air as she rubbed her sweat covered body.

I lowered myself on top of her, giving her a tired kiss before agreeing with her. "Yeah, it was pretty incredible, wasn't it?"

She flashed me a satisfied smile as I laid down beside her, wasting no time before rolling into me so she could rest her head on my shoulder.

"Thank you for my collar. I love it," she cooed as her hand reached up and caressed the soft leather.

"I'm glad you do."

"Am I your good girl?" she asked as she laid her tail across my chest.

I grabbed a handful of the fur and pressed my face into her fluffy softness. "Yes, you're my good girl."

CHAPTER
TWENTY-ONE

UNLUCKY PULLED his plane up as I pursued him from behind. I was able to see what move he was going to make and pull up before him so I could line up the kill shots. The Hak-17 I was piloting did as I asked and helped me to stay inside his climb. When the moment came for me to release a burst of gunfire, the air stayed silent, except for the sounds of our engines.

"I think you would be dead, Unlucky," declared a voice in my head.

"Well I'll be. I'm amazed at how much you have improved over the past few weeks, Rounder," the pilot of the plane in front of me said. He was First Lieutenant Felix Anderson, aka Unlucky, an older lionkin test pilot stationed at the Citadel.

"I'll say," said another male voice across my mind. "When Charlie brought you to us and demanded we help you improve, I assumed you didn't have as much flying experience as they said, since Captain Barnett beat you so easily."

The new voice belonged to Sergeant Carl Henderson, aka Turtle, and the other test pilot currently stationed at the Citadel. The harekin pulled his Thunderdrum up alongside the right wing of my plane and gave me a wave.

"We have been going for two hours now, are you ready to call it a day?" Henderson asked.

I gave him a thumbs up, showing that I agreed. Though I could hear them, they still couldn't hear me, so we had landed on hand signs and certain plane movements for me to respond to them. It wasn't a perfect system, but we had sort of come to perfect it over the past two weeks.

"*I agree with James. This has been enough entertainment for today,*" Anderson added.

"Alright then! What's that James? You want to buy us drinks at the officers lounge?" Henderson offered on my behalf.

I gave him the thumbs down sign to show that that would not happen.

"*Felix, help me out, thumbs down means yes, right?*"

"That sounds right to me," Anderson said.

Two against one. I shook my head and broke formation, pointing my plane in the direction of the Citadel. The other two quickly caught up with me as we flew in a loose formation.

I had been introduced to Henderson and Anderson through Charlie a few days after the duel between Hope and myself. On the day of the duel, most of the Citadel had placed bets on who would win, and almost all of the bets followed gender lines. The men of the Citadel had placed their money on me while the women had placed the eventual winning bet on Hope, all the women except one, lead mechanic Charlie Murphy.

As I had come to understand it, Charlie's plan was to place her bet on me, collect her winnings from her team of mechanics and engineers and then use that money to buy presents for Hope. Instead, the opposite happened, the women of her team won the bet, and Charlie and the few men under her command had to pay out a hefty portion of their base pay in order to settle their debts. After that, Charlie had taken it upon herself to get me trained up for the rematch for her own selfish reasons.

Carl, Felix, and I made our way to the dining hall after landing and completing our post-flight duties, which included meeting with the mechanics and filling out our post-flight reports. It was quiet in the dining hall, which didn't surprise me since most of the Citadel's personnel would get their meals to go and eat in their offices. The base had more engineers and intel analysts than it had actual soldiers and pilots, and those types didn't like to waste their time sitting around and visiting with others.

The Citadel was known in Thurnmarian lore as the *Secret in the Valley* though everyone knew what went on there to some degree or another. The Citadel served two purposes, one was research and development of new technology, the second was the headquarters for the TIA, the Thurnmar Intelligence Agency. Outside of the soldiers that acted as security, and the few test pilots, the rest of the base was filled with civilians with high military clearances.

It seemed like an odd combination to have at an installation like this, but as it was explained to me, it sped up research and development and the quick classification of secrets. When a TIA agent found something of interest in another country, their reports could be handed to an engineer who could take that information and begin applying it to new technology. On the other hand, if an engineer at the Citadel developed something new and innovative that could aid the war effort, TIA analysts could quickly be brought over to help classify and bury the research behind so much red tape, it would leave you looking like a mummy if you unraveled it all.

Because of all the secrecy on the grounds of the Citadel, there were a lot of well-trained minders on the base who trained those that worked there in ways of building mental blocks to prevent enemy minders from reading their minds. An engineer or analyst couldn't work on anything on the grounds of the Citadel without passing the minders mental block tests.

They were good mental blocks. However, I found that if I made physical contact with someone, I could easily pass through those walls and see what was on their mind. This was something I kept to myself though.

After dinner, we moved to the Officers Lounge for a night cap, and as we neared, a mind pattern appeared. It was familiar and comforting to me, though at the moment, it felt stressed and disturbed and was hoping someone would save her. I let out a little chuckle when I dug deeper and saw a scrawny ratkin was the reason for the stress.

"Good evening ladies," I said as we entered the lounge.

Hope and Charlie turned to greet us, the first jumping to her feet and rushing over to hug me.

"Thank the Goddess you're here! She's doing it again," Hope whispered as we embraced.

"Then it's a good thing I'm here. Don't worry, I'll talk with her."

She smiled and mouthed the words "thank you" as she held my hand and led me to the seat next to hers. "Charlie was just telling me about a dance hall in the nearby city of Ainsley that she said we should go to," Hope stated as we sat down.

"Is that so?" I asked the ratkin while gesturing to the bartender to bring us a round of our regular drinks.

"Yes...*we* should," she said with a sarcastic tone as she put her beer to her lips. "So I can push you down the stairs to the bathroom and steal your girl," she mumbled into her glass before taking a drink.

"What was that?" I asked.

"Nothing." She sighed as she kept drinking.

I shook my head. Charlie and I got along well until it came to dealing with Hope. She was madly infatuated with her because she was a wolfkin, which was now a rarity in every country except for the Crestia Empire. So far Hope had weathered Charlie's early advances, but the ratkin woman still tried from time to time. It was starting to get old.

"Are you talking about The Stable?" Carl asked as he and Felix pulled chairs up to the table.

"That's the place," Charlie said, "I haven't been in a while, haven't really had a reason to go, until now."

Hope cringed at the wink Charlie tossed her way while I stared daggers at the scrawny ratkin.

"I think it would be fun. So you like to dance?" Hope asked as she squeezed my hand.

"I do, and I'm pretty good at it," I said as I gently squeezed back.

"Humans can dance?" Carl asked with a chuckle.

"You bet your cottontail we can dance," I said to the harekin test pilot. "I'll have you know that I won a few jitterbug contests back on Earth during my down time."

"I like the jitterbug," Hope stated, "but the foxtrot is more my style," she added with a wink.

"Then how about we make it a date?"

"Sounds good to me," Hope said. "We can make it a celebratory date for when we get assigned to a carrier."

"Now that sounds like a plan," I agreed as I leaned in and gave Hope a quick kiss.

"You two make me sick," Charlie spat as she got up and headed over to the bar to sulk.

The bartender arrived shortly after with the drinks for Felix, Carl and myself. I thanked them once again for helping me train, and we drank a toast together before they got up and went to their own table, leaving Hope and I alone.

"Thank you for saving me from her," Hope said. "She seems to only get the point that I'm not interested when you tell her."

"I know, the two of us need to have a *come to Jesus* talk."

"Come to who?" she asked with a cute tilt of her head.

"It's an idiom from Earth. It means I'm going to make her stop."

"Ok...just don't hurt her."

I furrowed my brows. "I'm not going to hurt the girl!"

"I didn't say you were..."

I stared at her for a moment before changing the topic, "Any news on what carriers will be at the exhibition tomorrow?"

"Nope," Hope said as she shook her head. "They're being secretive about who we've drawn interest from, but I do have some news. I'm told there will be at least ten carriers that will have their captains and wing commanders present to observe our exhibition."

"That's good," I said as I took a sip of whiskey. "What hoops do they plan to have us jump through to show we are worthy?"

Hope smiled as she leaned in close to me. "Something everyone has wanted and you have been training for."

"A duel?"

"A duel! Except this time we'll have an audience. If you show improvement in your handling of a Thunderdrum and can get my plane as dirty as I am going to get yours, then they'll certify you as a fighter pilot and allow us to join a carrier."

"That should be easy," I said as I leaned forward, our lips moving closer to one another.

"Which part? Getting certified or losing to me again?" she asked as her breath tickled my lips.

I shook my head as I closed the distance and gave her a kiss. "I love your confidence, but after tomorrow, our extracurricular activities are going to start with me playing with your ears."

She sat up quickly and covered her ears as her cheeks turned a soft shade of crimson. "You are such a devious man."

I let out a laugh as she shifted in her seat. An unwritten rule on Dione was that you didn't talk about a woman's ears in public, which seemed strange since they were always on display.

She took a deep breath and looked at me once she calmed down. "If you're going to change your reward, then I'm going to change mine as well. When I win, I want a foot massage."

"A foot massage?" I asked.

"Yes, a foot massage. For a week," she added.

"Are you sure?"

"Yes I'm sure," she said as she leaned into me, "and I'm looking forward to it because I hear they feel wonderful."

"Charlie!" I shouted as I entered the hanger.

Every eye in the building looked at me, stopping what they were working on.

"Captain Walker?" the ratkin said, looking up from the table she was sitting at.

"We need to talk," I growled as I approached her. "I need you to leave Hope alone."

The sounds of people working slowly picked up, but I noticed many of the ears of the different beastkin in the room were focused on us.

On the table in front of the lead mechanic was a series of instruments she had pulled from my plane's cockpit.

"What are you talking about?" she asked as she set down her project.

I stood across from her and leaned forward on the table. "You know exactly what I'm talking about, your crush on Hope."

"Not so loud!" she hissed, lifting up her hands to get me to quiet down.

"What?"

"I don't need everyone knowing about that!" she said with a muffled breath.

"Charlie," I said as I pinched the bridge of my nose, "everyone on the base knows about it."

"No they don't," she blurted out.

I stood up and put my fingers in my mouth, whistling to get the whole hangar's attention. "Who knows about the Chief's infatuation with Captain Barnett?"

The room was silent as everyone looked around, and then one hand went up, then another, and another, until all the hands in the room were up.

"The easier question would have been who didn't know," someone called out. Laughter erupted from her crew of mechanics as they made jokes about Chief Murphy's crush on Hope and her love for all wolfkin in general.

"I hate you," Charlie said as she turned red from ears to tail and tried to hide by shielding her head under her arms.

"That's what you get," I noted with an air of smugness.

"Pshh, if that's how you feel, then let's see if we remember to put all the parts back on your plane when we reassemble it," she spat.

"You're joking, right?"

She sat up and shrugged.

"Charlie! Please tell me you are joking."

"Ughh, you know I am." She sighed. "I wouldn't be able to live with myself if my actions made Hope cry."

"Jeez, thanks."

She nodded back, beaming a smile like she had done something.

"But seriously," I said, "you're going to put my plane back together properly, right?"

"Yes, James, I have my honor as an expert mechanic to consider. I will make sure your first love is put back together properly," she said as she leaned back in her chair.

"What about Hope? Are you going to leave her alone?"

"Really?" she asked as she cocked an eyebrow up at me. "It's just a little bit of harmless flirting-"

"You think it's harmless, but it makes Hope uncomfortable and disrespects me. You need to stop," I said bluntly.

"But-"

"No buts, Charlie, Hope is my girl," I said as I leaned forward on the table. "I'm not going to say 'leave her alone or else,' because I don't believe in hitting girls, but Hope does."

The ratkin's eyes went wide. "She wouldn't hit me."

"You've heard the story of our escape from Crestia, right?" Charlie nodded.

"Hope wanted to kill the White Rabbit, I talked her out of it."

Charlie started chewing on her nails with her large front teeth as her mind processed if Hope would hurt her or not.

"Will you back off?" I asked.

"Yes," she said as she hung her head. "I'll back off. But I call dibs on the next wolfkin girl!"

"Deal," I chuckled. After a moment, I studied the equipment Charlie had been tinkering with on the table. "What are you working on?"

She shrugged as her eyes lazily scanned the boxes attached to wires. "We pulled this out of the cockpit of your plane. It is the only thing the two planes do not have somewhat in common, and for the life of me, I don't know what it is."

I looked down at the black box, it had five buttons for preset frequencies across the top and a knob to toggle between receive, transmit, or do both. It was my cockpit radio, something that I knew zero planes in Dione had on board.

"This is a radio," I said.

"A what?" she asked.

"A radio, on Earth we use these to communicate between planes and ships. We even use it to broadcast music."

She eyed me skeptically.

"Humans don't use telepathy."

"Ohhh," she exclaimed, "that's nifty, but we don't use those here so..."

"Charlie! That is a part of my plane!" I shouted as I stopped her from sliding the equipment into the trash.

"Tell me why you would need it on Dione?" she asked as she crossed her scrawny arms, "don't worry, I'll wait."

I pursed my lips as I thought. "For long range communication!"

"We have ringer cables that span the continent allowing one to vocalize with whoever they want in other towns and cities."

Did she just describe a telephone?

"What about ships that are long distances away?" I asked.

"Telepathy, my small-eared friend. The Communications guild trains their minders to talk with one another at distances greater than a thousand miles. Every ship has at least two, sometimes three."

As if to prove the point further, Hope reached out to me, *"Babe, where are you?"*

"In the research hangar talking with Charlie."

"Did you two 'come to Jesus?'"

I chuckled at the awkward way she used the Earth phrase. *"Yes, we did. She won't be messing with you anymore."*

"Yay! You're the best!"

"Anything for my good girl."

I felt her blush through our connection. As each day passed that we spent together, our relationship grew stronger, as did my ability to sense her emotions.

"Did you need me?" I asked after I felt her calm down.

"Yes! The exhibition is today, did you forget?"

"Crap!" I had forgotten. I had been so focused on dealing with Charlie, that it had slipped my mind. *"Where do I need to go?"*

"You need to come to Hangar 8, Grand Marshall Gill wants to meet with both of us before our exhibition starts."

"I'll be there in a bit."

I then turned my attention back to Charlie. "I need to go, do *not* throw the radio away. It's a part of my plane, and I don't want to lose any part of it. Don't throw it away, please."

"Fine, I won't," she said, giving in. "Good luck up there."

INTERLUDE 3: ADDISON

"WHAT'S TAKING SO LONG!" said a blonde lionkin with a raspy voice as she pulled back the cuffed leather sleeve of her aviator's jacket to check the time. "They told us they would start twenty minutes ago!"

"Aww, does the starlet of the sky have somewhere else she would like to be?" asked the black-haired zebrakin woman standing next to her.

"Shut up Jayden, nobody asked you."

"You still haven't learned to be patient, Addison? You always get so restless when things don't go the way you expect them to. You know, I blame your brother for spoiling you," said the tall muscular zebra girl as she looked down at the busty blonde.

"Do you want to get thrown overboard? Because that's how people end up getting thrown overboard," Addison hissed back with an annoyed side eye. She knew her brother spoiled her, but that didn't mean she needed it pointed out.

Both women were leaning on their elbows against the guard rails of the battle cruiser *Dark Griffin*. The sleek and deadly warship was positioned on the far end of the Citadel's proving grounds, just above the peak of one of the low mountains that helped form the Scarlet Highlands.

On the deck was a collection of men and women wearing either aviator jackets like Addison and Jayden, or officers' uniforms with the markings of the rank of captain on their shoulders. Addison's brother, Nathaniel, was somewhere in the crowd and wearing the latter.

She checked her watch again. Jayden was right, she was impatient, and the zebrakin knew it better than anyone else. The two had served in the same fighter wing together for two years before both were promoted to lieutenant colonels and went on to take command of their own fighter wings. Jayden had been assigned to the *Blue Snow*, and Addison was on her brother's ship, the *Astral Communion*.

While she waited, she reached in her jacket pocket and pulled out the folded up dossier she had been given on the two pilots they were there to observe. The first had the picture of a pretty wolf girl, Captain Barnett, who was born and raised in Thurnmar, and was considered a skilled pilot since she was a triple ace. However, some of those standing on the deck with Addison questioned the girl's loyalty, since she was a wolfkin. Addison shrugged when that was brought up. She didn't care about race, she only cared about if the wolf girl could help her. She also wanted the man on the second page, and if she would have to take the wolfkin as well, then so be it.

The man on the second page was why Addison had any interest in the exhibition at all. The attached picture showed a very handsome man who had cute little round ears on the sides of his head, a refreshing change from the normal men of Dione. He was what they were calling a human, and he came from another world called Earth. On Earth he was a minder and a fighter pilot, and he had attained the status of triple ace.

"He's handsome, but he has baggage," Jayden said as she looked over Addison's shoulder.

"Yes he is, and yes he does," she remarked. "Apparently these two have been through quite the ordeal with each other."

Jayden smirked. "I'll say, he shoots her down and then helps her escape execution. That's one way to sweep a girl off her feet."

"Are you jealous?"

Jayden sighed. "Maybe a little."

Addison reached over and rubbed her friends back, soothing the pouting zebra girl. When Jayden was feeling better, Addison went back to re-reading the dossier on the human.

"Captain James Walker, there is something special about you, isn't there?" she asked herself.

"He is a minder." Jayden pointed out.

"I know, but I feel like there is something that they aren't telling us."

"What do you mean?" asked the zebrakin with a puzzled look, pulling out her copy of the dossier and re-reading the same write up that Addison was looking at. "I'm not seeing anything. What are you talking about?"

"Oh come now, if you can't see it, then you might as well go back to the buffett in the galley and eat up before returning to the *Yellow Snow*."

"Don't be mean, it's called the *Blue Snow*," Jayden said defensively.

Addison was about to say more, but the buzzing sound of two Hak-17 engines echoed through the valley. Everyone on the deck stopped their conversations and turned to look at the exhibition that the two pilots would put on before them. Addison raised the pair of binoculars she had been given to her eyes and spotted the two planes. Both planes were painted similarly, but the tails were different. One had a red tail while the other had a blue.

"Red tail is the wolfkin, Captain Barnett, and the blue tail is the human," someone shouted out.

"Thanks for reminding us," replied one of the other wing

commanders who had moved closer to the rail with Addison and Jayden.

They watched as the two planes split, going wide and turning back on each other. The duel had started, and both planes quickly went into climbs to get above one another.

As the minutes ticked by, Addison was impressed by both of them. She had an informant in the Citadel who had told her about a previous duel between the two and its outcome. Based on that info, the human was doing very well. Both planes landed hits here and there, but neither had truly taken an advantage over the other.

Halfway through the duel, Addison lowered her binoculars and quietly slipped away from Jayden and the other wing commanders. She scanned around and found a blond male lionkin in a captain's uniform leaning against the bulkhead of one of the cruiser's heavy gun turrets. He saw her coming and straightened up.

"Seen all you needed to see, dear sister?" he asked as she approached.

"I saw more than you."

"What can I say, I brought you on to be my wing commander for a reason. I know fleet tactics, you know flying," Nathaniel quipped as he turned and moved toward the bow of the ship.

"If that's the case, I want them!" she said excitedly, bouncing next to him as they walked.

"Why? And I swear to Pumar, I will find a new wing commander if you say it's because he is handsome."

Addison bit her bottom lip and thought before speaking, "Well, yes, he is very handsome, but he is also a skilled pilot. I knew I wanted him-them before this even started."

"Oh?" her brother asked, raising a brow as he turned to look at her. "Please elaborate."

She pulled out the folded up dossier and pointed out the

bottom lines on the write up about James. "Right here. You see how it says he shot down Captain Barnett and her wingman, Captain Hyde, with relative ease when he arrived in Dione?"

Nate nodded to show he was paying attention.

"Well, I have a source inside the Citadel that informed me that these two had a duel two weeks ago. Captain Walker, flew a Hak-17, not the plane he arrived to our world in, and the result of that duel was that Captain Barnett mopped the floor with him. So what changed from when he shot her down to that duel?"

Nate thought about the new information he had just been presented, then his eyes went wide. "I think I see where you are going with this. You want them on board so you can have early access to the plane he came to this world in, once the engineers of the Citadel are done studying it."

"Bingo!" she said cheerfully.

"And what if the plane he came here in is not as advanced as you think? Or what if your source inside the Citadel was lying to you?"

"Priya would never lie to me!" Addison countered with a look of shock.

"She's the deputy director of the TIA. She's a spy, it is her job to lie," Nate noted as he rubbed his forehead.

"Why would she lie to me? we have been friends for years!"

"I don't know-hold on." Nate stopped walking while holding out his hand to stop Addison as well. "When did you even talk to her?"

"She came aboard the *Astral Communion* two days ago when we docked in Hopewell."

"And no one thought to tell me? How did she even come aboard without me knowing?" he demanded.

"Because she's a spy," she deadpanned. "You just said it yourself."

She had him there, so he stood there, crossing his arms and

scratching his chin. Addison's ears perked up as off in the distance, the pitch of the two plane engines steadied out and the sounds of the gunfire stopped. She started to get anxious that he wouldn't act in time to get the two of them, costing her a chance at the handsome human and his plane.

"Come on Nate!" she pleaded, "you know you are going to say yes, I know you are going to say yes, so say it already and go tell Grand Marshall Gill we want them!"

Nate looked at her for a moment before letting out an over exaggerated sigh. "Fine! I'll make sure we get them."

"Yay! Thank you!" the happy lionkin chirped as she gave her brother a hug.

He shook his head, smiled and ruffled her hair before straightening up and heading to the bridge to see Grand Marshall Gill.

CHAPTER
TWENTY-TWO

"DID ALL the flashes from the cameras affect your vision?" Hope asked.

"No, my vision is fine," I said as I changed lanes. "The problem is my navigator."

"I'm a pilot, not a navigator. Besides, I'm reading the directions as they were given," she said with a snippy tone from the back seat.

I held my tongue because for the past twenty minutes we had been driving around the city of Ainsley, looking for The Stable, a popular dance hall. We had just finished up another social event with members of the national press, and had snuck away so we could go on our much needed date.

"There!" Hope shouted as she pointed over my shoulder from the back seat at the street sign. "Page Avenue, turn left... left James!...You-you missed it."

"You do know you're supposed to tell me when to turn sooner than right when we come up on the street."

"Hey, I'm giving directions while getting changed in the backseat of a car, it's not that easy," she huffed before returning to her wardrobe change.

I pulled a u-turn in the olive green staff car and headed back the way we had come. "Page Avenue, right?"

"Correct," she said as she paused with her dress unbuttoned and recited the words on the paper. "Head north on 10th street and make a left on Page Avenue, then drive a half mile and it will be on your right."

"Got it," I said as I turned right on the street we had been looking for.

"I said turn left-" she squealed in the backseat as the car's inertia caused her to roll to her left.

"You said to turn left if we were going north, correct?"

"Correct," she grunted as she sat up and leaned on the back of my seat.

"We were going south because I made a u-turn, that means The Stable should be right-"

"There!" she shouted as she pointed at the neon lights that filled the forward windshield. "See? And you doubted my navigating skills," she boasted.

"Whatever," I said as I parked the car before turning to look at her. "Are you ready?"

"Ready," she said, her golden eyes glowing in the dim light.

I got out and moved to the back passenger door, opening it and offering my hand to help her out.

"Thank you James," she said as she stood up and straightened her outfit out. My jaw dropped.

Her silver hair was pulled back in victory rolls, and behind her right ear was a synthetic red orchid hair ornament that matched the red stain of her perfect lips. She wore a blue shirtwaist style dress with white polka dots that showed off more skin than I had seen on any woman in public on Earth. The dress had a low neckline that revealed the perfect freckled cleavage that sat below her collar and silver tag. The bottom of the dress ended just past her knees, showing off the perfect amount of her slender legs.

"You look beautiful."

"Thank you," she said with a bright smile. "I'm lucky that my personal belongings arrived this morning.."

During breakfast, Hope had received a notification that two crates had been delivered to her apartment. She was over the moon when we went to investigate and discovered that they were her things from her old ship.

"My clothes and my comic books!" she had shouted as she opened the two foot lockers.

"Comic books?" I asked as she opened a chest that was diligently packed with comic books stored in paper sleeves. I reached down and pulled one out. "The Green Tiger, Volume 3," I said.

"That's a good one!" she exclaimed. "The Green Tiger takes on space invaders from the World of Scales."

I chuckled as I flipped through the comic. "You're such a nerd."

"Yes I am," she said proudly as she snagged the comic book from me and gently stored it back in the foot locker.

She was very proud of her comic book collection, but she was also proud of her clothes. Her wardrobe was a colorful mix of dresses and outfits that accented her beauty.

"It feels so good to not have to go out in that uniform...Not that it looks bad on you. You look very handsome."

"Thanks babe, but the uniform does all the work," I said with a smirk.

I was happy for her. She had spent my first two introductory events in a military uniform, and tonight, she was finally getting to be my arm candy.

On the other hand, I was still in my tan officers dress uniform. I was not a fan of wearing dress uniforms for occasions like this, but it was all I had. Carl had sworn it would help me get free drinks and pick up single ladies, even though I was already taking Hope.

"Can't have too many!" he had said, which was weird advice to receive from a man who was single.

"I'm going to need to invest in some more nice clothes so I can take you out more often."

"Oh yeah? I'd like more dates, but first we need to finish this one," she said as she gave me a kiss on the cheek.

"Good idea."

We interlocked our arms and walked toward the bustling dance hall, cutting through a parking lot filled with more than a few cars with foggy windows.

"Get a room!" Hope whispered in my head as we passed one car that was having its springs properly tested.

"Why are you whispering?" I asked.

"I didn't want to bother them."

"You are using telepathy," I said flatly.

"Oh, you're right," she said with a shrug and a giggle as we approached the building.

There was a small line of mostly women waiting to get into The Stable when we got to the front door.

"You're Captain Walker, aren't you?" asked one of the burly doormen as we made our way to the back.

"Yes, I am," I said, turning to him.

"I knew it," the horsekin said excitedly, "and that means you're Captain Barnett, the Wolf of Thurnmar! I'm a big fan of yours."

"Really?" she asked with an astonished tone, "and is that what they're calling me?"

"Yes ma'am. Can I get an autograph from the two of you?" he asked as he pulled an autograph book from his back pocket. "I collect signatures and well wishes from famous pilots."

Hope and I exchanged glances before shrugging. "Sure, we'll do it," I said.

He handed me his book and I opened it, reading some of the names as I flipped to an empty page.

"Is that Addison Harris's autograph?" Hope asked as she looked on with me.

"It sure is. She's the Starlet of the Sky, and so pretty!"

"I'll have to take your word for it," I chuckled. "I haven't seen her yet. What's your name?"

"Horton."

I wrote a note about how I wished Horton success and happiness in all his future endeavors, then signed my name. Hope took the book next and thanked him for his support before signing her name as well.

"Thank you. Hey, Serah," he said as he turned to the rabbitkin sitting behind the ticket window. "These two get in for free."

"Again?" she squealed.

"Yeah, it's good."

"At this rate we're going to go broke!"

He rolled his eyes and nodded to the door. "You two have a good night."

The music washed over us as we entered The Stable, and the dance floor was the place to be. It was packed with couples dancing to the upbeat swing music that was being played by the big band on the stage in the middle of the room. Off to the edges of the dancefloor I noticed there were a lot of women standing around and watching. In fact, a closer inspection showed there were probably four to five women for every man in The Stable tonight, odds that any man back on Earth would find favorable.

I was also relieved to see that I was not the only person wearing a military uniform. There was a heavy mix of three different colors that represented the different services. There was the brown of the army, the dark blue of the navy, and the tan of the air force, that matched what I was wearing.

We turned a few heads as we made our way to a vacant table, and my skill as a minder was quickly put to the test.

There had been so many guarded minds on the Citadel that I had relaxed to the point that I wasn't trying to avoid picking up random thoughts. Now that I was around civilians, I picked up every stray thought in the room, including the ones that were targeted at us.

There were so many! Thoughts of jealousy, lust, fear and curiosity all mixed up in a whirlpool and funneled into my brain. I was overwhelmed and sat down at the table, furrowing my brows while I tried to tune them all out, and then I felt a hand on mine, and all the voices went away.

"Hey, are you ok?" Hope asked with a worried tone.

My eyes locked on hers as I found my equilibrium. "Yeah, I'm better now. Just had to tune out the voices," I said with a smile. "I'm going to go get us some drinks. The usual for you?"

"You know it!"

You gotta love a woman who drinks whiskey.

We loosened up after a few drinks and found our way onto the dance floor, holding each other as we danced to the different types of tunes the band was playing. We did stop from time to time to get more drinks and to catch our breath, but it was never for long and we were soon back at it on the dance floor.

Things calmed down when the band played a slower jazz song, allowing me to hold Hope closer to my body as we caught our breaths. She pressed the side of her head into my chest as we swayed to the gentle melody. I nuzzled against the furry ear that was pressed against my cheek, causing it to twitch and her to giggle.

"Stop! That tickles," she whined with a smile as she looked up at me.

As the song came to an end, I started to lean forward to kiss her when a man jumped on the stage with the band and blew a whistle, quieting the crowd and the band while drawing everyone's attention. "Oh yes, oh yes, oh yes, it's that time of the night! Time for the big jitterbug contest!"

The dance hall erupted in cheers as couples got up and moved to the dance floor.

"The grand prize? A silver loving cup! Those not tapped by the judges remain on the floor! Let's go!"

With that, the band jumped into a fast paced swing tune and the floor erupted into a mass of bouncing and twirling bodies.

"I'm sorry in advance!" Hope shouted over the music as she started bouncing around and kicking her feet.

"Why?"

"Because I'm not good at dancing!"

I didn't know where Hope got the idea that she wasn't a good dancer, because she was pretty light on her feet, and responded well to my cues for when I wanted to twirl, spin and dip her. We were having a grand time and made it to the final five when one of the three judges finally tapped me on the shoulder.

"And you said you weren't a good dancer," I teased as we made our way back to our table.

"Thanks hun!" she chimed, giving me a quick peck on the lips before sitting down in our booth and fanning herself off. "I'm really not a good dancer, but I enjoy doing it, especially with handsome company."

"Well it was my pleasure," I said as I grabbed a napkin off the table and used it to pat the sweat from my forehead. "I'm going to go get us another round of drinks."

She nodded, breathing heavily while she fought the urge to let her tongue hang out of her mouth.

By the time I reached the bar, the jitterbug contest was finished and the crowd had migrated back onto the dancefloor. As I leaned on the bar and waited for my drinks, a raspy voice to my right got my attention.

"Are you that human I saw pictures of in the paper?"

My ears perked up as well as human ears could when I heard the woman ask if I was a human. I looked to my right to see a blonde lionkin looking at me with emerald green eyes.

"Umm, yes, unless there is another man in the city with ears like mine."

"That's what I thought," she said as she took a drink of her martini.

I used that moment to check out the rest of her and holy hooters! The woman was wearing a green dress that was struggling to contain her full breasts. As for the rest of her body, I was sure she looked good, but my eyes couldn't stop looking at her tan cleavage.

She cleared her throat to get my attention. "My eyes are up here, fly boy."

"Sorry about that, ma'am."

She burst out in laughter. "It's ok, I'm just giving you shit. If I didn't want you to check out my chest, I wouldn't have worn this dress," she said with a little shake. I was sure if I had been paying attention, I would have heard the sounds of a few men in the room falling to the floor from the jiggle of her breasts.

"How are you enjoying Thurnmar?" she asked.

"Thurnmar good, very nice," I said simply as blood returned to my brain after her jiggling display.

"Do you always use so few words?"

"No ma'am, I was just...taken aback by..." I gestured to her.

She flashed a large smile that showed off her larger than normal canines. "Good to hear, maybe I can continue to take you aback? Back to your place? Or mine?" she asked as her hand gently traced a line from her collar bone, down her chest and the middle of her cleavage.

"Guhh...No, I-I can't, I'm here on a date," I stammered as I held up the two glasses.

"Oh? Got room for one more?"

"I'm afraid not. Have a good night ma'am," I responded before heading back to my table.

"She's a lucky woman. I'll see you around, Captain Walker."

I looked over my shoulder at the lionkin as I walked away and ran our interaction through my head. *Had I given her my name? No. Because then I would know hers. She probably knew it from a newspaper article about me,* I determined as I returned to wolf girl.

"Who were you talking to at the bar?" Hope asked as I placed her drink in front of her.

"Just some woman who wanted to meet Thurnmar's new and only human."

"I see, you sure that is all Miss kitty cat wanted?"

"Oh? Are you getting jealous?"

Hope ignored my question by looking out across the dance floor. The band was playing a slow jazz song while the man who had introduced the contest stood in front of the band, singing in time with them.

"Come on, let's dance some more," she said, taking my hand and leading me on to the floor.

As we moved in time to the gentle beat, I could feel her possessive emotions run across her mind. Hope was jealous of the lionkin woman who had been flirting with me, and she was trying to do her best to keep her emotions in check.

"Hey, don't be jealous," I whispered into her ear.

"That's not fair. Reading my mind any time you want to know what's wrong with me is cheating," she said, flattening her ears along her head.

"I'm sorry-" I had wanted to say more, but someone bumped into my back and almost knocked us over.

"Why don't you watch where you are going?" the voice of the man who had bumped into me said.

I turned to face him and saw that the voice belonged to a stout mulekin that was dancing with a petite brunette of the same race as him. He was wearing the brown uniform of the Thurnmar Army, and before it went any further, I knew how this would end if I didn't try to defuse the situation.

"I'm sorry about that pal," I told him, turning to walk away.

"Go figure, you pilots don't know how to get anywhere on the ground."

"He said he was sorry!" Hope snapped.

"Woah there, you better use that collar properly and keep your little dog on a leash. I don't want to get bit."

Hope touched her collar and was emotionally stuck between being angry and being ashamed. I on the other hand knew exactly where my emotions were.

To hell with diffusing the situation.

"I said I was sorry, and now you want to insult her? What's your problem man?" I demanded as I stepped up to the mulekin. The music around us kept playing, but no one was dancing.

"Oh? The weird looking fly boy wants to defend his mutt? Heh, what are you by the way?" he asked as he leaned forward, squinting his eyes at my ears. As this happened, the crowd started to shift as those in the brown and tan uniforms moved behind their respective side, and those in the blue backed away.

"Hey, it's that human. I saw a picture of him in the paper," a random voice said.

"Really? Well that explains the weird ears," another one shouted.

"And he's hooking up with a canid? Does he not know?" a ditsy voice said from the army side.

The voices continued around us. They were killing Hope's confidence, but adding fuel to the fire of anger that was building up inside me.

"So listen, jackass," I growled as I grit my teeth. "I'm going to give you the option to apologize before, or after."

"Aww, look at you standing up for your Crestia whore," he said, as the army boys behind him started to chuckle.

"After it is!" I yelled as my hand caught his temple with a right hook. He didn't see it coming and dropped like a sack of potatoes. There was a moment of silence, and then all hell broke loose. I had been in plenty of bar fights, and most of them were service vs. service, but nothing prepared me for what I saw.

Dionians were different. They were stronger and quicker than your average human, thanks to the animal traits they had. I saw a horsekin pick up a tigerkin and throw him across the room, however, in true cat fashion, the tigerkin oriented himself in the air and landed on his feet. A harekin kicked a pantherkin so hard that he flew backwards almost ten feet, and a birdkin was moving quickly around a lionkin, throwing punches quicker than I or the lionkin could see them.

I grabbed one of the army grunts that had been standing behind the jackass and punched him across the face before a bottle crashed down on the back of my head. As I fell to the ground, the sound of police whistles filled the air.

"James!" Hope shouted in the distance.

I tried to get to my feet but got kicked in my side, dropping me back to the ground when a pair of soft tan hands wrapped around my arm and helped me to my feet.

"Let's get you back to your date, Captain Walker," said the blonde lionkin woman from earlier. She led me over to Hope, who practically jumped in my arms when she saw me.

"Oh my goddess! I was so worried about you," she said, her tail wagging while we hugged. "Thank you for putting that ass in his place."

"It was an honor."

"I hate to break up the reunion," the lionkin woman shouted, "but you love bugs need to follow me if you don't want to end up in the back of a paddy wagon."

CHAPTER
TWENTY-THREE

"YOU KIDS SHOULD BE SAFE HERE," the lionkin woman said as we sat at a table.

Our new friend had helped us escape the ruckus at The Stable without getting arrested by utilizing an underground passage that connected the two buildings. As we moved along the passage, we saw that it was actually a part of the old catacombs of Ainsley, and was now being used to store alcohol for the dance hall. When we came up the other side, we found ourselves stepping out of the false wall into the men's restroom of the diner across the street from The Stable.

Luckily for us, no one was in the bathroom at the time.

We watched the pandemonium across the street through the window of the diner as men and women were being taken out and thrown in the back of two police buses. I ducked my head behind a menu when I saw the mule army grunt that had started it all.

"Good riddance," I muttered as he was dragged on the bus. I couldn't hear what he was saying, but I'm sure I made out the words "human" and "wolfkin" when reading his lips, which meant he was telling them to look for us.

"So are you two hungry?" the lionkin woman asked as she was looking through the menu.

I was about to comment on how she could eat at a time like this when Hope interrupted me, "Are you Addison Harris?" she asked with an excited whisper.

The busty blonde lowered the menu and looked over at my wide-eyed wolfkin. "You know your stuff, pup. Yes, I am Addison Harris."

"Oh my Goddess!" she yelped hysterically, bouncing in her chair and smiling ear to ear while the few people in the diner looked up at us.

"Are you ok?" I asked the giddy girl.

"I don't know, maybe? I-I've never met anyone famous before!" she said excitedly before turning back to Addison. "I'm your biggest fan! I saw all your movies, and then when you joined the Air Force, that's what made me decide I was going to be a pilot!"

"It's always nice to meet a fan," she said before going back to her menu. "I think I'm going to get the whale croc club sandwich, what about you two?"

"I'm not really that hungry, and are you really Addison Harris?" I asked.

"Babe! She is Addison Harris, who would lie about that?" answered Hope for her.

I looked at her as she continued to scan the menu, eventually feeling my eyes on her. "What?" she asked.

"Are you really *the* Addison Harris? The famous actress turned fighter pilot I've heard about?"

"Yes I am," she said with a wink.

"I don't believe you," I said, crossing my arms.

"Then read her mind," Hope offered. "If that's ok with you, Ms. Harris."

"Please call me Addison, and it's fine with me. Who knows, you might find something in there you like."

Her smile was erotic, but also terrifying. I felt like I was a mouse entering the cat's trap, but I needed to know for sure.

I reached out and entered her mind, skimming past memorias of her singing on a stage, acting in front of a camera, and fighting in the skies of Dione. Then came the memory of her getting ready for tonight, and how she wasn't wearing a bra...

"James...James! You're drooling," Hope said as she shook me.

"My bad...I believe you, Addison," I said as I grabbed a napkin and wiped my chin.

"Thank you, now are you two really going to sit there while I eat by myself? I'm buying!" she added quickly, as the waiter came to our table with glasses of water.

Hope's stomach gave off an audible groan, and on cue, mine answered with one of its own to agree with her. "Well if you're buying."

Hope ordered a meat and cheese sampler while I ordered something that sounded like a fried chicken sandwich.

"Did you get into the dance hall for free?" I asked the lioness after the waiter went to turn our order into the kitchen.

"Yes, after I signed that doorman's autograph book. Did he get you two as well?"

Hope and I nodded.

"It felt weird," Hope added. "It's been a while since anyone has been excited to meet me." She frowned.

I reached over and took her hand, giving it a little squeeze.

"Don't be surprised if more people get excited to see you," Addison said as she watched our hands. "You are the girlfriend of Thurnmar's human, you have become a celebrity overnight."

"Really?" she asked as her cheeks flushed a light shade of red.

"Yes, and if you need help dealing with it, don't be afraid to ask."

"Thank you." Hope said, her tail wagging behind her.

"Speaking of celebrity status, how did a famous actress like yourself end up as a fighter pilot?" I asked.

Hope let go of my hand and leaned forward, her mind jumping at the fact that she was going to get to hear her role model's story from her own lips.

"It all started with a photo shoot for the Air Force, and a cocky pilot offering to take me up in a two seat trainer."

"Yeah, that first flight usually does it," I quipped.

"It sure did. Granted, I was growing bored with acting," she sighed, "all the roles they had for me were the same. Some damsel in distress who needed to look pretty and sing a song."

She took a sip of her water before continuing, "I told my brother, who was my agent at the time, that I wanted to become a fighter pilot. He was against it at first, but once I made up my mind, there was no turning back. I joined the air force, and he joined the navy in hopes that our paths would cross on a carrier."

"Is that it?" Hope asked. "You just joined and boom, became an ace?"

Addison let out a chuckle. "No, when I joined, they taught me how to fly, but then wanted to use me for publicity."

"I can relate to that," I said, "my country did the same to me after I was shot down and returned home."

"I heard you were a double ace back in your world?" Addison asked.

"I am, and that's why they made me the face of many war bond campaigns around the country."

"Did you feel useless?" the lioness asked.

"Very useless. Why train me in how to fight and then not use me?"

"My sentiments exactly," she said as we shared a look of comradery.

"So what changed?" Hope asked. "How did you get into combat?"

"The bombardment of Tretshire."

Hope sat up straight, her ears fully alert when her hometown was mentioned.

"I was at the airfield singing for the pilots there when the sirens went off. The attack happened so quickly, Imperial planes attacked our position, killing many of the pilots. Something in me snapped and I ran to one of the undamaged planes, ordering the ground crew to get her started."

She paused for a moment as I watched the memory come back to her. "Myself and a handful of others took to the air. There were so many Imperial planes in the sky, and our counter attack caught them off guard. By the time the battle was done, I had brought down six enemy planes, an ace in a day, but it wasn't enough. Tretshire still burned from the destruction rained down by their bombs and long-range shelling."

Hope let out a sniffle as she grabbed her napkin and dabbed away the tears. Addison looked from her to me with a questioning look.

"Hope is from Tretshire," I informed her, "her parents died that day."

"Oh my God, I'm sorry," the lionkin said as she covered her mouth. "I didn't know."

"It's ok," Hope said through the tears. "I'm actually happy to hear that that is where you got your first combat. Propaganda reels before movies of your success from that day on is what inspired me to become a pilot. So, thank you."

"Awww," Addison let out as her eyes welled up. "I'm happy to hear that. It's always amazing to see what good can come out of something so bad."

The two girls smiled at each other for a moment before we were interrupted by the waiter with our food.

"This looks so good!" Hope exclaimed. "I'm so glad we got some food!"

"Right?" I said as I bit into my sandwich.

"It never fails. When you stay up late drinking, you will always need a late night meal," Addison pointed out between bites.

"So what happened after Tretshire?" Hope asked.

"I thought you were my biggest fan!" Addison chortled. "I went on to get forty seven more kills over the next three years and was promoted to lieutenant colonel and assigned to be the wing commander on a carrier."

"Which one?" I asked.

"The *Astral Communion*. It's my brother's ship!" she said proudly.

"So cool!" Hope gushed while chewing on a piece of sausage.

"Thank you."

"Is the navy not worried about nepotism?" I asked. "Why would the upper brass allow a brother and sister to work together as the commanders on a carrier?"

Addison furrowed her brows at me. "Are you saying we won't do a good job?"

"No, I'm just saying that he might show you favoritism, or not be as demanding of you as he would anyone else in your position."

"He better show me favoritism, I'm his sister!" she said as she missed my point completely.

"Never mind," I said before checking my watch, "well, it's getting late, and I don't want to keep you out too late, Ms. Harris-I mean, Lieutenant Colonel."

"James, when I'm out of uniform I would prefer you call me Addison," she said with a flirty smile.

"I can do that for you, Addison," I said with a wink.

She bit her lip as she batted her lashes at me. "Now I'm the one who was taken aback."

"Aback to your place, or mine?" I teased her.

We got lost in each other's eyes. Her's were lovely and sparkled like precious emeralds in the gentle light of the diner. I didn't have to read her mind to know what she wanted to do to me, but being able to read her mind made it all the more entertaining.

She wanted me to hold her while she demonstrated her flexibility, and how talented her tongue was. It was a wonderful image that was interrupted by the sound of a wolfkin clearing her throat.

"You're right, James, we need to go!" Hope said with an excited tone. She stood and grabbed my arm, pulling me to my feet, "Thank you again for your help Ms. Harris, it was a pleasure to meet you."

Addison stole a glance at my crotch as I stood, noticing the effect she had on me. "Hmm, the pleasure was mine." She then rose to her feet and gave us both a hug, Hope first, and then me. She pressed her large bosom against me as she leaned in. "I can't wait 'til I see you again," she whispered huskily in my ear before giving it a playful lick, followed by a kiss on the cheek.

"Indeed-"

Hope grabbed my arm and pulled me toward the door. "James! We gotta go!"

"You kids stay out of trouble!" Addison shouted with a final wave as I was dragged out of the diner.

We walked at a quick pace, Hope practically pulling me toward where we had parked the car.

"Hope," I said, trying to pull back on her to get her to slow down. "Hope, slow down. Why are you in such a rush?"

She glanced over her shoulder, checking to see if anyone was around before pushing my back against a wall and jumping into my arms. She wrapped her arms and legs around me and smothered my face with licks and kisses.

I caught the flying wolf girl and held on to her as she

greedily kissed, sucked and bit on my lip. "You want to fuck her? Don't you?" she asked between kisses.

"What?" I asked as I pulled my head back.

Her yellow eyes glowed as she stared at me, her tail wagging vigorously as she waited for me to answer her.

"Hope, I-I mean, yeah, Addison is beautiful, and she flirts like it's second nature, but I'm with you."

"That's not what I asked," she said as she ground against me, each syllable getting its own thrust. "Do you want to fuck her?"

"Yes, I do," I groaned.

Hope pressed her lips against mine and kissed me so hard that my head slammed against the wall. I winced in pain, grunting into her mouth as my head hit the same spot where a bottle had smashed my head just a few hours ago.

"Oh my goddess! I'm so sorry!" Hope cried as I dropped her.

My hand touched the back of my head, and checked it. Luckily there was no blood, but a nice bump had formed.

"How's your head?"

"This old thing?" I asked as I knocked on the top of my skull. "Let's just say it's going to take more than that to crack my skull!"

"Good, because I've grown attached to it, as well as the rest of you,"

"So I see. Do you plan on telling me what has gotten into you?"

She blushed and pressed the tips of her index fingers together while looking at the ground. "Well...let's just say that imagining sharing you with a woman like Addison Harris really got me excited."

"Really?"

"Yes...Why are you looking at me like that?"

I shook my head and scratched the back of my neck. "Sorry,

I'm still getting used to Dione I guess. The idea of one man having multiple women is still something I'm getting used to."

Hope leaned into me and wrapped her arms around my waist, pressing her face into my chest as her ears tickled my cheek. I wrapped my arms around her and she melted against me.

"Get used to it. I'm not selfish and want to be part of a big pack."

"Pack?" I asked as I looked down at her.

"Oh, I'm sorry," she said as she looked up at me. "It's what wolfkins call harems. We can call it whatever you want, I just want to be a part of it."

Her eyes sparkled up at me, begging to be kissed. I leaned forward and pressed my lips to hers. Our kiss was more controlled this time, but was no less passionate than the intense kissing she had engaged me in moments ago.

We stood in our own little world there on the sidewalk, lost in each other's embrace. One of my hands moved on its own up her supple back to her neck, over her hair until it found the soft warmth of her furry ear. My fingers gently rubbed the delicate fur of her ears, causing her to playfully growl into my mouth.

She pulled back from the kiss but held her head still, taking my other hand and guiding it up to her other ear. I was in bliss as I watched her eyes flutter and lips quiver, my mind picking one of her stray thoughts while I massaged her large ears.

"Call me a good girl! Call me a good girl!"

I opened my mouth to say what her mind was pleading for me to say when a cough from a passer by snapped us out of the moment.

"Oh, geez, sorry," I said as I pulled my hands away.

Hope didn't say anything. She bit her bottom lip, stared at me, and breathed heavily through her nose while she rubbed her thighs together.

"Car?" I asked.

"Car," she echoed with a wicked smile.

"We got a carrier!" Hope shouted as she ran up to me in the mess hall. She was an early riser, so she had been up a good two hours before me today. I usually got up shortly after her, but today I had enjoyed getting to sleep in, especially after the extra curricular activities we got into in the back seat of the staff car, and again in the shower when we got back to the apartment.

"That's great news," I said after I washed down my food with a swig of coffee. "What ship?"

"The *Astral Communion!*"

"That's an interesting name, I feel like I have heard it before. Doesn't it sound familiar?"

Hope shrugged as she swiped one of my pieces of bacon.

I really felt like I had heard that name recently, but the when and how eluded me. I joined Hope in shrugging it off and moved on, "When do we leave?"

"A car will arrive for us in the next hour, and it'll take us to Hopewell port, where we'll meet our wing commander at the dock."

"In the next hour?" I repeated back to her.

She nodded with a smile, and then it hit her.

"Oh crap! I need to go get packed!" she yelled as she got up and took two steps to leave before returning and giving me a kiss while stealing another piece of bacon. "They're picking us up at my apartment building, see you in an hour babe!"

I sat there and watched her hurry out of the mess hall before clearing off the table and heading to pack away my own things. There wasn't much to what I owned in this world, so there was no rush. Everything I had fit in my duffle bag. Hope on the other hand had two chests full of clothes to pack up, and luckily she hadn't gotten around to keeping any of them at my apartment.

Once I had everything packed, I headed over to the offices of the apartment to drop off the key to my quarters before going over to Hope's building. I took my time walking to where we would rendezvous, taking in the morning and the sights of the Citadel one last time. It was a nice base, and a part of me was sad I couldn't stay longer, but I had a job to do, and I was determined to succeed, not just for myself or for Hope, but to save this world from the threat that was on the horizon.

The images of what I had seen that day in Kampf's mind ran through my memories again, causing me to shudder. I had not been in this world for long, but I had met some interesting people, and the thought of the Nazis turning this world into their home away from home disgusted me. I wondered how my government would have reacted if they had been the ones to find the gate to this world first, especially since it was right in our front yard. I wanted to believe we would have done better by the people of Dione, but I wasn't sure.

My mind was running through scenarios of "what if" situations when I rounded the corner to see Hope standing next to a car with two trunks and a duffle bag, arguing with a pair of women, one a tigerkin, the other a horsekin. I wasn't able to make out what the argument was about, but as I got closer, I could start to make out what was being said.

"I literally just got my personal effects yesterday from my old ship, I'm not leaving them here to wait on Interservice Shipping again!"

"Captain Barnett, I understand, but there's no room," the tigerkin woman said as she gestured to the standard olive green four door staff car that the Thurnmar military loved to use.

"Get some rope!" Hope suggested. "I'm good with knots, we can tie them to the roof!"

"We're not doing that. Any scratches or damages will be

taken out of our pay," the horsekin woman said dryly. She seemed to have a lot less patience than the tiger girl.

"But...ladies...it's my stuff," Hope pleaded while making the biggest puppy dog eyes she could.

"I sympathize-we both do, Captain Barnett, but we can't," the tigerkin said with a sympathetic tone as she placed her hand on Hope's shoulder.

"What seems to be the problem?" I asked when I got close enough.

Both women took a moment to look me up and down before their thoughts started to go wild with what they wanted to do to me.

"You must be Captain Walker?" the horsekin woman asked with a flirty tone. "You are so much more handsome in person."

"I'll say, what is your opinion on stripes?" the tigerkin woman asked as she leaned forward and batted her eyelashes, her mind telling me that her stripes covered more than the areas covered in fur.

"What seems to be the problem here?" I asked again as I ignored their attempts to flirt with me.

Hope spoke up first, "These two are saying they won't take my luggage."

"That's not true," the horsekin blurted out. "Captain Barnett, we said we can't take your luggage because there isn't enough room."

"And why can't we tie them to the roof?" I asked.

The two took a deep breath and took turns listing off what could go wrong...

"You could scratch the paint."

"Dent the roof."

"They could fall off and hit a car."

"They could fall off and hit a kid!"

"Or an old lady-"

"Ok, ok, I get it," I said as I stopped them. I pinched the

bridge of my nose before I continued, "Ladies, please understand that Hope just got her belongings back yesterday after not having them for weeks. Imagine if you had to go almost a month without your personal effects?"

The two of them looked at each other. They were quiet for a bit, having what I'm sure they thought was a private telepathic conversation. I listened in, ready to say anything to help Hope's cause when the horsekin spoke up, "Fine! I'll get the rope. But you two are tying it up on your own, we're not liable for any damages, and you have five minutes."

"I'll only need two!" Hope declared, and sure enough, that's all she needed. We stood back and looked at her handy work after two quick minutes. The ropes were perfectly spaced out and the knots so well tied, they would have made any sailor jealous.

"Hope, how do you know how to tie knots so well?"

"I could tell you, but it would be more fun to show you," she said with a wink as we threw our duffle bags in the trunk before getting into the car. "*And by show you, I mean teach you."*

"*I know how to tie knots."* I fired back at her.

"*Like this?"* she asked as she imagined being gagged and laying naked in my bed while strands of light brown rope criss crossed the smooth skin of her supple body. Her arms were bound behind her back while her ankles were bound to the back of her thighs, restricting her ability to move.

The ropes that restrained her body were strategically placed, creating a beautiful harness to hold her flesh. Restricting cords ran under her breasts, around her hips, and over her shoulder, but the most visually pleasing part were the three strands that ran between her legs.

Three ropes were pulled tight against her womanhood. Two ran to the side of her dripping pussy lips while the third ran through the middle of her slit. This third seemed to be the most important one to me, since it was the one that ground its soaked fibers against her needy bud every time she shifted in her restraints.

"How do you know this?" I asked.

"Books."

"Books?" I asked skeptically.

"Yes," she replied as her cheeks took on a darker hue of red. "My aunt had books on the subject of Jordaran rope binding. They were very...graphic."

"I need to read these books."

The two hour ride from The Citadel to Hopewell Port went by quickly. Hope and I spent the majority of the time in the back seat blushing while continuing our mental conversation of all the fun we could have with a good piece of rope. I had to adjust myself more than a few times, praying the two women in the front seat didn't notice what I was adjusting.

By the time we pulled up to the docks, the two of us were breathing heavy from all the mental mind fucking we were doing to each other. My mind was in such a haze that I didn't catch the name of the commanding officer we were told to report to by the horsekin woman in the front seat.

"C-could you repeat that?" I asked with a dry voice.

"Commander Harris will meet you two in the dock masters office," she repeated, pointing at the small building that sat between us and the large warship.

"Got it, thank you," Hope said as she climbed out of the car.

I thanked the two ladies before getting out and adjusting myself one last time before helping Hope with her luggage. I made sure to grab the rope and stash it in my duffel bag before throwing it over my shoulder, looking over to see Hope blush as she caught me in the act.

"They said Commander Harris, right?" I asked as we entered the dockmaster's office.

"They sure did. It's good to see the two of you again," said a familiar voice.

We both looked up in shock to see a green-eyed lionkin woman with tan skin and blonde hair pulled into two dutch braids running down her chest, giving us a big dimpled smile. She wore a flight suit that showed off the curves of her hips and the thickness of her thighs. The zipper was pulled down enough to show off the tan skin of her bountiful cleavage as her tank top struggled to hold back the enormity of her breasts.

Addison Harris was a blonde bombshell who had looked gorgeous the previous night in her green dress when she had saved Hope and I from a night in jail. Now she gave off the sex appeal of a woman who knew she was beautiful, and knew she was in charge.

Now I remember why the ship's name sounded so familiar.

CHAPTER
TWENTY-FOUR

"THIS IS YOUR BUNK," Addison said as she leaned against one of the bunk beds in the squad cabin, pointing at the one on the bottom. The squad cabin was a room filled with six bunk beds, one for each member of a six person squad. As I had just learned, squads stayed in rooms together, so as not to wake up the pilots of the other squads if they were off duty and sleeping.

"Then the one above it is mine!" Hope declared, grabbing her rucksack and preparing to throw it up top.

"Oh no it's not," Addison said as she stood in her way, "your bed is that one over there."

She pointed to the top bunk of the set in the middle of the room. The six bunks were lined up in a row with the head of the beads all going toward the same wall. Across from the beds was the door to the bathroom and the six crew lockers, each locker going from floor to ceiling, with enough room for that member's personal belongings. In the bathroom were three roomy shower stalls and three toilet stalls, all set up for the user's privacy, since the rooms were coed. The room also had two sinks, one between each of the beds, with a mirror above them.

"Wh-why do I have to bunk here?" Hope asked with a concerned look. "Who's bunk is above James?"

Addison patted the mattress as she replied, "That would be mine."

"Oh boy," I mumbled.

"I see," Hope said with an accusatory tone, "you want to separate us while being able to tempt James with your feline flexibility every time you get in and out of bed."

"How dare you accuse me of doing this for my own personal gain," the lionkin commander said. She was definitely a good actress because I could see that Hope was spot on. "I separated you two because those who were staying in the apartments around you said you two fuck like squirrelkin in heat."

"Impressive," said one of the squad members from the bunk below Hope's, who happened to be a squirrelkin. She was introduced as Flight Captain Alyssa Hagerty, a cute little redhead with large blue eyes, small red ears with tufts of fur at the tip and a tail that was bigger than she was. She lowered the book she had been reading to get a better look at me, shooting me a wink before going back to her story.

I shook my head and started putting my things away while Hope and Addison went back and forth on the sleeping arrangement. By the time I had my personal items put away in my locker, the argument had ended with a simple, "I am the commanding officer, so you will sleep there because I said so!" from Addison.

"Yes ma'am," Hope said as she reluctantly started to put her things away.

"Well, since Hope has two trunks worth of stuff to store, how about I show you around?" Addison offered.

"Sure thing, see you later my little squirrel," I said as I gave Hope a quick kiss, drawing a chuckle from Hagerty before following Addison out of the cabin.

We entered a hall that led into the central room of the *Astral*

Communion's pilot quarters. The pilot accommodations consisted of a large mess hall at the center with doors leading off the sides that led to the squad cabins where over one hundred pilots slept. At the front of the pilots' mess hall was the ready room for mission briefings and debriefings and access up to the flight deck. At the back was a lounge with a few worn leather couches, dart boards, card tables and a balcony that allowed pilots to look out across the cavern of the hangar.

These quarters were for pilots only, so they sat at the front of the ship in the space between the ship's flight deck and the massive hangar underneath it. The *Astral Communion* was one of the newer air carriers that the Thurnmar Navy had rolling off the lines of their ship yards. She was slightly longer than the *Longbow*, the carrier we had landed on after escaping from Crestia, and had more guns and space on her upper and lower decks. In fact, she still had a wet paint smell about her, even though the ship had already completed a full eight month maiden deployment to the Oshory Abyss.

"It was a boring deployment," Addison remarked as we stepped out onto the pilots' balcony. "Since it was our maiden voyage, my brother is grateful that we didn't see any action."

I sat down in a chair on the deck while she leaned forward on the rail of the balcony, her ass and tawny tail with its black-furred tip practically right in my face. I was hypnotized for a moment by the lazy motion of her tail before I snapped back to reality. "Are you that eager for action?"

"Absolutely," she said with excitement as she spun to face me. "My place is in the sky shooting down the fighters of the Empire."

"I'm surprised you still fly, most wing commanders don't."

"My brother would probably prefer it to be that way, but I can't. Flying is a freedom only those of us who have done it can understand."

She closed her eyes and her mind went to the air, recalling

the memories of the first time she flew a plane, followed by her first time in combat. Though she had been in show business where fans adored her and studios paid her large amounts of money, she was meant for the air, as was I, and so many others out there.

"My father once told me that everyone wishes they could fly, some do it, and they are content, the itch was scratched, and they move on to the next desire or fascination." I paused to let the first part sink in. "But for a few, scratching the itch isn't enough. Doesn't matter if you have flown ten or ten thousand times, those individuals live to fly, and fly to live."

"He was a wise man."

"That he is. He's still alive."

"I take it you have the itch?" she asked as she sauntered to where I was sitting.

"I do, and you have it as well."

"That, and a few other itches that I need help scratching," she purred as she straddled my lap and lowered herself on top of me. "Let me see your hands, please."

Without much thought, I complied, raising my hand to her. She took my hand with both of hers and examined my palm while massaging my fingers.

"Your hand is so big compared to mine, and it feels strong. Mmm, I bet they could scratch my itch all night long," she cooed.

I was at a loss for words. I swallowed the dryness in my mouth as her thoughts made it hard for me to think straight. Things got even harder when she took my middle finger and licked it with her tongue before taking my digit into her mouth and sucking on it.

Her soft tongue swirled around the tip of my finger as she sucked and made its length appear and then disappear between her lips. It felt good, and my cock vibrated with jealousy as it strained against my pants, crying for it to be him and not a finger that couldn't truly enjoy her talents.

With my digit in her mouth, she unzipped her flight suit, exposing her tan cleavage. She pulled my finger out one last time and then licked my open palm from wrist to the tip of my wetted extremity, sending a shiver down my spine. My hand was then guided to her exposed skin and pressed firmly between her two large melons.

"Do you feel that?" she asked as my hand sank into her cleavage

"Yes."

"My heart has never raced like this before for a man."

"Your heart?" I asked as I was suddenly aware of her heartbeat, "Oh yes, your heartbeat...It's fast, and powerful."

She flashed a lustful smile at me as one of the fangs poked out of the left side of her lips. "I want you to read my mind."

"Are you sure?"

She moved my hand to the side, under her tank top and bra until the tips of my fingers brushed her nipple. "I am sure. Read my mind, tell me if you like what you see."

I nodded and dove in...

She was on top of me in my bunk, kissing on my neck and chest while she bounced on my cock. Sensations of pleasure washed over me.

"Can you see what I can do for you?" Her speed picked up as Hope appeared next to us. *"And I'm not a jealous lover, I can share, if she can,"* she added as she leaned over and pressed her lips to those of the silver-haired beauty. Seeing Hope and Addison kiss like that made my head race, it was without a doubt the hottest thing I had ever seen–

"Addison. Come to the bridge at once," commanded a masculine voice in her mind,

The vision of Addison and Hope kissing disappeared

abruptly, and was replaced by the mental image of a male lionkin that looked like her.

"Ughhh!!!" she roared as she stood up, freeing my hand from her chest. I sat there breathing heavily as she fixed her top and zipped up her flight suit. "Damn cockblock of a brother... Well, duty calls. Think about what you saw, and I'll see if I can help you with that," she said as she pointed to the bulge in my lap.

"Will do..." I gulped as I adjusted myself.

"When I get back, I'll introduce you to the squad. Until then, relax and get to know your surroundings," she ordered softly before leaning over and giving me a kiss on the same cheek as the other night.

She flashed me a smile as she left the balcony, and I was alone with my thoughts and a frustrated appendage.

"Do you need me to go over the rules again?" asked Addison as Hope and I stood in front of the small crowd that had gathered in the lounge. Spread out on the couch in front of us were the members of our air squad, the Black Lions. Filling in the spaces around them were the squad leaders of the fifteen other squads of the *Astral Communion*, and a handful of the pilots from those squads, who were mostly women.

Hope and I were the only two new pilots that were being added to the crew, so everyone on board already had an eight month head start on getting to know each other. I had taken part in weird hazing traditions and rituals before, but this one took the cake. It once again showed me how different Dione was from Earth, because no-one on Earth would take part in this in the open.

"Yeah, one more time for me please," I asked.

"Me as well," added Hope.

"I figured you would know this one," I projected to her.

"Nope! Each ship has their own weird games and traditions."

"The game is Answer, Drink or Kink!" Addison said from her perch on a bar stool behind the couch that held the rest of the Black Lions. "Flight Captains Barnett and Walker will be asked five questions each, one from each member of their new squad, so that means they will have to ask each other a question at some point. The member of the squad asking the question first must introduce themself, because this is a game to get to know each other, right?"

"Yeah!" shouted everyone as they hooted and hollered.

"When you are asked a question, you will have three options to choose from. You can answer the question, take a shot of the stone water or tell us a kink you are into."

A round of hoots and whistles went up around the room after she finished.

"I got it," I nodded, "but I have one more question, what is stone water?"

"A crazy strong liquor that does more than get you drunk," one of the spectators shouted.

"Its a strong alcohol that the Soothsayers of the Andona Theocracy drink to prophesize the future," Addison answered as she shook a bottle of clear liquid. She then handed it to a pantherkin on the couch who proceeded to set it on the table.

"Sounds delightful. Well I'm ready," I said to the crowd.

"As am I," Hope added.

"Very well." Addison proceeded to reach into a bowl, drawing a name. "Captain Cormer!" She then flipped a coin. "And your question is for...Captain Barnett!"

The only male on the couch stood up, he was a tigerkin with short orange hair and green eyes. He looked strong but also unamused by the whole situation. "Hello, I am Flight Captain Layton Cormer of the Black Lions, call sign Brainiac. Captain Barnett, how long have you been flying?"

Hope chuckled to herself, she had been preparing for the worst question ever, but had received a softball. "Nice to meet you Captain Cormer, I've been flying since I turned eighteen, so four, almost five years."

"Boring...Next!" Addison shouted as she dug in the bucket. "Captain Hagerty, you get to ask...Captain Walker! Take it away girl!"

The cute redhead squirrelkin from earlier rose from the couch, she was maybe five feet tall if you weren't counting her pointy ears. I actually think her fluffy tail was taller than she was.

She had a slender body, and was wearing chinos that fit tight to her small but strong legs. Up top she had on a black tank top that allowed me to see the freckles on the fair skin of her shoulder and the small cleavage of her petite chest.

"Hello again Captain Walker," she said with a melody like tone. "I'm Alyssa Hagerty, call sign Snoozer. I have a question about something that was said earlier. Commander Harris said the residents of the Citadel said you and Captain Barnett fucked like squirrelkin. Based on that, how many times have you had sex in one day?"

"Wow...ummm..." I felt my cheeks warm up as they turned red. Alyssa stared at me with a curious smile that made me feel like I was standing up there naked, but that's not why I was blushing. I wasn't a prude by any definition of the word, but what had me blushing was that every woman in the room, which was almost two thirds of the onlookers, wanted to know the answer as well. "I would say three, three times-"

"Four," Hope interjected.

I looked at her, then her mind flashed to a day we recently had off. "Right! It was four."

The women in the room murmured to each other, some nodding along and giving me smiles and winks.

"Impressive," Addison said before putting her fingers to her lips and letting out an ear piercing whistle, quieting everyone down. "Next, Captain Rose for Captain Barnett."

The beautiful and exotic pantherkin woman sitting next to Alyssa stood up. She was the first one of her kind I had seen since coming to Dione. She had lavender eyes and long purple hair that was braided and hung over one shoulder, but that wasn't the most unique thing about her. What truly stood out to me was her ink-black skin that looked like someone had tattooed her entire body. It matched the black fur of her tail and ears perfectly.

She was wearing the same outfit as Captain Hagerty, except her tank top was white and filled by a much larger chest than that of the squirrelkin. Her lean body moved gracefully as she stood, showing up off her delicious curves.

"Hello pup, I'm Lillian Rose, call sign Thorn. As a fellow predator, I want to know, have you ever accidentally eaten someone during a full moon?"

"Lillian!" Alyssa hissed as Addison slapped her hand to her face.

The room fell silent as everyone looked at Hope. Her eyes were wide, and her face turned pale. A memory that was from a few years ago surfaced. In it, she had hunted down a rabbit while in her wolf form, but woke up the next morning laying next to a female rabbitkins corpse.

She shuddered, grabbed a glass, and poured a shot of stone water, throwing it back before exhaling with a loud howl.

"You didn't say no," Lillian pointed out as she sat down. The room was still silent as all the eyes went back and forth between the wolf and the panther. Everyone knew the answer, but it seemed like Lillian had broken some unspoken rule.

"What about you?" I asked.

"What about me?" she asked smugly, "This is a time for us to ask you questions."

Her mind flashed two quick memories of her chasing down

horses while in her panther form. She had *accidently* done the same as Hope, twice.

"You didn't say no," I said as I smirked at her.

A chorus of "oohs" rang up around the room as Lillian glowered at me.

"Ok then...Oh look, it's my turn! And I get to ask Captain Walker!" Addison gushed. She stood up, still wearing her flight suit, but with the zipper open, exposing her cleavage. "Hey James, have you ever had a threesome?"

The atmosphere in the room livened up as everyone hooted and howled.

"Kink," I said. I could have answered honestly with a "no," but that seemed boring.

The room erupted with howls as many assumed that was a yes and I didn't want to answer.

"Nice," Addison said with a wink before going on, "Ok, tell us a kink you have."

"Well...legs. I love seeing a woman's legs, especially if she's wearing stockings."

My words had an effect on all the women in the room as they adjusted how they were sitting to draw more attention to their legs.

From there, the game sped up.

"Are you willing to share your man with other women?" Addison asked a swaying Hope.

"Yes, I am. I don't see a reason in hogging him to myself, but it has to be the right woman. No bitches," she added, shooting a side eye at Lillian.

Next was my turn to ask Hope a question. She looked at me with half-lidded eyes, the stone water making her look like she had taken three shots of whiskey in five minutes on an empty stomach. "Ear rubs or tail brushing?"

"Oh wow, that...that's the hardest question so far. Umm..." She tossed her head back and forth as she considered her answer, ears flopping each time before she excitedly gave me her decision. "Ear rubs! Because I can lay on you while you do it."

She then tilted her head toward me, staring at me with pouty eyes until I took one of her ears in my hand and rubbed it between my fingers. A chorus of "aww's" filled the room as the women couldn't help themselves.

Next was Hagerty, with a question for Hope, "Captain Barnett..."

"Call me Hope, you cute squirrel girl."

"Ok, Hope, how well endowed is Captain Walker?"

Most of the few men had left, so the room was mostly filled with women who had been quietly having their own side conversations, until now.

"How big is James? He's got a big dick, it's like, this long," Hope slurred as she held her hands shoulder width apart.

All the eyes in the room shot to me.

"Umm...she's over-exaggerating. It's not that big."

"But babe! Babe! *Babe*! It is big," Hope proclaimed, defending the honor I didn't need her to defend.

"Hello Captain Walker, I am Captain Cormer. Nice to meet you, how are you enjoying Dione?"

"I am enjoying it a lot, thank you for asking."

"Sit down Cormer, it's my turn," Lillian said as she stood up before Addison could announce if it was her turn or not. "Are you only into predators? Or does Snoozer have a chance?"

"Lillian!" yelped the blushing squirrel girl.

Lillian gave me a big shit-eating grin. She was proud of herself and seemed to enjoy living up to the call sign of *Thorn*.

"Who said I only like predators? I like all women, Captain Hagarty included," I said, as I smiled at the squirrelkin, causing her to turn as red as her hair. My expression then soured as I looked back at Lillian. "It's women who are bitchy that I can't stand."

Lillian's smile had dissolved into a look of annoyance as I subtly told her what I thought of her before she sat down in her spot, crossing her arms and pouting.

Addison rolled her eyes before looking at Hope. "So, the last question is for Hope to ask Captain Walker. Take it away wolf girl."

Hope bounced on her feet while clapping, before looking/falling into me. She looked up at me, her mind going in a million directions, but one question stood out, even to her drunk mind.

"Will you give me more head pats and call me your good girl this time?"

I smiled and hugged her tight, before taking a small step back and putting my hand on her head, patting it and ruffling her silver hair. "You are my good girl, Hope."

Her face lit up with a big smile and her silver tail wagged harder than I had seen it wag before.

"Awww," said the chorus of women in the room.

"Damn you two are cute," Addison said as she stood up and stretched. "This concludes Answer, Drink or Kink! Now take her to bed before she passes out where she is standing."

CHAPTER
TWENTY-FIVE

"I SEE you finally got your she-wolf in bed," Addison said as she saw me re-enter the pilots lounge. She was sitting in one of the sofas around a coffee table with Alyssa and Lillian still sitting on the couch that the whole squad had been on earlier.

Getting Hope into bed had been more challenging than it had ever been before. There were a few issues in our way that had not been there over the past month; one, we didn't have a private room; two, she wanted to have sex; and three, her bed was a top bunk. Somehow I stood my ground to her advances and was able to push her up and into her bunk, where she quickly curled up around her tail and passed out.

"Don't call her my she-wolf. She's my girlfriend."

"Same thing, just like I'll be your lioness one day soon," Addison added with a wink.

"Are you so sure about that?"

"Yes I am, I tend to get what I want. Care to join us for a drink?"

I looked at the table and was relieved to see that they were drinking whiskey, and not that ridiculously strong stone water.

"As long as it's whiskey, then I absolutely will," I said as I went to the sink and grabbed a clean mug.

"How's Hope doing?" Alyssa asked as I sat down on the sofa across from Addison.

"Oh, she's fine. She's curled up in a ball around her tail and sleeping it off. Y'all weren't kidding about how strong that stuff is."

"It's no joke, that's for sure," Addison agreed.

"It's not that strong," Lillian mumbled as she swished her drink around in her glass.

Addison jumped up and ran over to the cupboard. "Then let's keep the game going!" She grabbed the bottle of stone water and returned with four shot glasses.

The girls and myself made groans of protests, but she wasn't having any of it.

"This is the last night you can drink the good stuff on the boat, we set sail tomorrow and will be heading low to the Andona Theocracy. Our mission will be to assist them in holding off the Empire's attempts at invading the continent of the birdkin. What better way to ingratiate ourselves to their culture than to partake in their holy drink!"

"Somehow that makes sense," Aylssa said as she rubbed her forehead.

"I know I can handle it, but can captain big dick?" Lillian asked, throwing a thumb at me.

"If I can handle backwoods moonshine, I can handle this."

"I don't know what that is, but it sounds strong," Addison said. "Let's play a different game this time, how about... never have I ever?"

The three of us looked around before nodding in agreement.

"I don't mean to insult anyone's intelligence," Addison said as she sat forward in her seat, "but here are the rules. We each put up three fingers, every time you put down a finger, you take a shot of whiskey, when all three are down, you take a shot of stone water, and because he's new, James get's to go first."

All three of them looked at me as I thought about how I could get one up on them. Reading their minds had crossed my mind, but I decided to play fair. "Ok, never have I ever had someone pull on my tail."

All three put a finger down as they took a shot of whiskey.

"I like having my tail pulled," Addison purred in my direction.

"Someone get the spray bottle for the kitty in heat over there," Lillian muttered before looking at me and wondering if I even had a tail.

"I do not have a tail, Lillian," I answered with a coy grin.

Lillian froze and looked at me, then at Addison.

"Oh yeah, he's a minder, so guard your brains ladies."

"Of course he is," the pantherkin groaned. "Well then it's my turn, and I got one for our new *friend*. Never have I ever shot down a Thurnmar pilot."

"Glad to see you like to read the newspaper," I said to the pantherkin after taking my shot.

"A girl needs to stay up on her current events, especially when a strangely attractive man from another world is involved." She smirked.

"You think I'm attractive?" I asked the panther girl.

Her eyes went wide as her cheeks took on a purple hue. "I-No...well...I-I...it-it's not your turn to ask questions!"

The sound of an empty shot glass being placed on the table saved Lillian from further embarrassment. Alyssa had taken a shot and lowered her finger, and tried to sit there like nothing happened.

Unluckily for her, we all saw it.

"Oh? Did our little squirrel girl have a case of friendly fire?" Addison asked. "What happened?"

"Ummm...it was my first time seeing combat, and before I could pull the trigger, a pilot in our squad who was a rookie like me swung in front of me to steal the kill. I might have gotten a little angry and…"

"Sounds like he had it coming," Lillian said.

"Did he survive?" I asked

"Yes, he did survive. Now it's my turn anyways," Alyssa said, cutting off Addison who was preparing to ask something. "Never have I ever been shot down."

Addison and I both put a finger down and took a drink.

"I didn't know you had been shot down, Commander," Alyssa said.

"Same. The propaganda reels they showed before movies said you had never been shot down," Lillian added.

"Well that is the point of propaganda. I have been shot down twice, but they can't let the public know that the 'Starlet of the Sky' has been bested."

"That makes sense," I said as I rubbed the stubble of my chin. "You know, you girls keep trying to take me out but are slowly whittling down your own numbers as well."

"Well don't you worry about any more friendly fire ladies! I have just the one that will take out Mr. Human," Addison said as she sat up straight and prepared a glass of stone water.

"Never have I ever had sex!"

I put my finger down, but noticed that the girls still had their fingers up.

"Really?" I asked as I grabbed the shot Addison had prepared for me.

"Yes, what kind of girls do you think we are?" Alyssa asked.

"Ones that wanted to know the length of my dick and how many orgasms I have had in one day," I replied, staring down the red-headed squirrel girl.

"That's a fair assumption," she said with a laugh. "I'm just a girl with a healthy libido that is waiting to be satisfied by the right man."

"You and me both," Addison sighed.

"So...now that I'm done, are you three going to keep playing?" I asked as I brought the drink to my lips and prepared to down the drink that had knocked out Hope. I inhaled the strong citrus and botanical smell of the alcohol before throwing back my head and letting the clear liquid surge across my tongue and down my throat.

"Holy cow!" I wheezed as my voice came back to me after I swallowed the ridiculously strong liquid.

"Here, whiskey helps," said Addison as I stuck out my tongue, trying to get the sterile taste of the alcohol off of it.

I slammed back the shot of whiskey and shook my head as the familiar smokey taste of the brown alcohol washed away the blandness of the stone water. It had barely been a minute, but I could already feel the effects of the stone water grabbing a hold of me.

"Oh gosh, why? Why do y'all drink that?"

Before answering, the three of them had each poured a shot of their own and downed it before chasing it with a shot of whiskey.

"We drink it because it makes you feel good," Addison purred as she pressed her hands to her cheeks before rubbing herself from her neck to her luscious breasts.

"No, it's because it makes you feel warm," Alyssa said as she fanned herself off.

"Wrong! We drink it because we don't know any better!" Lillian added, flashing a toothy smile.

"No we do not," I said in agreement with a chuckle.

We all laughed at that and then sat in the silence that surrounded us. I checked my watch, it showed that it was just past ten, but no one looked like they were ready to call it a night.

"So how many kills do you girls have?" I asked as my head felt light.

"You know mine! Fifty three kills."

Alyssa raised her mug to the lioness. "That's why you are the wing commander. Six for me."

"And I am sitting at four, one away from Ace. What about you, Captain Human?" Lillian asked with a mocking tone.

"I'm looking for my seventeenth kill at the moment."

"Are you counting when you shot down Hope and her wingman on day one?" Addison asked.

"You did what?" Lilliana and Alyssa asked in unison.

"No, I'm not, because that was an accident."

"Hold on," Lillian screeched, "you mean to tell me you shot down that pup, and now you two are dating?"

"It was an accident," I groaned. "I also helped her escape from execution in the empire," I added.

"Aww, that's so romantic!" Alyssa said with her soft tone.

"Still, I call bullshit on you being a triple ace," Lillian slurred as she leaned forward. "There's no way you're a better pilot than me."

"It's not bullshit, and I am," I said, leaning forward and glaring back at her.

"I'd chill if I were you Lillian," Addison said, "I've seen him and Captain Barnett fly. They are both very skilled."

"Oh really? How many kills is the pup at?"

"Nineteen," I said.

"That girl is also a triple ace?"

"You didn't think I brought them on for James's good looks alone, did you?" Addison asked.

Lillian sat back, crossing her arms and pouting. The drunk part of my mind started to wander over to hers, just to see what little miss attitude was thinking-

"Don't even think about reading my mind."

"I won't," I said, relaxing into my chair.

The rest of the night went by in a blur. We spent the next few hours being goofy and talking way too loud about nothing in particular before we got the sign that told us we should call it a night. The sign was the heavy breathing of Alyssa, who was passed out where she sat on the couch and was using her tail as a blanket.

"James, you...you're gonna have to carry her," Addison said with a drunk laugh.

Addison and Lillian laughed after they tried to pick her up themselves, but failed. I was feeling the effects of the special drink, but not to the degree of the girls. Maybe it was because I was a man, or a human, maybe both? I wasn't sure.

I scooped up the little squirrelkin and carried her in my arms while the other two followed behind me. She was incredibly light and looked adorable as she wrapped her arms around my neck and buried her head into it, her breath tickling the skin under my chin.

"Which bunk is hers?" I whispered as we entered our squad cabin.

"The bottom one under your wolf girl," Lillian answered while she was doing more to carry Addison at this point than Addison was doing to carry herself.

I gently lowered her into the bed and set her down, but when I attempted to pull away, her arms were still wrapped around my neck. When I tried to free myself, her grip got tighter.

"Alyssa," I whispered, "time to let go and go to sleep."

"I don't wanna," she said as she shook her head.

"Alyssa, stop hogging him," Addison whined from behind me as she struggled to get undressed.

"Ok, but I want a kiss," declared the squirrel girl softly in my ear.

"Fine, but just one, and on the cheek," I said as I leaned in and gave her a little peck on her soft skin.

"Mmm, that felt nice," she said as she released my neck and gently fell into her pillow, snoring before her body came to rest.

I stood up and saw Lillian looking at me. "Let me guess, you want a good night kiss as well?"

"You wish," she said as she crawled into her bottom bunk on the far side of the room.

"I'll take a kiss," came a voice from behind me.

My eyes practically jumped out of my head when I turned and saw the busty tan lionkin sitting on my bed in her black bra and panties.

"Wow…"

"I take it you like what you see?"

"Absolutely I do."

She lifted her hand, curling her fingers in the gesture for me to come closer. Trapped by her gaze, I closed the distance between us, stopping just in front of her. The way her emerald eyes looked up at me froze me in place, yet warmed my soul at the same time.

Addison rose to her feet, grinding her body against mine as she did so until she was face to face with me. "I've been wanting to do this since last night," she whispered as she put her lips against mine. The kiss started out simple, but quickly evolved into something more passionate as our lips parted and our tongues met. She tasted like whiskey and cinnamon, and I loved it.

My hands grabbed her hips and pulled her body against mine, causing her to moan into my mouth. They then roamed up and down her back before settling on her perfect ass, cupping and squeezing her peachy cheeks while her lion tail swished back and forth.

I was ready to go further, when she pulled away from me. "Help me up into my bed."

I did what she asked, and lifted her up onto the bed above mine, where she sat with her legs dangling off the edge, spread just wide enough for me to get a good view of the wet black fabric between her tan thighs.

She reached down and gently caressed herself through the fabric, drawing a moan from her lips and an anxious grunt out of mine. I was hypnotized by the circular motion of her fingers, and could do nothing to look away, not that I wanted to.

"Do you want a taste?" she asked as she pulled the fabric to the side, exposing the puffy lips of her shaved pussy to me.

I inhaled deep and took in her scent. "I do. I really do."

"I know you do," she whispered, spreading her valley with one hand and rubbing her finger of the other against her clit and down into the tunnel of her sex, coating them with her slick juices before pulling them free. She extended her soaked digits toward my face, holding her fingers out for me to lick them. My tongue reached out and licked at the spiced nectar on her fingers, tasting her sweetness. I wanted more, but before I could take another lick, she withdrew her hand and rolled up into her bunk.

"Goodnight James," she said as she pulled her blankets over herself, taking away my view of her gorgeous body, and turning her back to me as she got comfortable.

"Wait...what?" I hissed.

"I said goodnight, Captain Walker," she said as she looked back over her shoulder at me and gave me a wink. She then laid her head down on her pillow and started breathing heavily like she was asleep.

"Ohhh, you're bad," I said as I sat down on my own bunk, taking a few deep breaths, trying to get my body back under my control before I laid down and closed my eyes.

CHAPTER
TWENTY-SIX

"CAPTAIN WALKER, *Rounder, what do you think of your call sign?*" Addison asked as we flew along the underside of the continent.

I don't like it.

"*Hmm, I guess you don't like it,*" Addison said.

I shook my head. *Yeah, that's what I said.*

It had been two days since the *Astral Communion* had set sail from Hopewell Port and set a course to move under the continent as we headed north east towards Andona. Addison wanted Hope and I to see how she preferred under patrols to be carried out while we were still within Thurnmar airspace.

It was simple enough, be aware that you only had two to two and a half miles of space between the ocean below and the floating landmass above you. Look out for the jagged pieces of greyosite that can protrude up to fifty feet out of the land mass above. Keep track of where the planes flying with you were compared to your position. Fly in long drawn out left and right banking turns that allow you to look down and scan the air out and below you.

"*What was your call sign back on Earth?*" The lionkin asked.

It was Yellow Rose.

There was silence for a moment before she spoke up.

"*You know what, I'm getting tired of looking at you,*" she said with an annoyed tone. "*Take up position on my backside. You can't ignore me if you're looking at me.*"

I'm not ignoring you-wait, can she even hear me?

This wasn't good. I did what she told me to do, dropping back behind her in our formation.

"James, what are you doing?" Hope asked.

She had been flying in the back and had to make room for me as I moved back and Addison took the lead.

"Addison is mad at me. She thinks I'm ignoring her, but I've been responding to her."

"Why can't she-oh no..."

"What?" I asked.

"I'm the only person you can talk with telepathically, remember when we connected in that jail cell back in the Empire?"

Oh crap, she was right. It had been so long since I needed to talk to anyone telepathically, except Hope, that I'd forgotten I needed to connect with Addison to communicate with her telepathically.

"Hope, you need to tell her."

"Me?"

"No, the other wolf girl I sleep with," I deadpanned. "Yes you! You're the only person on this planet I can talk to telepathically, it has to be you."

I could feel that she was worried about how Addison would respond.

"*Commander Harris,*" Hope said nervously, "*Captain Walker wants you to know that he can hear you.*"

The lionkin let out a mental growl before responding. "*Of course he can hear me, I'm projecting to him. He's the one being rude and not responding.*"

"*He's not being rude, ma'am.*"

"*Then why are you responding for him?*" Addison asked.

I could feel the tension in the air as Hope took a gulp and answered her. *"James can't talk to you telepathically because you and him don't have a...connection."*

"What?" Addison yelled, her plane visibly rocking. *"He's felt me up, and he's seen my snatch! How do we not have a connection?"*

"Excuse me?" Hope asked.

I wasn't sure if she had projected that to both of us, but I knew it was directed to me. *"It was after you passed out the other night. I should have told you."*

"That explains that smell. I thought it was odd you smelled like cinnamon."

"I'm sorry," I said to my silver-haired beauty, my heart racing as I started to panic about losing her. *"I should have told you."*

"Yes, you should have, but I'm not mad. I know she wants you, I just wanted to talk to her about it first."

"Really?" I asked.

"Stop ignoring me!" Addison screamed in our heads. *"If you two are having a private conversation about me, then you better fucking fill me in!"*

Sorry-crap.

"Hope, tell her we're sorry."

I felt Hope sigh from her cockpit. *"Commander, we're sorry. We were talking about something else, but not you."*

"Liar!" I projected to Hope.

"Fine! I just want to know how we got in the fucking air without knowing that James couldn't project to me?" Addison asked.

I thought for a moment on how to answer her respectfully.

Hope had a different idea. *"Because you didn't ask-"*

"I shouldn't have to ask!" Addison retorted, her plane rocking from side to side again. *"He's a fucking minder! What kind of minder can't communicate telepathically with anyone at will?"*

She had a point. I needed more training.

Things got quiet as we continued our practice patrol. While

we flew, I started paying more attention to the continent above us.

Some would expect the underside of the floating continents of Dione to look like the roof of a cave, jagged rocks, stalactites and a palette of brown and gray, but that was not the case. I was surprised to see vegetation, and a few small settlements hanging here and there around massive dark gray gemstones pointing down to the ocean with small airships mining them.

"So that's what greyosite looks like?" I asked Hope.

"Yes," Hope answered. "That's the mineral that allows ships to soar in the air when an electrical current is sent through it."

That magical rock was something anyone on Earth would love to get a hold of...shit, it was probably the resource Major-General Kampf had been referring to. A shiver ran down my spine as I thought of what the Nazi's could do with ships that could float on air and not need some hydrogen gas bag to keep them aloft. They could carry enough bombs on a single ship to make the Blitz on London look like a slap to the face compared to the punch that it actually was.

"James, be sure to keep an eye on your distance from Captain Barnett and myself as you swing your plane," Commander Harris projected, snapping me back to reality.

Yes ma-damn it, I cursed before reaching out to Hope. "Hope," I said with an irritated tone, "Please relay to Commander Harris that I understand, and I am fully aware of where you two are."

"Don't be snippy, you know she's as irritated by this as you are."

"Doubt it," I said to myself.

"Commander, Captain Walker said he understands and once again would like to apologize for this inconvenience."

"Liar!" I hissed at Hope.

"What is done is done," Addison replied, "at least he can hear me, which is even better because he can't say anything back... Hmmm."

There was a pregnant pause as I felt her mind working. I

was slightly trailing off her right wing, and was close enough that I could pick up what her mind was putting off.

"James, did you know felines are more flexible than canids?"

"Commander, that is a lie made up by your people and you know it!" Hope said frantically in defense of her own race.

"How do you know?" the sexy lionkin asked with a sultry tone. "I have yet to demonstrate my superior flexibility to you, or the handsome Captain Walker."

The two women had been bickering back and forth for the past two days, and I was the reason. It wasn't that they were angry with each other, or fighting over me, it was that both Hope and Addison wanted my attention. They both wanted it one hundred percent of the time, while having no idea how to handle sharing it fifty-fifty. I guessed there were no books in Dione on how two women or more should date one man, and I couldn't help them. On Earth, the only harem I had ever heard about was the one that was created by Genghis Khan, and I didn't know what was real and what wasn't in that story.

As the two women bickered about who was more flexible, I thought about cats and dogs back on earth.

We had a dog that lived with us while growing up, Duke, but there was a stray cat that my father had taken a liking to that slept in the pilot's seat of his plane while it was in the hangar. As I recalled, that cat had shown great flexibility when it came to cleaning itself, while Duke seemed to spin around in circles when trying to chew on his own ass.

"Hold on...can Addison-"

"James...James!"

"Yes, Hope, I'm here."

"Jeez, what are you daydreaming about over there?"

"I know what he's daydreaming about," Addison said playfully, her mind showing me just how flexible she was.

"No he was not!" Hope protested.

"Actually...I was thinking about cats and dogs back on Earth and how cats could lick all the way back to their-"

"Lalala, I can't hear you. Lalala," Hope screamed.

"What did he say?" Addison asked.

"Oh...umm-he was saying how he prefers canid style to feline in bed."

"Bull shit, no way he said that."

"What is a feline style?" I asked, but never got an answer as the two went back at it, arguing over the pros and cons of the two respective positions and making it hard for me to focus on flying.

Back on the *Astral Communion*, Addison was sitting across from me at one of the tables in the pilot's mess hall while Hope sat to my right. The lionkin's emerald eyes were locked on mine. We sat there, staring at each other in silence for minutes.

"Are you even trying?" she asked in her smokey tone.

"Yes, I'm trying."

"Then why isn't it working?" she asked, directing the question to both of us.

I leaned back in my chair and rubbed my face while Hope tried to recall what had happened that night in the Crestia jail cell. It felt like that night had been a year ago when it had barely been a month, although there were flashes in my mind that felt like it had happened yesterday. I did my best to recall that event, that moment we connected, when Hope stepped in for me.

"We were sitting across from each other, looking into each other's eyes," Hope said, pausing to think. "Umm...I know! I told him not to use his mouth and to only use his telepathic abilities, then I heard him-um and...he...um..."

Addison and I looked at Hope as she trailed off. Her face

was a bright crimson as she crossed her arms tight across her chest and chewed on her bottom lip.

"What did he say?" Addison asked as she leaned closer.

"He said I have beautiful eyes."

The details started to return as the fog that had been blocking those memories receded. The thread! There was a thread that I could see with my mind's eye when I was focused on Hope. I had to find that thread with Addison.

I reached across the table and took Addison's hand in mine. "Let's try this again."

"Yes, let's," Addison cooed in my mind.

I closed my eyes and took a few shallow breaths, clearing my mind and focusing on the mental images I was getting from Addison. It wasn't the first time I'd seen so clearly into her mind, and it was vivid and creative. I saw her looking at me, and felt her desire to have a connection as close with me as I had with Hope. She was used to getting what she wanted, and not having this link was starting to bother her.

I opened my eyes and looked into hers, and while I fixated on her green hues, I saw that thread and grabbed it...

"Your eyes are like emeralds."

Addison jumped as her eyes went wide. *"Go on, keep going..."*

Feeling emboldened, I decided to give her what she wanted.

"I want to taste your lips, feel your skin, and explore your body."

Her grip on my hands tightened as she started breathing more heavily. *"Yes! Yes! Don't you dare stop!"*

"There are so many things I want to do to you, but what I desire most..." I paused and looked up at the large round ears on her head, covered in soft tawny fur. *"What I want to do the most is take your ears between my fingers and feel how soft they are."*

"Oh, Captain Walker!" she cried, letting go of my hands and covering her ears as she turned away from me, blushing and giggling like a little school girl.

"James, you didn't..."

"He did! He asked to rub my ears!"

The mess hall got silent as all the pilots who had been milling around stopped what they were doing and looked at us. Now it was my turn to be embarrassed as I remembered that Dionian women didn't like having their ears talked about in that way, at least not in public. I tried my best to shrink into my chair, but there was nowhere I could go to escape their glares, or their thoughts.

I am not a pervert!

"Sorry," I whispered. "I guess I still need to learn to control myself."

"No no, it's fine," Addison said as she fanned herself and took a few deep breaths. Eventually the onlookers in the mess hall went back to minding their own business. "It's fine, just never had anyone be so forward with me like that."

"Really?" Hope and I asked in unison.

"Yes really. A lot of men and women are intimidated by my success and beauty. They think I need to be slowly courted, but James, wow, you just went for it."

"And I like it!" she said, switching to telepathy. *"I can't wait to make you all mine!"*

"Excuse me?" Hope interrupted.

Addison had sent that to both Hope and I and it did not sit well with the wolfkin. She moved closer to me, grabbing my hand as she let out a growl toward Addison. The lioness moved back in her seat due to the territorial display that the wolfkin was putting on, but she met Hope's glare with one of her own.

"Easy Captain Barnett. No reason to flash fangs in public."

Hope relaxed her face enough to stop snarling, but kept her eyes locked on Addison.

"I don't mind the flirting and the teasing," Hope said, *"in fact I enjoy the thoughts of him being with you, but this is one time you will not get your way."*

I looked from beauty to beauty as the conversation took place telepathically.

"I assure you that that was never my intention. I am fully aware that you and James have something more than puppy love between you two."

"What is your intention?" I asked bluntly. I didn't mind the flirting and the teasing ether, but I wanted to know where she planned on taking this. Was it a game, or did she want more?

Addison closed her eyes and took a deep breath, relaxing her face before continuing. *"I think it's obvious, James. I'm very attracted to you. The handsome you on the outside, and the sweet and considerate you on the inside. You're a caring and compassionate man, and Hope is lucky to have you."*

I squeezed Hope's hand. "That's kind of you to say."

"Yes, thank you Commander."

"I want that in a mate. I want you as my mate," she continued. But then she paused and took a deep breath, turning red before she added, *"And I want head pats!"*

"What?" I asked.

"I want head pats!" she demanded. *"We all saw the way you rubbed Hope's ears, jostled her hair, and then finished it with the gentle caress of her cheek before you kissed her forehead! Oh gods! James, please pet me like that!"*

I was at a loss for words as I looked across the table at the blushing lioness. She leaned forward in her seat as she stared at me with hopeful eyes, she desperately wanted me to say yes. Addison had just made this big declaration of her feelings, and it all boiled down to head pats? Is that what all Dionian women were starving for? A man who will rub their ears till their legs kicked while they drifted off to sleep? It couldn't be that simple...could it?

"Is that really all you want? Headpats?" I asked.

"I mean...I want more than that in the long term." She sighed as she sat back. "Thurnmarian men have grown lazy in their showings of affection. Many think that because there are so many women, they don't have to be sweet or caring, and the worst part is many women allow that."

Hope squeezed my hand. I could tell she didn't think I was like any of them, and the more Addison went on, the more her own feelings grew for me. I looked into Hope's golden eyes and a warmth filled me from the inside as I admired her. It wasn't love, not yet, but my silver beauty was getting closer and closer to saying it, and so was I.

"See...I want that." Addison said softly as she watched us.

I shook my head. "I want it too."

"As do I," Hope said before turning to Addison. "That just leaves one small piece of business that Addison and I have to agree on."

Addison and I looked at the wolfkin as she sat up straight, waiting for her to continue.

"If you truly want to pursue a relationship with James, then there are two things you must agree to. One, you must acknowledge that I am his alpha female, especially if and when he decides to add to his harem."

"Hmm...what if I want to be alpha?" Addison asked with a teasing tone.

"Then go find another man," Hope said out loud, showing her fangs again. Her ears stood tall and alert as she continued, "I was here first, I already have a connection with him that you're hoping will develop between the two of you. It only makes sense that I be his alpha."

The two stared at each other as they were locked in a silent battle of pride, but we all knew who would win. The most difficult part was going to be for the spoiled woman to admit that for once in her life she wasn't going to get her way.

"Fine!" Addison relented, breaking first and looking away while rubbing the back of her neck.

"Then say it," Hope demanded with a kind smile.

"You are James' alpha female. I am his beta."

I took a drink of water as the air around Hope settled. She smiled ear to ear while celebrating her success internally.

"Beta, yuck," Addison said with disgust like the word tasted disgusting on her tongue. "What's your second condition? You said there were two."

"Right, I get to have James' first child."

The whole dining hall turned to look at our table, again, this time because I was choking and coughing after Hope's declaration caught me mid gulp.

"Obviously," Addison said with a shrug, "you're his 'alpha,' so the honor of his first child should go to you. Besides, I'm not ready for a child yet."

"Hold on," I gasped after I made sure I wasn't going to drown, "you want to have a child?"

Hope looked up and smiled, her yellow eyes sparkling. "Not right now, but one day, yes, I want to be a mother...if that's what you want."

Worry filled her mind as she thought she had said the wrong thing to me, but it couldn't be further from the opposite. I wrapped my arm around her and pulled her into my chest, hugging her tightly. "I'd be honored to have a child with you, Hope Barnett. In fact, I'm kind of surprised I haven't gotten you pregnant already."

"You are?" Hope asked with a small laugh.

"Yes, we've had a lot of sex, any woman back on earth would be pregnant five times over by now."

Hope gave me a confused look before asking, "Is it that easy for humans to have babies?"

"Wow, the priests of your world must be mixing fertility elixirs all the time," Addison added.

"Easy? Fertility elixirs?" I asked while the three of us looked at each other with confusion.

"Yes," Hope answered, "you have to take a fertility elixir to get pregnant. Do humans not do that?" she asked as her eyes widened and ears stood up.

"No...hold on, do Dionians?"

They shook their heads in unison before Addison stepped in with an explanation. "The Gods of Dione didn't want the planet to become overpopulated, since our gestation periods are so different from race to race, and can span from two months with a rabbitkin to three months with canids like Hope, and four for felines like me.

"So the priests were given the instructions for creating a special elixir, one that they keep secret, and when a female Dionian takes it, it awakens her reproductive abilities and makes her extremely fertile-"

"And extremely horny and aggressive," Hope added.

"Yes, that too," Addison said as she continued. "In fact, you're required to chain up any woman who takes the elixir because she will become too ravenous and sexually aggressive. This is for her partner's safety as well because she *will* try and fuck him to death."

I sat there staring at them, wide eyed and mouth agape as I imagined what being "fucked to death" would feel like.

I would probably be dried up like a prune...

"Is he ok?" I heard Addison ask Hope.

"Yeah, he does this from time to time, just give him a second."

I shook away my thoughts and turned back to the girls. "So let me get this straight...you have to go to the church to get a magic elixir that makes you able to have babies, and it makes you salacious?"

"Yup," they both said in unison.

What the...what kind of world had I been teleported to? I had come to terms with the animal features, was beginning to understand the minder abilities and was intrigued by the full moon transformations of everyone around me...but this?

"That's wild." I chuckled.

"Is it? Because you just told us humans don't need this elixir, so y'all must be having babies like crazy," Addison pointed out.

Thankfully we had time for me to explain human reproduction and how conservative Earth was on the topic of sex compared to Dione. By the time I was finished, both women had looks of pity on their beautiful faces.

Hope shook her head, "That sounds miserable."

"Nine month pregnancies, and it isn't guaranteed?" Addison added.

"And the women keep themselves covered up? The men must hate it."

"The women must hate it! Not being able to show off to get a mate!"

"And they get...what did you call it...periods?" Hope asked.

"Yeah, I think he said every month, uhh, just kill me."

"Agreed." Hope nodded. "Definitely kill me over living like that."

I shook my head as the two of them wrapped their minds around Earth. Then a thought I had pushed away came to the surface. Would I ever see Earth again? Did I want to? Here I was a combat pilot and surrounded by beautiful women who were crazy about me.

On the other hand, on Earth I was an airshow pilot who never stayed in one place long enough to put down roots of any kind. Yes, my dad was still alive, but he wouldn't blame me for staying here.

A soft hand took mine.

"Hey, James, are you ok?" Hope asked.

"Yeah, sorry, I was thinking about back home."

"Oh...do-do you want to go back?" she asked, pulling her hand away and looking down at the table.

Oh crap. Her mind was starting to head down a dark path, and even Addison was looking away from me.

"Hope, I want to be wherever you are, and I want to have kids with you, but first, I have one condition."

She looked up at me with longing eyes.

"I want the mother of my children to be my wife. I don't want to have a bunch of bastards running around."

Her mind began to run wild and her eyes got huge as her tail started to wag frantically.

I smiled at her reaction as I continued, "This doesn't mean I am proposing, not yet, instead, think of it as a promise, to you, my...alpha female." That felt weird to say out loud. "When I'm ready to have a child with you, I'll make you my wife. How does that sound?"

"I do."

"Excuse me?"

"I-I mean yes, that sounds wonderful!" Hope said, pressing herself against me, the soft fur of her ear tickling my cheek.

Addison cleared her throat. "Don't forget about me." I could tell she wasn't used to being ignored, or coming in second to other women, but she was doing her best to not be the spoiled girl that everyone thought she was.

"Do you really think I could forget about you?" I let Hope go and leaned forward, taking Addison's hand in mine. "I promise that before we have a child, I will make you my wife."

"I do," she said, flashing a smile and a wink at Hope before looking back at me, "but you better take me on a date first."

CHAPTER
TWENTY-SEVEN

"DAMN IT FEELS *good to be in the open air again!*" I shouted as my Hak-17 climbed toward the blue heavens above.

Being able to climb my plane as high as I wanted without the limitations of a massive continent looming overhead was a more liberating feeling than it probably should have been. It had taken a week for the *Astral Communion* to travel the underside of Thurnmar to reach the open air between Midar, the home continent of Thurnmar, and Hightar, the home continent of the Andona Theocracy.

The entire squad was on patrol when we broke free of the shadow of the continent, and I wasn't the only one buzzing around. Our squad of six had been broken into two teams of three, a tactic that Addison said worked better than pairs of two. I was teamed up with Hope and Alyssa, and when they saw me pull up and climb once in the open air, they were quick to join me.

"The sky always feels so big after spending time flying under the continents," Alyssa said.

Hope pulled her plane up and spiraled toward the clouds. "I one hundred percent agree with you."

"You don't realize how small two miles are until you have to stick within a corridor like that for a week," I added. "It feels weird being able to pull up so high."

"Right, that was your first time. Now that it's over, how do you feel?" my silver-haired beauty asked.

"I feel like I never want to do it again. I recommend we take the high heading next time."

That earned an agreement from Hope and Alyssa before a new voice joined the conversation, "You know, taking the low heading under the continents is a better way to conceal fleet movements, and is the preferred method of cruising for navy's on both sides of the conflict."

I shook my head before replying with a polite tone, "Thank you Captain Cormer."

"You mean thank you captain buzzkill," Lillian prodded, jumping in on the conversation.

"Clear the minds and keep your eyes open Black Lions," Addison ordered, her tone more business-like as compared to her usual flirtatious nature. "Now that we're in open air, and leaving Thurnmar airspace, we could run into a patrol from the Empire at any time, so stay alert."

"Yes ma'am," replied the squad in near unison.

That meant that the patrols would mean something now, so I settled in to take it more seriously, but a part of me doubted I would see anything.

"Hey Captain Walker, want to make a bet?" Lillian asked.

"Sure, what you got?"

"If we spot an enemy patrol and I shoot one down before you, I get to rub your ears."

A chuckle came from all the squad members, even stick in the mud Cormer was laughing. One of the running jokes of the past week was how I wanted to touch everyone's ears. This was because asking that question seemed to be the catalyst that locked the thread in place that allowed me to communicate with others telepathically. After connecting with Addison, I needed to connect with the rest of the squad and the ship's air traffic controllers, I just didn't want to do it in public...again.

We had moved the connection process to the squad cabin so I could connect with the other members of the Black Lions without drawing the attention of the other pilots on the ship. I already had enough rumors about me running around the ship, and I didn't need to add to it.

Alyssa was the first one up, and she was amazingly receptive to the process.

"Alyssa, can I touch your ears?"

"Sure, as long as Hope is ok with it," she said with a wink.

I turned and looked at her, "She said she was ok with it if you were."

"Not right now," Hope said as she rolled her eyes.

"Rain check then?" the squirrelkin asked.

"Definitely," I said with a nod.

Lillian followed her. She sat in the chair across from me, and once again I quickly made the connection, asked the question and then received a quick slap to the face.

"Think twice before you ask me a question like that again," she hissed as she got up and walked to the other side of the cabin. Once she got to her bunk, I saw her steal a glance back at me. There was a strange hue of red showing on the cheeks of her onyx skin, and when we made eye contact she gave me a meek smile before turning away. What was it with that woman?

Next were the four women who worked as the air traffic controllers for the *Astral Communion*. They thought it was weird that I needed to make a connection with them first before I could communicate with them, but in their minds, they weren't complaining. Their reactions were the same as all the other women in this world, but because I didn't have any type of interaction with them before this moment, it was awkward as all get out.

The last person to come through was Captain Cormer, the only other man on the squad, and if things were awkward with women I had never met, it was twice that with him.

He sat down across from me and crossed his arms while the girls of the squad were trying their best to hide their laughter around us. It was hard to focus on him for two reasons, one, he was a guy, and I wasn't a fan of staring at guys, and two, his brain was not easy to access. It felt like he was putting up one of those mental blocks that I had come across when meeting high ranking officials, but it was crudely built.

"Captain Cormer, I can't make the connection if you have mental blocks up."

He squinted his eyes at me. "I don't know what you mean. I'm not doing anything to block you."

"Really?"

"Yes, but I'll try and relax my mind further if that will help you access it."

"Thanks...I guess," I said, pinching the bridge of my nose.

"You can do it babe." Hope giggled as she struggled to keep herself together. "Just tell him how pretty he is."

The other girls burst into laughter.

"It's probably not wise to mock a man who can read your minds and look into your most embarrassing memories," I said to them.

"Sorry," they said collectively before going silent.

I took a deep breath and reached back out to Captain Cormer's mind. When I came into contact with it this time, that poorly built wall was down and I could hear his thoughts, and was not surprised by what he used to relax. "*The Hak-17 Thunderdrum has a flight speed of 325 miles per hour, the current C variants are fitted with four .50 caliber machine guns with four hundred rounds per gun. The climb rate is...*"

Having enough of that, I quickly located the mental thread and grabbed it, opening my eyes and looking at Captain Cormer.

"Damn...this is going to suck..." I said as I dropped my head. *"Can I touch your ears?"*

"I'm sorry Captain Walker, but I don't like men in that way."

The whole cabin erupted into uncontrollable laughter as I died a little on the inside.

"Sounds like a deal to me, Captain Rose. But keep in mind, if I get a kill before you, I get to rub yours."

"Deal," she agreed before whispering, *"Like hell are you touching my ears..."*

And so the patrol continued as we pushed east out ahead of the warship, and sadly for both of us, we didn't spot anything. We also didn't spot anything during our patrols on the next day, or the one after that. By the time we had made it all the way to Andona and taken the under route below the small continent, there hadn't been so much as a distant spotting of an Imperial fighter or ship.

"That's how it is sometimes," Addison said as we undressed after another long and uneventful patrol. "But don't get lulled into thinking they aren't out there. Just when you relax, the Empire will show up."

After a few more days of no action, the *Astral Communion* entered a holding pattern. All patrols were canceled as all the air squads were called to the pilot's mess hall. Addison and a few high ranking ship officers stood at the front of the room while everyone settled into their seats. Usually meetings were held in the ready room at the front of the pilots quarters, but that room wasn't big enough for all the pilots at once.

I was sitting toward the front of the room with the rest of our squad, holding open the seat next to me, waiting for Hope. She was usually punctual, but today was running late.

"Made it just in time!" she said as she rushed to the chair next to me, plopping down and scooting it closer to me.

"Where have you been all day?"

"Oh, you know, here and there," she said as she waved her hands around. "Just walking around the ship...oh, some of the girls showed me where they like to go layout and get some sun on the upper bow below the flight deck."

"I see, and is that where you ran into some brown and purple paint?" I asked, rubbing away the smear on her neck with my thumb and showing it to her.

"Oh...umm...they were...painting the hallway on one of the decks, I must have gotten some on my hand and touched my neck and not noticed. Clumsy me, right?"

"What hall is being painted in these colors? Everything is gray."

"In the marine quarters. You know how they are," she said with a big smile that was begging me to stop asking questions. I wasn't ready to let her off the hook yet. I opened my mouth to speak-

"Attention!" Addison shouted, raising all the pilots to our feet. Her brother entered the room followed by a short petite rabbitkin woman who I assumed was his secretary.

"At ease," he said calmly, moving to the podium and waiting for everyone to settle down. This was the first time I'd seen the Captain up close, and I could see the family resemblance between himself and Addison. Like her, he had blond hair and sharp emerald eyes, but unlike her, he was taller, in fact, he might have even been taller than me, but with a less athletic build.

Ship Captain Nathaniel Harris was a rising star in the Thurnmar Navy, known for being a brilliant mind in the tactics of fleet maneuvers. He was also rumored to have a bit of a sister complex as well, not in the weird backwoods of Kentucky kind of way, but more in the spoil her rotten kind of way.

"As many of you are aware, it has been an uneventful voyage from Hopewell Port to just off the western edge of Andona. Now that we have made it this far, I can unveil our true mission."

His secretary turned out the lights, pitching the room into darkness before turning on the projector. Displayed before us was a map of the open air east of Andona and North of the Empire. There was a mark that represented where we were that was labeled "Waypoint Zulu" and south west of that, close to the twin peninsulas of Floray, in the north end of the Empire, were multiple markings in the oceans.

"We will be taking part in Operation Monolith, a multi-pronged attack on multiple Imperial fuel depots set up on well-defended core lands. It is no secret that Crestia has set their eyes on invading and conquering the Andona Theocracy, in fact, they have begun amassing their invading forces on the western side of Twins of Floray"

He pulled a telescoping pointing stick out of his back pocket and pointed at the western side of the peninsulas that made up the "Twins of Floray." He then pointed at the marks east of the land mass, and south of our waypoint.

"These markers represent the fuel depots we will be hitting. Some would say it is a foolhardy plan to attack Imperial targets while they have gathered so many resources nearby. However, others, myself included, believe that striking out at these valuable fuel depots could have multiple positive effects. Of those, delaying their invading force and destroying the valuable resources needed to carry out that invasion stand at the top.

"We have joined up with two other carriers, along with their accompanying escorts, and will carry out our first of many strikes tomorrow morning. Commander Harris will give you your squad instructions from here. This is the first military operation that the *Astral Communion* will take part in, and while some of you have seen combat before, this is the first time we will fight as a family. Do not let down your brothers and sisters."

His secretary scrambled over to the light switch, flicking on the lights and blinding us without warning. While our eyes cleared, Captain Harris collapsed his pointer and gave the room a salute. Without prompting, everyone rose to their feet and returned the salute before he exited the room. His secretary quickly scrambled after him and started commending him on how good his speech was before the door had closed all the way.

Addison took the podium her brother had vacated and began going through the plan for the attack we would be taking part in. I was glad we would finally get to see some action because I wasn't going to get any closer to my "One Hundred Kills" guarantee if we never saw any enemy aircraft. I had been wanting to get a proper measure of how good the other members of my squad actually were when it came to combat.

I knew what Hope could do, and Addison's reputation preceded her. All I had seen from the other three were that they could fly, but I had to trust that Addison knew her stuff when it came to recruiting pilots. This was her squad on the ship she was the wing commander of, and while it was her first posting, she seemed to be well prepared for the job.

"Operation Monolith will begin mid morning tomorrow. Be sure to get a good night's rest, and take care of any business that is going to make you sharp for tomorrow," she said, looking at me when she said it. "I need this entire air wing at one hundred percent. Understood?"

"Yes ma'am," the room said in unison.

Once dismissed, I turned to Hope who quickly gave me a kiss. "I gotta go! Got something I need to finish-handle...something I need to handle."

"Hope, is everything ok?" I asked

"Yes, why wouldn't it be?"

"Because you're acting strange," I said, placing my hands on her shoulders. "Are you in trouble?"

She gave me a comforting smile and leaned in to hug me. "Babe, everything is fine, I'm just in the middle of a personal project."

"Can you tell me about it?"

"Not yet," she said before pulling away from me quickly. "And please don't go snooping in my head. Here, snoop around in her head instead."

She grabbed Addison and pulled her in front of me before darting out the room. "I love you, see you later!"

Did...did she just say she loved me?

I felt my heart flutter at those words as I held on to the memory of how she said it.

"I love you too," I called out to her.

I didn't see it, but I felt her jump with excitement through our connection.

CHAPTER
TWENTY-EIGHT

ADDISON STOOD there in front of me, her eyes big as she was confused on what she was supposed to do. She started nodding her head, clearly a sign that she was having a private telepathic conversation with someone. When I listened in, I found that someone was Hope and caught the tail end of their conversation.

"*...please do this for me!*"

"*You know I am your commanding off-*"

"*You are also my beta! Listen, you wanted time with James, well here you go. Thank you! Love you! Bye!*"

With that, Hope cut off the connection and Addison let out a big sigh.

"Everything ok?" I asked, feigning ignorance.

"Yes, everything is just peachy," she replied, flashing me a well-practiced smile. "You know, you and I have not had a lot of one on one time recently."

"I'll say. For someone who claims to be one of my girlfriends, I tend to only see you when we go on patrols, or when I see you come to bed late or leave early."

Her smile dissolved and transformed into a frown. "I know. I've been a terrible girlfriend. It's just...this job has so many responsibilities, it's exhausting!" she said as she rubbed her face and let her body slouch.

I looked around and noticed the room had a lot of her subordinates in it. "Addi, maybe we should go somewhere a little more private if you are about to vent about your job."

She lifted an eyebrow as she looked up. "Did you just call me Addi?"

"I did."

"Hmm," she grunted, "I like it. Just don't use it in formal settings."

"Can do," I said with a wink. "Now about that private spot..."

She straightened up and tapped her index finger to her lips as she stared up and off into space. She was lost in thought for a moment before her whole face lit up. "I know just the place!"

The lioness took my hand and led me toward the bow of the ship. Our destination was one of the most breathtaking views I'd seen since I arrived in Dione.

"This is where I like to come to be alone and take cat naps," she said as we leaned against the guard rail.

Addison's spot was a secluded deck on the forward exterior of the ship, just below the flight deck. We needed a key to open the hatch that led to the walkway made of perforated steel that was barely wide enough for two people.

"Just how secret is this place?" I asked as I noticed a weather-tight chest next to a hammock that was hanging from the support beams of the flight deck above.

"There are only two people on this ship with this key."

"Let me guess, the other is your brother?"

She nodded. "My brother set it up for me so I could have my privacy on the ship if I ever needed it. He has his own private room, since he is the captain, and I...turned down my own private quarters."

"What was that?"

"I turned down having private quarters."

"Why would you do that?" I asked.

She shrugged. "I didn't like being so far away from my pilots. I had grown to enjoy the camaraderie I got to experience by being around everyone. So, I told him he could give it to one of his officers, and I was going to take a bunk in my squad room."

"Do you think being wing commander would be easier if you had your own private quarters?"

"Maybe. But the work would still be there, and it's not hard work, it's just tedious work."

"Tell me about it."

She took a deep breath. "Every day I have to approve squad patrols, look over maintenance reports to see what planes are in and out of commission, which is small seeing as we haven't seen any combat. Then I have to meet with my brother, inform squad leaders of changes, give briefings, yadda yadda yadda. James! I-I hate this job!"

She started breathing heavily as the anxiety of the job started to engulf her. Her mind felt like it was drowning. She had done so well at appearing to be on top of everything, but now I saw the side she kept hidden from everyone.

I closed the small distance between us and wrapped my arms around her, pulling her in tight with my embrace. She gladly accepted and tried to bury herself as deep into my chest as she could.

"You know I'm here if you ever need anything. You don't have to carry your burden as commander alone."

She didn't say anything, and while we stood there, I felt her body relax and the anxiety melt away. She started to purr a little, which was a sensation I was still getting used to, her being my first catgirl and all, but the vibrations were soothing in a way.

I moved my lips to her ear. "Are you feeling better?" I asked softly.

"Mhmm," she replied, nodding against my chest.

"Good, do you want to take a cat nap with me?"

Her purring stopped and she slowly looked up at me. "Yes, but you have to follow my rules for cat napping."

"Ok, what are they?"

She left my embrace and opened the chest on the deck. "Rule one of cat napping, you don't tell anyone about where I go for cat naps." She pulled two blankets out of the chest and threw them over the hammock. "Rule two of cat napping, you lay out soft comfy blankets to avoid rope burns on your skin."

"Rope burns? You're wearing clothes, how do you get rope burns?"

She let out a chuckle as she began removing her clothes. "Rule three of cat napping, one has to do it naked!"

Her green eyes watched me as she slowly undid the buttons of her tan officer shirt before throwing it back off her shoulders and letting her bountiful breasts bounce. My mouth slowly dropped towards the deck below while the lioness continued, lifting her tank top over her head, and then removing her green satin bra.

"I love how you look at me," she purred before turning her back to me.

She peeled her tight pants and panties down her legs at the same time, exposing more and more tan skin, bending at the waist so her apple bottom pushed toward me. Her tail made a playful flick as it freed itself from the tail hole in the back, bobbing its black tip in the air before settling down.

Her tail slowly swayed, allowing me teasing glimpses of her ass crack down to her smooth puffy pussy lips. My own pants were now tight from the sultry strip tease she had given me, but she wasn't finished.

Turning to face me, she reached behind her and unclasped

her bra, and rolled her shoulders forward, freeing her voluptuous breasts with a bounce. I licked my lips at the sight of her large pink nipples. They sat perfectly on top of their own tan mountain.

She was deliciously fit and curvy, and I had to have her.

"Care to join me?" she asked after stashing her clothes in the chest and jumping into the hammock.

I began to remove my own uniform, choosing to let my actions be my answer. She watched me as I stripped down and crawled into the hammock with her. I sank into the blanket and the webbing, and Addison brought her legs up and over mine, curling into the space between my arm and the side of my body as best as she could. I helped her out by wrapping my arm around her, allowing more of her soft skin to make contact with mine while she wrapped us both in the blanket.

"It's beautiful up here," I said softly, taking in the panorama before me. Out in front of us was nothing but blue sky, clouds, and the waters of the ocean core below us. Fresh air blew against us in the form of a gentle breeze, rocking our hammock.

"I know. It's even better because the ship is at hold and no patrols are being conducted."

"Is this where you sleep when you don't come to bed in the squad cabin?"

She shook her head. "I didn't know you were keeping that close of a tab on when I came to bed."

"I wouldn't say I was trying to, it's more that I'm a light sleeper and stirred enough to see you undress and pull those long legs up into the bunk above me."

"But you've been watching me?" her raspy voice asked with a playful tone.

"Guilty."

"Good," she said, adjusting so our legs became more tangled and my growing erection lodged between our lower stomachs. She let out a soft sigh and pressed her chest firmly into mine as she relaxed in my arms.

"Do you always nap naked?" I whispered into her ear.

She let out a cute little laugh before answering, "Yeah. Your girl is a bit of an exhibitionist."

"Nothing wrong with that."

The gentle swaying of the hammock mixed with the heat of her body and the gentle purring she created made my eyelids heavy. I saw why she came here for her cat naps and found myself falling asleep with her in my arms.

I'm not sure how long I was asleep, but the sensation of gentle licking, kissing and sucking at your neck was without a doubt the best way to wake up. As I stirred, I became aware of the sensation along the shaft and tip of my cock. Her soft fingers gently caressed my length, ending at the tip where she massaged my swollen head. She was a wonderful little tease.

"Good morning..." I said, still half asleep.

"More like good afternoon," Addison giggled.

"Are you enjoying yourself?" I asked, looking into her emerald eyes.

"Very much, especially if you enjoy it."

"I do."

"That's what every girl likes to hear," she said before leaning into me and pressing her lips against mine and seeking out my tongue. As we kissed, her hand worked harder and faster at stroking my shaft as it was nestled against the heat of her slit. My free hand found a toy of its own to play with, grabbing a hold of her large breasts and kneading them in my grip.

We both moaned as the ecstasy of each other's touch washed over us. The pace at which we made out went from sweet and gentle to passionate and energetic. I had wanted to claim this girl since the night she first teased me, and here I was, ready to bury myself deep within her and make her mine. Make her a part of my growing family.

I pulled my hand free from her breast and reached down to guide my hardness into her waiting pussy, but when I thrust forward with my hips to enter her, she moved with me, keeping my sword from impaling her. My eyes opened as she continued to back away from me and sit up, allowing the blanket to fall off her shoulders and expose her skin to the sunlight.

"Easy there stud. You don't gain entry just because you woke up."

I nodded my head in agreement while I took in her beauty. The silhouette she cut into the setting sun behind her was a masterpiece to behold. Her full chest raised and lowered with every deep breath she took, her pink nipples ready for attention. As I admired her, she made a gesture for me to rotate my body so I was laying on my back across the length of the hammock.

"Have you ever had sex in a hammock?" she asked.

"Can't say that I have, have you?" I replied as I got myself situated the way she wanted me.

"No, though I have read a book written by early sailors who were very experienced in the act. The ships back in the helium days before greyosite were much smaller, so the sailors slept in hammocks to save space."

By now, she had spun so she was sitting on my stomach with her back to me. I reached out and rubbed her tan skin, running my hands down her muscles to the base of her ass and slender tawney tail.

"I'd like to read this book so I can learn their ways."

"No need. I've read it enough for the both of us, I've just been waiting for the right man to practice with. I think we should start with what they call the *Dog's Instinct*," she said as she moved her hips back toward my head.

I quickly got the idea of what she was doing and helped guide her knees out to the side of my head, and lowered her beautifully smooth pussy down onto my waiting face, opening my lips to meet her lower ones with a passionate kiss. As my tongue licked out and split the folds of her slit, I felt her grab the base of my cock and stand it up at attention before her lips met the tip and opened for my swollen head. She sucked and toyed with the tip of my dick before lowering her mouth further down my shaft. The slick heat of her tongue and throat soon gripped all of my length.

A moan escaped my lips but was muffled out by the grinding of her wet valley against my face. My tongue explored her folds and lapped up at her nectar. It was a sweet taste, and one I had on my mind since that night she had given me the smallest of samples. The sample had been great, but now the entire buffet of her pussy was at my lips and I wanted it all!

Our moans mixed in the breeze as we both eagerly licked and sucked on each other's sex, neither wanting to stop, both wanting to bring the other to the peak of our pleasure. I was going to be the first to break, her tongue was something else. It was moist and warm like any woman's tongue should be, but each lick felt like it was tugging and pulling at the sensitive parts of my cock, and I was ready to explode.

I groaned out a warning that I was close, pulling her soaked pussy from my lips long enough to warn her.

"Good!" she said, releasing me and letting my orgasm-loaded cock slap against my belly while she pressed her whole weight into my face. "How about making me cum while junior takes a break."

My cock tensed in the cool breeze, twitching for the last bit it needed to release, but it wasn't enough. I wanted to press her off me to protest, but found I didn't have the leverage to move her like I would have had on a bed.

Oh, this tease!

If she wanted to cum, I was going to make her gush.

I reached around and spread her lips wider, giving my lips and tongue deeper access to her inner tunnel while my fingers massaged her clit. Her pearl was flicked, rubbed and pinched while she bucked her hips. I let her moans and the feedback from her mind guide me, staying with what got the best reaction. After a few minutes of this, I felt her thighs grip my head like a vice and heard her let out a roar....

"Nyah...by the gods! That's it-that's it...ohhh.....ohh...."

My face was smacked with a rush of her fluids as she came on my lips, soaking me with her juices as she collapsed forward. She disconnected her pussy lips from mine and lay on top of me, my still hard cock now nestled between the cleavage of her breasts. Her body was starting to relax from the waves of her orgasms that had washed over her, but I wasn't going to let her get out of this that easily.

Her ass was still up in the air, leaving her dripping and tensing pussy exposed to me, and it was begging to be touched some more, so I gave it what it wanted.

"Ohh...fuck, babe, let me c-catch my...ohhh..." she cried out as my fingers began to blast at her slit. I started with two, my index and middle finger, while my thumb rubbed at her pearl. She moaned like a lion in heat as I coaxed repetitive orgasms from her. By the time I let her catch her breath, my cock was twitching aggressively between her cleavage, begging for a release of its own.

"What's the best position for the finale?" I asked.

"Umm...hold on, let me think," she said while still trying to catch her breath.

Since we were already making skin to skin contact, I let myself dive into her mind, and I didn't have to go far. On her surface thoughts were the drawings from the book she head read, over fifty different spicy depictions of how to fuck in a hammock circled around me, and they all looked like a lot of fun. However, one stood out because it would be easy for us to get to from how we were laying already.

"Let's see how much fun this jaguar position is." I growled.

Her tail stopped the hypnotic swishing it was doing and froze in mid air, she slowly turned and looked at me, pushing sweat-soaked hair from her face. "Truly? That's the position you chose?"

"Yes, is there a problem?"

"Not at all, it's the one I've wanted to try most!"

She crawled forward in the hammock, letting my cock drag along the soft and slightly damp skin of her stomach until it peeked out from between two red wet lips. She raised herself up so she was sitting on my hips while slowly grinding her soft wet folds against my throbbing shaft, looking back at me over her shoulder as she did so.

"Are you ready? Stud?"

"I've been ready since the first time I saw you."

She reached between her legs and grabbed my cock while she pressed up on her knees, rising to get the distance needed to guide my length into her tunnel. Her smooth lips greeted the tip of my rod as they parted to allow me to enter. She slowly impaled herself, inch by inch, until the base of her ass was resting on my hips again before gyrating and feeling me move inside her damp folds.

"My gods, it feels even bigger than it looks," she cooed.

I grunted a "thank you" that was quickly transformed into a moan of pleasure as her internal muscles squeezed on my shaft.

Her hips started to move front to back as she slowly pulled herself forward till she had a hold of my ankles. Now her front to back motions translated into up and down ones as she bounced her hips on mine, causing her ass and tail to jiggle in front of me. It was a sight to behold, and a feeling to embrace! She knew just how high to rise before slamming herself down on my cock again and again.

I grabbed her ass as she picked up speed and aided her in slamming down on my cock harder and harder. My mind was spinning but wholly focused on my organ deep inside the sexy lioness' tight folds. I wanted the feeling to last forever in this ecstasy, but I knew that I couldn't. She wanted to milk me for every drop, and I wanted to give it to her.

I moaned her name over and over, screaming it to the heavens and whatever deity might be listening, or watching.

"I-I love when you scream my name! Make me yours! Make me yours!" she screamed with me.

My hips began to match her movement as we bounced in the hammock and tested its resilience, and what had simply been the healthy sound of two people making love turned into thunderous claps of fucking as our now moist skin slapped against each other again and again. I was going to claim her, here and now.

I grabbed the base of her tail as my balls tightened and clawed at her perfect back as my cock erupted like a geyser inside her. I felt her body shake in what I now knew was her signature display of an orgasm. My lap became drenched as our rhythm fell apart and she slumped back on to me, my cock still emptying the last of what I had to give into her tight pussy.

We lay there, her back on my stomach, my arms wrapped around her and my cock still inside her as she refused to let me go. The breeze rocked us as we caught our breaths, and a shiver from my lioness told me that the sweat left on her skin from our love making was now making her cold. I wrapped the blanket around us as she moved to a more comfortable position at my side, both turning to hold each other.

"So cat nap, and then let's get dinner?" I asked.

"No," she answered lazily, "cat nap, then round two, then another nap, then round three. I'll have my brother bring us food and leave it at the hatch."

I didn't have to look down to tell she was being serious. "You are so spoiled."

"I know, and you're going to enjoy spoiling me."

CHAPTER
TWENTY-NINE

THE GENTLE SNORING of the lionkin laying on my chest slowly pulled me out of my slumber. Sleeping in a hammock, naked, with my arms wrapped around a beautiful woman was amazingly tranquil, and I highly recommend it to anyone who was considering trying it. The gentle rocking as we swayed in the breeze had lulled us both into a deep sleep...after we were worn out from spoiling each other.

As I became more alert, my eyes began to lazily scan my beautiful partner. Her golden locks were splayed over her back, free of the double braid she usually kept them in. The sultry face she always wore around me was now at peace and relaxed, decorated with slightly smeared makeup that did nothing to take away from her beauty. My eyes followed a path past her exposed shoulder, down to the dimples of her back, to her luscious peach of an ass and tawny tail with its black tuft of fur at the tip.

While I admired her, I became aware of her soft skin pressed against mine, her tits pushing into my stomach, her thigh resting over my cock, which was more awake at the moment than I was.

Damn morning wood, that little guy was never satisfied, god love 'em.

"I feel someone trying to wake me up," the sleepy voice of my lover said.

"He has a mind of his own. I was content watching you sleep."

"Aww," she said as she lifted her head and looked up at me with heavy eyes. "But now that I'm up, and you're up, how about we get in one more for the road?"

"I think you're being greedy," I groaned. "My spirit is willing but the body is sore and needs sustenance."

"I'm all the sustenance you need," she said as she crawled on top of me and buried my face between her lovely mountains.

My hands reached out and took them in my hands out of instinct. I was ready to give her what she wanted when the sounds of a commotion in the hangar deck below us reached our ears. It didn't seem like anything to be worried about, but all the voices belonged to women, and they were hooping and hollering as though a male model was walking around shirtless.

"What is going on down there?" Addison asked as she leaned out of the hammock and looked down. She couldn't see what was going on, her spot was protected from prying eyes, but curiosity had gotten a hold of her.

While we got dressed, the ruckus grew louder, and now I swore I could hear men's voices mixed in with the women. I listened to the thoughts of the crowd below us and started to put together that there were some paintings that had been done on the side of some planes. Everyone was calling out to their friends to come to the hangar deck to see them.

Lillian was the first to reach out to us. "Hey Commander, are you and the human awake?"

"We're up. What's going on in the hangar?" Addison demanded

as she stashed her blankets in the chest and nodded for me to follow her.

"Well...I could tell you, but showing you would be so much more fun. Hurry up! You gotta see what the pup did."

Lillian only called one person "pup."

"What did she do?" Addison asked me.

"I have no idea." I shrugged.

She gave me a look that said she didn't believe me.

"I honestly have no idea. She asked me not to go looking in her mind, so I didn't."

Addison rolled her eyes at me as we stepped out her secret door into the corridor.

What did that girl do?

The stairwell down to the hangar deck was busier than usual, but the crowd moved quickly since everyone was heading to the same spot. Once we stepped out on the deck, I looked across the cavern of planes with their wings folded up and saw where everyone was gathering. They were splitting into two groups and encircling two planes, one plane surrounded by men, the other by women.

As we got closer, those who had already seen what they came to see passed us with their eyes focused on me as they walked by. Stray thoughts came across my mind as they went by. The men were jealous of me and wished they had a girl like that, while the women wondered how they could get some alone time with me and if I really looked like that.

That?

"Babe! I was wondering when you would make it," Hope shouted as she ran up and jumped into my arms, smothering me with a good morning kiss. "You smell like sex. Did the commander do a good job at distracting you?"

"You could say that again," I said as Addison blushed and fidgeted under our gaze.

Hope moved over and hugged the lionkin. "Good job, my trusty beta! I knew I could count on you."

"Don't call me that in public!" Addison hissed.

"Aww, you're no fun," Hope teased. "So how was he?"

"Captain Barnett!"

That didn't stop her as she continued to tease the blushing lionkin. Hope seemed to be in rare form this morning as she was jittery with energy, and looked exhausted. Her face, hands and arms were covered in little smudges of paint, and some had even gotten on her tail, but it didn't seem to bother her.

"I guess you got your personal project finished?" I asked.

"I did, come on!" she said as she grabbed my hand. "Let me show you your plane!"

Hope led me toward the plane with the tail number that I had been assigned, guiding us through the men who had gathered around the aircraft. She shouted at a few to move or she was going to bite them, which got us to the front of the crowd quickly.

"Ta-daa!" she shouted, holding out her hands with the familiar gesture that accompanies that phrase. I was silent for a moment as my eyes took in the painting before me. She had painted a pinup of herself on the side of my plane. It wasn't bad, in fact, it was really good!

She was wearing a purple bra and panties, a matching garter belt attached to ripped stockings that ran down her sumptuous thighs to her exposed feet. She had on her aviator's jacket while giving a salute and a playful smile to the spectators. Her silver hair and tail were pulled back by the rushing wind as she straddled a falling bomb like she was riding a bucking bronco with the words "Fox Catcher!" written out below her.

"How did I do?" she asked as she stood next to the plane and gave me the same salute she had painted herself giving on the plane.

"It's...wow. You never told me you could paint...This is awesome!"

"So you like it?" she asked, her paint-covered tail wagging as she bounced over to me, staring at me with full hopeful eyes.

"I love it," I answered, leaning down to give her a kiss before pulling her in for a big hug.

She melted into my grasp, happy that I was praising her.

"Hey Hope," Addison shouted as she interrupted our embrace. "I noticed you only painted one side of the plane. What do you say to painting me on the other side?"

Hope looked at Addison, then back at me. "Is she worthy?"

"Hmm, I'll have to think about it."

"Think about it?" Addison huffed. "What is there to think about after last night?"

"I said I'll think about it," I repeated as I walked up to her and gave her a pat on the head. "I mean having a girl painted on the side of your plane after only knowing her for a couple weeks seems kind of fast. I usually wait a month before giving her that honor."

I'm not sure if Addison was aware that I was playing with her, but she nodded her head with a determined smile. "Fine! But in thirteen days, these tits," she said as she grabbed her breasts, "and this ass," she added as she slapped her butt, "are going on that plane!"

"I think that's doable. How does that sound, Hope?"

"Sounds like a plan!"

Having settled that, I turned to the crowd of women that were two planes over. "So if you are painted on my plane, does that mean..."

"Yup!" Hope said with a big smile that said she was proud of herself.

"Hope, you didn't," I asked.

"I did, do you want to see?"

"Shit, might as well," I said, throwing up my hands. "Lead the way."

Hope took my hand again and led me to her plane while Addison fell in behind us. The crowd of women was much larger than the crowd of men, and as we approached, they got silent and made a path. Their eyes locked on to me as some stood there with their mouths open, others licked their lips, and a brave few tried to reach out and grab at me for attention. Addison and Hope were both quick to slap their hands away.

We got to the front of the crowd and I froze, my eyes wide with shock as I processed what I was looking at on her plane. It was...me...a very well done painting of me. My muscles were larger and more well defined than I thought they were, and my hair was long and flowing, like some Swedish man I had met once back in England. I was leaning against a wooden fence with my hands behind my head wearing Hope's interpretations of cowboy boots and a cowboy hat with a pair of white boxers and the words "Wolf Tamer" painted out below it.

I felt awkward as I looked at the painting that stood before me. To make matters worse, the more I looked at it, the more details I picked up. From the sweat dripping down my skin to the massive bulge threatening to escape the white boxers. I was flattered and embarrassed.

"Wow..." I somehow managed to say.

"Wow?" Hope asked anxiously.

"Wh...wh..."

"...Wow, that looks amazing, right?" Addison said from behind me.

"Thank you Addi-I mean Commander Harris," she said, accepting the praise.

"Yeah...Wow...Amazing..." I said, still in shock.

Addison stepped forward to get a closer look. "We need to talk about getting one of these on my plane."

"Wait...what?" I asked, finally snapping back to reality. "You want one too?"

"Absolutely I do, maybe not in this pose, but in a different one, like in a hammock?"

The ladies around me nodded in agreement, a few going as far as to throw out some suggestions of their own...

"He could be carrying an ax like a lumberjack."

"Or working on some pipes!"

"He can work on my pipes."

"He should be bent over wearing an Oshory Kilt!" a familiar voice shouted. I looked over towards that voice and saw Lillian for a split second before she ducked out of my field of view.

"Can you do my boyfriend?" one woman asked Hope.

"Oh, mine too!"

The women around me started swarming forward to ask Hope if she could do a painting for them. I could see that she was happy to have positive attention, but was starting to get overwhelmed and looked at me.

"*Babe, help!*"

When your lady asks for help, you help her.

"Ladies...Ladies!...LADIES!!!" I yelled as loud as I could.

The hangar got quiet as the woman turned to look at me.

"Thank you. Captain Barnett would be more than willing to paint pin ups on your planes, however, it won't be free and it won't be today. Please come and find her after the operation to make an appointment."

The throng of women were understanding and soon dispersed, allowing a group of men who had been waiting in the back to move toward us.

"Same applies to you guys as well," I said before they got too close. "Set up an appointment and she will get to you when she can, *after* the operation."

They nodded in agreement and went back to their duties.

"Thanks babe!" Hope said as she hugged me tight. "You're the best."

"You know I'd do anything for you."

"What about me?" Addison asked, not wanting to be left out of the moment.

"Yes, you too," I said as I grabbed her and pulled her into the hug.

I really would have done anything for them, and I knew that they believed me when I said it. I couldn't fight all their battles for them, but I could support them and help them where and when they needed it.

"So since I'm now officially in the pride, I get my painting first and for free, right?"

"Pride?" Hope and I asked in unison.

"Yeah, pride! It's what we lionkin call our family."

"I know that, but why do you assume we would be a pride and not a pack?" Hope asked.

"Wishful thinking," Addison said.

"James hasn't told us what his family will be called, but also he hasn't asked us to join it. Right now, we're just two girls he's sleeping with," Hope said as she shrugged her shoulders.

Addison took a deep breath. "By the Gods, you're right. Hope!"

"What are you two getting at? Do you two need me to ask? I figured y'all already knew."

"Of course you need to ask!" Addison growled. "It's not polite to assume."

"If you didn't ask, then any girl could claim to be a part of your pack," Hope added as she dropped her ears. "Then it wouldn't be special."

"Right, but you don't have to call it a pack–"

"Or a pride," Hope said as she interrupted Addison.

"...correct, or a pride. You need to call it whatever you humans call a group of humans."

I rubbed my chin as I thought about what she asked. I knew about the names for the groups of a few animals. Dogs and wolves were packs, lions were prides, crows were a murder and monkeys were a troop, but what did we call a group of humans?

"I got it!" I said when it hit me.

Both girls leaned in close to hear what I had to say.

"There is no set name for a group of humans, but if I had to choose, I want us to be a clan."

"A clan?" Addison asked.

"Yes, a clan. It's a large collection of families, all with one common interest. The vikings used them back in my world and they were bad ass."

"Vi-Kings?" Addison repeated.

Hope tapped a paint-covered finger to her lips before speaking up. "The Walker Clan...I like it."

"It does have a ring to it," Addison agreed. "Now all you have to do is ask us to join."

"Ok, do you two want to join my clan?"

The looks I got said the two women were not amused by my basic proposal. I scanned their minds and saw that it needed to be more formal than that, so I took a step towards them and took a knee. "Hope Barnett, you were the first honest person I met in this world. You've been loyal to me every step of the way since we started talking about planes. I cherish every moment spent with you and can't wait to spend many more."

I then turned to Addison. "Addison Harris, it's been a short but enlightening time. You keep me on my toes with your constant flirting and teasing, and I hope you never grow tired of spoiling me, just as I plan to never grow tired of spoiling you."

Standing, I extended my hand to both of them. "Hope, Addison, would you do me the honor of joining my clan?"

Hope smiled and wiped away a tear before dropping to her knees in front of me and taking my hand. "I, Hope Barnett, accept and promise to be loyal to you for forever and always."

"I also accept," Addison said as she lowered herself to her knees and took my other hand, "and I promise to spoil you as much as you spoil me," she added with a cheeky grin.

That seemed a little more formal than I thought it needed to be. I helped them both to their feet before giving each a deep and passionate kiss. I then took one in each arm and led them off the hangar deck. "I'm starving! Let's get some breakfast."

"Hey Addison, do you think there's enough time to fill out the name change forms before the operation?" Hope asked after a moment.

I looked at her with a puzzled look.

Why does she need a name change form?

"I don't think so, but we can do it after we get back," Addison answered.

"Ok. Hope Walker," she said as she hugged me tighter. "I like how that sounds. It sounds like they were meant to be together."

"Ohh, so does Addison Walker! I'll have to let my brother know!"

"Hold up...what just happened?"

CHAPTER
THIRTY

"*SHOULD* we have the party on the ship or on land?" Hope asked Addison and I as we flew in formation with the rest of the squad.

I shook my head. "*I think we should focus on the mission first so all three of us are still alive to make it to the party."*

"I'm going to have to agree with our husband on that one, Hope," Addison replied. "*We will work out the details after we land."*

"Fine, but I like how you called him our husband!"

"I know! I got chills after I said it!" the giddy lionkin said.

I shook my head and focused forward. By Dionian customs, I was now a married man with two beautiful wives. Apparently, asking a woman to join your harem was the same as asking her to marry you back on Earth, the big difference being Dionians didn't see a reason for engagement periods or weddings. In Hope's words, "Why put it off? You asked, we agreed. You are our husband and we are your wives." All that remained was to fill out official paperwork and announce it to everyone so we could have a party and get gifts, and the sooner the better apparently.

Addison's brother was the one who had insisted we put off announcing it to everyone. It made sense to me, having his sister/wing commander change her name the day of a major operation was unprofessional.

"Your brother didn't seem to be happy that you got married so suddenly," I said to Addison.

"He'll get over it," she replied with a mental shrug. "He is a little mad that you didn't ask his permission first, but understands since you're not from this world."

"I'm guessing you left out the part where you tricked me into asking," I said to myself and the instrument panel in my cockpit. It didn't really bother me that much, I was head over heels for the two of them and felt a warm feeling inside when they called me their husband, or I called them my wives. Still, I didn't like having someone being mad at me for something I wasn't aware of.

Shaking my head, I re-focused on the mission at hand when Addison called out to all squad leaders. "This is Wing Commander Harris to all squadrons, check in for final approach, we're five minutes out."

We were part of a two pronged attack with two other carriers, the *Vision at Night* and the *Blue Snow*, as well as their escorting ships of our combined strike groups. The wings of the *Astral Communion* and the *Vision at Night* were carrying out this strike while the fighter wings of the *Blue Snow* stayed back and protected the carriers.

The plan was to escort the six rocket bomber squads of the *Astral Communion* and watch their tails while they launched their dual one thousand pound rockets at their targets. Once they were done, the escorting fighters were allowed to conduct mop up strikes on any target of value. Fighters, fuel tanks, radar stations, ships, you name it. We would have ten minutes to make the best use of our loaded ammo before hightailing it back to the carriers.

I focused on my breathing as I heard the squad leaders check in with Addison. We were getting closer. Intel gathered by the early morning scouting run did not expect there to be a large defensive force because the Empire wouldn't expect an attack out there. However, you should always be ready for the unexpected.

"*Three miles out, climb and begin phase one!*"

The engine of my plane roared as I increased the power and climbed to 10,000 feet. Banking right to keep an eye out for targets, I got my first good look at the atoll we were attacking.

In the middle of the ring of islands was a set of offshore oil rigs, three in total. The largest island of the atoll had a fuel refinery as well as an airstrip and almost two dozen large storage tanks. Along the smaller islands of the chain were defensive buildings with anti-aircraft guns that were not yet manned, and on the second largest island, another airstrip with two rows of six fighters.

None of that worried me, what did was the battle cruiser and four destroyers that floated overhead. The cruiser sat almost directly over the oil rigs in the middle while the destroyers were spread out just past the island rings. I was sure some ensign on board one of the ships was getting his ass chewed for not spotting our attack.

I hoped the spotters understood that what was about to happen was not their fault. We were the ones pulling off a crazy attack deep in Imperial territory. If only I could see the faces of the panicking soldiers who thought this was a tropical retreat while their precise fuel processing capabilities went up in flames...

"*RS 1 and 2, your target is the cruiser. RS 3 through 6, target the destroyers, RS 3 will take the northernmost, 4 the east, 5 the south and 6 the west. Make those shots count!*"

"*Roger!*" said the collective of bombers as they and their escorts split up.

Each rocket squad, or RS, was assigned two fighter squads to protect it, except one, RS2. Our squadron, the Black Lions, was assigned to escort RS2. We were flying with them toward the massive cruiser hovering over the middle of the atoll. As we drew closer, I saw flashes from the ground as the land based anti-aircraft guns came to life, quickly followed by the anti-aircraft guns of the cruiser we were bearing down on.

No planes had taken off from the ground, but I noticed a few patrol planes that were supposed to be looking out for an attack were quickly taken down by other squads as they desperately tried to help their comrades on the ground. All we could do was buzz around the cruiser, hoping to distract their anti-aircraft fire while the rocket squads did their work.

"Avoid getting shot, avoid getting shot," I repeated to myself as I hassled the cruiser. A few shots glanced off the side of my plane from time to time.

"RS1 beginning final run from the port side."

"RS2 doing the same from the starboard side."

The cruiser saw the bombers lining up their attack and popped a series of shells into the air, releasing a torrent of smoke that engulfed the ship in a cloud two times larger than it. The haze hid the ship from our view, which would allow them to maneuver unseen, however it also obscured the gunner's views of our incoming planes. This didn't stop the bomber squads as they pushed into gray gloom before them.

"Hold your lines!" shouted the squad leader of RS2.

Sporadic gun fire came out of the haze in every direction.

"Taking heavy fire! Shit, I'm hit, engines on fire!" shouted one of the bomber pilots before his sentence was cut off in time with the glow and sounds of an explosion from within the haze.

"Hold your course!" the squad leader shouted. *"Release in three, two, one, release!...Pull up! Pull up! Pull up!"*

I saw the flashes of the rocket engines ignite within the cloud, and seconds that felt like minutes passed before a series of explosions boomed from the smoke screen as our bombers climbed up and out of it. The haze was blown away and what we saw was a welcoming sight. The large ship was spewing flames and smoke from both flanks while listing to the starboard side as she dropped. This began a slow spiral downward toward the oil rigs below it, smoke leaving a trail of where the mighty ship had been.

Explosions from across the lagoon grabbed my attention next. The destroyers were suffering the same fate as their command ship, the other squads finding similar success. Today was easily showcasing the advantage swarms of aircraft had against larger ships with no fighters of their own to defend them. No doubt we were going to return with a few losses, but the Empire losing a cruiser and four destroyers was greater than a handful of fighters.

"Wing Commander, this is Sparkles, fighters are starting to scramble on the ground of the main air strip"

"This is Sleepwalker, same here on the northern side."

"Understood," Addison replied, "the ships are dropping, and with any luck, that cruiser will smash those rigs. The timer on mop up operations has officially begun. As commanding officer I am issuing a decree. The squad that returns with the most rounds of ammo has to do The Dance! Happy hunting, and good luck!"

There were mental shouts of excitement as the fighters of *Astral Communion* took turns diving at the fuel refinery and its adjoining storage tanks, peppering them with enough machine gun fire to trigger air-rattling explosions.

I made my way over to the northern airstrip, intent on taking out as many Imperial planes as I could so I could begin to chip away at my one hundred kills. I prepared to start my strafing run, my first victim in my sights when a plane with a familiar lewd painting on its side dove in front of me and opened fire on the same target.

"Hope!" I shouted as I pulled back on the stick, canceling my run.

"I'm sorry hubby, were you planning on shooting them?"

"*I was, are you trying to be a bad girl?*"

"*Maybe,*" she said mischievously. "*Can I hunt with you darling?*"

"*Of course you can, as long as you don't poach another of my kills. Just so you know, I almost shot you by accident.*"

"*Wouldn't be the first time,*" Addison pointed out as she joined us.

We took turns diving on the airfield, pumping the red and gray planes with as much lead as we could with every attack. Some had their engines spinning up, others had their pilots running out to them, one was even taxiing to take off. It didn't matter, they all exploded the same once we shot them enough.

Boom!

An explosion from the middle of the lagoon shook my plane in the air. The sinking battle cruiser had finally dropped on top of the oil platforms below it, setting off a massive explosion with many smaller ones following it. The flames from the chaos burned so hot that I could feel the heat through the glass of my canopy.

"*Wow,*" Alyssa called out.

"*That perfectly sums up the scene,*" Lillian added.

"*Would you guys stop gawking and empty your mags?*" Addison hissed. "*The wing commander will not be doing The Dance!*"

We all agreed in our own way and got back to causing destruction.

Beers flowed freely as everyone cheered and laughed in the hangar while the members of the *White Unicorns* did *The Dance*. It was their punishment for coming back with the most ammo. Pilots, mechanics and sailors alike were crammed into the massive hangar, just so they could see the spectacle that was *The Dance*.

What was *The Dance*? It was something akin to the chicken dance back on Earth, played to a similar tune on any instrument that was available, which with this collection and size of crew, meant a few violin and accordion players. *The Dance* went on for five seconds for every round they returned with, and they had brought back two hundred and three rounds, which added up to seventeen minutes of dancing non-stop.

It wasn't really the dance routine that was bad, it was the outfit. The dancers had to strip down to their underwear and then tie feather dusters to their bodies to look like feathers. One to the head to look like the crown of a rooster, and a few others to their wrists and ankles.

The *White Unicorns* were an all women's squad made up of two rabbitkins, a horse-, tiger-, lion- and birdkin. They were attractive, as most women in this world seemed to be, even though their skin was flushed red from a mix of exhaustion and embarrassment and covered in a sheen of sweat.

Addison was sitting on the wing of a nearby plane, overseeing the action with a silver pocket watch in her hand. I found myself leaning against the same wing, Addison's legs dangling on both sides of my shoulders while Hope leaned back against me, my arms wrapped around her.

"Five more minutes," my lioness shouted from above. "Keep it up! Y'all are doing great!"

"Please...commander," panted the birdkin with a large C painted on her back and chest, a little extra punishment for being the squad leader of the losing squad. "Can...can we please...take a break! My feet are killing me!"

"Of course you can take a break," Addison shouted.

The music stopped and so did the dancing girls. They doubled over and placed their hands on their knees as they caught their breaths.

"However," Addison continued, "for every second you rest,

that is a second that I add to your dance. So take as long as you need."

"What!? Commander!"

"You knew the rules!"

The girls looked at each other before nodding to the makeshift band. The familiar song of the chicken dance started and the girls were back to it, bouncing around while flapping their arms and clapping their hands.

Their time finally came to an end and the six of them collapsed on the ground, breathing heavily while everyone cheered and gathered around them, lifting them back to their feet. The band started playing different songs that they knew just to fill the atmosphere with sound while the crew of the carrier mingled around and indulged in their drinks.

"Did you get any kills?" Addison asked as she ran her fingers through my hair.

"Two," I grumbled.

"Ninety eight to go!" Hope pointed out as she laid her head back against my chest, her tail gently moving from side to side between my legs. "I got two as well, if that makes you feel any better."

"Same for me," Addison added from above as she continued to mess with my hair.

The world around me seemed to fade away as I got lost just being in the presence of the two women I cared about the most. It had been a month and a half since I arrived in Dione, and other than the weird first week in Crestia, my time on Dione had been pleasant. I was not cast to the sideline to raise money for the war effort, instead, I was getting to do what I was good at.

I was a fighter pilot, and a damn good one. Yes I had to get one hundred kills, but I was excited to see if that was attainable, and I liked my chances of getting that number as long as I was in a squad with my two beautiful wives, Hope and Addison.

The celebration came to a halt when the ship's speaker croaked to life, grabbing everyone's attention.

"Attention crew of the *Astral Communion*. Prepare for an address from Ship Captain Harris," said the soft voice of the Captain's secretary.

Seconds later the captain addressed us, "Pilots and Sailors of the *Astral Communion*, I want to commend you all on a successful first mission for this mighty ship. I also want to take a moment to recognize those we lost during the mission."

Everyone got silent and stood at attention as the names of the five pilots we lost today were read off. Following that was a moment of silence before the Captain came back on again.

"Tomorrow we will continue Operation Monolith as we strike deeper into the Empire's northern fuel fields. Every refinery we put out of commission, every oil rig we set ablaze, and every fuel tank we blow up helps the Coalition and eliminates resources from the Empire. Enjoy today's victory but don't forget that we still have a job to do. Continue to fight for your brothers and sisters. That is all."

The hangar stayed silent for a moment before those around us picked up their conversations where they had left off. However it didn't last long and soon everyone began to file out as they returned to their respective areas of the ship. The pilots needed to rest, the mechanics needed to see to the planes, and the sailors needed to make sure we stayed in the air.

My girls and I joined the flow and climbed the stairs to the pilots quarters, bypassing the lounge and mess hall and cutting a beeline straight for our squad cabin. Luckily for us, the cabin was empty.

"I don't know about you two, but I need a shower. I still have the scent of last night's activities on me," Addison said with a wink as she tossed off her jacket and began removing her flight suit.

I leaned in close and hugged her, kissing her neck while

taking in her scent. "I don't know if I should be disgusted or turned on."

"Disgusted," Hope said as she removed her clothes. "I have the most sensitive nose on the ship and I have been able to smell her since we landed."

"Oh gods, is it that bad?" asked the beautiful blonde as she sniffed her pits before removing her bra and panties.

"Don't listen to her, she just has a sensitive nose," I said, giving her a peck on the cheek as I moved past her toward the shower. "Besides, Hope still smells like paint from this morning."

"My bad," Hope said, blushing as she crossed her arms over her chest. "I thought I would have more time to shower before the-"

"Ladies!" I said as I waved my hands in the air to get them to follow me to the bathroom. "I personally don't mind how y'all smell, but the good news for both of you is we can fix it in the shower."

"I'll wash your back if you wash mine," Hope said with a smile and a wink.

"I'm hoping he does more than wash my back," Addison purred.

CHAPTER
THIRTY-ONE

PHASES two and three had gone as well as phase one for Operation Monolith. We had delivered a massive blow to the Empire's fuel refineries across multiple atolls in three days. During that time, our carrier wing had taken part in one more strike and one defensive rotation where we had to protect the ships of the strike group while the other wings were out.

I recorded only one kill during phase two. *One closer to one hundred,* I told myself. Patience was going to be the name of the game on my quest to one hundred kills. Not every sortie would net big numbers, in fact, averaging at least one kill every offensive mission I flew was considered incredible by Earth standards.

Today was the morning of the fourth phase. All the pilots of the *Astral Communion* were gathered in the mess hall for the quick briefing from Addison on what we could expect on this attack.

"As you can see," she said as she flipped through the slides on the projector, "late night reconnaissance shows that this will be the most difficult raid of the operation."

The photo showed a large crescent-shaped island with a massive oil refinery facility being fed by a half dozen offshore rigs in the bay created by the inside of the crescent. In the sky overhead was an Imperial carrier that was accompanied by a strike group made up of two battleships and eight destroyers.

"Ma'am, what are those two boats in the water?" one of the squad leaders asked.

"Our onboard TIA analysts do not know," Addison responded as she pointed out the boats in question. "We've never seen water-bound ships like these before, but they don't seem to be heavily armed."

Boats in the water were nothing new to the people of Dione, but large water-going vessels were odd. Odd to everyone but me, and the silhouette of these ships was very familiar to me.

"Nazis," I said out loud, causing all eyes to turn to me.

"Nazis?" Addison asked.

"Do you mean the bad guys from your world who are helping the Empire?" Hope asked.

"The one and only."

"Well, lucky you," Addison said as she took back everyone's attention. "We're going to be the tip of the spear today so you'll get a chance to take a shot at them. We are only going after this one large installation, so the wings of the *Astral Communion* and *Vision at Night* will be conducting the attack together while the wing of the *Blue Snow* will defend the carriers..."

There was more to be said, but I had tuned out everything around me and focused on the image of those two boats. If I could take them out, I could help the war effort back on Earth and do my part as an American.

I will destroy those boats.

Our planes flew low to the water like we had with each of the previous phases. There were more planes around us as we had joined up with the fighter wing of the *Vision at Night* and were flying quickly toward the large imperial fuel facility.

My eyes were locked forward, and soon a speck on the horizon appeared and began to grow.

"*Five minutes out,*" Addison projected to everyone. "*All squads get ready. Nothing has changed. Hit the defending warships, destroy the facilities, mop up anything we can hit and get out.*"

We got closer and closer, and the shapes on the horizon grew larger and larger. I could make out two, maybe three destroyers, a few air defense blimps tethered to the ground and the towers and tanks of the refinery. I scanned the scene before me, but from this height, I couldn't see enough detail, I needed to climb higher to see if *they* were still here.

"*Three miles out. All planes climb to attack height and begin!*"

I quickly pulled up on the yolk and climbed into the air before banking right so I could get a better view, and then I saw them. In the water, two gray ships with a central conning tower, a large deck gun in front and two smaller anti-aircraft guns to the back. Only a small portion of these crafts were above water, while the rest of their mass was just below the surface. I knew what they were, but the red flags with the black swastikas left no doubt.

"*See the dock north of the main refinery?*" I said privately to Hope and Addison. "*Those are Nazi U-boats.*"

"*With the red flags?*" Addison asked.

"*They look kind of small,*" Hope added with skepticism.

"*Most of the boat is underwater. It can submerge to get away,*" I said to them. "*We need to take them out.*"

"*We will, my husband, but first we need to carry out the mission,*" Addison said sternly. "*Stay focused, stud. I'll make sure you get your prize,*" she added, privately.

I shook my head and looked for the rocket bomber squad we were in charge of escorting. Orders of what to attack had already been divided up between the twelve rocket bomber squads that were sent with us. We moved into defensive positions and that is when I got a strange feeling.

For being such a large facility, it was less defended than the small atolls we had attacked days earlier. Yesterday's scouts had informed us that there was a carrier stationed here, which meant an escorting strike group of supporting ships, but as we flew in the air above, she and her escorts were absent. I scanned the sky around us again to make sure we weren't missing anything.

There were our combined fighter wings, a thunderstorm to our north, and the three destroyers I had spotted as we approached. The bombers of our wings were starting their runs on the destroyers, and at any moment, I expected their air defenses to come to life, but as the bombers got closer, the destroyers stayed silent. In fact, the only anti-aircraft guns that were firing were around the main refinery.

"What the hell is going on?"

The three bomber squads made their calls as the rockets on their underbellies dropped, lit up and raced towards the quiet destroyers. The missiles screamed toward their victims, impacting their sides and passing right through them with no explosions.

"*What happened?*" Addison asked. "*Were they duds?*"

"*No, they hit. They passed through and out the other side,*" replied a random voice.

"*Ma'am, I think they are balloons-er...blimps.*"

I looked closer, and sure enough, the nearest destroyer was sagging, like it was deflating.

"*What's going on?*" Lillian asked.

"*I'm not sure,*" Addison replied. "*Begin taking out ground targets-*"

Before she could finish, I pulled back on the stick and banked hard to the left, cutting a B-line straight for the two U-boats. G forces pressed down on me as I pushed the Hak-17 to its limits and, engine screaming, I raced toward my prey.

"James! Where did you go?" Hope shouted.

"I'm going to say hello to some old friends!"

"Don't worry pup, I'll keep an eye on him," Lillian called out. "Wait for me, human!"

I felt her mind fall in line behind me, curious to see what I would do.

The crews of the two U-boats were scrambling on the deck as we approached. Some were untying their lines to push the boats away from the dock while others were preparing the anti-aircraft guns. They were too late. I lined up the gun sights and let loose a spray of lead and watched as Nazi sailors dove for cover.

As I pulled up, I looked back and saw Lillian's plane pepper the boats before pulling up to continue following me.

"I'm not stopping till we send those shit boxes to the bottom of the ocean!"

"Works for me! I kind of like it when you're this way," she said with a wicked tone.

"You would," I replied as I turned my attention forward to focus on my climb.

Up ahead was the building storm. I had zero plans of going into it, but then I spotted a group of red and gray planes emerge from the large ominous cloud overhead. More and more started to swarm out of the cloud before they went into a dive, heading right for us.

Oh crap...

"Lillian...do you see what I see?"

"Fuck, are those all Imperial fighters?"

"Addison!" I called out. "We have company! Imperial fighters to the north, coming from the storm!"

"Shit! Attention all squadrons, the empire sent us some dance partners! Bogies coming in from the clouds to the north."

My mind raced on what to do. I was in a bad position. The enemy planes were diving toward me while I was climbing, anything I did would expose the full profile of my plane.

"*What do we do James?*" the pantherkin behind me asked with a nervous tone.

"*We play chicken. Don't shoot, just increase your throttle and fly right at them. They are too clustered together to open fire on us. Once we clear them, wing over and pursue them.*"

"*That's fucking insane!*"

"*The best plans usually are.*"

"*If I die, I'm haunting your ass!*"

"I'll probably be there with you..." I said to myself

I increased the throttle and focused on the sky behind the swarm of enemy fighters that were quickly barreling toward me.

Just fly straight. No pilots are suicidal. They'll move...I hoped.

The first planes zoomed past us. Some of the lead planes tried to take shots, but were moving too fast, just as I predicted. More planes dove out of the cloud that seemed to get darker as I climbed toward it when the twin bows of an air carrier broke through.

"*Located the missing carrier. It was in the storm,*" I shouted as I got way too close, winging over to put distance between me and the ship before her anti-aircraft guns could open up on me. Lillian did the same and we dove after the planes that had gone past us, gaining on them quickly.

Below us, the beginnings of the aerial battle had begun between the fighters of Thurnmar and the Crestia Empire as Lillian and I started to catch up to the last few enemy fighters that were in the rear.

"*You ready, Thorn?*" I asked, using her call sign.

"*Is a pig's ass pork?*"

I lined up my shot on my first customer and let off a quick burst. The four guns of the Hak-17 lit up the plane in front of me along its left wing, causing the fuel tank to ignite and blow off the wing, sending the plane into a death spiral. Without skipping a beat, I adjusted my angle and found my next target, letting loose another barrage of lead right before they pulled up. The rounds shattered the cockpit and the plane dove right into the ground, creating an impressive explosion as I pulled up. Dirt and sand were kicked up in my wake as my plane came within mere feet of meeting the ground itself.

Using the momentum I had gained from the dive, I climbed again, looking for my next target while my mind scanned the sky for my girls. I trusted that they could handle themselves, but I needed to be sure, and thanks to my connection, the two of them stood out in my mind like the needle of a compass pointing north.

"Hope, how are you doing?"

"*Lone Wolf!*" she reminded me. "*I'm having the time of my life! It's like shooting fish in a barrel!*" The painting of my abs sped past my field of vision.

I watched her for a brief second as she dove, spun and peppered an Imperial fighter with hot .50 cal rounds before it exploded in mid air as she climbed in search of another target.

"*Damn, I love watching you fly!*"

"*You can watch me fly anytime babe!*" she hollered back in a husky tone.

"*I'm fine too,*" Addison pointed out, interrupting the combat flirting between Hope and I. She was high above the combat zone, flying defensively more than offensive.

"*Need any help?*" I asked as I whipped in behind a Crestia fighter that was tailing one of our planes from the other carrier wing. I could tell the enemy pilot wasn't aware that I was behind him, and positioned myself to intercept his next move with a wall of gun fire.

He made his move to the right, I pulled the trigger, he flew through my spray of bullets and kept banking to the right until his plane slammed into the ground. A grateful "*Thank you,*" was projected to me from the pilot who's butt I had saved.

"*I could use some looking after while I coordinate the counter attack,*" Addison shouted. "*We need to clear a path for our bombers to make a run on that carrier.*"

"*I got you,*" I said as I spiraled up to where she was.

"*Brainiac is here as well,*" Cormer added as his plane popped up level with mine.

From this vantage point we could see that there were more of us than there were of the Crestia fighters. They dove on our combined air wings with all the air speed advantage they needed to catch us off guard. While they had done some quick damage to our numbers, we were slowly turning the tide against them.

"*Commander Harris! Enemy escort ships are moving in on the combat zone.*"

"*Copy that. Bomber squads, check in, let me know how many candles we still have to burn.*"

Two battleships and eight destroyers were moving into the airspace over the island, their anti-aircraft guns filling the skies with flack. That was going to be a pain in the ass to deal with. I hated dealing with flack because you didn't know for sure where it was, and flying through a cloud of falling shrapnel was good for no one's engines.

While I loitered there, I spotted a Crestia fighter climbing up toward us and dove off to intercept him. I fired for a split second as I screamed past him, not sure if I really did any damage. As I pulled up to circle back for another pass, bullets ricocheted off the sides of my fuselage. I didn't need to check my mirrors to know a Crestia fighter had latched onto my tail.

I picked up his thoughts and discovered he was a cocky little shit, confident that he was going to get me. His frustration grew as our cat and mouse game went on and he struggled to get a shot on me, so he started guessing. Since I could see his thoughts, I just had to stay ahead of his guessing, which of course, made him even more angry.

"*I'll get him off your tail in exchange for another kiss!*" said the sweet voice of Alyssa in my head. I looked ahead and saw her flying at me, instantly catching on to what she had planned.

"Deal!"

"*Break left on my count...three, two, one, break!*"

I dove left just in time to miss the hail of bullets she fired. They found a home in the engine of my stalker, causing smoke and flames to spew from the front of his plane as his propeller locked up. He was quick to bail after he dove away from Alyssa's assault and realized he was piloting a burning glider.

"Thank you, Snoozer!"

"Anytime, Rounder."

"*If you have time to flirt, you have time to kill!*" Lillian shouted as she buzzed past my plane.

"I think Thorn is jealous," Alyssa fired back.

"I-I am not!" cried the flustered pantherkin.

"Ladies, cut it out," Addison barked at everyone. "*Don't forget, we have a job to do.*"

She then switched her broadcast to our entire flight wing, "*Fighters of the Astral Communion, rendezvous south of the oil platforms. We will provide cover for the bombers to take out the incoming escort ships. I'd love to go after that carrier, but we need to take the easy targets as they present themselves, and allow the escort ships of our strike group to hunt down the carrier.*"

A round of confirmations rose from the many pilots as we started moving into position.

"*The battleships are our number one priority. They pose the biggest threat to our fleet,*" Addison commanded as we locked into formations around the remaining rocket bomber squads and escorted them toward the targets.

We closed in on our targets, and I couldn't help but notice the elegance of the Crestia battleships in comparison to those of the Thurnmar navy. They looked to be the same size, but while the Thurnmar ships looked logical and to the point, the ships of the empire had a beauty to them that almost made me feel bad for what we were about to do...Almost.

I had three kills from that battle, and was more than happy to sit back and watch our rocket bombers add three battleships to the *Astral Communion's* kill count. I couldn't wait to see the elegant ships that were used by the Empire be sent to the planet surface below. It was what they deserved for siding with Nazis-

"Attention all fighters of Astral Communion and Vision Of Night! Attention all fighters of Astral Communion and Vision Of Night! Return immediately! Return immediately! The strike force is under attack! I repeat! We are under attack!"

INTERLUDE 4: JAYDEN

"*DON'T GET TOO COMPLACENT, we need to stay alert,*" Jayden called out to her fighter wing as they patrolled the skies over the three carriers and the escort ships of the strike group.

This was the second security patrol for the *Blue Snow's* wing since Operation Monolith had gone underway, and after completing two attack missions over the previous few days, she was bored. She wished her wing could have been selected for today's mission. The targets were the biggest ones yet, and she knew that Addison was going to brag about how well her wing did when they returned with a carrier kill.

"She'll get the biggest prize and that man," she said to herself in her cockpit.

She hadn't met this 'human' that everyone had talked about, but she had heard rumors and seen pictures of him. He was handsome, a gentleman, and apparently a generous lover. He checked all the boxes that the tall zebrakin had when it came to finding a man, yet she doubted he would like her. Not many men liked girls like her.

Jayden was not a girly girl, in fact, since she was the

youngest of four, and the only girl, she had been raised by her dad to be like one of the boys.

"I'd just raised three boys, so it was easier to raise you like a boy as well," he had told her when she was fifteen.

She wasn't mad at him for it, but it had made things difficult for her.

The zebra girl was strong, athletic, and preferred to fight and show off her strength over gussying herself up with the girls. "Tomboy," was what they called her. Men didn't like muscular tomboys, they wanted their women to be soft and delicate. Even in a time where women had to do more of the daily jobs because of the war, men still preferred beauty over brawn.

She sighed as toxic thoughts crossed her mind, ignoring the warning she had issued out to her pilots mere minutes ago. Not like there was anything to be alarmed of. Other than the thunderstorm moving past them to their west, the skies were clear.

Jayden was about to bank to her right and fly through the middle of the fleet when a shadow inside the passing thunderstorm got her attention. For a moment, she thought she saw the triple barrels of a battleship, but the swarming tempest was moving around so much, she could probably have seen anything if she focused-

Boom!

The clouds of the thunderstorm lit up, as though multiple cannons had all been fired at once. The vibrations from the shockwave shook her plane, and then her eyes went wide as the starboard side of the *Blue Snow*, her carrier, exploded.

"*What the fuck was that?*" called out one of her pilots.

"*I don't know. Was there an accident on board?*" asked another.

Jayden didn't answer them. Her eyes were glued to the storm to her left, and the shadows that were emerging from them.

"*It's an ambush! enemy ships in the storm to our west!*" Jayden announced to the fleet, but her warning was too little too late.

The guns of the emerging battleships unloaded another volley at the sides of the unprepared warships of the Thurnmar strike group. Once again, the *Blue Snow* took the brunt of the fire, along with two of the escorting destroyers. The ships were barely a mile from each other, which meant the damage caused by the Empire's 18 inch guns was beyond brutal.

She watched in shocked horror as her ship started to list to the starboard side and fall from the sky. Planes, equipment and crewmen fell from her decks into the open sky below as black acrid smoke bellowed from her sides.

"*Abandon ship! Abandon ship!*" cried out her Captain.

She wondered how many would be able to get to the air rafts with the ship tilting the way it did. Her wondering didn't last long as another blast from the Imperial battleships splintered the *Blue Snow's* flight deck before an explosion from within rocked the entire fleet.

Her air carrier was gone.

"No...Achew! Not now...not now! Achew!" she screamed in her cockpit as she started to panic. This was a terrible time for the anxiety trigger that gave her the call sign "Pepper" to show up. All around her, a chaotic battle was taking place, and she could do nothing because she was sneezing!

Her mind was filled with voices as orders, questions and cries for help were projected out from everyone. On top of that, the booms from the guns of the Imperial and Thurnmar ships rang in her ears. She had to get a hold of herself. She had to breathe.

One voice in the chaos stood out as it called to her. "*Commander Bombay, Commander Bombay, this is Captain Harris of the Astral Communion, can you hear me?*"

Captain Harris? That was Addison's brother. His tone was

calm as he called out to her, and it somehow helped calm her down enough to stop sneezing.

"Th-this is Commander Bombay. I read you loud and clear Captain Harris."

"Commander, I need you to organize your fighters and begin strafing runs on the enemy ships. I'm sorry, but your ship is gone. Right now we need to defend the rest of the fleet. Addison is on her way back and her bombers still have rockets that they can use on those capital ships, but she needs time. Can you buy us that time?"

She grit her teeth, machine guns couldn't do anything to a battleship! But she had to try. Mosquitoes never stopped anyone in their tracks, but they could slow you down.

"I'll do my best," Jayden replied.

"That's what I like to hear. Addison always spoke highly of you. We are counting on you."

"Roger that," she said as she took a deep breath before projecting to her fighter wing. "All fighters of the Blue Snow. Gather high and begin strafing the bridges of those capital ships! We can't let them get away with wiping out our home."

She pulled back on her yolk and climbed above the combat zone. She was soon joined by the more than fifty remaining fighters of the lost carrier. They took turns diving down toward the Crestia battleships below them, unleashing a .50 caliber storm of bullets on the thinly armored topside decks.

Jayden wasn't sure how much damage her fighter wing could cause with only heavy machine gun rounds, but she knew that if they concentrated their fire on the command towers, they could knock out the bridge and fire control. Without their commanders, these battleships were no more than floating hunks of metal.

As her fighters did what they could, the Thurnmar ships regrouped and fell back as the smaller escort ships and battleships put themselves between the Imperial attack and the two remaining carriers that were trailing smoke and limping away from the battlefield. From her vantage point up high, Jayden could see the numbers of both sides; the Empire did not have any carriers in this fight, but they did outnumber the Thurnmar forces in battleships and cruisers.

"*Commander Bombay, my squad is out of ammunition,*" called out one of the squad leaders.

"*Mine as well,*" said another, and another as her remaining pilots checked in.

Her numbers had been cut in half by the anti-aircraft guns of the capital ships. Their reward was meager as only one battleship was sitting dead in the air after one of her squad members drove her plane into the bridge as she was going down. They were doing so little, and now that they were out of ammunition, they could do even less.

"*What do we do now?*" one of her younger pilots asked.

Two thoughts had crossed her mind. One, they could try and land on the two remaining carriers and resupply, but that had many complications. What if the other fighter wings returned and needed to reload and refuel while they were on deck? They also became a larger target as the carriers would have to slow down and stop carrying out evasive maneuvers to avoid a hit from the guns of the battleships just so her planes could land.

The second option was the one a pilot only considered when there were no other options. She couldn't order any of her pilots to sacrifice themselves, and even bringing it up to them felt taboo. But the way Jayden saw it, if she could do this and help keep her best friend's ship and brother safe, it was a sacrifice she would make.

"*Ladies and gentleman, it...*" She took a deep breath as all the voices quieted down and focused on her. "*...it has been an honor to call myself your wing commander. I can't ask anyone to join me, but just because I am out of ammunition doesn't mean I am done fighting.*"

All communications were silent before one of her pilots spoke up, "*If you can still fight, then I can still fight.*"

"*Me too.*"

"*For the Blue Snow!*" echoed the less than three dozen remaining pilots of her air wing.

Were they as insane as she was? Maybe they didn't know what she was saying.

"*Guys, you do know I'm talking about-*"

"*Commander. We know.*"

So it was settled. She tightened the straps on her harness and took a deep breath.

"*Captain Harris,*" she said as she reached out to her best friend's brother. "*Please tell Addison that I am glad I got to call her my friend. I hope she meets a good man, has a happy marriage, and that they are blessed by the Gods to have many kids,*" she said as she lifted her goggles and wiped tears from her eyes. "*We will be reunited one day on the Silver Planes.*"

"*Or, and hear me out,*" a familiar voice said, "*we could reunite in the pilots lounge of the Astral Communion and see who can handle the most stone water!*"

The combined wings of the *Astral Communion* and the *Vision at Night* were coming in fast from behind the pursuing enemy warships. Before they knew what hit them, the stern sections of the Imperial ships were exploding in flames, shutting down their forward propulsion and leaving them dead in the air. The hunters were now sitting ducks for the Thurnmar guns to get in a bit of target practice and revenge.

EPILOGUE 1:

"WE NEED to get this going before anyone notices we're gone," Captain Nathanial Harris reminded me as we walked down the aisle of the ship's chapel.

"I know," I replied as I followed him to the platform at the front of the room.

A day had passed since the empire had set up a trap for our battle group during phase four of Operation Monolith. After getting a count of who had been lost and who had survived, it was decided that we needed a celebration of life. We would share drinks and food with those who survived, while paying tribute to the memories of those we lost.

It was during this time that Hope and Addison decided that we absolutely needed to have a proper wedding to signify our unions. Remarkably, they were able to pull everything needed for the ceremony together in a few hours, and now here we were.

"Thanks again for doing this," I said to Nathan.

"Think nothing of it," he said as he stepped up and took his spot in the middle of the platform. "I always wondered when I would get to officiate a wedding on my ship, I just never assumed it would involve my sister."

"I'm glad we could make your dream come true," I chortled as I stood next to him, looking back toward the chapel and the door at the back.

He leaned toward me. "Promise me you'll take care of her."

"I promise," I said as I turned to him. "I love her, and I will do whatever it takes to protect and take care of her."

He gave me a nod and an approving smile as we turned to face the chapel and the small audience that had gathered for the occasion.

Captain Harris and I were wearing our officers dress uniforms, his navy blue, since his service was to the Thurnmar Navy, and mine in the tan of the Thurnmar Air Force.

The chapel was small, with three rows of seats and an aisle running down the middle, and each row had room for three people to sit comfortably. On both walls were paintings of the five Gods of Dione, each one looking more animal than human, compared to the Dionians who worshiped them.

Sitting in the seats were Alyssa, Lillian, and Layton, all dressed in their tan officers dress uniforms like me. They were a small audience for what we were about to do, but they were the only ones that mattered to my girls and I.

Addison had wanted her friend Jayden there, but we decided against it since she was dealing with the loss of her ship and so many of her pilots. We would tell her when she was in a better state of mind.

"Are you girls ready?" I asked, calling out to Hope and Addison.

"I am," Hope replied. *"But Addison looks like she's about to have a panic attack."*

"I am not! Let's do this," Addison said.

I smiled, looked over to Alyssa and gave her a nod. She got up and went over to a record player, turned it on and set the needle of the player on the spinning record.

A lone violin began to play a tune that sounded similar to

the *Canon in D* back on Earth. The squirrelkin then moved to the door at the back of the room and held it open as our witnesses turned back to look at my two lovely brides.

Addison and Hope stepped into the room side by side and looked absolutely stunning. They were barefoot and wore matching white lace dresses that featured a simple low-cut neckline. A corset back allowed the luxurious curves of each girl to be shown off in ways that made each unique. The sleeves of the dresses were long and flowing, creating an elegant effect that was reminiscent of the wings of a swan as it landed on the still water of a pond.

The silver threads of Hope's hair were tied up in a bun on the back of her head, while Addison wore her golden locks in the same double dutch braids that hung over her chest, like always. Both wore a crown of white flowers that sat between the soft fur of their ears.

In their hands they held a bouquet of white roses accented by the yellow of daisies and the purple of petunias, a Thurnmar tradition.

"You look amazing, Hope," I said to my wolf girl. She gave me a radiant smile when our eyes met, which caused her large silver tail to start to wag gently behind her.

"And you look positively stunning, Addison," I said to my lioness, who bit her red-stained bottom lip as her eyes started to tear up when my gaze met hers.

They continued their barefoot march down the aisle until they stood before me. Two pillows waited on the ground in front of them, and they both lowered themselves to their knees on the pillows and bowed their heads. This was similar to how they did on the day I had asked them to join my family, but there was more ceremony involved this time.

Nathaniel stepped forward. "Friends, we are gathered here today to witness the union of Hope Barnett and Addison Harris to James Walker. They do so before the witnesses gathered here, and the eyes of the Gods above."

He reached out with an open hand. "Hope, may I see your hand?"

"Yes," she answered as she raised her hand, her head still bowed.

Nathaniel took it. "James, take Hope's hand."

I took her soft hand in mine, holding it gently.

"James, do you accept Hope into your family, to carry your name, bear your children, and spend your remaining days with until you both depart for the Silver Plains?"

"I do," I said, giving her hand a gentle squeeze.

She looked up at me, her golden eyes wide with tears that she was doing her best to hold back.

"And do you, Hope, accept James's offer to join his family, to carry his name, bear his children, and spend your remaining days with until you both depart for the Silver Plains?"

"I do," she said as she blinked away a tear.

He then turned to Addison, who was breathing heavily. "Addison, may I see your hand?"

Addison used the sleeve of her dress to wipe away her tears before raising a shaking hand.

"Addison, are you ok?" I asked.

"Peachy...I'm just trying to keep from turning into a blubbering idiot in front of everyone."

Nathaniel joined her hand with mine, and I gave it a soft squeeze. *"Take a deep breath, you are doing great."*

Nathaniel repeated the lines he had said for Hope with Addison.

"I do," I said.

"I...d-do," Addison said between joyful sobs.

"By the powers invested in me by the Thurnmar Republic, and the Gods above, I declare you husband and wives,"

Nathaniel said. "Ladies, please stand. James, you may kiss the brides."

Hope stood up slowly, her hand still in mine, but Addison jumped up and launched herself at me. "I'm so happy!" she cried as she pressed her lips to mine, sniffling while her soft lips peppered me with kisses. It was strange to see the usually coy and flirtatious lioness behave this way, but it was refreshing, if not a little overwhelming.

"I'm...happy...too," I said between kisses, doing my best to match the love of my lionkin wife.

Hope waited patiently, but she reached her limit and cleared her throat.

"Oh, sorry," the blonde beauty said before she stepped away. "Hold on Hope, let me clean him up."

She grabbed her tear soaked sleeve and wiped away the moisture left behind by her tears and kisses.

"Go get your she wolf," Addison said when she was done.

My eyes turned to Hope, who smiled at me while holding back her own tears, but one escaped and ran down her flawless cheek. We had been through so much since we first met, going from almost enemies to lovers.

I stepped to her, taking the back of her head in my hand as I leaned in to kiss my silver-haired wife. I felt her love radiate while we embraced, warming my soul as I poured my love into her.

I pulled back and smiled at her, squishing her tight against me while reaching out to hug Addison in the same way.

"I love you girls."

EPILOGUE 2:

IT WAS a dreary morning when the *Tattered Wings* pulled into the port city of Glasgar on the western edge of Oshor. No one paid any mind to the mid-sized clipper from Ildor as it docked in a Coalition nation port. The Ildory were neutral in the global conflict and notorious at keeping their purple-stained fingers clean and out of trouble. All who did trade with them found they were trustworthy and reliable, and because of this, they were the best smugglers in the world.

As goods were offloaded from the cargo hold of the clipper, a hooded woman in a large coat and carrying a small suitcase disembarked and moved past the dock workers as she headed into the city. Once clear of the port and its fog, she removed her hood, exposing her large white fox ears and white shoulder-length hair. No one paid any mind to her for Oshor was home to the Enclave, an anti-Crestia collective of foxkin who were citizens of Oshor and swore to right the wrongs carried out in the name of the Goddess Crestia by the Empire.

Madeline moved casually through the city, admiring the goods in the windows of the shops she went by and even purchased a meat skewer from a street vendor. She waved to those who waved at her, and greeted anyone who wished her a good morning with one in return. Her smile was genuine and brightened the day of the few she flashed it to, but on the inside, she wished death on everyone who said hello to her.

"I can't stand the Oshory accent," she groaned to herself.

After walking for a few blocks, she arrived at her destination, the Travelers Bureau of Glasgar. Checking to see that no one was around her, she stepped into an alley and quickly shifted back to her rabbitkin form before heading to the entrance to the Travelers Bureau.

The three story sandstone-clad building was the local headquarters for the purchasing of any tickets on one of the ship lines that sailed out of the port. The inside was warm and welcoming and filled with reception areas for the five competing ship lines, including the Gold Star Line of Thurnmar.

"Good morning ma'am," chimed the cute rabbitkin woman behind the ticket window for the Gold Star Lines, "how may I assist you?"

"I'd like a ticket of passage to Thurnmar," Madeline asked in her version of an Oshory accent. "First available ship please, destination does not matter."

"Of course! Let me see, the next available ship is the *Kashmir*, she departs tomorrow morning before noon. What level of accommodations would you like?"

"Third class will do fine."

"Very good, it will cost fifty-eight trade bills and I will need to see your travel papers."

Madeline reached into her inner coat pocket and pulled out her wallet and an envelope. She fished out the required fare and her falsified travel papers, sliding them through the gap at where the window met the counter.

"I'll be right back," the ticket agent said as she took the money and the documents and went into the processing room behind her.

While she waited, Madeline pulled a folded picture out of the envelope and smiled. She was thankful that Shasta had gotten the pictures from that night developed. She looked beautiful, and James was so handsome. That was the night she had fallen in love.

Yes, it had been over a month since she last saw him, and yes, he had run away with that dirty gray wolf bitch after they had tied her up, but her body and soul still yearned to be with him.

"I know you will come to love me just as I love you," she whispered softly as she kissed his image multiple times.

"Umm...Ms. Farrell, sorry to interrupt."

Madeline looked up to see the ticket agent standing there, blushing as she watched her make out with the picture.

"Sorry about that..."

"Oh no, Ms. Farrell, it's all right," said the ticket girl as she leaned closer to the window. "I have a man of my own that I'm also pretty crazy about, but he's on the other side of the continent at the moment."

Her smile would have been adorable, if she hadn't been trying to one up Madeline.

"I'm sure he's special to you," Madeline stated as her red eyes glared at the rabbit girl, "but he's nothing compared to my James."

How dare this bitch compare her man to James! This girl was smitten over some long eared, cotton tailed dimwit while Madeline was in love with the most unique man on the planet! To compare the two would be like comparing a bicycle to a plane. Yes, a bicycle was fun to ride, but a plane took you for the ride of your life while lifting you to new heights!

"I-I'm sure that's right," stuttered the ticket girl under Madeline's killer stare. "H-here are your p-papers. One third class ticket on the *Kashmir* for Tabitha Farrell, departing tomorrow morning and heading for Sorcel, Thurnmar."

Madeline took a deep breath letting out a sigh before flashing a fake smile at the girl. "Thank you so much, I really do appreciate all your help. Have a nice day," she added at the end as she grabbed the ticket and her travel papers, putting them away before grabbing her suitcase to leave.

"Sorcel," she said to herself as she walked down the street. It had been almost two years since she was last in the capital of Thurnmar, and she hated it there. The food was bland, their accents were weird and the absolute peak of the loathsome mountain were the politicians! They were the absolute worst, always saying one thing but doing another with not a single honest bone in their body. "Yuck!" Oh, but she could tolerate it. She could tolerate anything for James.

She was still in her rabbitkin form when she woke the next morning. She got a bit of shopping done before boarding the *Kashmir* so she could have snacks for the voyage. The sky liner would feed the passengers on the almost week long voyage across the skies of Dione, but third class meals were often meager, and didn't include sweets or alcohol.

After making the necessary purchases of Chocolate Marbles, the Oshory version of Choc Um's, and wine, she worked her way toward the sky liner docks. The ship would not leave for a few more hours, but by boarding early, she could freely move about the decks while the crew was busy preparing to set sail.

The ship was nice, not as nice as any of the Crestia Skyliners, but still nice. A large black hull with a single set of massive contra-rotating propellers at the tail, white passenger top decks crowned by two smoke stacks painted purple. And then there was the gold trim. The damn Thurnmarians loved their purple and gold, in contrast to the red and silver preferred by the Empire and Madeline.

She opened a package of Chocolate Marbles and tossed a few of the candy-coated chocolates into her mouth as she waited. She grimaced as the milk chocolate melted in her mouth, Choc Um's were so much better than this knock off.

That's when a sight on the other end of the port grabbed her attention.

A Thurnmar Aircraft Carrier with the name *Astral Communion* painted on her bow was being lowered into the dry dock saddles of the Coalition military yard; it was beaten up and looked like it had just returned from battle.

"Serves you right," she spat at the wounded ship. "I hope they sink you next time."

She leaned on the rail and tossed another Chocolate Marble into her mouth when a pair of crew members, one male, one female, walked by. She paid them no mind, but listened in on their conversation out of boredom.

"It's a shame we are leaving port on the day the *Astral Communion* arrives. You know Addison Harris is stationed on her," the male horsekin said.

"Like you would have a shot with Addison Harris!" laughed the female pantherkin.

"Maybe? You never know! You miss one hundred percent of the shots you don't take."

"You are something else. Granted, I did want to see that human that they got on her," sighed the pantherkin. "I hear he's really handsome. My cousin saw him in Hopewell and said he made her tingle in ways other men never had."

Madeline's ears perked up, did she say human? Was she talking about James? She quickly focused on the woman's mind and searched her memories for this "human."

That's James! Why is he wearing a Thurnmar military uniform? She thought when she saw memories of the newspaper article the pantherkin had read. The headline read "Thurnmar's Newest Pilot is Not of This World!"

No, James...what did you do?

She turned and followed the two, her sensitive rabbitkin ears allowing her to hear their conversation while she kept her distance.

"You sure that furless man is on that ship?"

"As sure as my tail is black. My cuz saw him board the *Astral Communion* with some silver wolf girl."

"He's still with her?" Madeline shouted.

The two crew members turned to look at her, but only found empty space. Madeline had heard enough and took off for her cabin, grabbing her suitcase and belongings before making her way to the gangplank to get off the *Kashmir*.

James is here! He came to me! Yes, he was still with that she wolf, and he had joined the Thurnmar Air Force, but that could be fixed! As long as she could talk to him, she could fix his mistakes.

Then Kampf's words echoed in her mind..."You will go to Thurnmar and bring him back to us. Prove your value to us and your father, or we turn off the machine and let your next death be your last."

She rubbed her neck, she could still see Kampf's smile when he had strangled her to teach her a lesson. She could still see her fathers disappointed look in his eyes after she had shape shifted for the first time when she turned fifteen.

"I will bring him back to Crestia," she said to herself as she transformed back to her foxkin form. "Even if I have to sneak on to that damn ship and kill everyone on board, I will bring him back to Crestia, and he will be mine!"

**The story will continue in
Wings and Tails No. 2.**

If you enjoyed this book, please leave a review on Amazon and one or more of these awesome groups.

https://www.facebook.com/groups/pulpfantasy/
https://www.facebook.com/groups/dukesofharem/
https://www.facebook.com/groups/haremlitbooks/
https://www.facebook.com/groups/MonsterGirlFiction/
https://www.facebook.com/groups/HaremGamelit/
https://www.facebook.com/groups/monstergirllovers

Thank you for reading. This has been a labor of love for me, and I hope that you enjoyed reading it as much as I enjoyed writing it. I came up with the concept a few years ago while sitting in a meeting and daydreaming instead of paying attention to my boss. I'm a nerd, through and through. I watch anime, read manga and pulp romance for men and love Warhammer 40K Lore.

Please follow me on one or all of my socials.
X (Twitter) : https://x.com/isaacwrites27
Facebook: https://www.facebook.com/Isaac.Lee27

ACKNOWLEDGMENTS & THANK YOU

Mrs. Lee: My wife has heard every idea and concept before they got on the pages of this book. She encouraged me through the hard times where I wanted to quit, and always told me when something I did was dumb.
    I Love You.

Eli Lorenz: One of my best friends. He's a nerd like me and helped me think outside of the box that I created for this world.

Gwen Grayson: My editor and friend, she helped my chapters come to life by demanding more, and helped fix my grammatical mistakes.

Nini: The artist who created my amazing cover and brought my words to life! She has so much skill as a painter and digital artist.
    Go check her out on X(Twitter) @NinouilleSFW

Thank you to my Beta Readers. Their criticism and suggestions were a great help. Thank you to the authors and readers of **Pulp Romance For Men Community.** There is not a more helpful group of individuals than this. They are fun, hilarious, honest, and always there for encouragement.

Isaac Lee

Printed in Great Britain
by Amazon